W9-CYC-624

Praise for Tessa Harris and her Constance Piper Mysteries

The Angel Makers

"A nail-biting story full of suspense and mystery."
—*Fresh Fiction*

The Sixth Victim

"Constance is an unusual protagonist with a special gift. Harris's treatment of the working class's spirituality and belief in ghosts will attract fans of Sharyn McCrumb's 'Appalachian Ballad' mysteries. Readers who follow Jack the Ripper theories may also enjoy."
—*Library Journal*

"A reinterpretation of Jack the Ripper with a supernatural touch . . . [Harris] still combines two perceptive points of view with a convincing portrait of London's seamier side with a neat twist of an ending."
—*Kirkus Reviews*

Books by Tessa Harris

Dr. Thomas Silkstone Mysteries
THE ANATOMIST'S APPRENTICE
THE DEAD SHALL NOT REST
THE DEVIL'S BREATH
THE LAZARUS CURSE
SHADOW OF THE RAVEN
SECRETS IN THE STONES

Constance Piper Mysteries
THE SIXTH VICTIM
THE ANGEL MAKERS
A DEADLY DECEPTION

Published by Kensington Publishing Corporation

THE ANGEL MAKERS

TESSA HARRIS

KENSINGTON BOOKS
http://www.kensingtonbooks.com

KENSINGTON BOOKS are published by

Kensington Publishing Corp.
119 West 40th Street
New York, NY 10018

Copyright © 2018 by Tessa Harris

All rights reserved. No part of this book may be reproduced in any form or by any means without the prior written consent of the Publisher, excepting brief quotes used in reviews.

To the extent that the image or images on the cover of this book depict a person or persons, such person or persons are merely models, and are not intended to portray any character or characters featured in the book.

If you purchased this book without a cover you should be aware that this book is stolen property. It was reported as "unsold and destroyed" to the Publisher and neither the Author nor the Publisher has received any payment for this "stripped book."

All Kensington titles, imprints, and distributed lines are available at special quantity discounts for bulk purchases for sales promotion, premiums, fund-raising, educational, or institutional use.

Special book excerpts or customized printings can also be created to fit specific needs. For details, write or phone the office of the Kensington Sales Manager: Attn.: Sales Department. Kensington Publishing Corp., 119 West 40th Street, New York, NY 10018. Phone: 1-800-221-2647.

Kensington and the K logo Reg. U.S. Pat. & TM Off.

First Hardcover Printing: June 2018

ISBN-13: 978-1-4967-0659-1 (ebook)
ISBN-10: 1-4967-0659-5 (ebook)

ISBN-13: 978-1-4967-0658-4
ISBN-10: 1-4967-0658-7
First Kensington Trade Edition: August 2019

10 9 8 7 6 5 4 3 2 1

Printed in the United States of America

To Lucy, the bravest young writer I know

There can be no keener revelation of a society's soul than the way in which it treats its children.
—Nelson Mandela

ACKNOWLEDGMENTS

This book would not have been possible without the help, support and inspiration of so many people. These include the writer and paranormal expert Lynn Picknett and David Bullock, author of *The Man Who Would Be Jack.* Also recommended for anyone wishing to research further into these murders is *Amelia Dyer: Angel Maker* by Alison Rattle and Allison Vale. For an overview of life in a Victorian slum, I recommend *The Blackest Streets* by Sarah Wise. Paul Begg and John Bennett's *Jack the Ripper: The Forgotten Victims* concentrates on murders contemporary with the canonical five attributed to the Ripper. There were many gruesome unsolved murders around the world at this time, some "Ripper-style" copycat cases, and these form the focus of this intriguing book.

Angela Buckley's walking tour of Amelia Dyer's old haunts in Reading brought the whole dark episode to life for me, and her book *Amelia Dyer and the Baby Farm Murders* is highly recommended. Thames Valley Police Museum at Sulhamstead, near Reading, also has exhibits pertaining to Amelia Dyer.

By far the best online resource for all things Ripper-related is www.casebook.org, the world's largest public repository of information on the subject. Here you'll find hundreds of fascinating tidbits, newspaper reports, postmortem reports, and articles and essays relating to the Whitechapel murders, as well as a photographic archive.

Finally I'd like to thank my editor at Kensington Publishing, John Scognamiglio, and my agent, Melissa Jeglinski, my friend and fellow writer Katharine Johnson, and my husband, Simon, and children Charlie and Sophie for their support.

Chapter 1

London, Saturday, January 12, 1889

Constance

Two blasts. Two blasts from a copper's whistle is all it takes. I shudder to a halt, my breath burning my throat. Behind me is my ma's beau, Mr. Bartleby. I hear his heavy footsteps pull up sharp. I turn to see his anxious eyes clamped onto the back of my head; his mouth lost under the thatch of his big moustache. We both know what the whistles mean. They've found something. My stomach catapults up into my chest. Two more blasts cut through the fog like cheese wire, then it all kicks off. The air's filled with the shouts and sounds of men running: a dozen pairs of boots trampling over wet stones.

"Flo!" I call softly at first, then louder. "Flo!" Then again, until I'm screaming her name over the mayhem that's breaking out all around me. More whistle blasts. More footsteps. More shouts, too.

"Clarke's Yard!" I hear someone yell.

Clarke's Yard? I'm knocked off balance. Could she be there?

She's not supposed to be there. Clarke's Yard is where they found poor Cath Mylett just before Christmas.

We're out of Whitechapel, in Poplar, up toward East India Docks, but this is still Jack's patch. There's some who think it was him who strangled poor Cath just a hundred yards up ahead. I'm not so sure. Knew her, we did. She was Flo's good friend and we was with her the night she was strangled. But what's Flo doing up here now?

Mr. B's caught up and we swap looks. Neither of us says a word before we both break out into a run. The high street looms through the patchy smog. Buildings are blurred and smudged, but we can see a couple of coppers making a dash. They're heading for the builder's yard. There's boarded up shops lining the road, but in between an ironmonger's and a tobacconist's I know there's a narrow alley that leads to workshops and stables at the back. Daytime it's safe—as safe as anywhere can be in this part of London. Come the night, it's a different story. It's where men pay to have their way. That's where they found poor Cath.

I'm hot and cold at the same time and my heart's barreling in my chest. The air's so thick with grit and grime, you could spread it on your bread. I throw a glance back at Mr. Bartleby as I run. He's no spring chicken and he's gulping down the dirty murk like it's going out of fashion.

"Over there!" I pant. I pause for a moment as, narrowing my eyes, I make out people pouring onto the street. The women stand on their doorsteps, arms round their little gals, while the men and boys rush over toward the yard, setting the dogs barking.

I start to drag myself as fast as I can toward the din and the gathering crowd. Mr. B's doubled over, his palms clamped on his thighs. I can't wait for him. My dread mounts and I start to pray.

"Please, no. Please let her be all right. Please, Miss Tindall," I mutter. She was my teacher. She won't let any harm come to Flo. If it's in her power to save her, I know she will. Jack shan't touch a hair on my big sister's head. Emily Tindall won't let him. I swear she won't let him.

I'm almost there, level with the lamppost that casts a grubby yellow glow on the opposite side of the street. I reach the edge of the crowd. The lads with the flaming torches who've come over with us from Whitechapel are already there.

I'm glad to see one of them is Gilbert Johns. It was him who cared for me when I fell into a faint in the street a few weeks back. A full head taller than most of them, he is, with forearms like Christmas hams.

"Gilbert! Gilbert!" I cry.

He whips round and latches onto my face. Plowing through the gathering crowd like a big shire horse, he edges toward me.

"Miss Constance." He's looming over me, and for a moment I feel safe, but then there's more shouting and we both see the coppers won't let no one into the yard. There's two of them at the mouth, barring the way.

"Keep back!" one of them cries. The other rozzer gets out his truncheon and starts waving it in the air, but it's too late. One of the Whitechapel lads—one with a torch—makes a break for it and bolts down the alley. The murmurings start to swell and the coppers can't hold their line. The crowd surges forward, funneling down the passage. Gilbert and me are among them. His arm's around me. Beside us, a little nipper takes a tumble, but no one stops to pick him up. We push on, like rats along a gutter, but a second later everyone's stopped in their tracks, not by the rozzers, but by the shout that bellows from one of the lads up ahead. It's a sound that makes all of us stand stock-still and catch our breaths; it's a sound that causes time to stop still and all around us fall away. It's the cry I'll never forget. It's the cry of "Murder! Murder!"

Emily

You may wish to look away. There is blood. Much blood. It is Florence's, but I am with her, watching over her. I was here to see the flares from the young man's torch illuminate the sodden earth and show a steady trickle of syrupy liquid. Blood-soaked stockings are visible where the muddy hem of her skirt has ridden up to her knees. She is slumped against a wall, her head lolled to one side, her legs splayed.

What most of the crowd who've clustered in the yard do not yet know, however, is that as well as a stricken young woman, a few yards away there also lies a brutally slain body. Jack is here, indeed, lurking in the shadows, waiting to pounce on his next helpless victim. This is, indeed, his domain. Five he's killed already. Five he's cut and gutted. That is why Constance is so desperate to find Florence before he does. But what she is yet to discover is that, this time, the murder victim is not a hapless prostitute, nor, thank God, is it her sister. It is a man. His body has been discovered not fifty paces from where Florence lies, in a blacksmith's forge. Yet despite his sex, there is a similarity in the manner of killing with the fiend's alleged female victims. Just like Mary Jane Kelly's, not two months before, his face has been mutilated beyond recognition.

More constables, never far away in these dark days when terror is stalking the streets, are speeding to the scene. When news of this killing seeps out into the gutter press, there will be another frenzy in the East End, in London, in England, in the world. More lurid headlines will be plastered across newspapers; more accusations of incompetence leveled at the Metropolitan Police and Scotland Yard, and Constance will have to suffer yet more pain and anxiety. For the moment, there is no way out of this quagmire. For the moment, everyone is sucked in. For tonight, you see, they will think the very worst. Tonight they will fear that Jack the Ripper has struck again.

Chapter 2

Four weeks earlier, Wednesday, December 19, 1888

Constance

"Cheer up, my gal. 'Tis the season and all that!" Flo winks as she pats our friend Cath's arm, then slugs back her second large port and lemon of the night. Or is it her third? Either way, it's coming up to Christmas and my big sister's full of spirit, strong as well as festive, if you take my meaning. So, if a good-looker shows her a sprig of mistletoe, those lips of hers'll be on him like a limpet. 'Course we know it's all a show. She's just putting on a brave face, like the rest of us. It's six weeks now since Mary Kelly felt his knife, but we know he's still about.

"Deck them halls, that's what I say!" Flo slams down her empty glass and nudges me. "Whose round?"

Cath and me stay quiet. She's no money, and me, I don't take drinks off strangers. We're in the George Tavern, on Commercial Road in Poplar, not far from the docks. The pub is full of sailors and dockers, and there's a lech in the corner who's barely taken his eyes off us girls. On his hand, he's got a big tattoo of a naked woman. From the look she gave him earlier, I think he might be one of Cath's regulars. He catches me eyeing his tattoo and suddenly his leathery lips part and he slides his tongue in between them. He rolls it up at the edges and thrusts it in and out of his mouth. I snatch away my gaze and hear him laugh out loud at my fluster.

It's coming up to ten o'clock and we ain't seen a friendly face all evening. It's not Flo's usual spit-and-sawdust, but she was stood up by her intended, Daniel Dawson. He's been called to work late at the Egyptian Hall, with it being the festive season and all that. I'm not sure I believe him. Slippery as an eel, Danny is. If I know his sort, he'll be out with a girl from the chorus. But Flo's managed to twist my arm as usual. She's acted all down in the dumps and persuaded me to come and see what her old pal Cath Mylett is up to.

Cath is what the French might call "*petite.*" Round here, we'd say she was a sparrow. She's been working in Poplar this last month. A good few years older than Flo, she is, but they always seemed to have a laugh together. Even named her first daughter after her, she did, but all that was before *he* came a-calling earlier on this year. It's like there's this great shadow cast over London Town and its name is Jack the Ripper. Cath is a working girl, see. In Whitechapel, she's known as Drunken Lizzie Davis, on account of her being partial to a tipple, or Rose—that's her favorite, but here in Poplar, she's changed her working name again, for a fresh start. Fair Alice Downey, they call her. She reckoned she'd be out of Jack's patch if she went nearer the docks.

Flo thinks Cath's got a man round these parts, too, but he's married, so she sees him on the sly. But new man or no, she still has to earn her keep out on the streets.

"Like it over here then, do you?" I ask Cath. She's not one for the gab, not like our Flo, so I try and make small talk. She shrugs and turns to the direction of the lech.

"Whitechapel or Poplar, one man's prick is the same anywhere," she says in a loud voice, so as he can hear. She talks like she's got dirt in her mouth. "Leastways Jack's less like to get me 'ere," she adds.

There's an odd look in her eye, and when I shoot her a questioning glance, she bends low and points to the side of her boot. I catch sight of the wooden handle of a short knife. I've heard a lot of working women are arming themselves with hatpins and the like. And who can blame them? A girl's got to do all she can to protect herself these days. What's more, from the look on her face, I know she'd use it, too.

So we're sitting in the corner, minding our own business, when I see Cath tense. I follow her gaze and who should I see but Mick Donovan, Gilbert Johns's friend. He's the Paddy with the funny walk, who worked at Mrs. Hardiman's Cat Meat Shop. There's sprigs of sandy hair sprouting under his nose, but it'll take more than a 'tache to make a man of him. He's having a word with a bloke at the bar, but as soon as he sees us three gals, he's over in a flash.

" 'Evening, ladies," says he, like we're the best of mates. But Cath is in no mood for boys like him, even if he could pay for his pleasure. She gives him the cold shoulder, so his roving eye soon settles on our Flo. Punching above his weight, if you ask me. Nonetheless, in two shakes of a lamb's tail, he's offering to buy her a drink.

"Had a win with a filly at Kempton, so I did," he tells us. He's a gambler, all right, but I've no interest in helping him spend his winnings in case he wants something in return, if you get my drift. Flo, on the other hand, never refuses a free bevy and accepts his offer.

While she's making chitchat with Mick, Cath and me are left to our own devices. Seems she's not up for a night on the tiles. She's edgy and upset about something and keeps looking over to the bloke at the bar, the one with his back to us. The drink's not working on her like it usually does. Her skin's all pale and papery and it's creased between her eyes by a ceaseless frown. This time last year, she lost a baby girl. Hazard of the job, you might say. Sometimes not all the douching in the world will stop one of those blighters hitting the mark, if you'll pardon my being so frank. But I know she loved this little one—Evie, she called her—just as much as she loved Florence, her first, the one she named after our Flo. But just like with Florence, she had to give her away. Somehow she managed to scrape together a fiver and put the poor mite up for adoption. The minder told her there was a good home for the little soul, but Cath was pining so much that the next day she decided she wanted her back. So she called in, only to find Evie had become an angel overnight. Whooping cough, they told her, even though she seemed healthy enough when she left her the day before. Buried, too, before Cath could say farewell.

Sometimes Cath dosses in Spitalfields, sometimes in Poplar. If I was a betting person, I'd wager she's not got her doss money for tonight, neither. She'll need to work before she lays down her head. My eyes dart to the lech with the tattoo again. He'd have her in an alley as soon as look at her. The thought sickens me.

I turn back to Cath and see she's suddenly all teary again. She's watching a young mum feed her babe in the corner and it's like she's picked a scab. She dabs her eyes with a torn hankie. She's still raw and I clasp her hand tight. You see, I know the pain of loss, too. It's less than two months since I found out about Miss Tindall's cruel fate. She was my old Sunday school teacher. Only she'd become so much more than just that. Miss Emily Tindall was my friend, my mentor, no, my guardian angel. Murdered, she was, but no one can be brought to justice and my own wounds aren't even beginning to heal.

I gaze at Cath, mourning for her baby Evie. "The little mite's in a better place now," I say. I'm trying to reach out to her, but then I hate myself for sounding so glib and smug, like a parson.

Do I mean what I say? Do I really believe that good people go to heaven when they die, or is it a lie made up to comfort those of us left behind? I'd like to think it's true, but I hold my tongue and watch Cath's face as the heartache screws it up like an old brown paper bag and her tears fall.

A moment or two passes before she lifts her face again and dabs her cheeks. "It's not right," she sobs.

Suddenly I'm not sure what she's on about. There's something more. "What's not right?" I ask.

"The babes, dying so young." Her face is all puffy and she begins to sob again. "So little and helpless."

In my mind's eye, I'm picturing sickly little infants, whimpering and moaning before giving up the ghost, but I'm not sure what it is she's seeing.

"Cath?"

Her grief has suddenly turned to anger. There's something of a strange look on her face and her eyes grow wild, like she's fresh out of Bedlam. She stands up and steadies herself against the table. Wiping more tears away with her sleeve, she sniffs. "I best be off," she says. "I've got business to do." I picture her up against a wall, her skirts round her waist, and all so she can sleep in a bed tonight. She reaches for her bonnet and places it firmly on her head.

Flo's neck whips round. "You off then, Cath?" She's been looking for an excuse to escape Irish Mick, who's turning out to be even creepier than Danny, touching her at every turn.

"Yes," says Cath, leaving her bonnet ribbons to dangle under her chin. She pats the stiff, velvet collar round her neck to see it's done up against the cold.

"Business," I say.

Flo nods and pulls a face. "Got to earn your keep, I s'pose."

"Good-bye," I tell her, standing up to give her a hug, but she stiffens, like she doesn't want me to touch her, so I just say: "It'll be all right." She shoots me a peculiar look, like she's back in the madhouse, but she don't say nothing. "Take care," I call after her as she shuns a cluster of dockers by the bar and disappears into the night.

"What's got into her?" asks Flo. Mick's made his excuses and has gone. Turns out he's up here delivering geese and turkeys for Mr. Greenland. So now she's left with me, but her face is as flushed as a spit jack's. She's downed a few too many.

"She's still grieving," I say. Sometimes I wonder at my big sister's thoughtlessness. When she's had a glass or four, she spouts a lot of claptrap and no mistake.

"But it's Christmas!" she protests. "Christ-mas!" she shouts loudly, turning round and waving a hand in the air to all and sundry. It's the signal to leave, I think. A couple of sailors start to close in, and the lech with the tattoo perks up, but I manage to wheel Flo toward the door before any of them makes a move on her.

I don't know which is worse, the 'baccy smoke inside or the fog out. It's a mile-and-a-half walk back to our house in Whitechapel and I'm dreading it. It's starting to drizzle, too, and, worse still, Jack's out there, lurking. I hook my arm through Flo's and she breaks into another Christmas carol. "'God rest ye, merry gentlemen, let nothing you dismay,'" she trills. I manage to drag her a few hundred yards, but she's getting hoity-toity with me. We're sticking to Commercial Road, so there's plenty of people about, and a few wagons and carts, but Flo keeps wishing every passerby the "compliments of the season."

By the junction with Sidney Street, we've moved on to "Hark! The Herald Angels Sing," but the smog's still as thick as thieves and I'm wondering how on earth we'll tackle the rest of the journey. Another cart with its lamps lit rumbles past us and I'd pay no attention if it isn't for the feathers rising up from the trailer. At first, I think the rain's turned to snow. The feathers are like big flakes, whirling in the wind. But when I look closer, I see it's a poulterer's wagon. What's more, the driver's looking at us. As the glare from the streetlamp lights up his face, I recognize who it is. And he recognizes us.

"We must stop meeting like this, ladies," jokes Mick Donovan, raising his cap. He fancies that he's God's gift to womankind. That he certainly is not, but I'm still pleased to see him. He tugs on the reins, bringing the cart to a halt just ahead of us.

Flo lifts her gaze and narrows her eyes at him. "Con! Will ya take a look at that? If it ain't my Paddy hero!" she blurts out. I could clock her one, I honestly could, the way she flirts. She knows I hate it when she calls me Con, too. My name is Constance. That's how the vicar christened me, and that's how I want to be known.

Mick bends low from his perch as we draw alongside. "I'm off back to the shop to get more fowl," he tells us. "Want a ride? It's not fancy, but on a night such as this, it . . ."

He hasn't finished his sentence before I've dragged Flo by the arm and am waiting by the tailgate. Mick jumps down, slides back the bolt, and helps us climb up. The cart's still full of feathers and a few empty sacks. There's a whiff of dead fowl wafting about, too, but I don't care and nor does Flo. She's already leaning on my shoulder as Mick jiggles the reins and we're off, showered in a snowstorm of feathers, but headed back for Whitechapel and the safety of our home.

It's still cold in the cart, and jerky, too. We're tossed from side to side now and again, but the drizzle has petered out and it's a darn sight better trundling along like this than gritting our teeth against the biting cold if we'd staggered back. I cover my face in my shawl as we go. I'm just settling into the ride, and then, from out of the corner of my eye, I think I see Cath. She's clamping her hat on her head, minded toward the junction of East India Dock Road. I know her lodgings lie that way. She's moving fast and I call to her, but my voice comes out all muffled from behind my shawl and is silenced by the fog and the noise of the traffic. The cart just clatters on, jouncing over the muddy ruts, splashing through the filthy puddles, taking us back to Whitechapel, back to Jack. Or so I think. But for Cath, the night is yet young.

Emily

Constance has done the sensible thing by accepting a ride from Mick Donovan. With Jack still prowling around Whitechapel, she and Florence are safer by far than walking home. But it is their friend Catherine who needs to be vigilant tonight. I find myself shadowing her as she hurries past the Eagle Tavern in East India Dock Road. A sudden gust of wind blasts down the street, setting empty barrels rolling and shop signs creaking; and in its wake, it takes off Catherine Mylett's hat. Slowly, as if in a daze, she turns to see it tumble to the ground and roll along the road. She lets out a little moan, but she does not choose to pursue it. It joins the blown sheets of newspaper in the gutter. There is no attempt to retrieve it. Instead, she turns and resumes her journey, counting her bonnet as but a trifle, counting it as lost. I fear 'twill not be the only thing that is lost this cold winter's night.

Ever since the death of her daughter, Evie, Catherine has been living but half a life. So knotted with grief, she was forced to enter the Poplar and Stepney Sick Asylum earlier this year. Her weight plummeted and sleep eluded her. When she was finally discharged, she may have been physically stronger, but mentally she was still most troubled. She also had to go back on the streets.

Moments later, Catherine is turning into a neat row of terraced houses off Poplar High Street. It's more respectable than anywhere she's ever lived. These London brick abodes are bigger and more solid. They stand in a long line with steps leading up to their smart front doors, with a bay window to one side. The panes are not boarded and the guttering doesn't hang from their roofs. There are thick curtains up at the windows and inviting gas lamps burn, instead of measly tallow stumps. For a moment, I think myself in the wrong place. There are no doss houses here. This is a decent neighborhood.

It's then that I notice Catherine is acting oddly, avoiding the glare of the infrequent streetlamps, hiding in the shadows. She stops at a house in the middle of the row. Since she discovered this new address, she's stood here once or twice before, just looking—looking and wondering and trying to pluck up the courage. She will do what she is about to do for her dead Evie, and for all the others there have been before her and since. Tonight she has decided she has looked and wondered enough. She bends low and reaches down to her right boot. Glimpsing behind her, she satisfies herself that no one is around before she climbs the steps and seizes the door knocker. She raps three times. She holds her breath. The blood pounds in her ears, so that when the door opens, she is not quite sure what the man in the smoking jacket says at first, although she can tell he is shocked to see her. By the light of the gas lamp in the hall, she watches his lips form a round "o" shape and she imagines him saying the name she used at that time.

"Rose?"

She does not respond at first, but sways a little on the doorstep.

"Rose," he says a second time, more assuredly, but with a look of disgust on his face. It's a look she has seen so many times before. From somewhere inside, she hears an infant cry.

"Where is she?"

"Where's who?"

"The old Irish bitch that killed my Evie."

"You're drunk," he sneers. He cannot smell her breath, only the reek of smoke on her clothes, but she is not welcome. He is about to slam the door in her face, when she suddenly lurches toward him. The blade glints in the candlelight as she raises the knife.

"No!" cries the man, pushing her away from him.

But she flies back. "She killed her!" she wails. "And all the others." There's a scuffle. He clasps hold of her wrist, but she manages to struggle free and plunge the knife down toward the man's chest. There's a sickening shriek. Blood blooms on flesh and splatters onto the wall. Catherine cries out. The man grunts. The knife clatters to the floor.

Constance

We're at the end of our street. It's too narrow for the cart to turn round, so Mick jumps down and helps us out of the back. The cold air's sobered Flo up. She started to jabber again when we trundled past St. Jude's Church. The jerking must've rumbled her innards 'cos the next thing I see is her spewing up over the side. Luckily, I don't think Mick heard. Anyway, we're back safe and sound and I'm grateful for our ride.

First Mick sees Flo down and then takes my hand, all firm like. There's something in his eyes that makes me blush. I'm hoping he can't see me color in the shadows. Flo's a few paces ahead of me, staggering toward our door. "Thank you. It was kind of you," I mutter, dipping my eyes to the slippery cobbles.

He whips off his hat. "The pleasure was all mine," he replies with a smile. I notice the bristles on his top lip rise; then without warning, he bends low and tries to find my mouth. I manage to turn my head away and feel only his coarse hairs against my cheek. Startled, I jerk my hand up to my face. I'm half expecting to find a rough patch just above my jaw, where his lips snagged me.

I look up to see he's swallowed his smile and regards me all strange. "I'd best be off then. More geese to deliver up Poplar way," he says.

There's an awkward silence between us that's suddenly filled by the howling of an unseen dog.

"Good night," I tell him, sounding stern as a schoolmistress. The sharpness of my own voice surprises me. But what he did just gave me the creeps. He don't reply; he just snorts and walks back to his cart, like he's wasted his time on me.

"Come on, Con," groans Flo, leaning up against a wall. I walk the few paces back to my front door. My legs feel like twigs. There's nothing I want more than to feel safe behind the bolted door of my own home. I suddenly think of Cath, out alone on the streets at the mercy of any man who wants to use her. I say a little prayer aloud: "Please, God, don't let anything bad happen to her."

CHAPTER 3

Thursday, December 20, 1888

EMILY

I do not choose what I see. I am sent and I am shown. I am a revenant. I used to live here in Whitechapel, among this squalor and deprivation, among this seething, disparate mass of people whose dreams have long been snatched from them to be replaced by the daily nightmare of despair. But I am returned and I speak through Constance Piper. We were close when I walked this place in my human form. There was a bond between us. I was her teacher. She was my pupil, but there was also a sisterly intimacy that transcended the boundaries of our respective births and classes. However, my death, instead of dividing us, has brought us closer together.

I am present much of the time and have returned to this district, sometimes with Constance's knowledge, but many times without it. She has no notion that I am here tonight. Nor that I am sent to witness yet another murder in this godforsaken dis-

trict of London. As the night creeps on, I fear something terrible is about to happen.

In the living accommodation above the East India Arms in Poplar High Street, the landlady, Mrs. Thompson, is woken by her dog. His bark's worse than his bite, but he's kept chained in the courtyard to ward off thieves. Slipping from between the rough blankets on her bed, she shivers, then shambles over to the window to look out. She screws up her eyes to peer into the blackness, but sees nothing. She returns to her snoring husband.

And so the night wears on. A shop manager, bogged down by paperwork, tallies and tots up into the early hours. His grocery store backs onto a builder's yard, just off Poplar High Street. It's called Clarke's Yard. The ventilator in the shop has remained open all night, but he has heard nothing out of the ordinary. Nor has the letter carrier, whose bedroom looks onto the same yard.

It's just gone four o'clock when Sergeant Robert Golding and Constable Barrett pass by on patrol. It's been a relatively quiet night, save for the usual drunkards and the odd brawl. Yet as he draws level with the narrow mouth of the yard, something catches the senior officer's eye. Lying by the wall is a shape. He approaches and crouches over it.

"Give us your lamp," he orders the constable, who duly hands it over.

The glow that emanates from the bull's eye lantern reveals that the shape is that of a woman—and, what's more, a woman already known to the police. Seeing her face, Sergeant Golding recognizes her as a local unfortunate, although he can't put a name to her. He feels her neck for a pulse. Her body is still warm, and she is lying on her left side. I can tell that it strikes him that the attitude of the body is somewhat reminiscent of that of the Ripper victim Annie Chapman. The left leg is drawn up and the right stretched out, although on this occasion the clothes are neither torn nor disarranged in any manner. Nor is there any obvious sign of injury.

Sergeant Golding rocks back on his heels and stands in thought.

"Another of Jack's, sir?" the constable asks anxiously. The mere thought has caused him to tremble.

Golding shakes his head. "I think not." He looks about him. "Lift the lantern, will you, lad?" he instructs. Constable Barrett holds the lamp aloft to the woman's face. There's a trickle of blood from her nostrils, but she's not been cut. It doesn't look as though this is Jack's handiwork, and for that, he is grateful, but he still needs assistance. He takes out his whistle and blows two sharp blasts. Within seconds, more constables have arrived.

CONSTANCE

The bed creaks as Flo stirs, rolls over, and starts snoring again. At least the booze has brought her sleep. My own head throbs not because of strong drink, but through my own anxiety as it spews out endless thoughts. I had a dream. No, a nightmare more like, and for the past hour or more, my mind's been fixed on Cath. I worry that she's still on the streets. The thought of leaving her in the state she was in is keeping me awake, niggling in my brain. It's times like these I need Miss Tindall most. For a short while, I found comfort in the notion that I thought she could still speak to me from beyond the grave; I was her spirit medium, although now I think I must've been mistaken. I'm still feeling all strange. Something happened to me, you see, and I ain't been myself for a while. I've not felt like Connie Piper, the flower girl, since I went to the Egyptian Hall and saw a strange man called Mesmer the Magnificent perform his act on stage. I know it sounds daft, but he tried to put the audience into a sort of trance. That's when something flipped inside my head. My brain went all mushy, like mashed-up marrowfat peas, and I started to see, well . . . things.

I always fancied myself as a shopgirl in the West End one day, working behind the counter of one of them fancy stores. They'd call me by my real name: Constance. But Miss Tindall, my old teacher, she said I was better than that. If I spoke right and learned my lessons and my manners well, I could one day be a lady. Flo used to tease me; said I had "hairs and grasses" or "airs and graces" to say it proper. Maybe I used to, but not no more—or "anymore," as Miss Tindall would have corrected me. She's gone, and everything I thought happened before was only in my mind—my poor, stupid, deluded mind. I'm telling myself it's all been a dream, or a nightmare, more like. So now I think my grief got the better of me and made me believe foolish, fanciful things that comforted me in my time of sorrow and loss. I ain't heard from Miss Tindall since they laid her—what was left of her—in the ground.

"Tell me Cath is safe. Tell me, please," I say, over and over. But there's no reply. I can't even comfort myself with the thought that if anything bad, I mean really bad, had befallen Cath, then Miss Tindall would have told me. It seems that everything strange that's happened has all been in my own sad mind.

Dawn is a way off. It's dark in the room. There's a candle stump on the nearby chest of drawers. I reach for it and strike a lucifer. The candle flares into life and I ease myself out of bed. Flo groans. She'll have a sore head this morning and won't be in any hurry to be roused. I am afraid, but I know what I must do. I force myself to shuffle sideways. I pad toward the looking glass that hangs on the wall near the window.

I haven't gazed at a mirror since that night at the Cutlers' house when I stared into one and saw not my own face, but Miss Tindall's. The memory of it chills me and comforts me at the same time. I move closer to the frame. I have to do this. I close my eyes, take a deep breath, and position myself in front of the glass. With my eyes still shut, I whisper her name. "Miss Tindall, are you there?" I ask, keeping my voice low. My heart's thumping in my chest and a cold shiver creeps down my spine.

Slowly I open my eyes and stare. And there, staring back at me, real steady, is the reflection of myself. I look how I imagined I might. My brown hair is twisted in a rope over my left shoulder. My body is slight, and if I squint hard, I can see my lips are chapped and cracked. I am what I am: an East End flower girl.

"Who you talking to?" comes a voice from the bed. Flo's head has bobbed up, but flops down again in an instant. "Bloody hell!" she groans, clutching her temples.

"Don't worry yourself," I tell her. She rolls over and falls silently to sleep once more. I only wish I could.

Emily

The blood on the hall floor at Woodstock Terrace has been mopped away. Some smeared the walls, too. That has not been so easy to clean. For a flesh wound, there really was rather a lot of blood.

That's not to say that the man who was on the wrong end of Catherine Mylett's knife is not suffering. His left hand is throbbing. He's staunched the flow as best he can, but the wound will have to wait to be properly dressed. He does not wish to wake his mother-in-law, a trained nurse. The cut was only an inch away from the artery in his wrist. He'll live, but more than anything, his pride is injured. It hurt having to hand over all that money to a whore.

CHAPTER 4

CONSTANCE

We're on our way to the flower market when I find myself stopped outside Mr. Greenland's shop. Under the cover of a red-and-white–striped awning, dozens of plucked turkeys and geese are strung up by their scrawny legs. The poor creatures have kept their heads, but they've lost their feathers, so their bodies are all pink and pimply. Through the window, I see the old poulterer, Mr. Greenland himself, looking dapper in his straw hat and striped apron. He's busy about his bloody work. Chitterlings bubble and spill over the slabs; the offal jigs in front of my gaze. And there's the music; the *swish–swish* from the sharpening steel as it caresses the blade of the old man's knife. I'm mesmerized by the sound and the sight of the meat and the guts, even though the scene fills me with horror and disgust. It makes my own innards roil and yet I can't take my eyes off the bright red flesh. It makes me think on how Miss Tindall met her end. She told me herself how her killers cut her up and threw her body parts away, and as I watch the cleaver chop off a turkey's head, I hear a scream escape from my own lips, only it's like it's coming from someone else.

"What the . . . ?" Flo spots me with my face pressed up to the window and grabs me by the arm. I thought she'd be feeling the worse for wear after last night's little escapade, but she's back to her usual self. She drags me away. "What you think you're doing, Con?" She gives me a right dressing-down. "What's got into you?"

The truth is I don't know. Last month with Mary Kelly's murder, last night with my worries over Cath, and today—it's like there's a stone in my chest that I'm dragging round with me. All I'm sure of is, I'm not the girl I was a few weeks ago.

"Cat got your tongue?" Flo wants an answer.

"Let's go back to Poplar," I say suddenly.

"*Back to Poplar?*" Flo repeats before her full lips curl at one edge. But it's not a smile she shows me, more of a sneer. "You're not worried about Cath, are ya? Aaah, bless." She pulls at my cheek like I'm a baby.

For a moment, I feel ashamed; then I straighten up. "Is that so wrong?" I hear myself say. I sound a bit cocky, but I've said what I needed to.

Hands on hips, she smirks. "Surely, if Cath was lying dead somewhere, you'd know?" She's talking to me like I'm a five-year-old, but then she puts her face close to mine. "What with your *special powers* an' all!"

I don't like the way she teases me, and when I shoot back a glare, she backs off. "Tomorrow, maybe," she says. There's as much bend in her as the bristles on a hearth brush. She knows it's dark before five o'clock and no woman with any sense ventures out alone after that. I don't reply. I'm not brave enough to go all the way to Poplar by myself in the dark. She's won.

CHAPTER 5

Friday, December 21, 1888

EMILY

I stand at the shoulder of yet another police surgeon. In the early hours, when Catherine's body was discovered, a Dr. George James Harris was called to attend. He was not a happy man, for who would be, dragged out of a warm, comfortable bed before dawn? The assistant divisional police surgeon's examination at the scene was cursory, to say the least. At the time I willed him to look more closely at Catherine's neck, but the light was poor, the night cold, and he was eager to return home. So, seeing no signs of foul play, the doctor pronounced life extinct. He then gave orders for the body to be removed to the mortuary as quickly as possible. I accompanied it, but remained hopeful that the truth would out.

A few hours later, I was gratified to see the mortuary keeper and assistant coroner seemed much more able. The latter, a solid, humble man by the name of Chivers, is accustomed to dealing with Poplar's poor. It was he who first discovered the mark around Catherine's neck and the scratches above it. And now it is time for the postmortem proper. Dr. Matthew Brownfield stands poised by the corpse, like some hierophant about to perform an ancient ritual. But he does not cut first. He examines and inspects, and the neck is of particular interest.

"Ah, I see, Chivers," he says to the assistant coroner, musing over the marks on Catherine's throat. He produces a ruler, then takes measurements. Next comes out the magnifying glass. He peers and he prods. "Evidently caused by a cord being drawn tightly," he announces.

"My thoughts too, sir," replies Chivers.

"Help here." Brownfield glances up to the porter and together they turn Catherine over onto her front. The surgeon takes a handful of her tousled hair and lays it to one side to expose the back of her neck. "As I suspected."

"Sir?"

Brownfield beckons the assistant and points to the telltale signs. "A cord, four-threaded, I'd say, drawn tightly from the spine to the left ear." His finger hovers over the line, then traces it. "And these here, thumb and finger marks."

"Yes, sir." Chivers nods in agreement. "Strangulation?"

"No doubt of it." The surgeon stands back and skirts round the table to the other side. "She couldn't have done this herself." Bending over, he turns Catherine's head to the left and beckons Chivers to look closer. "Whoever did this must've stood to her left and"—he holds up both hands—"holding the cord like so, he must've thrown it round her throat, crossed his hands, and thus strangled her." He crosses his own hands and pulls an imaginary rope with a theatrical flourish, then nods emphatically.

"Murder, pure and simple," he says.

Constance

It's another day that thinks it's almost night in Whitechapel. We ain't—sorry, we haven't—seen the sun for weeks now, or so it seems. It's hard for it to shine through the thick layer of coal smoke that hangs above us all.

"Chin up, my gal. You'll be sorry if we come home empty-handed," Flo chides, tugging at my sleeve. She's stern, but I know inside she's all quivery, like a jelly. We're out and about again, but we're all still on our mettle. We all know he's out there, somewhere, sharpening his knives, just like Mr. Greenland. And Old Bill is as useless as a bucket with a hole in it.

I'm still feeling sick with dread, but I paste a smile on my face as, armed with a basket of mistletoe—it always sells well this time of year—I stand on Farringdon Street junction. I thrust bunches of green, waxy leaves under the noses of passersby, and bawl over the din of the traffic, "Mistletoe. Mistletoe for your sweetheart. Ha'penny a bunch!"

Flo loiters by me, ready to relieve an unsuspecting punter of a penny or six. It's a routine we've performed over the past few years, ever since our dear old pa died, in fact. I don't like doing it, but Flo says it helps keep a roof over our heads. So that's how the day passes; me putting mistletoe into hands and Flo taking money out of pockets. Swings and roundabouts, as they say.

Toward four o'clock, when the cold has crept into my boots and I can't feel my poor feet no more, Flo decides to call it a day and we begin to head back toward Whitechapel. As we walk along Ludgate Hill, there's a little street rat trilling away. He's got no shoes on his dirty feet. " 'Christmas is a-coming and the goose is getting fat,' " he sings, thrusting a ragged old cap in front of us. " 'Please put a penny in the old man's hat.' "

Flo looks at him, all put out. "You'll be lucky," she sneers as we pass. "Geese don't get fat in Whitechapel. None of us does."

You can't blame the poor nipper for trying to earn a few pennies to keep the wolf from the door. It's what we all do here. We get by as best we can. Miss Tindall used to tell me that poetry is food for the soul, that's as maybe, but it don't stop your empty stomach aching.

We've just reached Liverpool Street Station when a newsboy catches my eye, or rather my ear.

"Dead body of a woman found in Poplar!" he shouts.

I feel the muscles in my chest clench, and Flo and me look at each other. Without a word, we dash up to the boy. Flo hands over one of the coins she's just lifted from a cull. "Give us one," she orders.

We stand under the gleam of a streetlamp not two yards away. With shaking hands, I read the front-page report.

"What's it say?" jabs Flo, all jittery.

My tongue sticks to the roof of my mouth at first. I can barely speak, and when I do, the words come out all dry and raspy like sawdust. "They found a body in Clarke's Yard, in Poplar High Street," I tell her.

Even though her face is part in shadow, I see her go pale. "Who?" she murmurs. "Does it say who?"

I shake my head and scan the words that start to blur in front of me, but somehow I manage to focus and read on. "The landlady of the East India Arms says she heard her dog barking very loudly around three o'clock, but couldn't see nothing," I tell her, adding: "There's to be a postmortem."

Suddenly Flo snatches the newspaper from my hands. I don't know why. She can't read. It's like she's got to do something, so she hits out at me. I snatch the crumpled pages back and carry on. "It says there was 'great discoloration of the face, neck, and arms, but no marks on the body.'" But the worst bit is yet to come. I look up at Flo and frown.

"What is it?"

The words come clattering out of my mouth. "It says, 'Her age was stated to be twenty, but she looked older.' You don't think . . . ?"

"Oh, Christ!" murmurs Flo.

EMILY

At Commercial Street Police Station, the headquarters of the Metropolitan Police's H Division, news of the death of yet another unfortunate is taken as a matter of course. The force is used to dealing with at least three such unexplained deaths each month; although behind closed doors, every policeman will tell you that these whores bring it on themselves. Addled by both gin and the pox, it's hardly surprising they're often found dead in the gutter. The new recruits are told to expect to encounter them on their beats, especially in the early morning. It's an occupational hazard in these parts. Besides, the officers of H Division have bigger fish to fry. They are on the trail of none other than the man whose name is on everyone's lips.

The Criminal Investigation Department team is a close one, more like a small battalion than a whole regiment. Up until last year, being stationed in Whitechapel was seen as an unenviable posting. Now any ambitious young detective would give his eyeteeth to have a crack at hunting down England's most notorious murderer. Such ambition does, however, breed rivalry among those who are assigned to the investigation.

A large room has been set aside to accommodate the eight detective sergeants and eight detective constables assigned to this, one of the four stations in H Division. While the headquarters are in Leman Street, Commercial Street is, to date, closest to where the Ripper has struck. Each detective has his specific role. One, for example, is liaising with Scotland Yard; another two are sifting through the dozens of letters that arrive each week, purporting to be from Jack himself. (The vast majority are, of course, hoaxes, but need to be investigated, nevertheless.) The others have each been assigned to follow up on the various leads members of the public give them. Not entirely unsurprisingly, a handful of the same names emerge several times over. One such is that of Montague John Druitt, a former barrister-turned-

schoolmaster who is living in Blackheath, although just why this particular character should be of such interest defeats the detective sergeant who has been delegated to investigate him. Superintendent Arnold is, however, adamant, and Detective Sergeant Thaddeus Hawkins must follow his orders.

Thaddeus Hawkins was formerly stationed at K Division in Whitehall. It was he who, as a relatively new member of the Criminal Investigation Department, played a central role in the identification of my own remains in the case that is now known as the Whitehall Mystery. His subsequent rise was in no small part thanks to his willingness to believe Constance's remonstrations. So impressed with his work were his superiors that he was given a promotion and posted to Whitechapel but three weeks ago. He has been dropped in at the deep end with strict instructions to leave no stone unturned when it comes to this Druitt fellow. Unlike his other colleagues, who seem incapable of organizing their various notes and files into some semblance of order so as to facilitate their travails, Sergeant Hawkins likes to work neatly and methodically. Whereas loose sheets of paper seem to proliferate on the other detectives' desks, he files them away in alphabetical order. He has a system that serves him well, one taught to him by his father, who was a librarian at a boys' school. (And who also had more than a passing interest in Greek mythology, hence his son's nomenclature.) Names, places, dates, et cetera, are written on a standard-sized piece of card and arranged in a long box in alphabetical order. Such a system of data organization is expandable, can be rearranged easily, and added to if necessary. These innovative methods have, of course, caused much ribaldry among Hawkins's colleagues, some of whom—especially the older men—regard him as nothing but an upstart grammar-school boy, who knows nothing about the realities of life in one of the vilest and most notorious districts of London.

"Wouldn't know a bedbug if it bit him on the arse," he'd heard another detective mock when he didn't see he was near-

by. Of course, he did. His mother had died when he was ten, and his father lost his job soon after. Father and son had been forced to move to an area where the rents were lower and the chances of being robbed in the street much higher. The mocking didn't bother him. The name Thaddeus means "courageous of heart," and his father always reminded him that he needed to live up to it.

There are times, however, when he wonders what his efforts are all for. His pursuit of Mr. Druitt has produced several cards and he has cross-referenced these with the witness accounts of all of the Whitechapel murders to date. As yet, however, his system has not produced any conclusive leads, and he knows that if he doesn't find some meaningful evidence shortly, his boss, Detective Inspector Angus McCullen, will soon be breathing down his neck. So, when he sees him striding over to his desk this morning, he naturally tries to avoid eye contact. Too late.

"You. Hawkins. In my office now, laddie!" orders McCullen in his guttural Scottish accent. He's a small, stocky man, built rather like a bulldog, with a bite to match. No doubt a redhead in his youth, the copper tinge to his hair, both cranial and facial, has long since faded, although anyone who knows him would testify that his accompanying temper has not.

Glennister and Leach, two of the senior detective sergeants, swap smirks as Hawkins rises hurriedly and enters the lion's den.

"Shut the door," growls McCullen. He's just about to divest himself of his topcoat and tartan scarf, when he suddenly remarks, much to his annoyance, there is no fire in the grate. He decides to remain wearing his outer garments. "This whore in Poplar," he begins.

Hawkins was afraid he would be the one to be singled out over this latest death. "Yes, sir. As yet unidentified."

"The very same. Have you heard anything?" McCullen slumps down behind his desk, rubbing his hands together for warmth.

"A prostitute, so they say, sir. Died of natural causes, according to the officers who found her." Hawkins stops himself. "Although . . ."

"Although what?" McCullen blows on his fingers.

"A reporter from the Evening Standard *was apparently asking . . ."*

"Och! Flies on shit!" The inspector slams the desk with both palms. "Brownfield's writing his report as we speak and I don't think it's going to make good bedtime reading."

Hawkins arches a brow. "He thinks it was murder?"

"Aye, laddie. I'm afraid he does, which is nonsense, of course." McCullen shakes his unremarkable gray head and leans over his desk. "You're a bright lad," he tells Hawkins candidly. "I don't need to tell you that if word gets out another East End whore's been slain, the finger will point at Jack again and then all hell will break loose. So, until the inquest, it's your job to keep a lid on it. Understand?"

"So I'm to say no one else was involved?"

McCullen nods with a smile. "You're learning quick, laddie."

"Yes, sir," replies the detective sergeant. For the moment, he will simply have to suppress the doubts that have already begun to surface about the woman's death.

CHAPTER 6

Saturday, December 22, 1888

CONSTANCE

Neither Flo nor me has had much sleep. We're both worried about Cath. There's seven women been slaughtered in Whitechapel this year. Eight, if you count my own dear Miss Tindall. And now there's a ninth. Of course, I'm praying it's not Cath, but there's been no word yet on who this latest victim is. The inquest opened yesterday at Poplar Town Hall. Mr. Wynne Baxter is the coroner. He's the gent who was in charge of the inquests into the murders of Polly Nichols and Annie Chapman and Liz Stride, so he knows what he's about, but he's adjourned proceedings until the new year.

I wondered if we should go to the mortuary, but Flo told me we could get nabbed if the coppers recognize us and we might even end up doing three months' hard labor in the clink. "Then what would Ma do?" she'd asked, putting on her teary-eyed act. Instead, she said she'd get her friend Sally Richardson, who grafts in Poplar, to ask around.

So that's why we're headed toward the West End and away from where the latest body was found, where I think we should be. We're leaving Whitechapel behind for the day and looking out for richer pickings among the ladies and gents of the better-off districts of this teeming old metropolis. With it coming up to Christmas, the toffs have more money in their wallets than usual. They say the streets of London are paved with gold. Well, that's not true. Everyone knows it, but the West End is paved with silver, all right. There's more florins and crowns jangling about in swells' pockets in Regent Street and Oxford Street than wives in the king of Persia's harem. They're too busy gawping at the fancy shop windows, dressed with their bells and red ribbons, or listening to the carolers, to notice anything else. So Flo will relieve them of just a little of it; it's sort of like giving to charity, spreading festive cheer, only the first they'll know of it is when they open their purses or look in their pockets to find their half crowns have gone to a more deserving home.

It's the last Saturday before Christmas, so everyone's out and about. We're being carried along with the crowd as it flows toward Commercial Street. "This place is crawling with blues," mumbles Flo. Her eyes are darting left and right. "The sooner we get out o' here, the better."

Just as we're about to cross the road, a shout goes up. We both look behind us at the same time to see two coppers struggling with a ragged bloke, who's spitting and cussing. We know they're nabbing another one they think might be Jack. Last week, they took someone down the station just 'cos he had a peak on his cap, like a witness said. Old Bill is getting desperate, clutching at straws. We hurry on, plowing our way toward the omnibus stop, like a couple of gritty mastiffs, when Flo suddenly lightens up. She's caught sight of her friend Sally Richardson, the one she was going to ask about Cath.

"Oi, Sal!" Flo shouts over the din.

Sally turns a freckled face toward the call. Flouncy like a pair of curtains in a tart's boudoir, she is, in a bonnet with a sprig of holly in it. Flo lunges through the crowd and reaches out to take her elbow. She stops her outside the baker's.

"Just the person I'm looking for!" yells Flo. Sal lets out a squeal when she realizes it's her best friend and gives her a hug. It doesn't take long before they both forget I'm there and my eyes start to wander. We're in the lower half of Commercial Street, near St. Jude's Church, and it brings back memories of Miss Tindall. Only a couple of months ago, I was trawling these parts looking for her after she went missing. Frantic I was, asking shopkeepers and hawkers and the like if they'd seen her. I was told she'd gone back to Oxford, that she'd left without saying good-bye, but I knew she wouldn't do that; not to me. Turned out I was right. They buried her remains only a few days ago. I hope she's at peace now. I fear I can't be, knowing how she suffered. Every time I think of it, it's like someone's pressing on a fetid wound, it hurts me that much. So I try to hold my thoughts firm, lest they bring on angry tears. But here, in this place that stores so many painful memories, it's hard not to. And just as I'm thinking I've blanked out her image, the strangest thing happens. Lo and behold, there she is again. Miss Tindall! She's standing there, calm as you like, in broad daylight at the end of Fashion Street. It's her. I know it is, even though her back's to me. That's her hat and she even's got her trusty green brolly hooked over her arm.

"Miss Tindall!" I cry.

There are market stalls on the other side, spilling out from Petticoat Lane. Barrow boys are bawling and yelling and adding to the roar of the traffic. They're selling bags and ribbons and umbrellas, and a sea of people is lapping all around her, but she's not budging. She just stands there, looking calm and serene, as the cries and shouts whiz past her like artillery fire. Then she turns, slow like, and I see she's holding something in her arms. She's cradling a bundle of some sort, although I can't make out what.

A quick glance to my left tells me Flo's still gassing with Sal, so I take my life into my own hands and head off across the street toward her. I swerve in front of a hansom and the air turns blue with the driver's hollering. Another cabbie joins in as I weave past his carriage, but just as I'm almost over, a wagon crosses my path. I have to lean back so I don't get clocked and in an instant she's gone. I screw up my eyes and look first left, then right, then left again. Miss Tindall's nowhere to be seen. I scoot up Fashion Street, peering into the shops, then back down again, quick as I can. But it's not quick enough. Blow me. She's really gone. I'm whirling around like one of them dervishes in the Crimea when I hear Flo's yell. She's spotted me and she's definitely not happy.

"What you playin' at?" she squawks. She's followed me across the road.

"It's her," I say. "I saw her."

"Who?" She's scowling at me. She knows very well who I mean.

"Miss Tindall!"

Flo shakes her head. "We're not startin' that funny business again!" She grabs me by the arm again. "You know she's dead."

"I tell you! I saw her," I protest.

But she's having none of it and she marches me along by her side like I'm a naughty nipper.

"Come on, Con. We're late." I wince at being called Con, but Flo's in charge now. We're trotting back down Commercial Street again. I glance back just one more time in the vain hope of proving I'm right, but just as I do, I spot a copper with his eyes locked onto me. A bent old hag in a head scarf is by his side.

"There," she cries, lifting her arm and pointing at me. "That one!"

Flo looks daggers at me. "Scarper!" she yells. I panic. She

goes left. I go right. It's what we usually do when Old Bill's onto us. Ofttimes we just nip down an alley, or hide in a doorway. It don't take much to outwit a copper, but this time it's different. My legs feel like they weigh a ton, like they're stuck in thick mud, and I can't move. I watch helplessly as Flo disappears round a corner, leaving me to the mercy of the approaching rozzer.

"You!" he calls after me. It's PC Tanner. He's our regular down White's Row, where we live, and the look in his eyes tells me I'm in big trouble. I quake in my boots, even though I've not helped Flo lift anything this morning. The bent old crone is catching up. "That's 'er," she huffs as she draws close.

"Me?" I wail. "I ain't done nothing!"

My pounding heart is thundering in my ears as the copper grabs my arm and forces it behind my back.

"What the . . . ?" I feel the cold steel of the cuffs grip my wrists.

"Constance Piper," says PC Tanner, all formal, "you're under arrest!"

"What for?" says I, struggling vainly.

A cluster of people has gathered round to watch. Handcuffs locked behind my back, the constable glowers at me. He's a different bloke from the one who's sweet on Flo.

"Don't come the innocent with me," he snarls.

"What for?" I ask once more as I feel my tears well up.

And then he looks at me from under his helmet and tells me straight.

"For the murder of a newborn child."

Suddenly I see stars. In a heartbeat, the world blurs in front of me.

EMILY

I am not far away. Just across the road, in fact, watching events unfold as I'd planned. Had the child's body been found aban-

doned on a rubbish tip or on the banks of the Thames, as is quite commonplace these days, then not many would have raised a brow. Few newspapers bother to report such findings anymore, eschewing the thorny subject of child cruelty for the more titillating gossip circulating in government or, better still, in the royal circle. An Act of Parliament to protect infant life was passed a few years ago after the shocking case of two "baby farmers" who murdered their charges. For a payment of five pounds, these women would take in babies whose mothers were unable to keep them and would neglect them so woefully that they only lingered for a few weeks in most cases. Oh, there was righteous outrage at first, as there usually is as long as such events remain at the forefront of our consciences, but then, of course, they slip out of our minds and are put to one side until the next calumny is exposed. At the moment, inquests into such infant deaths are deemed to be an irrelevance, and, more often than not, the verdict will be "found dead" and no inquiry is made as to by whose hand the child might have died.

It pains me to see Constance bundled away like that, cuffed by the police and shouted and jeered at by the growing crowd that thinks she has killed a babe. Desperate young women take desperate measures, including slaughtering their own, to survive. That is surely the crime the baying mob that now gathers thinks Constance has committed, but she will soon be able to prove her innocence.

She was not mistaken. She did see me carrying a paper parcel. I secreted it under the costermonger's barrow, but she was the only one who knew I was there. She will have to endure another hour or two of discomfort before she is exonerated and set free. But by then, a train of events will have been set in motion that will save countless lives, as long as she is prepared to be guided by me.

CHAPTER 7

CONSTANCE

I'm not sure how I got here, but I'm in the local nick. I can't see straight; there's little stars tripping before my eyes and everyone is shouting and ranting around me. I suddenly think of Flo. I need her, but she's nowhere to be seen. Then I remember. She scarpered off in the opposite direction as soon as Old Bill put the finger on me and now she's left me to their tender mercies. PC Tanner's face is still swimming in front of me and there's another copper now, all gruff and meaty, peering at me. He's sporting white muttonchop whiskers that are yellowed by tobacco smoke. I catch a whiff of him. Smells like a bonfire, he does.

"What's all this then?" booms Whiskers, standing behind the front desk.

PC Tanner tugs at his blue tunic and then I hear him say it. "This here young woman's accused of killing a baby, Sergeant Halfhide, sir."

His words don't register with me at first. It's like he's talking about someone else. He knows my name, so why don't he say it?

Whiskers throws a look toward the station entrance, where

there's people trying to get in and there's coppers trying to stop them. But they can't quiet the jeers and the caterwauls and I'm beginning to panic. Then I do a stupid thing. I start to struggle and I dive for the door, but from out of nowhere, another two or three coppers are on me in a second and drag me back to the big desk. I lift up my bowed head, but it's no use. The sudden surge of energy I felt has deserted me and I start to slide down the side of the counter again until a beefy copper tries to heave me onto my feet. I'm floppy as a rag doll, still I manage to bleat pathetically: "I didn't do nuffink, I swear."

"Let's be 'avin' her then," barks Whiskers. All stern, he is, and the two coppers fix their arms under mine and heave me across the flagstones and through a door that leads to the cells.

Soon I find myself sat at a table in this little room. The hairy sergeant comes in and sits down opposite me. He leans forward and taps the charge sheet with his stubby yellow fingers.

"Infanticide," he says. It's a word I don't know. I frown, so he repeats himself, only slower. "*Infant-i-cide,*" like I'm a kid at school. "Child murder." Then he adds: "It's a hangable offense."

My heart's in my mouth. I try and leap up. "I never . . ." But PC Tanner and his beefy mate tug me down. Whiskers gives one of his men a nod and sends him off and out of the room.

"I don't know what you're talking about," I whine. "I ain't killed a baby. I couldn't kill a baby." I feel tears running down my cheeks and I wipe them away with the back of my hand. I think of the bent hag with the head scarf who accused me. "It's that old bunter's word against mine," I wail.

My pleas fall on deaf ears. "Yours was it? Or someone else's?" Whiskers' stare bores through me like a drill. It gets into my very core. I'm scared.

"No! No!" I'm shaking my head when PC Tanner comes back in again. This time, he's holding a brown paper parcel, like the one I saw Miss Tindall carrying, and all of a sudden, the room's filled with this pong. But it's only when Whiskers folds back the wrappings that I realize what's inside. I barely catch a glimpse of it, but that's more than enough. It's a sight no one should have to suffer. I gag at the stink that bursts into the air. It's a baby. A dead baby wrapped in dirty cotton rags. I try and blink away the bulging eyes, the blue lips, and the little balled fists. I can't tell if it's a boy or girl, but it put up a fight. Yet the worst is to come. Around its tiny neck is a piece of flowery yellow ribbon tied and pulled tight. The little mite was strangled.

"God in heaven!" is all I can blurt.

My head's still in my hands when I hear someone else come into the room. A sniff. Whoever it is knows the reek of death when they smell it. There's the scraping of the chair as Whiskers stands to his feet sharpish. I look up and I'm that relieved to see a familiar face that I feel myself springing up from my seat.

"Constable Hawkins!" I cry.

Emily

No wonder Constance is so relieved to encounter Thaddeus Hawkins. As a detective constable with K Division, he was present at the mortuary when Pauline Beaufroy identified my torso. I know the memory of it still flashes into Constance's mind every day. He was kind to her in those most trying circumstances and, what's more, he had faith in her. He attended my memorial service, too. I saw him pay his respects. He was not so important or so pompous as to forget that at the end of the day, when we take off our clothes and our tongues are at rest, we're all Adam's offspring. We have the same hopes and fears; and we all bleed. At heart, he's a good man.

I think he's taken more trouble with his dress than when he was stationed at the King Street Police Station: The neatly tied cravat, the waistcoat, and is that the sheen of oil on his pate? Perhaps that is because he has just been promoted. There's a light in his eyes, too. He thinks he recognizes Constance, although he remains uncertain.

The hirsute sergeant catches the glimmer in the young man's eyes. "She's already known to you?" No doubt he's eager to pounce like a cat on a mouse on any criminal record Constance may have.

I am relieved to see the detective nod. "We have met before." It's not a question, but I know he still can't quite place her. Yet I also know Constance will prompt him.

"I was with Miss Beaufroy, at the mortuary, sir." From his expression, he still needs more, so I can tell she has to force herself to say it. "The torso, sir."

"Miss Piper. Yes?"

It is done. The memory floods back into the detective's mind. I will still need to explain everything to Constance, but she has started well.

Constance

I'm that thankful. I didn't think he'd recognize me, let alone remember my name, but then, of course, he saw me as Miss Beaufroy's companion—all dressed up like a lady—not what I really am. Or was. The truth is, I'm so confused after what's happened, I really don't know myself. Am I a flower girl or a lady?

"Constable Hawkins," I reply. I can't think of anything else to say. He's looking at me all curious, like he's not a clue why I'm here. He pulls out the chair and sits down at the table.

"It's Detective Sergeant Hawkins to you," snarls Whiskers. I'm not surprised that he's climbed the ladder, but I'm the one who gave him a leg up—me and Miss Tindall, of course. If it wasn't for us, the Whitehall Mystery, as the papers called it, would remain unsolved. I'm hoping he appreciates that.

"The charge," says Whiskers, slipping a sheet of paper under Detective Sergeant Hawkins's nose.

He reads it, then shoots me a horrified look. "*Infanticide?* What is the meaning of this, Miss Piper?"

"A mistake!" I manage to cough out before Whiskers cuts me off.

"Seen trying to rid herself of that parcel." His nostrils flare in disgust as he nods at the brown paper package, which has been placed on a smaller table a few feet away. "She's all yours, Hawkins," Whiskers adds as he heads for the door.

"Thank you, Sergeant Halfhide," the detective calls after him, although he's still keeping his bewildered gaze on me. "You may leave us, too, Constable," he tells PC Tanner, adding: "And perhaps you'd be so good as to arrange for that to be taken to the mortuary for examination." He switches to the reeking parcel.

"Sir." Tanner nods and picks up the package, holding it at arm's length like it's a ticking bomb.

I understand Sergeant Hawkins wants to wait till the door is shut firm before he speaks to me, but I can't wait no more. "I can explain," I tell him, even though I've no idea how. He nods his shiny brown head and looks earnest. Authority becomes him. He wears it well, like a Savile Row suit. He sits at the table, then picks up a pencil and plays with it in his fingers. He has gentleman's hands. His fingernails are clean and short.

"Yes. I'm sure you can, Miss Piper," he says calmly. He sounds like a doctor telling some poor sod they've only got a few weeks to live. The old Constance tells me I'm done for, but then something strange happens. As I watch his gesture, a shaft of light lances through the high window and hits me like a bolt of lightning. There's a flash before my eyes and I suddenly make sense of all this: of the dead baby and why I'm here, answering to a detective in the Metropolitan Police force. And in that moment, I think I can explain. I'm no longer a suspect facing her inquisitor, but on equal terms. Silly, I know, but it's almost as if I feel I've known Detective Sergeant Hawkins all my life. He leans back in his chair and an easy silence fills the gap between us, that and the gentle ticking of the fob watch that peeks from his waistcoat pocket. The seconds slow to a trickle and it's all because of Miss Tindall. She has sent me here. It's all her doing. I close my eyes and try and imagine her, listen to her voice. She's there, all right. I can't see her, but I feel her presence. It's flooding into me, lighting up the dark corners of my mind, so that everything becomes quite clear. I close my eyes.

"Miss Piper," I hear Sergeant Hawkins say in a soft, concerned tone. "Miss Piper, are you quite well?" But I blank him out and listen only for Miss Tindall.

A moment later, I reopen my eyes. "Yes, I am quite well, thank you," I say. Yet it's not my reply that causes him to raise his brows so much as the manner of its delivery. The fluster and bluster has gone from my demeanor. I am quite poised and my diction is crisp. I have become a lady once again. I may still be wearing the shabby garb of a flower seller, but I am the same as I was when we first met in the company of Miss Pauline, and I know exactly what I must do.

"You understand, Sergeant Hawkins, I had nothing to do with this baby's death," I say with such a certainty that my statement takes the detective back a little.

I'm worried I sound too pompous, but no. Quite the opposite. It seems the detective accepts my sudden change of fortune without question. He nods. "Of course, Miss Piper."

"I am glad of it."

"Yes. A misunderstanding, I'm sure."

"*Yes. A misunderstanding*," I echo. "A case of mistaken identity." I can hardly believe what I'm saying. He keeps his eyes on me and nods. I feel my spine stiffen. I am emboldened. "So I am free to go?"

Sergeant Hawkins nods and I push away from the table to rise. As I do so, I feel more words land on my tongue from out of nowhere and fall from my lips. Before I leave, Miss Tindall is reminding me to ask about Cath. "I'm sure you must be busy, especially after the murder in Poplar," I say.

He's standing, too, but as he pushes his chair toward the table, his head jerks up. "*Murder,* Miss Piper? What makes you think we are dealing with a murder?"

"I read in the newspaper . . ."

He smiles, which I wasn't expecting. "Surely, Miss Piper, you know you mustn't believe everything you read in the press." It's like he's disappointed in me for swallowing the spiel they print. "The officers who found the body say the woman died of natural causes," he tells me.

That's news to me, but I gulp it down because another question is hovering on my lips and I need to get rid of it. "Do you know the dead woman's identity?"

"No." He shakes his head. "Only that she was an unfortunate."

There's that word again: "unfortunate." All the *unfortunate* women in Whitechapel aren't on the streets through bad luck alone. The Wheel of Fortune is spun by powerful gents. Miss Tindall told me that. Their women don't have to sell their bodies to get by. It just suits men that street girls do. I feel the blood drain from my face as I think of Cath, but my look goes unnoticed because just then there's a commotion outside. To my shock, I see Flo's head bob up and down through the small grille in the studded door.

"Con! Con!" she yells.

All of a sudden, I'm a Whitechapel flower girl again.

Sergeant Hawkins looks at me and frowns. "You know this woman?"

I worry Flo's put her foot in it again. "Yes. She's my sister," I hear myself say in my usual voice, and I know, for sure, that Miss Tindall's spell is broken.

Sergeant Hawkins rises, stalks over to the door, and half opens it. Immediately Flo's head squeezes through, looking beyond him to me.

"You all right, Con?" she calls before turning to scold the detective. "You got no right to 'old 'er 'ere. No right!" she cries, wagging her finger at poor Sergeant Hawkins. She bobs up again. "We'll get you out o' 'ere. Don't you trouble yourself, gal!"

Even though I've no need of her help, it's good to see Flo. I knew she wouldn't leave me in the clink. She must've been watching from round the corner when the coppers cuffed me. Her dander's up, and when that happens, she's like a clucking hen. You don't want to mess with her when she's in that mood.

"You leave 'er alone. She ain't done nuffink. With me all morning, she were," insists Flo, now wedged firmly over the threshold of the poky room. "That old crone didn't know what she was on about. Half a brain if you ask me," she jabbers. "She's innocent, I tell ya."

"I know," replies the sergeant.

"*Innocent,*" stresses Flo.

"Yes. I know Miss Constance is completely innocent of this terrible crime."

Flo's eyes open wide. "You do?"

"Yes. She is free to go."

She claps her hands together. "Then what are you waitin' for, my gal?" she asks me.

Sergeant Hawkins gives a shallow bow, trying to hide a smile.

"Good day to you both, ladies."

Flo's suddenly all coy. "Good day to you, er . . ."

"Hawkins. Detective Sergeant Hawkins," he tells her.

Of course Flo's no idea about rank in the police force. "I'll put in a good word for you with Sergeant Batty, down at Limehouse," she tells him cheekily.

I catch the detective's amused expression. I'm glad he's not taken it personal. "Good-bye, Miss Piper," he says to me, then lowering his voice, he adds: "I shall keep you informed of any developments regarding the baby's case." We have understood each other. I am glad.

As we pass the counter on our way out, Flo spins round to

PC Tanner. She can't help herself. "Ashamed of yourself, you should be," she scolds. It's like she's telling off a cheeky schoolboy and the constable seems all hangdog.

And me? I arrived here accused of killing a baby, but then Miss Tindall came to help me. She's back. I wasn't dreaming. Not only did she return, she showed me the way out of my difficulties. But she's still not told me about this death in Poplar, and now I hear it might not be murder, after all.

As Sergeant Hawkins escorts me to the main door, a little way behind Flo, I turn before we reach the front steps.

"The dead woman, in Clarke's Yard . . . ," I say. I picture Cath, lying cold on the mortuary slab, and my expression betrays my fear.

"Tragic business," he offers by way of sympathizing with my feelings. I think perhaps he detects there is more to my inquiry than meets the eye because he follows his commiserating with a suggestion. "Several people have been visiting the local hospital"—he pauses to think of a delicate way to frame his meaning—"to see if they can be of assistance." He is trying to make it easier for me.

I nod. He pauses, then says: "Good day, Miss Piper." He resumes in a more businesslike manner with a bow of his head.

"Good day, Sergeant," I hear myself reply, just how Miss Tindall would, but there's nothing "good" about this day in the East End. A baby has been strangled and another woman found dead on the streets.

As I descend the police station steps, my lips move in a prayer for the latest poor soul. "Please don't let it be Cath," I whisper.

Chapter 8

Emily

A young woman by the name of Louisa Fortune gazes forlornly out of the train window. She is not alone in the compartment. Beside her sits an elderly woman in a large hat with purple feathers and opposite her a clergyman wearing a monocle and a stern expression. He peruses a copy of the Daily Telegraph.

Louisa catches sight of one of the headlines and suddenly strains her eyes to read. Today Jack the Ripper is Russian, according to a report from Vienna. The words leap out at her: His monomania was that fallen women could only be redeemed and go to heaven if they were murdered.

She feels the sharp point of a blade between her ribs. Is she so fallen from grace that death is her only hope of redemption? The thought riles her and she looks through the window, fidgeting with her hands, tugging at the fingers of her gloves, then smoothing them back again. There is a novel on her lap, but it remains firmly shut. After seeing the newspaper, she no longer has an appetite for reading.

I, however, can read her face as if it were an open book. It tells the story of despair and loss. Her eyes are glassy, and shad-

owed underneath, while her lips are flat and tight, as if she is trying to stifle the cry of the constant pain she feels inside. This pain has irked her ever since she gave up her son for adoption. She'd had him baptized, against the midwife's advice. "Best leave that for me, dearie," the old Irish minder had told her.

Nevertheless, she was determined that her son should have some memento of her, even if he was never told of her existence. So she'd bought a silver christening cup and engraved it with the boy's initials. She'd called him Bertie for short and told herself that the gift would be a testament to her love for him, and if he had his own children, then she would like to think that he would pass on the set to his offspring. It is her greatest sorrow that she will never see that day. She loves him so much that she thought her heart would break when she handed him over, swaddled in his silken shawl, together with a five-pound note, to his minder, Mother Delaney. He'd cried when he'd left her arms, her warmth, and her scent. She had cried, too. Not in the Irishwoman's sight, but alone, on a bench in a churchyard.

And now she is on her way to see her Bertie again for one last encounter. At least she can be sure that Mother Delaney is of good character. Or so she tells herself. She spent a total of three months in her home, prior to and after the birth, and has been assured that this kindly old woman will adopt the boy. And yet she is still having doubts, grave doubts. She is due to see Mother tomorrow, to hand over the final five pounds to secure Bertie's adoption. This meeting was intended to satisfy her that her son is being properly cared for and thriving under the nursemaid's supervision before he is lost to her forever. But now she is not so sure that she can bear to let him go.

As soon as the city of Oxford comes into view, however, her melancholy expression lifts. The dreaming spires prick her memory and she recalls happier times at Lady Margaret Hall and she thinks of me. We who are remembered fondly in this way never die. She lifts her fingers up to the grimy glass of the pane, as if trying to touch me. She's recalling the day we first met in the college gardens: me, a stiff, priggish young woman, who'd never before left home; she, self-assured, well-traveled, and altogether more worldly.

Suddenly the locomotive lumbers to a halt, sending its steamy breath over the platform in great clouds.

"Oxford! Oxford!" calls the guard.

The clergyman rises, folds his newspaper, and leaves. The woman in the purple-plumed hat also disembarks, so that Louisa is left alone in the carriage. Heavy doors swing open, then shut. Suitcases bump and scrape along the platform. With her head propped against the window, she watches friends meet, wives greet husbands, mothers embrace sons as the whistle blows and the train chugs out of the station. She can control herself no longer. The dam bursts.

Constance

As we walk home, Flo's full of herself. "I told 'im, I did," she says as, for the third or fourth time, she replays what went on in the police station. I'd rather forget it all, but I can't. I'm trying to make some sense of what happened: the dead baby and the nameless woman lying on a mortuary slab. Somehow I know Miss Tindall is trying to tell me something. She was there with me in that tiny room. I know she was, but I can't work out what she wants of me. What with the clatter of hooves, the traffic's din, hawkers calling and Flo squawking, I think my head will explode. Suddenly I stand stock-still and cover my ears with my hands.

"Con?" Flo frowns at me. She's shocked. "What's amiss, Con?"

I fix her with a look that only sisters can fathom and she knows straightaway.

"This is about Cath, ain't it?"

I nod. "I need to know if it's her, in the hospital."

To my surprise, instead of getting on her high horse and telling me to pull myself together, she nods. “You’re right.”

A sigh escapes from my pent-up chest. I don’t need her approval, but it helps. I twitch a smile, then catch my arm in hers and together we set off toward the docks and toward the infirmary. We’re going to the mortuary.

CHAPTER 9

EMILY

The Poplar Hospital for Accidents stands just across the road from the imposing entrance gates to the East India Docks. As might be gleaned from its name, the staff there are more used to dealing with the crushed limbs of dockers than with the bodies of women found dead on the street. It's dangerous work shifting cargo. A winch can fail; a capstan recoil; ropes can lash and burn. And you won't find many of the gentler sex on the dockside. It's men's work, hard men's work. Yet it is here that Catherine Mylett's body is laid out in the mortuary, although, of course, no one yet knows that it is she, perhaps not even her killer. She is not really known in these parts, having lived until relatively recently in Whitechapel. So, for the past two days, people have been coming and going. Some have steeled themselves to look upon her bloodless face; a few have taken a voyeuristic pleasure in it, as if she were some exhibit at a freak show. Some have gasped at the sight, even though she appears quite peaceful. Many have shed tears, but none has been able to identify the young woman found in Clarke's Yard. None until now.

CONSTANCE

When we arrive, I do the talking. I tell the deskman that we're here to try and put a name to the woman they found in Clarke's Yard. His eyes are so crossed I can't even tell if he's looking at me or not, but he doesn't seem put out in the least. It's like I've asked to buy a bag of sugar. He just slides a piece of paper in front of me.

"Can you write?" says he. I can't tell from his look if he's asking me or Flo.

"Yes. I'll write for both of us."

I think I surprise him. "Then leave your names and addresses here, will ya?" His spindly finger points at a blank space at the bottom of the paper. I see from the list, we're two of many who've come along to see if they can "be of assistance," as Detective Sergeant Hawkins put it.

A flat-faced nurse appears behind Flo from out of nowhere.

"Nurse Pringle'll take you," says the clerk, and on a nod, we fall in behind her and are led down the corridor, past a flaking sign that points to the mortuary.

It's the smell that hits us first; sharp as tin cans, it is. The metallic, chemical tang stings our nostrils. I know it's better than the stink of rotting corpse, but it still takes your breath away. There's a bank of drawers ranged along the wall. I guess that's where they keep the other dead bodies. At least we know she's not been cut; her face's not slashed like Catherine Eddowes's or Mary Kelly's. I don't think I could have looked at them. The thought of it turns my guts.

The box isn't fancy. Just plain pine. I'm grateful I don't recognize the copper on guard, but, more important, he don't seem to recognize us. He just nods and we edge closer to the coffin. Flo clasps my hand. We both take a deep breath and together we lean over. A second, I tell myself. Half a second. That's all it'll take to know. I tighten my toes to keep my balance as I look on the face. Flo gasps and her head shoots away, and I feel my stomach clench as I see the familiar mask, eyes closed, which once was Cath. For the second time in the same day, my world becomes a blur.

Emily

Meanwhile, across the city to the west, lugging a small valise, Louisa Fortune trundles toward a shabby hotel less than half a mile away from Paddington Station. She cannot afford to stay in the Great Western Royal Hotel. This is not a salubrious area; not an area she would have chosen to frequent back in the days before her fall from grace. The peeling facades of the buildings, the drunken shop signs, and the reeking, waist-high dung heap on the roadside conspire to unnerve her.

She has to remind herself that she is from a good family. This is not where she belongs. She has studied at Oxford. She has traveled a little: to France and Italy, to the usual palaces and museums. To me, she always appeared a little wild and exotic: the way she wore her red hair loose, not in a chignon, or how she eschewed stays under her petticoat. But in the end, she had been forced to face reality. Her allowance dried up and she had either to take up a post as a governess or face a loveless but respectable marriage arranged by her mother. She chose the former and immediately found herself in a twilight world, where she was neither equal nor inferior to her employers.

How has it come to this? you may ask. Two years ago, she landed herself a position in the household of a well-to-do family with a large estate in Essex. The father, a wealthy businessman with wide property interests in London, had been widowed for several years before he took his second wife, who was younger by at least thirty years. Not only was his new spouse beautiful, she knew she was, and with this knowledge came a haughtiness that succeeded in belittling any woman who threatened her su-

periority. This dominant position was further strengthened by the fact that she was also proving extremely fertile. The businessman's first marriage had produced but one son, now an adult. Only eight years into his second, three girls and one boy had already appeared, and there was another on the way. This meant that Louisa Fortune's services had been very much in demand; although unfortunately, as it turned out, the children did not keep her busy enough.

The adult son, Robert, returned from Cambridge and occupied her idle hours. They fell in love. Despite the fact that it was a love expressed in stolen moments, in fleeting touches, and in secret assignations, it flourished. One summer evening, six months into their relationship, all decorum had been abandoned on a bed of sweet hay in a stable.

Suspecting that his eldest son had feelings for this young governess, the father dispatched Robert to London to learn the workings of his own vast business empire. But such a move, it seems, came too late to prevent a pregnancy.

Mercifully, Louisa managed to keep her secret for as long as possible both from her master and from his son. Yet, without employment and unable to face the wrath of her own strict family, she was forced to leave her post and lie low for the last few weeks before the birth. She knew that after her delivery, the only course open to her was to offer up her child for adoption.

Six weeks ago, a son arrived—perfect in every way, with her own brown eyes and flame-red hair and his father's nose. He was born in Stepney, East London, in an ordinary suburban house, in an ordinary suburban street, and his life would surely be both ordinary and suburban. No one would know of his true parentage. That was the way of the world. It was cruel and unjust, but she could no longer fight against it as she had when she was younger.

At Oxford, she and I would attend lectures and rallies. We called for equal rights for women, for universal suffrage, be-

cause we were free to think for ourselves. Now, however, the yoke of womanhood weighs heavily upon her shoulders, but endure the burden she must. Tomorrow is the day she must suffer the cruelest part of it all; tomorrow she must say good-bye to her little son, to her little Bertie, for good, with the sole consolation that Mother Delaney will pass on regular updates on his welfare.

This is what has brought her to this room with its threadbare rug and barely enough coal to last the evening. The smell of damp mixes with grime and she can see springs poking through the side of the mattress like thorns. The walls are so thin, the grunts and occasional shrieks of laughter from the next-door occupants are easily heard. The sounds make her feel even more alone. Her small valise is open, but remains untouched. She has not the energy to unpack it for the moment.

I feel for her and watch as she sits on the only chair in her room and looks increasingly disconsolate. It's then that she spots the well-thumbed novel she could not bring herself to read on the train. It lies on the bed, too, and she leans over and picks it up. It is the copy of Jane Eyre *I gave her when I heard she was to take up her post as a governess. I signed the flyleaf:*

> To My Dear Louisa,
>
> Remember what Helen says to Jane: "If all the world hated you, and believed you wicked, while your own conscience approved you and absolved you from guilt, you would not be without friends."
>
> You may count me as one of your truest, too.
>
> Emily

It is the volume she consults whenever she feels down or angry, or both. I think it gives her hope. It tells her that all will be well if she is strong and shows courage. I hope she is not misguided. I fear she may be.

Chapter 10

Sunday, December 23, 1888

Emily

To the casual observer, the scene might appear rather touching: an elderly woman in a plaid shawl, presumably a grandmother, billing and cooing over the baby she's just been handed by a young woman. The two of them sit on a bench in a small square, just round the corner from Westminster Abbey. There's a service going on. It's a little more sheltered here than out on the street, and obviously more discreet, but the cold is raw, nonetheless.

"She's a bonnie little thing," says the older woman to the baby's mother, a shivering stripling of a girl, who can be no more than eighteen. The mother is wearing a large-brimmed hat so that any passerby cannot see her eyes. They are red and wet with tears. Her clothes are shabby in contrast to the baby's. She's brought a small bag with several stitched napkins, two pretty little smocks, and a pink pelisse for when her daughter is a little older and can be taken out for a stroll in a perambulator—the one that her own mother could never dream of affording.

As the old woman cradles the child, she fusses with the embroidered shawl she's swaddled in. "Let's keep you warm, dearie," she says, pulling it up to cover the child's fine blond hair. "We don't want you catching a chill now, little Susan, do we?"

As if the thought of her baby being ill has triggered a memory, the young woman brings out a folded paper from her bag. "I've her smallpox vaccination certificate here," she volunteers, waving the document around. "Her arm's still a little sore from the needle."

The old woman shakes her head. "Don't you worry now," she says with a smile. It amuses her how so many of these mothers take care to vaccinate their babies before handing them over to her. "She'll be fine with me, so she will. And you know you can visit anytime you like."

The young mother smiles as she dabs her eyes. She's been greatly buoyed by the friendly tone of the old woman's letters, even though she's more advanced in years than she'd imagined. Yet, this first meeting has reassured her that her darling Susan is going to a loving home. She does not hesitate to hand over her five pounds when asked.

Still supporting the baby's head, in a maneuver that shows, to the young woman, her experience in handling infants, the matron reaches into her bag and deposits the money. For a moment, she hands the child back to her mother, so that she herself can rise from the bench. The young woman seizes the chance for one last hug, one last caress, of her sweet little Susan.

"Oh, my love," she whispers before her baby is taken from her arms.

"So we're done," says the matron, back on her feet, with the babe held in the crook of her left arm. Her words sound a little too final for the young woman and tears spring forth once more.

"Thank you, Mrs. O'Brien," she splutters.

"There, there, dearie," comforts the matron. "I'll write to you and tell you how's she's faring, so I will."

The tearful mother nods. "Oh, please do."

Mrs. O'Brien is not the old woman's real name, you understand. It is just one of the several aliases it behooves her to use in her line of work. She smiles, nods, then waddles off into the crowds of a London street. The young mother remains a moment longer, grasping at the last sight of her little girl. She is desolate. How she will make it back home, she really has no idea. How will she ever be happy again? She cannot say. All she knows is her darling baby deserves more than she can ever give her.

CONSTANCE

Ma and me are in St. Jude's for the Sunday service, but I can't concentrate and my mind's straying from the sermon. I keep harking back to yesterday at the mortuary. When the duty copper saw me half swoon and Flo start to blub, he rattled us and told us to wait until another constable arrived to "accompany" us to Commercial Street Station. 'Course I asked to speak to Detective Sergeant Hawkins, but he weren't there, so we ended up separated. Some older bloke tried to dig the dirt on Cath. Important, he seemed. I think they said he was an inspector. He had a funny accent, too, like he was speaking with a biscuit in his mouth. Scottish, I think. I don't recall his name. He just kept firing questions at me about the night Cath died.

"How much did you see her knock back? Was she drunk? What was her mood? Would you say she was anxious?" It was clear he was leading me down a dead end. There's only one way he wanted this investigation to go. He fancied Cath had died like so many of her sort die in the East End. They are cold, or starving, or ill, or, most like, all three, so they drink themselves into the grave. That's the way it is round here. A fact of life. A fact of death. But he's closing his ears to the word on the street. Everyone thinks that Cath was murdered, and a lot of us fear by Jack.

By the time the service is over, it's almost one o'clock. Cold enough to freeze the tail off a brass monkey, it is, yet there's still a long queue outside Wolf's, the baker's. Does a roaring trade roasting joints on a Sunday, he does, for those of us that don't have an oven. And you should taste his gravy. A halfpenny a ladle, it is, but we'd pay double that, it's so good. We dropped a nice bit of brisket off before church and it should be done by now, so Ma gets in line, while I go home to boil the spuds.

I've just shut the door behind me when the first thing I notice is Flo's hat on the floor; then a bit farther on, her coat's been flung down at the foot of the stairs. It's like she's torn them off in a hurry. I know she was off seeing Danny, instead of being in church—and who could blame her?—but I sense something's amiss.

"Flo," I call up. "Flo, are you there?"

"Go away!" comes the muffled reply.

Of course, I ignore her. I know her better than she knows herself. I stride up the stairs to find her lying, facedown, on our bed.

"What's he done now?" It's that greasy dolt Danny. I'm sure of it.

Slowly she lifts up her head. She's been crying. She props herself up on her elbows; I can see another tear break loose. "I shouldn't never have gone to Poplar that night," she tells me.

I sit down beside her on the bed. I've read her wrong. Cath's death has hit her hard. "You can't blame yourself for what happened," I tell her. "We couldn't have known *he'd* be in Poplar, too."

Her head jerks up and she looks puzzled. "What you on about?"

"Jack," I dart back. "Poplar's not his normal hunting ground." But it's soon clear to me that I'm the one who's got the wrong end of the stick. It's Danny she's got the hump over.

"It's nuffink to do with the murders," she whines. "It's Danny. He got to hear from one of his mates that I was . . ." She dips her head in shame. It's not something she does often.

". . . making eyes at other men." I finish the sentence for her.

She nods and brushes more tears away with the back of her

hand before she swings round on the mattress and sits upright by me. "One of 'em saw me and told 'im. We rowed." She lifts her moist eyes to mine and I see a purple bruise blooming on her cheek.

"He didn't!" I raise a hand to her jaw. I'm angry for her, but she seems accepting. Her weary nod tells me Danny has hit her. I'm sure it's not the first time, but I know there's more to her sorrow.

"It's over," she tells me through trembling lips.

At the news, I'm ashamed to admit that I feel glad. How dare that low-down greasy rat hit her? I know she's a flirt, but that doesn't give him the right to treat her like that. They were never a good match, and she deserves better, but I try and keep my own counsel. At times like these, it's best to tread careful for fear of causing offense. I think that deep down Flo knows he's just a Jack the Lad. He's got a roving eye, just like she has. Neither of them's ready to settle down. That's why I'm so alarmed when she suddenly flings herself at me and starts to sob like her world has ended.

"What am I going to do?" she cries. "What am I going to do?"

I pat her on the back. "It'll be all right," I tell her; then it slips out. "You're too good for him, anyway," I say. But she just sniffs and sobs even louder. So we sit, side by side, my arm around her heaving frame. "Don't cry so. It'll be all right," I tell her, stroking her tousled hair.

But no matter what I say, there's no consoling her and suddenly I find my own tears falling, too. A great wave of sorrow washes over me as I think about poor Cath, the dead infant at the market, and about Miss Tindall as well. It's like Flo's sadness is a sickness that she's passed on to me. I feel guilty, too, when I think on that Wednesday night at the George. Cath wasn't herself—all fretful and wild. We should've seen her back to a doss house. But "should" is a big word when you're tired and cold and a long way from home and afeared that Jack will rip you.

CHAPTER 11

EMILY

The family, though small, could be any number of comfortably-off families standing around a dining table about to enjoy their Sunday roast. Mother Delaney says the Catholic grace. "Bless us, O Lord, and these, thy gifts, which we are about to receive through thy bounty. Through Christ Our Lord. Amen."

"Amen," says Mother Delaney's daughter, Philomena, or Philly as she's known. "Amen," responds her husband, Albert, even though he does not share their Roman persuasion.

Mother and daughter have, in fact, not long returned from Mass at the Catholic church in Whitechapel. Due to certain recent difficulties, the nearest church in Bow is out of bounds to them, so they've had to find a new one where they won't be challenged. Who knows how long they'll be able to visit this one? But Mother always feels better after she's received the Host at Holy Communion.

As for Philly, Mass is just a good opportunity to don her Sunday best and compete with other female celebrants in the fashion stakes, even though there is actually very little competition. It strikes her that most Catholic women look poor and down-

trodden. Sometimes she wishes she were of the Anglican persuasion, where the bar is much higher. Today she wore an elegant forest green two-piece, topped off with a neat bonnet embellished with velvet ribbons, from her husband's store, of course. And she was sure her new suede gloves didn't go unnoticed. She felt like a rose between thorns.

As I mentioned earlier, the man of the house and Philly's husband, Albert Cosgrove, is not a member of the Catholic Church; he's not a member of anything, in fact, although he does have a secret hankering after admission to the Drapers' Guild, but he accepts that, under the circumstances, it is out of the question. His face is long and his hair is parted down the middle, while his chin is shaped like a trowel, coming to a point at the bottom. Aesthetically speaking, it would surely benefit from the cover of a bushy beard. Instead, however, Cosgrove has opted for wispy light brown sideburns that are crying out for a good trim.

For the past three hours, a large sirloin of beef has been roasting in the oven. Lotte, the maid, a docile young woman, broken in under a much harsher household, can turn her hand to most things, including peeling vegetables, and she soon has the meal on the table.

Little Isabel joins the adults in her high chair. She's a pretty, plump girl, aged no more than eighteen months, with large red ribbons nestling like exotic butterflies in her golden ringlets.

Napkins are unfurled, wine is poured—only on the Sabbath, you understand—and all four of them are ready for Cosgrove to carve the joint. Only, of course, he cannot. His hand is still bandaged from the unfortunate incident a few nights before, so it is up to Mother to step up to the plate. This she does expertly with the steady hand of a woman used to suturing wounds. With thick slices apportioned and smothered in gravy, and vegetables served, there is, however, just one thing missing from the table. Amid the tureens of mashed potatoes, peas and carrots, and the gravy boat, the cream of horseradish is notable by its absence.

"Lotte!" Cosgrove, surveying the array of dishes a second time, can find none. "Lotte! Horseradish sauce, girl, and quick about it."

The crestfallen maid, her thin face all angles and lines, dips a curtsy and rushes to the pantry. Two minutes later, however, the plates of beef remain and there is no sign of the horseradish.

"Where's the girl got to?" asks Cosgrove, irritated. "The food's getting cold."

As if on cue, there comes the quick patter of feet. "Mother!" exclaims Lotte, glaring at the old woman.

"What is it?" she growls, the look of eager anticipation suddenly vanishing from her face.

"One of the babes is taken real bad," the maid replies breathlessly. "Turned all blue, it has."

The pantry, you see, is not only home to all manner of jars of jams, ketchups, and pickles, sacks of flour, tins of biscuits, and bottles of vinegar and wine. It is where most of Mother Delaney's charges—her babies—are kept. But instead of following the girl to see what ails one of the infants, the matron remains seated and her smile reappears as she tucks her napkin under one of her many chins.

"Don't worry yourself, Lotte. It'll be a touch of colic, that's all," she assures the girl before her gaze settles on her plate once again. "And 'twould be a crime to let all this food go cold now, to be sure."

CONSTANCE

It's a bellowing voice outside that shakes Flo and me from our sorrow. I rush to the bedroom window and look below.

"Have no fear, ladies. I bring festive cheer!"

Together we let out a sigh and round it off by shaking our heads. It's only Mr. B come to call. I hurry downstairs to let him in, but when I open the door, all I see is a mass of green spikey leaves and branches.

"Merry Christmas!" is all we can hear from behind the thick boughs of greenery as they're shoved over the threshold.

He's met Ma on the way home and for a moment our house is full of mirth. She's all flushed and laughing like a little girl. "Oh, Harold!" she chuckles as Mr. Bartleby maneuvers himself and the tree inside. "You are a one!"

If he'd had a white beard, Mr. B could pass for St. Nicholas, he's that red in the face, and jolly, too.

"Merry Christmas, my dears," he booms again, setting down the tree in the center of the room. "If it's good enough for Her Majesty at Windsor Castle, then it's good enough for us. That's what I say," he announces. He takes off his bowler and stands back to admire the tree.

"It's very fine," says Ma, clearly impressed.

Suddenly he remembers the bag in his pocket. "There's candles with holders, too," he adds.

"For the tree?" asks Flo.

He nods. "For the tree. For the Christmas tree," he tells us, making a meal of the word "Christmas."

We'd not given decking the house much thought this year, even though my sprigs of mistletoe have been selling like hotcakes for the last week or more.

"Well, I never," says Ma, clasping her hands to her bosom. I think I see tears of joy in her eyes, and for a moment, I forget all my woes. But it's not long before I'm reminded of them. Flo snaps Mr. Bartleby's false cheer like it's a twig under her foot.

"You know it was Con and me who said it was Cath Mylett they found dead in Poplar?" She doesn't mention she's finished with Danny. I've promised to seal my lips. But Flo's done it good and proper. She's wiped the smile off Mr. B's face quicker than you can say "Jack Frost." He shoots a look at Ma and tries to redeem himself.

"That's why I thought you could do with some cheering up."

"It's very thoughtful of you, Harold," Ma tells him sheepishly, but after Flo's put the kibosh on the proceedings, it's hard to be merry. "Let's all have a tipple, shall we?" she suggests. She's trying too hard, but, of course, never one to say no to a cup of cheer, a moment later Mr. B's sitting down in our only armchair, a whisky in his hand. He stares into his glass as Flo and me start clipping the candleholders to the spindly branches of the tree, even though it's the last thing we feel like doing.

The drink doesn't seem to lighten his mood, although it is loosening his tongue. "I'm sorry about your friend, girls," he tells us. He glances up. "About Cath."

Flo looks over at him and tips him a nod, as if to say, "I should think so, too."

He takes another gulp of his whisky to give himself more courage, and the next moment, we find out why. "You should know there's a meeting called for tomorrow." Mr. B reckons himself a bigwig in the Whitechapel Vigilance Committee, which has been set up to help protect us women on Jack's patch.

Ma's been standing by the tree, handing us candles. Her eyes widen. "Harold, they don't think it was . . . ?"

Mr. B's back stiffens and he puffs out his chest, like he suddenly feels important again. I can tell he's trying to quash any trace of a smile, but I know it's there. "Rumor's going round it is, and we've got to look at all the possibilities, I fear," he tells her, sounding all grave, like he's some fancy lawyer or judge.

Flo and me have both stopped still.

"They don't even know she was murdered for sure," I snap. I'm the devil's advocate, even though, deep down, I know she was. "The coppers say it was natural causes." I suppose I should be grateful that poor Cath wasn't slashed and ripped, but I just hate Mr. B's smugness. I glance at Ma. Her lips are suddenly straight and her face ashen.

Mr. B is deadly serious, too. "If there's a chance that it's 'im, then we'll need to extend the patrols."

"Oh, Harold." Ma wrings her hands. "And to think the girls was with Cath the night she died."

Mr. B nods and slugs back the rest of his whisky. "They've certainly had a rum do of late," he agrees as he strokes his 'tache. It's then that he shoots me a queer look. "In three days, Con here has been one of the last people to see Cath Mylett alive, and then she's accused of killing a baby." He tilts his head and fixes me with a frown. "Funny how you couldn't see all this coming, Con. After that night at the Egyptian Hall, I thought you had special powers. No?" He raises his big hands into the air and wriggles his fingers, all scary-like, his gold rings flashing in the candlelight.

I bite my lip, but this time it's Ma who comes to my aid.

"It ain't no joke, Harold. The poor girl's been through enough without you joshing her."

Mr. Bartleby leans back in his chair, like he's been hit by Ma's scolding tongue. But I can tell it's all an act. He likes to put the frighteners on me. That's why when Ma and Flo go out of the room to boil the kettle, he taps me on the arm and says: "They say that bad things happen in threes, Connie dear. All I'm saying is you'd best be careful."

Chapter 12

Monday, December 24, 1888

Emily

Philomena Cosgrove, dressed in her new coat with a fox-fur collar, has been out and about early this morning. She can't trust Lotte with all the shopping for tomorrow's festive meal. At least Greenland's delivered the turkey and the pheasant the other day, but there's still much to do. She's just purchasing her parsnips and potatoes for roasting when she hears the newspaper boy's cries. He's calling out the headlines from the first edition of the Star. *What he's yelling makes Philomena stop and listen. "Dead woman named. Poplar dead woman named."*

Of course, she'd heard that a prostitute had been found dead in the early hours of Thursday morning, not half a mile away from her own home. Normally, she'd have thought little of it. Those sort of women die on the street all the time. But that, of course, would have been a few hours after that wretched girl had turned up on their doorstep and tried to kill Albert. Curse her! Surely, it couldn't be . . . ? Rose, or Catherine, or whatever she called herself—the woman whose child she'd helped bring into the world and disposed of almost as quickly. The thought rears its head, retracts, then reemerges when she remembers her husband said he gave the woman money when she threatened to expose them. A great deal of money. She pays her tuppence to the newsboy and sees to her shock that the dead woman was, indeed, Catherine Mylett, also known as Rose. At first, she is relieved. At least the slut won't be returning to demand more from them, but then comes the worry.

Arriving home in a state of high anxiety, Philomena catches her husband and mother at the breakfast table. "It was her," she gabbles. "The dead woman we heard about the other day." She lowers her basket of vegetables to the floor and rushes over to the table, brandishing a copy of the newspaper.

Mother Delaney's eyes slide over the story. "She got what she deserved," she grunts, then shoves the paper over to her son-in-law, who scans it quickly. Aware that the gaze of his wife is boring into him, he looks up, munching his toast. He shrugs to show he's not interested.

"What if the coppers come calling?" presses Philomena.

"It says she died of 'natural causes,'" Mother Delaney points out, snatching back the paper.

"Oh." Her husband nods. "Oh, well. That proves something then," he says glibly.

"You mean that we've got nothing to worry about?" asks Philomena, seeking reassurance.

Albert smiles at her. "It means, dear Philly, that you and your mother are right. There is a God, after all." And with that, he wipes his moustache with his napkin and rises to leave for work.

CONSTANCE

It might be Christmas Eve, but I'm feeling as festive as one of them geese hanging in Mr. Greenland's window.

"So you're off to the City?" Ma huffs cheerily. Her chest's tight again, but she's settled down to sew silk flowers.

Flo's told her she's heard some of the bankers get an extra guinea in their pay packets today. "Rich pickings," she crows, a look of delight in her eyes, like someone's shoved a box of chocolates under her nose and told her to take as many as she wants.

"I need to go get some mistletoe first," I say. "Or green stuff." I'm looking at the Christmas tree as I speak and then I have an idea. "A few sprigs wouldn't go amiss, would they?" I nod at the foliage.

Ma lets out a little cough. I think she'll object at first, but there's still a sort of sisterly conspiracy between us. "I don't see why not. I'm sure Mr. B won't mind," she says with a shrug.

"He won't notice," says Flo, and she immediately starts to break off some of the shorter branches near the top. "Bit of red ribbon on this and a sprig or two of holly and I reckon them City gents will pay at least tuppence for one."

So we have a plan. I fill my basket with a few branches from the Christmas tree and together Flo and me set off for the flower market to see if Big Alf can give me some berries or such like on the cheap. But first I need some ribbon—red ribbon for the trimming of the buttonhole sprigs.

"Let's stop off on the way," suggests Flo, putting on her bonnet.

I nod reluctantly. I don't fancy going near the market after what happened. And I certainly don't want to bump into that bent old bag with the head scarf who accused me of murder.

We set off and join the brewery boys and the starch workers, the shopgirls and the dockers, as we all stream out of our homes for another day's hard toil. Heads down, shoulders braced against the chill, we join the river of people that flows down Commercial Street. There's not much Yuletide cheer around, just the slow, hard clanking of the factory machines, which does my brain in sometimes, and the clatter of wagons.

I'm hoping they'll be a jollier lot in the City; jolly enough, at any rate, to spare tuppence for my Christmas buttonholes and sprigs.

I look up at the sky. It's gray, as usual, but it's not cold enough for snow. I wish it would—snow, that is. At least everything would look cleaner for a few minutes before the brilliant white of a heavy fall is covered in soot and grime again. Everything gets soiled in the end in Whitechapel, that's just how it is.

Up ahead of us are the stalls where they found the baby the other day. The smell of roasting chestnuts covers the usual stench of horse dung, but I can taste fear on my tongue. My eyes swerve from left to right, scanning for sight of the woman who pointed the finger at me. lt don't feel right walking along the rows of stalls, like everyone'll be watching me, judging me. Instead, as we pass a haberdasher's shop, I call to Flo.

"I'll buy my ribbon here," I say, pointing to the window decked out in red and green. There's a sleigh in the center and it's loaded with presents, all wrapped up in bright paper.

"What's wrong with the market?" Flo protests, but the look I give her reminds her of what happened. She nods and agrees to wait outside as I pluck up the courage to go in. I'm not that used to shops, you see, especially not ones that sell fancy goods such as this.

The bell above the door jangles open. The shop's dark inside. It's lined with wooden shelves, crammed full of rolls of material that look like ancient scrolls. There's rows of little button drawers, too, and inside the big glass counter at the front lie card upon card of ribbon and lace and bindings. It's just like a magical cave full of jewels or a sweet shop's window. There's all the colors of the rainbow and patterns, too. Stripes and spots and flowers and swirls all scramble for my attention. Different shades of the same color as well. I didn't know there were so many blues and they're all labeled: *peacock, azure, turquoise, sapphire, cobalt.* Greens too: *emerald, forest,* and *spring.*

The bell summons a thin man with a long face, who appears

from the back. It's like a spell's been broken and I'm suddenly nervous. But then I remember what Miss Tindall always told me. "Have confidence," she'd say. "Hold your head high and the rest will follow." So I try and forget I'm wearing a tattered old jacket and a patched-up skirt and I stick out my chin and muster enough courage to smile politely.

As the shopkeeper moves out of the shadows and into the pool of light cast by a large oil lamp, I see that his limp whiskers cling to his jaw, making him look like one of them codfish on a fishmonger's slab. I twitch a smile, but he doesn't return it. There's no Christmas cheer on his lips.

"Yes," he says, all grumpy. I feel like I'm a bad smell in his lovely shop.

I clear my throat and think of Miss Tindall. "I wish to buy some red ribbon, if you please, sir."

He arches a brow and narrows his lashless eyes. "Let's see the color of your money first," he sneers, clearly thinking I'll do a runner as soon as the ribbon's in my hand.

I feel my cheeks blush. I'm just thankful I'm his only customer. I pull out two pennies from my apron pocket and place them on the counter. I half expect him to bite them to check they're not fakes. He doesn't. Instead, he takes out the ribbon card and unravels a length to measure it on a ruler, which runs the length of the counter, and rather than telling me to scarper, he leans over, poised on the wooden edge. I notice one of his hands, the left one, is bandaged.

"How much?" I ask.

"A penny a yard," says he.

"I'll have two, if you please."

But as I watch him unwind the ribbon, something strange happens. My eyes are drawn to the row of cards nearby and there's this flash. Suddenly I'm looking at the dead babe at the police station. I hear myself gasp for breath as I remember the binding round its neck. Suddenly terror takes me by the throat and shakes me.

"Something wrong?" the shopkeeper asks sternly as he snips one end of the ribbon.

I look up with unseeing eyes, then down again to the glass counter; my gaze settles on a flowery yellow binding on the side of the display. I can barely breathe.

"You all right?" asks the shopkeeper again.

My head jerks up. "What? Yes!" The words struggle out of my mouth as I realize what I've just seen and take fright. I have to get out of here. I need to see Sergeant Hawkins. I swirl round to face the door and start to run.

"Here! What about this?" the shopkeeper calls, brandishing the red length. I turn to see him holding up the ribbon. It looks like blood is streaming down his arm. I don't reply.

"Your money!" I hear him call as I grab the door handle and fall out into the street. I don't care about the tuppence. All I care about is telling Sergeant Hawkins what I've just seen.

"What the hell?" Flo's still outside and I snatch her hand and pull her away from the shop. "What's going on?" she yells.

I catch my breath. "The binding!" I pant.

"*Binding?*" she echoes. "What you talkin' about?" She's growing impatient with me.

"It's the same as was round the dead baby's neck!" I blurt. I suddenly feel sick at the saying of what I've just realized.

But instead of listening to me, Flo just rolls her eyes. "'Ere we go," she says with a sigh. "You're going all physic on me again?"

The way she reacts makes me angry. "*Psychic,*" I correct her as she tugs at my arm and pulls me back along the street.

"You what?" She's battling through the crowd toward the main road, jostling toward Commercial Street, but I stand firm. She jerks her head back.

"The word's *psychic,*" I repeat crossly. "I have to tell the police."

She looks at me and gives me one of her cheeky smiles. I

think she's softening for a moment, but then I hear her say: "You're sweet on that Sergeant Hawkins, ain't ya?"

I feel my nerves stretch, but I hold my tongue. I say nothing and we walk on, fighting our way through the sea of bobbing heads. There's people all around, clamoring, yelling as Flo takes hold of my arm again. I search the faces round me, hoping I just might catch a glimpse of Miss Tindall close by. But of the one person I know who's looking out for me, the one person who understands, there's no sign. I'm on my own again.

CHAPTER 13

EMILY

The meeting is arranged for midday by the entrance to Platform One on Paddington Station. Rush hour is over, but the station is still busy with families getting away from London to spend Christmas with relatives. Nevertheless, it's not hard to spot an elderly woman in a plaid shawl and black bonnet, carrying a baby in her arms. Mother Delaney suggested the venue in her last letter. She thought it would be convenient as Louisa's train terminated at the station, although Louisa herself would have been more than willing to travel to the old woman's new abode. She would have preferred it, in fact, so that she could check up on the conditions in which her little Bertie is being kept and ensure that standards are being maintained.

Mother Delaney's previous house, the one in Stepney, where she'd spent her confinement, had been clean and comfortable. It was a refuge for her from prying eyes and gossiping tongues. You'll remember it's been six weeks since she labored through the night to bring forth her perfect boy. He'd latched onto her immediately and sucked so well. The thought of it makes her breasts tingle and she feels her milk flow beneath her camisole, just as freely as her tears have flowed since leaving him. She'd remained at Mother Delaney's for a further two weeks after the birth. Now a month has passed since she left him in the elderly matron's care. She wonders what her baby'll look like. Will he have more hair? Will his little cheeks have plumped? Will there be bracelets of fat around his tiny wrists?

She trusts that Mother Delaney has looked after him well. She is a kindly woman, used to nurturing hundreds of little ones over the past three decades, so she was told. But one can never be too careful, she reminds herself as she approaches the platform. The truth is, she is wavering. She is not sure that she can go through with this. She is not sure that she can say good-bye forever to the person she has loved most in her life. She is thinking she might come to another arrangement: one that is not as final as adoption; one that still allows her to see her son whenever she can, and one day, perhaps, to have him back with her for good.

In her gloved hands, she holds a Christmas gift for Bertie: a little wooden rattle, painted in red and yellow, and wrapped in red tissue paper, for his amusement. But just where he will spend tomorrow, she is still uncertain. Will it be with Mother Delaney or with her?

"Miss Louisa. But how well you look, to be sure!" the old Irishwoman greets her. She's shaped like a beer keg and not much taller. She is warm in her salutation. Her lined face crinkles into a broad smile and her thin lips open slightly to show stained teeth. In her arms, she holds a cream blanket and swaddled somewhere inside is Bertie. Or, rather, a baby she says is Bertie.

Louisa has been firm up until now, but her resolution is fast crumbling. If she holds the child one more time, she fears she might never let him go. The transaction, if it is to go ahead, must be businesslike. No tears. No recriminations. She will simply hand over the last installment of the payment, the final five pounds, and walk away, leaving her son behind, and with him, of course, her heart. That is what she had resolved, although now she is not so sure. Events, however, do not go according to plan.

"Mother Delaney." Louisa's greeting does not match the Irishwoman's in its effusiveness, but her expression is benign enough, albeit understandably strained, given the circumstances. Yet her gaze soon switches to the bundle and the light returns to her eyes. Without thinking, her arms raise, and before she knows it, she has broken the promise she made to herself. She has to hold Bertie. In this moment, her life depends on it.

The swiftness of her almost involuntary action takes the old woman by surprise. "But . . . oh! Careful now!" she splutters as the sleeping child leaves her arms and is enveloped by Louisa. Yet, the fire that blazes in the young woman's eyes is doused almost instantaneously, to be replaced by one of horror.

"What the . . . ?" She looks incredulously at the old woman. "This isn't my baby. This isn't Bertie!"

Mother Delaney lets out a nervous laugh. "To be sure, it is, Miss Louisa." She shakes her head as she peers over the cream folds at the fair-haired baby, who has just been rudely awoken. "They change a lot in a month, don't you know?" She places one hand under the child and takes him back into her own arms.

Louisa freezes. The color drains from her face until her instincts take over and she snatches back the boy. "That is not my baby!" she wails. "Bertie has red hair, like mine."

Mother Delaney is adamant. "It's grown lighter." The baby starts to whimper. "There, there," says the old woman, jiggling the child in her arms.

"No!" snaps Louisa, lunging for the bundle once more. "This isn't my Bertie."

Mother Delaney's brow arches. "Bertie, is that his name, now?" Her question is tinged with a sneer before her mouth suddenly sets hard. This one's a tricky customer, *she is thinking. She is forced to lay down the gauntlet. "Prove it," she goads. "If you're so sure it's not yours, prove it."*

Louisa is up to the challenge. "My son has a birthmark on his left thigh," she cries. Unwrapping the blanket, she lifts the baby's gown to reveal his leg. It is pale pink and mottled with blue veins, scrawny in appearance, but without a blemish. "You see!" There is a hint of victory in the young mother's voice as she points to the thigh. Then the panic takes hold. "Where is Bertie? What have you done with him?" Her voice rises an octave and an arc of her spittle lands on the old woman, who wipes it from her face with the back of her hand.

There is an awkward silence before, quite suddenly, Mother Delaney's lips lift into a smile. "A mistake," she says softly.

Both Louisa's brows shoot up. "A mistake?"

"I've five other babbies to look after at home, and I'm not as young as I used to be." The old woman touches her temple. "I just don't know how I could've done such a thing."

There is contrition in her tone. She is owning up to her mistake, *thinks Louisa.* A genuine error. A stupid blunder. An easy fault. We all make mistakes. *The tension in her chest slackens a little. She will give the old nurse the benefit of the doubt. After all, did they not spend many weeks living under the same roof? There was a trust between the two of them. It should not be broken lightly.*

"You must bring him to me as soon as possible." Still, there is an urgency in Louisa's tone that smacks of desperation.

"To be sure, I will. But what with Christmas and all, does Friday suit?" Mother Delaney suggests, forcing a smile.

Louisa takes comfort in this offer. "Yes." She wills her pounding heart to slow. "Yes," she repeats. "Same time, here." She points to the ground.

The old nursemaid nods. "Very good," she says, rocking the grizzling child a little as she recovers it. "And that?" She nods at the parcel Louisa is clutching.

"Bertie's gift," she explains. "For Christmas." She hands it over willingly and watches as it is stashed in a large carpetbag the old woman carries. "Friday, it is, then," she confirms after a moment.

"Friday, it is."

"Good day to you, Mother Delaney," says Louisa, forcing a smile. But just as she has turned on her heel to leave, the old woman calls her back.

"There is one other thing," she says.

"Yes?" Louise glances round.

She tilts her head. "Could you be seeing your way to parting with a little of the balance? Three pounds, say? Just to be going on with?"

Louisa's eyes widen. The old woman's words snag on her like thorns on lace. Unable to believe what she has just heard, she swivels round. Did she hear right? Mother Delaney's expression tells her she did. The effrontery of the woman! *she thinks.*

She advances toward her, straightens herself to her full height, and glowers down on the fat little matron. "You'll not have a ha'penny more until I see my child!" she hisses from between clenched teeth. "Not a ha'penny more!"

The Irishwoman's mouth droops in a look of resignation, as if she is the one who has been wronged. "Very well, Miss Louisa," she concedes, a little more humbly than before. She turns and walks away.

Louisa watches her go before she herself wheels round and marches across the concourse. Only once she is safely out of the station does she allow her angry tears to flow.

Chapter 14

Emily

This time of year it grows dark early, or perhaps I should say it grows even darker. Yet, Detective Sergeant Hawkins does not notice that the sky has long blackened, that the streetlamps are lit, or that the shadows on the office wall are long. Nor does he take notice of the carolers singing outside Commercial Street Station. Since Mary Kelly's murder, day is blending into night and vice versa. He has slept little, eaten sparingly, and returned to his police lodging house hardly at all. His landlady, Mrs. Moony, sent word to the station, asking if all was well, when he didn't return home last night. He appreciates her concern, and regrets his thoughtlessness at not informing her of his decision to stay at work. He has recently had cause to consign all domestic considerations to the bottom of his list of priorities.

His recent secondment to Whitechapel is proving more difficult than he'd realized. He knew it would not be easy fitting in. He is, after all, younger than most detectives of the same rank. Nor do they share many interests. He prefers poetry to pints and fencing to football. Even now, he knows that some of his men—and, indeed, one or two of his fellow officers—resent his gram-

mar-school education. Yet he has, thus far, proved himself a very able detective. None other than Inspector Frederick Abberline has placed much faith in him after his work on the Whitehall Mystery. He may not have solved the murder, but at least his detection did allow the victim's family to give her a decent burial. That, at least, must have offered them some comfort, *he tells himself. He's thankful, too, that this latest death of an unfortunate, this Catherine or Rose Mylett or Alice Downey or whatever she calls herself, seems to have been self-inflicted. That's the line the force is taking at the moment.*

He, Hawkins, has been instructed by his commanding officer to deal with all the ensuing paperwork. It's an open-and-shut case, or at least must be treated as such. Foul play is not on the cards and, for the moment at least, the young detective is happy to fall in behind Inspector McCullen's order. Cath Mylett wouldn't be the first prostitute to drink herself to death, and she won't, unfortunately, be the last.

There will, of course, be an inquest, but it should be a straightforward affair. This way, he and his colleagues can be left to pursue the real enemy of the moment: the man who calls himself Jack the Ripper.

Inspector McCullen has assigned this young detective specifically to Montague Druitt, a suspect who, it seems, has caught the eye of none other than Superintendent Arnold himself. It's Hawkins's job to dig deep into this singular gentleman's background and to wheedle out any facts he thinks pertinent to the Whitechapel murders.

The other detective sergeants are all family men: Glennister, Leach, Smith, and Harrison. He is not; hence, he has volunteered to work tonight and tomorrow when most God-fearing folk will be marking the Lord's birth. He's sent word to his uncle and aunt in Highgate that he regrets he will not be able to spend the festivities with them. With two deaths within his jurisdiction in the last seventy-two hours, he has more than enough weight on his shoulders. Little wonder that he cannot rest. And now PC Tanner is about to add to his woes.

"Copy of today's Star, sir," says the constable, laying down a newspaper that has clearly been thumbed by many a policeman before making its way onto the detective's desk.

Hawkins reads the headline: IS HE A THUG? A STARTLING LIGHT ON THE WHITE-CHAPEL CRIMES. THE ROPE BEFORE THE KNIFE. Momentarily forgetting Tanner's presence, the detective lets out an involuntary expletive. The constable shifts awkwardly and Hawkins is reminded he is not alone.

"That'll be all, Tanner."

The constable gives a shallow bow and is about to leave when it occurs to him that he will not see his superior tomorrow. "Merry Christmas, sir," he says with all the cheer he can muster.

"What?" snaps Hawkins, looking up from the newspaper with a furrowed brow.

"I shan't be in tomorrow, sir," Tanner reminds him. "Christmas Day."

Hawkins nods. "Of course." Embarrassed at such an aberration, he touches his head and clears his throat. "Merry Christmas to you and to your mother, too, Constable," he manages.

Seemingly satisfied, Tanner takes his leave. Hawkins watches the policeman go, no doubt straight back to his widowed mama and a hot meal, while he is left to study the rest of this sensationalist article by the sickly light of his single lamp. With mounting consternation, he reads the interview that Dr. Brownfield has given to the unworthy rag. The good doctor postulates that the self-styled Jack the Ripper may, in all probability, have been responsible for Catherine Mylett's death. In disgust, the detective reads aloud: "'All the facts seemed to combine to one suggestion—that this was the work of the Whitechapel murderer.'"

In an uncharacteristic show of anger, Hawkins hurls the newspaper to the floor. He knows that Brownfield's outburst will trigger another wave of hysteria among the Whitechapel populace, let alone London and the rest of the country.

Inspector McCullen will, no doubt, be incensed when he sees the report. He has given specific instructions to treat the death as "self-inflicted." Assistant Commissioner Anderson also believes that to be the case and is firmly of the opinion that this latest prostitute was not killed by anyone's hand at all: she simply fell down in a drunken stupor, was choked by her own collar, and died.

Hawkins knows that happens in the East End. Self-destruction through poverty is a common cause of death in these parts. He himself, however, is not so sure. Somewhere on his desk, which is groaning under the weight of files and index boxes, is a copy of Dr. Brownfield's report. Sergeant Halfhide brought it in earlier in the day, but he'd been sidetracked and had yet to read it. Seizing it triumphantly as soon as he spies the salient black folder, he hunches over to examine it intently. His eyes are sore and he massages his temples as he scrutinizes the account. Halfway down the second page, the words leap out at him: On the neck was a mark which had evidently been caused by cord drawn tightly round the neck, from the spine to the left ear. Such a mark would have been by a four-thread cord.

He reads on: There were also impressions of the thumbs and middle and index fingers of some person plainly visible on each side of the neck. . . .

Hawkins looks up and shakes his head. It baffles him how the constables who found the body could not have seen such marks. One of the problems is, of course, that no ligature was recovered from around the dead woman's neck. If it had been, the task of finding out exactly what happened would surely have been so much easier. He is raking his fingers through his dark hair, contemplating his next move, when there's a knock at his door. Tanner appears once more.

Hawkins is puzzled. "I thought you'd left."

The constable nods. "I was going, sir, but there's one of them Piper girls to see you. The younger one."

"Miss Constance?" Hawkins frowns.

"I didn't want her to trouble you, sir, but she says it's urgent."

The remark seems to annoy the detective. "May I remind you, Constable, that Miss Piper is the person who identified Catherine Mylett's body. She may have valuable information. She is no trouble." He rises, pulls down his rucked-up waistcoat, and reaches for his jacket, which is draped over the back of his chair. "Show her in, if you please."

Constance

My nerves are tight as piano strings; I'm that on edge. Sergeant Hawkins can see that as soon as Tanner shows me into the office. He shoots "mummy's boy" a scowl, which is as good as telling him to clear off, and waits until we're alone before he invites me to sit.

"Miss Piper, what can I do for you?" He sits down, too.

As I said, I'm all flustered, but I need to be sensible as well. It's important that I'm—what's the word?—credible. I think Sergeant Hawkins already respects my judgment, so I don't want to disappoint him.

"I have something that might interest you, sir," I say in my best voice. I fill my lungs with breath and launch off. "I've seen something."

Sergeant Hawkins squints at me. "Something?"

"Something to do with the dead mite."

"The baby?" Looking puzzled, he leans forward over the desk and picks up his pencil.

I lean forward, too. "I saw some ribbon today. It was just the same as the sort round the little child's neck," says I.

"Interesting. And this was in Whitechapel?" He nods eagerly.

"Yes."

Sergeant Hawkins's pencil suddenly stops moving and he looks up at me, intrigued. Among all the papers that sit on his desk, there's a box. I've seen it before. It's the one that contains the clothes and effects of the dead baby. He takes off the lid and there's that reek again. He wafts it away from me with another file, then delves inside. A length of ribbon lies on top. He takes it out for a closer inspection under his oil lamp. "Something like this?"

I'd twisted my head away from the smell, but now I turn back to see the limp binding in the spotlight. The sight unsettles me and fills my guts with the horror of seeing the dead mite again.

"Yes," says I, taking out my handkerchief and holding it to my face.

"I'm sorry," says Sergeant Hawkins, realizing too late that he should've been more mindful of my sensibilities. Just because I'm Whitechapel-born-and-bred don't mean I don't have feelings. Trouble is, I think I'm a puzzle to him, and all. The first time he saw me was with Miss Beaufroy. He took me for a lady's companion. I was all polite and well-spoken. Then, a few weeks later, I turned up in one of his cells an East End flower seller. Sometimes I'm a lady in my speech and manners, if not the dress; at others, I'm your typical Cockney girl, with dirt under my fingernails and on my tongue. I'm what Miss Tindall might call "an enigma."

"Where did you say you came across the binding?" he asks, looking at the ribbon.

"The haberdasher's in Bull Court," I tell him, watching him return it back to the box. "That's what killed the baby, ain't it?" I correct myself, "Isn't it?"

Sergeant Hawkins nods and sighs, but he don't seem all that grateful. I'm glancing at the box as I speak. He's watching me and I've reminded him that it's still open, so he returns the binding and shuts the lid. His actions are slow and deliberate, as if he's playing for time, as if there's something troubling him. I worry he'll try and pull the wool over my eyes, but then he sends a bolt out of the blue.

"To be frank, Miss Piper, the matter is out of my hands."

"What?" I blurt. I can't hide my shock.

He looks at me all coy, like he's embarrassed. "I've been specifically seconded here to investigate a certain suspect in the Whitechapel murder cases and now"—he throws up his hands and surveys the piles of files and papers on his desk in despair—"and now the baby and Miss Mylett. I don't know what to think because I have neither the time nor the resources to look into either case with the rigor they both deserve." He slumps back in his chair to draw breath and looks at me in a way that makes me feel both angry and sorry for him.

"But you don't buy what they're saying about Cath? You don't believe it was the drink that killed her, do you, Sergeant Hawkins?" I'm eager for his reply, but it don't come soon enough. Slowly he shakes his head, like he's giving up.

"I understand," I say softly after a moment. "I understand that it's hard for you, Sergeant. Life in Whitechapel is cheap, and you . . ." I'm not proud of myself for accusing him of belittling us East Enders, but I'm feeling let down.

He breaks me off. He's hurting, too. "Miss Piper," says he. "Please believe me when I say I will do everything within my power to uncover the truth about what happened to your friend, but, as I said, my remit and my resources are finite."

Is he wanting rid of me? I think I'm being dismissed. I stand and make myself as tall as I'm able. "Very well, Sergeant Hawkins," I say. "Have it your way. You're the expert and I'm only a flower girl," I tell him. There's acid on my tongue and I can see my words burn him.

He screws up his face into a scowl and shakes his head. "No, Miss Piper. I appreciate your assistance, I really do. I'm so sorry if you thought otherwise." I manage a smile before I bid him good night. He's on his pins again and I think he's understood my feelings. Perhaps that's why, as I'm turning, he adds: "I will, of course, make inquiries at this haberdasher's. In Bull Court, you said?"

His words put more heart in me. A cautious smile blooms on

my face. He returns it and a sort of understanding fills the space between us. For a moment, I think it's like he doesn't want me to leave, that he wants me to keep him company through the long night that lies ahead of him. But, of course, he does not. He just fixes me with this look and from out of nowhere says: "It was a girl."

"A girl?" He's lost me.

"The dead baby was a girl. About three months old," he tells me,shaking his head. "She'd even been vaccinated. Why would you vaccinate a child, then kill it?"

I'm not sure why he's telling me this. It's like he needs to make sense of the little one's death. But then he adds: "I made sure she had a Christian burial."

For a moment, I'm lost for words, but I feel my eyes start to mist as I'm touched by the thought of his act of kindness. In the end, "thank you" is all I can manage, but I'm sure he knows that it comes from the bottom of my heart.

"Good night, then, Miss Piper," says he after a moment.

"Good night, Sergeant Hawkins," says I. Once more I turn.

"Oh, and merry Christmas!" he calls.

I switch back, surprised by his greeting. "Merry Christmas," I say in a hoarse whisper, even though it don't feel much like Christmas to me.

EMILY

If Londoners could rise above the layer of smog that seems to perpetually cover the city this winter, they might just see a star in the east, the brightest of all, that heralds the birth of Christ on earth. It is the night before Christmas, when those children lucky enough to have a loving family and a warm bed have gone to sleep. They are dreaming of what toys they might find in their stockings hung by the fireplace when they wake. Not all children, however, are so fortunate.

Let me take you back to the terraced house in Poplar, not two miles from Whitechapel, where Mother Delaney lives. In the cold of an upstairs room, without heat in the middle of winter, there is no evidence of Christmas, although there is a poignant parallel with the Nativity. Just like Mary, the mother of Christ, a young mulatto girl is in the throes of labor. She lies on a filthy bed. Despite the freezing temperature, her golden brown forehead is dotted with sweat.

Between her teeth, she bites on a rag that muffles her agony. She arrived earlier in the afternoon, her water already broken. The old midwife was careful to ask for her fifteen shillings before she ushered her upstairs and bid her lie on a mattress covered in newspapers. "Best not dirty the sheets," she'd explained to the frightened girl, who by this time was in too much pain to quibble.

And so the labor continued; the vise around the young woman's belly tightening and loosening every few seconds for the next twelve hours. Afternoon turned into evening, evening into night, and around midnight, a newborn girl took her first breath. It was swiftly followed by her last.

Mother Delaney, with more lines on her forehead than teeth in her gums, leans over the bed. The mulatto remains dazed.

"My baby?" she bleats. "Where's my baby?"

The old woman smiles and, stroking the young woman's head, says softly: "Your baby, darlin'?" as if the answer wasn't already a foregone conclusion. "Why, she's gone to be with all the other angels in heaven."

CHAPTER 15

Tuesday, December 25, 1888

CONSTANCE

Christmas Day. It's one of the two days of the year—today and Easter—when me and Ma manage to coax Flo into St. Jude's. But it's been harder than ever this morning. Mr. B once joked that a bolt of lightning would strike my big sis next time she sets foot on hallowed ground, but I know it's not his silly remark that's turned her sulky. She's lying in bed. Her skin's all pallid and she just hides her head under the blanket.

"Come on, Flo," I say to her. "It's Christmas and you're always the one for making merry." I'm not sure she's listening to me because suddenly she throws off the covers, dives for the commode from under the bed, and throws up. I wince as she wipes a spool of spittle from her lips with a corner of the blanket.

"Must be that milk we had last night," she groans, her face all wan. "I thought it tasted queer."

"How come Ma and me ain't sick, then?" I ask unthinkingly.

She shrugs and falls back onto her pillow. "So you'll not be coming to the service?" It's a dull question, I know.

"Not unless they want puke in their collecting bowl." She can be a right madam sometimes, can our Flo.

The thought of her spewing up in the plate convinces me that she's doing the right thing by staying at home. Truth is, I wish I wasn't going, neither. I've not been at all comfortable in St. Jude's since I found out what went on at the Sunday school there—how Mrs. Parker-Smythe allowed the fairest of them girls to be preyed upon to service the pleasures of wealthy men. For all I know, it still goes on.

We'll be in the free seats at the back, well away from Mrs. Parker-Smythe and her like, who pay for their pews. I don't know how they can sit in church, looking for all the world "holier than thou," when really they've the blackest of hearts. If there's any justice—and I'm still not sure there is—they'll burn in hell. But not today. Today the stench of the rotting innards of this Christian community will be masked by the wafting of incense as together we mark the Savior's birth.

My prayers for snow haven't been heeded. It's cold, but not that cold, yet everyone who herds inside St. Jude's front doors is grateful for the shelter the church offers. It's packed with families. Everyone's made an effort. Faces are scrubbed. Collars starched. Those that have gloves wear them. We're celebrating the birth of the Christ child and it seems that's enough to put a smile on even the gloomiest faces.

The Reverend Barnett himself is giving the sermon. I've only heard him once or twice before from the pulpit, but I know Miss Tindall held him in very high regard. So when he starts to speak, I listen, and when he puts the question "Why did God come to earth as a newborn?" it's like he's asking me direct. A tingle runs down my spine as, once again, I see that little baby with the binding round its neck; its tiny fists still balled as it fought for life.

I listen to the reverend. "If the Lord had come to us as a grown man, would we have understood his sacrifice? Even here, in Whitechapel, so many die daily of disease, of poverty, of cold, of exhaustion." He is looking out over the congregation, his eyes fixing here and there. He is speaking directly to every one of us and I say to him in my heart, *Or are murdered.* Of course, he doesn't know of my feeling about Cath's death. He carries on: "Jesus was both man and God. He was born of a woman and came to us as a child."

My mind strays back to the tiny girl, wrapped not in a swaddling band, but in a paper parcel, tied with twine. She wasn't in a hay manger, like the infant Jesus, but shoved in the shitty gutter under a market stall. She wasn't just dead, like the dozens of babies found all over England every year. She was more than that. She was a sleeping angel in our midst. Just as the organ strikes up again for another carol, it comes to me. It's like something bursts into my brain and I suddenly understand why I saw Miss Tindall at the market. She was leading me to that baby. She put the parcel there, knowing full well that I'd be arrested for the little mite's murder. It was her way of telling me that it's my task to find out who killed her and then bring them to justice.

When the service is over, Ma soon finds some friendly faces in the congregation. There's dear old Mrs. Greenland, the poulterer's wife, salt of the earth, she is, and nosey Mrs. Puddiphatt. Together they make their way toward the church door to join the queue to shake Reverend Barnett's hand. His wife, Henrietta, is there, too, wreathed in smiles. But me, I just want to weep. I walk to the little side altar, where the children of the Sunday school, the little group that I used to help Miss Tindall teach, has made a crib scene. There were some of the stricter ones at St. Jude's who argued such a scene was "too Roman," but Mrs. Barnett said it would remind us that we were all children once and how important they are. So now, in this quiet corner of the church, little brightly colored plaster statues of

Mary and Joseph, the shepherds, and the Magi are gathered on the altar. There's even an ox and an ass. The scene is as pretty as a picture, all bathed in the warm glow of a dozen or more candles.

And at the center of this quaint scene is the Baby Jesus, looking all pink and plump and contented. There's not many babies born round here that look that well, I can tell you; and, yet again, I'm reminded of the dead little girl. I kneel down and say a prayer for her and I thank God that Detective Sergeant Hawkins saw to it she was given a Christian burial. She'll be in heaven now, a little angel. I ask Miss Tindall to take care of her, too, and it's then that I have this strange feeling. It's the feeling you get when you sense there's someone close by, as if you're being watched.

"Miss Tindall?" I whisper.

There is no reply; only the faint sound of Christmas greetings at the main door at the far corner of the church. "Miss Tindall," I say again, under my breath. I'm thinking she'll show me the way; somehow she'll tell me what I need to do to track down the baby's killer. But I hear nothing. She is not here.

After a while, I stand up and smooth my skirts before turning wanly to see if Ma is ready to leave. Just as I do, I catch sight of someone standing in the flickering shadows, beside one of the pews. My heart leaps. A woman—a lady by her bearing. It's too much to hope for.

"Miss Tindall?" I say out loud this time. In the gloom, I shuffle toward her, feeling my way through the pews. It's her. It has to be. My heart beats faster. My pace quickens. But as I grow closer, I realize I was mistaken. It's not Miss Tindall who stands before me, but a woman of probably about the same age. Her dark green coat is too thin to keep her warm in winter, and her hat has a fine veil that she draws back in front of me. Yet, I can tell simply from her deportment that she is not one of us. The candlelight catches the glint in her eyes and I realize she is staring at me. She wears a haunted look. I draw closer. I can see why she wears a veil. She has been crying. And then she speaks.

"Miss Piper?" she asks. Her voice even sounds like Miss

Tindall's, only thinner, as if it's been crushed underfoot. "Miss Constance Piper?"

"Yes," I reply softly. Something makes me reach for her hand and she offers it. "Yes. I'm here." And in that moment, Miss Tindall comes to me and I know that this lady has been sent to me, and that I must help her through her pain.

EMILY

Another connection has been made. Constance will try her hardest to help my dear friend Louisa through her heartbreaking experience. Whether or not she succeeds, I cannot say, for now. All I do know is that Constance will leave no stone unturned to find Louisa's lost child, and in earthly life, that is sometimes all that a person can do. One must try one's utmost because, very often, fate will conspire against you.

CONSTANCE

It seems like this lady—she tells me her name is Louisa Fortune—and me have spent hours together. Her manner is mild and her speech free of the harshness of my sort. In a voice as smooth as silk, she's told me her sorry tale. She's related how, as a governess, she fell in love with her master's son and became pregnant with his child.

"So you left their home?" I ask.

She nods, twisting her handkerchief as we speak. "I had no choice. I was desperate." She pauses, like she wants me to sympathize with her, and I do.

"What did you do next?"

She fumbles in her reticule and brings out a scrap of newspaper. "Here." She hands me the torn square and I squint to read it: *Respectable woman and her doctor husband seek up to four children to call their own. Good food and sound education guaranteed. Terms from £10 for adoption. Address "Mother", Post Office, Stepney.*

As I read, she carries on. "So I sought out this couple and found rather an elderly woman who lived with her daughter and her husband. She cared for me and even delivered my baby. But then"—she turns away from me, like she's ashamed and starts to chew her lip—"when it was time to . . . to leave my son with her, I thought I would die of sorrow."

I know it's hard for her. It was hard for poor Cath, too, and all the other women who've had to give up their own. "I couldn't see a way out," she tells me, wringing her hankie again. "So I left him with her, but then I had a change of heart—" She breaks off to let a sob shudder through her whole body. "I was going to see if there was a way that I could perhaps keep him. I was going to ask her if . . . if she could mind him for me, instead of adopting him."

"So what happened?"

"We arranged to meet at Paddington Station. I was to have handed over the final payment, but I just couldn't bring myself . . . Oh, God!" She raises her face to the altar, like she's pleading the Almighty direct. "When I asked to see him, she'd brought the wrong child."

"The wrong child?"

"It wasn't Bertie she had!"

"I don't understand."

"She said she must have made a mistake. She was minding other babies, too, you see. But then she had the temerity to demand more money from me." Her tears have turned angry.

"What did you say?"

"Naturally I refused and she agreed to meet later this week and bring Bertie, of course."

"But you worry that she will go back on the agreement?"

She nods and takes a deep breath as she dabs her eyes. "I fear for him. There was something in her manner . . ."

It seems this last meeting with the old woman has made her feel so uneasy that she'd changed her plans. She didn't return home to Cheltenham, after all, but was, she tells me, "persuaded" to stay in London over Christmas Day.

"Persuaded?" I repeat. "Who *persuaded* you, miss?"

Suddenly her expression changes and she shakes her head. "You'll think I'm insane," she says, her voice dropping to a whisper. "But I knew I had to find you."

Thinking of Miss Tindall, I hold my breath, but it's not how I first thought. Not exactly.

"I am a friend of Miss Beaufroy, Miss Pauline Beaufroy," she tells me.

I breathe out. The pieces of this puzzle are suddenly falling into place. She was the beautiful lady who was such a rock to me in my quest to find out Miss Tindall's fate.

"She and I have long been friends. I met her through Emily Tindall, you see."

I gasp. "Miss Tindall?"

She nods. "I believe you knew her, too." Her eyes tell me that she knows something. She sighs. "When I told Miss Beaufroy of my . . . my predicament, she said if I needed help while I was in London, I might find you in St. Jude's." She nods. "So here I am."

For a moment, I am stunned into silence. I knew we were meant to meet. Miss Tindall may not have brought us directly together, but she will have had a hand in this. She will have guided Miss Louisa's thoughts. I know it. As we sit in the soft light of the candles by the crib, I feel her presence again and my doubts melt away like wax.

"Do you think you can help me?" I hear Miss Louisa ask. I switch back to her. "Miss Beaufroy said you were"—she hesitates before she finds the word—"*special.*" She shoots me a tentative smile, to see if the description meets with my approval.

I take her hand. "If I am *special*, it is because Miss Tindall chooses to talk through me," I tell her.

Then she says something that doesn't surprise me. "We were at Oxford together. I heard she was . . ." She stops herself from repeating what we both know.

"So you know she's been in touch with me since," I ask, to make sure we understand each other.

She nods. "I do. So if anything . . ." She halts for a moment, trying to compose herself. "If anything bad has happened to my little Bertie, then you would know, because Miss Tindall would tell you?"

I can see that she struggles to speak of her worst fears. I take her other hand. I must remain calm for her. It is my turn to be her rock.

"You've arranged to meet this woman, this Mother Delaney, again at Paddington on Friday?"

"Yes. But I fear . . ."

I feel my finger lift and place itself on my own lips and her mouth is stilled. "Fear will do you no good," I hear myself say, even though I know it is Miss Tindall who's speaking. She is here. She is by my side. "Have faith," I urge, although I'm not sure how I can help her.

As we've talked, it's felt like time has stood still, only it can't have, because from out of the corner of my eye, I see the Reverend Barnett has only just greeted Ma, and now she's on her way back toward me. I stand suddenly. "I'm sorry, I must go." I hope I don't sound too stiff, but I think Miss Louisa understands.

She glances over at Ma as she approaches. "Yes, so must I," she says, rising and giving Ma a bow of her head as she rustles by.

"An old friend of Miss Tindall's," I explain as Ma watches the governess head for the church door.

She just chuckles. "Peas out of a pod," I hear her murmur, but my eyes are fixed firmly on the plaster statue of the newborn Jesus in the crib. So this is it. There is a connection between Miss Louisa's baby and the dead child in the market. There has to be. Why else would Miss Tindall have sent her to me? I know it's up to me to track down the baby's killer and to reunite Bertie with his anxious mother. I also know that I must allow myself to be guided along this new path by Miss Tindall's hand. I'm sure she won't desert me.

Chapter 16

Emily

While the good burghers of Whitechapel and the surrounding districts pour out of churches after celebrating the Virgin birth, there are others for whom Christmas is just another day. Despite the fact that the trains are all silent, the omnibuses are in their garages and the dray horses have been given the day off, there is still life in Poplar.

It's a cut-through to the East India Docks, and, of course, the many Jews who live in the district do not observe the Christian holy day. There are Christians, too, who go about their affairs as if the coming of Christ as flesh does not warrant marking. Detective Sergeant Hawkins is one such. Naturally, he would have paid his twice-yearly visit to church—Christmas and Easter—had he not had more pressing matters. As he strides along Poplar High Street and passes a family ambling home from a service, his mind flits to his aunt and uncle's festive table from which he is, regrettably, absent. He knew they would be disappointed, but at least the roast goose can be eaten cold and the plum pudding warmed through another day.

Hawkins is on his way to Clarke's Yard, the place where

Catherine Mylett was discovered dead. He has not visited the scene itself, because according to the testimony of Sergeant Golding and Constable Barrett, no crime had been committed—with hindsight that was remiss. In fairness, Inspector McCullen had only assigned him to the case three days ago with the explicit brief that this was not another murder to be added to his already heavy responsibilities.

As he walks along, head bowed, he recaps the facts of the matter. No weapon was recovered. No ligature. No obvious injuries were visible, apart from a little blood at the victim's nostrils. The ground around was relatively undisturbed.

Clarke's Yard lies just off Poplar High Street. Up until a few months ago, it was secured by high wooden gates, but these mysteriously disappeared. Since that time, the now-open alleyway has become a well-known meeting place for those of ill repute. It takes Sergeant Hawkins less than half an hour to reach the yard from the police station. As he approaches the mouth of the narrow passage, he hears banging and tapping. Someone is about. The yard is used to store building materials, but several tradesmen rent out workshops, although how they can see to carry on their business in this ill-lit, squalid corner is beyond him.

He accepts he is taking a risk, venturing into this godforsaken warren, but his conscience has been pricked by Constance's words: "Life in Whitechapel is cheap." He wanted to prove to himself, as much as to her, that he didn't think it so. Every unexplained death deserves investigation, he'd told himself. That's why he wants to search the area, just to make sure nothing has been overlooked. For this purpose, he has brought with him a lantern. It is not even two o'clock in the afternoon, and yet, in this gloomy alley that has witnessed all manner of unspeakable acts, there is barely ever much light. He strikes a match and his lamp flares into life. Lowering it, he sees vermin at his feet, scuttling off beneath a doorway. Lifting it, he sees the passage opens out, up ahead. He presses on and steps out into the courtyard.

A gruff voice suddenly rasps against the gritty air: "What you want?"

Hawkins is momentarily startled. The glow from his lamp picks up a craggy-faced man holding a hammer.

"Police," he replies stiffly, fumbling for his identification badge in his breast pocket. The man, his cheeks smudged by soot, is a stocky artisan: a blacksmith by the looks of him. He wears an eye patch over his left eye—flying sparks present an occupational hazard—and sports a large leather apron and thick gauntlets. He's been working in one of the sheds. The hammer is lowered.

"You 'ere about the dead woman?" he growls. His thick accent is familiar to the detective. Hawkins nods. "You got a warrant?"

The sergeant looks the man in the eye. "I am come to examine the area where she was found. That's all. Mr. Braithwaite, isn't it?" He's read Sergeant Golding's perfunctory report. "A Yorkshireman. Yes?"

The man narrows his good eye, then slowly nods. "Aye. Come to this hellhole from the Moors."

Hawkins smiles at the blacksmith's quip. "Perhaps you would show me where the body was found, if you please?"

The smithy, his armor penetrated, concedes and walks a few paces into the courtyard. On one side, there are stables that offer shelter to the dray horses that pull mainly brewers' carts. There are half-a-dozen ramshackle workshops, too. Without a word, the Yorkshireman leads the detective to a high wall that encloses the area at the back. He points to the ground. "Round 'ere."

Hawkins crouches down to inspect the earth, shining his lamp on the mosaic of cart tracks and hoofprints, not to mention footprints. The crime scene has been compromised. It may as well be the center of Spitalfields market. He scoops up a little of the soil and weighs it up in his hand. It is moist and clings to his fingers. He sniffs it. He does not know why. Standing up again, he sluffs his hands together in an attempt to dispel any lingering dirt, while at the same time surveying the layout of the yard. It is then that he walks over to the wall. It is sturdy, made of brick. He lifts the lantern, tracing a course with his hand back toward the entrance. The bricks are cold and slimy to the touch. He looks up. He looks down. He has followed the wall into a corner, and now turns sharply at right angles. From the stink, he can tell that this is the area where the workmen often urinate. Avoiding the patch of soggy ground, he follows the bricks by eye.

The blacksmith, who has been observing the policeman from a distance, now approaches him from behind and peers over his shoulder.

"Where were you that night, Mr. Braithwaite?" asks Hawkins, his gaze still fixed on the wall.

"Me?" asks the Yorkshireman, caught off guard by the inquiry. "I were at home," comes his defensive reply. "I told the other coppers. I didn't see 'owt. Besides," he adds, with a shrug, "it's the drink that did for 'er, so 'tis said."

Hawkins shrugs. "We shall see," he replies. Of course, he has found nothing of material interest, but his encounter with this blacksmith has been most revealing. "We shall see, Mr. Braithwaite," he says again, thoughtfully, before heading back to the police station.

CONSTANCE

Ma and me usually rely on Flo to bring the cheer into our humble home. But now that she's split from Danny, and she's feeling green around the gills as well, we ain't—sorry, we *haven't*—got much to be cheerful about. Course this time of year, it's harder with Pa not around, too. There was always a stocking for us each, with some sweets and an orange in the toe. Then when we were grown, he'd strike up on his old squeeze box. Carols, we'd sing. "Silent Night" is Ma's favorite, but Flo and me would ask him for jolly songs like "Jingle Bells" and "We Wish You a Merry Christmas." Flo used to stamp her feet when we called for figgy pudding and then sang, "We won't go until we get some." And Ma would tell her to calm down, otherwise we'd have grumpy old Mrs. Malakey banging on the wall. But this year, well . . . it's not the same. Instead of Christmas cheer, fear's festooned like paper chains over Whitechapel. Nevertheless, we'll do our best.

By the time we arrive back from church, Flo's up and doing. She's lit a fire and it's no coincidence that the tree's looking a bit thinner. I know she's used some of the lower branches for kindling, but it's made the room smell nice and fresh; it's how I imagine a forest like they have in fairy tales might smell.

Our Christmas dinner is just like most other dinners: a sausage each and some cabbage. Ma brings out some beer, but Flo says she's not up for it, and I'm certainly not in the mood. Most families round here join the goose club so they can be sure of one good meal a year, but we're saving our bird for Mr. B's visit tomorrow. He's spending today with his married daughter and her husband and their three children over in Bermondsey. (I'm not sure what happened to Mrs. Bartleby, but he never speaks about her.) It's one of the few times I wish he was here. He's annoying when he pokes fun at me, and he's pompous, but he can raise our spirits when he's a mind to.

While Ma and Flo are in the kitchen, washing the pots, I'm left in charge of tending the fire. I give the glowing ashes a good poke, but there's not much life in them. The coal scuttle's empty, but there's an old newspaper by the grate, so I reach out and grab it. I tear off a sheet and am about to roll it into a ball to throw on the embers when, for no reason, the fire suddenly flares and I feel a sharp pain in my hand. Without thinking, I immediately drop the paper onto the hearth. When I look down, I see it's caught light at the edge, even though it wasn't near the flame. It's a sign. I know it is. I peer down at the print and it starts to glow before my eyes, but it's not burning. The writing is plain as day. It's an advertisement that reads: *Respectable woman and her doctor husband seek up to four children to call their own. Good food and sound education guaranteed. Terms from £10. Address: Mother, Post Office, Poplar.*

I shiver. The words are familiar to me. I've seen them before. I saw them on the piece of folded newspaper that Miss Louisa showed me in church this morning. Only the address has changed. Now it's Poplar, not Stepney. The old woman she seeks—the old woman I know I must find—has moved close by.

EMILY

So it is done. Constance knows what she must now do: track down the baby farmer to her new abode. That is where I now find myself, in Poplar. Whereas most pantries in the comfortable houses that line Woodstock Terrace are accommodating what remains of today's festive fare: the half-eaten roast turkey, the remnants of a braised pheasant, or the crumbs of a pudding that Cook insists can be used in trifle, the leftovers at Number 9 are having to share their shelves. Granted, there is still an untouched Stilton cheese and an unopened tin of water biscuits. And, of course, there is a sack of potatoes and one of Brussels sprouts, but most of the space is taken up by items never normally found in a pantry: infants.

The windowless room, where the temperature barely rises above ten degrees Fahrenheit, is perfectly suited to the task, according to Mother Delaney. At least the chill keeps the smell at bay. On a row of deep shelving at the far end of this room sit six crates of varying sizes. In all, bar one, lies a sleeping infant. The old matron knows the baby that is causing the fracas: Bertie is his name. At seven weeks, he's the oldest—and the loudest—at the moment. Not only is he noisy, he keeps kicking his legs, too, so she's had to swaddle him tightly. But he is by far the healthiest of her charges, so she's earmarked him for special treatment.

"You've a fine pair o' lungs, to be sure!" says Mother De-

laney, waddling over to the farthest drawer to peer into it. As she does so, she holds her nose. The child has soiled himself . . . again. She shakes her head as she traverses the tiled floor to a wall cupboard from which she retrieves a brown bottle. Back with Bertie, she pours out a spoonful of syrupy liquid. Mother Delaney swears by laudanum, both for her charges and for herself. She pinches the child's face so that his mouth opens and down the medicine goes.

"There, there, darlin' boy," she soothes.

She returns to the cabinet, bottle in hand, but before she puts it back, she eyes it longingly. "Don't mind if I do," she says with a chuckle, and, uncorking the stopper once more, she takes a large swig. "It is Christmas, after all."

Chapter 17

Wednesday, December 26, 1888

Emily

I return to Commercial Street police station. It is still quite early, but already Detective Sargent Hawkins is back behind his neatly-kept desk, while all around him lie unruly collections of reports and papers. Despite having returned to his own bed in the section house last night, he slept poorly. His head's feeling as thick as an East End fog; so when Constable Tanner brings him a steaming mug of tea, he relishes the thought of the hot liquid soothing his dry throat.

"Most welcome," he says to Tanner as he primes himself for the first sip.

"Sorry, sir," says the constable. "You might have to leave that for the moment, sir." Tanner's eyes dart to the tea.

"Why?" Hawkins croaks.

"Because the boss wants to see you," he replies, rolling his eyes toward Inspector McCullen's office. All thoughts of the re-

viving powers of a brew are banished. As Hawkins heads toward his superior, the constable mutters to himself: "And he ain't happy."

As soon as he opens the office door, Hawkins is greeted by the broad shoulders and stocky build of his boss.

"Sir, you wished to see me."

Detective Inspector McCullen paces up and down, muffled against the cold in his office by a large scarf. Yet again, someone neglected to light the fire before his arrival this morning. Although a match has since been set to kindling, the room remains only marginally above freezing. But it is not only the temperature that makes McCullen feel the need to pace up and down, hands behind his back. His face is set in a scowl. He means business and Hawkins soon finds out why.

"Shut the door!" he barks. A greeting is eschewed in favor of an expletive. "What the bloody hell did Brownfield think he was playing at?" He slaps a copy of the Christmas Eve edition of the Daily Star *down on the desk and waves a derisory hand over the text. "'Is he a thug? The work of the same man.'" He spits out the headlines. Hawkins is uncertain as to how he should react, so he waits silently and is rewarded with a change of tone. "At least my Christmas wasn't ruined entirely," volunteers McCullen, now holding his palms to the fledgling fire.*

"Sir?"

The senior detective's lips twitch into a half smile. "Dr. Bond has come to our rescue."

"How's that, sir?"

McCullen now stands with his back to the fire and lifts his coattails to warm his rump. "He finally found the time to examine the dead woman's body late on Christmas Eve, and, according to the learned surgeon, although death, indeed, was by strangulation, it was not at another's hand."

Hawkins shakes his head in puzzlement. "Then how . . . ?"

"Bond says the wretched whore fell down while filthy drunk

and choked herself on her blasted jacket collar!" snorts McCullen. He turns round to face the fire.

Hawkins is surprised, but, he admits to himself, relieved. This news was not expected. He looks about him. The inspector's office is neat and ordered, not at all like the cluttered space he shares with his own colleagues. "So the cord? The marks on her neck? All circumstantial, sir?"

McCullen nods. "Indeed, and, as you know, Bond's opinion carries as much weight as all of the London knife men put together. It suits the assistant commissioner to believe it, too." He walks toward his desk, picks up a folder, thumbs through it randomly, then flings it down again. "And what's this I hear of the woman's nickname? Drunken Alice?"

There is little, it seems, that escapes Inspector Cullen's forensic mind, but the question, coming as it does completely unexpectedly, throws Hawkins a little. "The medical report says she was sober at the time, sir."

McCullen returns to warming himself by the fire; then, after a short pause, he throws a glance over his shoulder. "Well, maybe we ought to ignore that, Hawkins, so we can get the guvnor off our backs." He rubs his hands together in thought, making things up on the hoof. "Mylett drank herself to death and fell down in a drunken stupor. Let's put that theory out to the press, shall we? See how they chew on our bone."

It takes a moment for Hawkins to digest what his commanding officer has just ordered him to do. The Metropolitan Police Service is already a laughingstock. Another murder, let alone another Ripper murder, is the last thing that's needed. McCullen is angling for this whole business to be dusted up and brushed under the carpet. This unfortunate's death will be scooped up into a metaphorical dustpan and neatly disposed of, filed into the refuse bin. He will get a pat on the back from Assistant Commissioner Anderson and everyone can concentrate on what really matters: catching Jack.

His sergeant's silence causes McCullen to turn away from the fire and look at Hawkins straight. "I can see I've offended your principles, eh, Detective Sergeant. Holier than thou, are we?"

The younger man flounders; then after a moment, he replies: "No, sir, but perhaps we're being a little premature."

"Premature?" *McCullen repeats, and Hawkins immediately regrets using the word.*

"Hasty, sir," he jumps in.

McCullen glares at him. "Don't come the grammar-school boy with me, laddie." He clenches his fist and punches the mantel-shelf. "We've got bigger fish to fry than bother with some drunken slut. Until the coroner says otherwise, this Mylett woman brought her death on herself, you hear me?"

Hawkins tugs at his waistcoat and straightens his back as if standing to attention. "Yes, sir."

The maneuver causes his commanding officer to lift his lips into a half smile. He knows this young man to be shrewd. He'll go far, but he still needs to learn how to play the game. McCullen takes a deep breath. "How are you doing with Druitt?"

The sergeant shifts awkwardly. "He's not been seen for the past two and a half weeks, sir," he replies stiffly. "I'm working on it."

"Working on it?" *McCullen echoes, shaking his head. "Not good enough, laddie. I assigned you to him because I thought you had more wits about you than the rest of 'em." He touches his temple. "I need results, Hawkins, and fast, or you'll be back in Whitehall as a constable sooner than you can say 'Jack the Ripper.'"*

Constance

The papers is full of what they're calling the "Poplar Mystery." I buy a copy of the *Daily News* and bring it home to read. Flo and Ma sit by me as I tell them what's written. It don't make happy listening. "Says here the police have been 'unsuccessful in tracing anything like a connected chain of the deceased's antecedents,'" I say out loud.

"What's them when they're at home?" asks Flo.

"Any relatives," I explain.

Ma's forehead crumples into a frown. "Does that mean they ain't told Maggie?" she asks. Ma knows Mrs. Mylett from way back, but they haven't been in touch for a while. She shakes her head. "I'd best go round to Pelham Street," she says.

The truth is, Cath went by so many names and lived in so many places that it was hard to keep track of her. Like a lot of women in this neck o' the woods, she could never put down roots. She was always at the mercy of others.

EMILY

Meanwhile in the parlor of his home in Woodstock Terrace, Albert Cosgrove sits in a comfortable chair by the fire. He is wearing tartan slippers and a red satin smoking jacket, which his mother-in-law gave him for Christmas to replace his other one that was unfortunately rather badly stained. She's told him he looks quite the gentleman in it, even though she thinks she should have bought a bigger size. He glances down at his left sleeve. He's been told his wound is healing nicely. It'll be a relief to have the bandage off. The sleeve, however, he finds a little too short for his liking. The garment may even be somewhat lacking across the chest as well.

Nonetheless, Mother Delaney's son-in-law appears at ease as he puffs his pipe and reads the latest copy of the Draper's Record. *While most men are content to relax during the festive holiday, he would rather use his time profitably. Success, he's learned, does not come from idleness. He is catching up with the latest ladies' fashion trends. He may only manage the shop, but he still does all the ordering. Lace is very* a la mode, *according to an article in the magazine, especially for children. And, as if on cue, just as he had read the sentence, one of the "brood," as he calls them, starts to cry. He has ignored the irritating whimpering for a while, but now that it is a full-blown guffaw, he can let it pass no longer.*

"Quiet!" he shouts, turning his face to the closed door. The bawling continues. "Quiet, I say!" He smooths his paper again and resumes reading. This second time, his command is heeded. Silence reigns in the parlor once more.

Back in the kitchen, Philomena stands at the wooden table, glazing a boiled ham. She's as thin as her mother is fat and as fine-featured as the older woman's face is coarse. In her right hand, she holds a brush; while on her bony left hip, she balances Isabel. Philomena is relieved to be preparing cold cuts this evening, especially having given Lotte time off. Yesterday's festivities were very taxing. They were only supposed to be minding three children over Christmas, but two of the adoptive mothers changed their minds at the last moment and will not now collect their charges until tomorrow.

At the sight of her grandmother, Isabel bleats and thrusts out her arms. "Issy," says Philomena by way of reprimand.

Mother Delaney tuts, then smiles. "Come to Maimeó,*" she coos, and her daughter passes over the child in a well-practiced maneuver.*

"Let's go and play, shall we?" says the old woman, brushing the girl's cheek with her rough lips. "Father Christmas brought you lots of new toys, didn't he?"

Philomena wipes her forehead with the back of her hand before her eyes settle on the open carpetbag on the windowsill. "And there's that one, too," she says, pointing to something brightly colored peeping out from the bag. With Isabel on her hip, Mother Delaney walks over to fetch the small parcel wrapped in red tissue paper. She remembers she should've put it under the tree when she brought it home with her on Sunday. She also remembers something else.

"What did ya get for that silver cup I gave ya?" she asks her daughter.

Without bothering to look up, Philomena replies: "Six shillings."

"Six shillings? *'Twas worth twelve if it were a penny," huffs Mother, reaching for the gift from her bag.*

"The man said it was less because 'twas already engraved with initials."

For a moment, the old woman seems disgruntled, but her attention soon switches back to her granddaughter.

"What have we here?" she asks her gleefully as she prizes apart the red wrapping. Of course, she knows full well. "Will ya look at this!?" she exclaims. The little girl's face lights up as her grandmother shakes a red-and-yellow rattle before her eyes. "Aren't you the lucky one?" she says with a smile.

CONSTANCE

Earlier today, at one o'clock sharp, Mr. Bartleby came to dinner with us. Ma insisted we save our goose for him. Flo didn't feel like eating, anyway, so we're having the bird with bubble and squeak. Mr. B's doing his best to lighten everyone's spirits. He cracks a few lousy jokes and Ma and me titter now and again.

"Here's one for Con," he says. "Who is the greatest chicken killer in Shakespeare?" I shake my head and shrug. "Macbeth," he replies, "because he did murder *most foul.*"

He laughs like a drain at that, and I admit I chuckle, but Flo's still wearing a face as long as the Old Kent Road, pining after that no-good Daniel of hers. She's finally told Ma about the breakup, but, of course, neither of us says anything to Mr. B, so he's got no idea what's happened. He thinks she's just being plain sulky, like she can be at times.

Afters is figgy pudding. It was hard as the knocker of Newgate, but the custard softened it a bit. Anyway, I'm just clearing away the dirty plates when Mr. B announces he's brought presents for us all.

Ma's face lights up. "Oh, Harold, you shouldn't!" She beams.

I know he shouldn't and all. He certainly won't have paid good money for them at a store. Whatever he's got us will have been lifted and fenced at that shop of his in Limehouse, like the mantel clock he gave Ma last Christmas. No, I'm not happy about taking Mr. B's presents, but as soon as I've put the plates in the kitchen, I return to the table with a smile on my face. He's brought a cloth bag with him, and from out of it, he brings a small brown parcel with a red ribbon round it.

"This is for you, dear Patience," he says, handing Ma the present with a flourish, like he's some *maitre d'* in a music hall.

She takes it from him with a flutter of her eyelashes and peels back the wrapping to reveal a blue oblong box. It looks fancy, like a necklace case. I hear her wheeze with excitement as she opens it up and, sure enough, there on a little bed of silk sits a silver locket with a chain.

With eyes wide, she looks up at Mr. B. "Oh, Harold! It's beautiful!" she squeals. He gets up from the table and walks round to where she's sitting.

" 'Ere, let me put it on for you," he says, scooping it out of its case with his finger. I watch as he unclasps the chain, then loops the necklace over Ma's head so that it falls round her neck. She leans forward a little to allow him to fasten the clasp. I watch the chain lift and tighten slightly against Ma's chest. She touches the pendant with her fingertips, then brushes her neck. I see this all in minute detail, like it's been slowed down in time and I think of Cath the night someone put something round her neck, too. And then I see her. It's like she's right in front of me, gasping for breath, fighting for her life, and her fingers are grasping at her own throat and at her collar.

"Lovely, ain't it, girls?" I hear Ma say, but her voice seems far away. I don't reply. I can't reply. I'm still picturing that night in Clarke's Yard. "Con. Connie, love. You all right?" Ma's voice is louder now.

"What? Yes." I manage a smile.

"You've gone white as a sheet, my gal," says Mr. Bartleby, taking his place back at the table. He nudges me lightly in the ribs. "Don't that suit your dear mother?"

I nod. "You look a proper lady, Ma," I say.

Mr. Bartleby laughs and slaps the table. "Didn't I tell ya I'd give you something classy, Patience?"

Ma smiles and nods her reply. "You're too generous, Harold," she chides.

"Nonsense," he replies, bringing out yet another parcel from his bag. This time, it's Flo's turn. "And for you, Miss Florence. . . ." He hands her a larger parcel. She looks at him warily, but we all know she can't resist a pretty trinket. Soon she's tearing at the paper like a terrier. It's a gold bracelet inlaid with mother-of-pearl. She gasps with delight at the sight of it.

"It's . . . it's beautiful." I know it's hard for her to show gratitude to him, but I can tell she's not faking it when she says: "Thank you so much."

It's then that Mr. B goes and puts his foot in it. Just as Flo's about to slip the bracelet round her wrist, he goes and says: "I thought you could wear it on your wedding day."

Flo's head jerks up. Ma gasps. I freeze. Mr. B frowns. "What've I said?" he asks innocently. It's not his fault that we haven't told him about the broken engagement, but Flo's not hanging around to explain. She just bursts into tears and runs upstairs quick as a flash.

"Oh, dear! Oh, dear!" moans Mr. Bartleby, shaking his head, but I can see a smile hovering on his lips. It's clear he won't lose sleep over his little *faux pas,* as I think the French call it. He's soon back on the case and handing me my gift. "Now you gave me a bit of trouble, you did, Connie," he tells me as I start to open a small cardboard box. "I know you're not one for pretty things, so I settled on that."

I'm a little puzzled as I pull out a little silver cup from the box. It's engraved with leaves and squiggles, and when I turn it over in my hand, I see initials etched on it. That's when it dawns on me. It's a baby's cup—the sort that rich people give as christening gifts. I study the initials once more. *RLF.* Should they mean something to me? My next thought makes me shudder. The *'F'* could stand for Fortune and the *'R'*, well that could be for Robert. That's short for Bertie, ain't it? It's like the cup's been sent to me by Miss Tindall.

"Nice, in'it?" says Mr. B, trying to coax some reaction out of me.

I force a smile. "Very," I reply. "Thank you." He's got a nerve, palming me off with poke like this. It's obvious that Ma's and Flo's jewelry was stolen, too, but this cup, complete with the initials of some little kid, takes the biscuit. I don't even want to be in the same room as him anymore. It's only for Ma's sake that I don't fling it down in disgust and run upstairs to join Flo.

CHAPTER 18

Thursday, December 27, 1888

EMILY

Number 9, Woodstock Terrace, is quieter than usual today. That's because when Mother Delaney opened the pantry door this morning and checked on her charges, she found not one, but two babies had passed in the night. Naturally, Philomena sent directly for Dr. Carey, but he had been unavailable, apparently called away to his own sick father, so another physician will attend this morning. He is a much younger man, newly qualified, in fact, and eager to make his mark on the world. So eager that he's even done a little research into the case notes of the household he is about to visit and is rather concerned by what he has seen.

In his spidery writing, Dr. Carey has recorded the deaths of no fewer than three infants over the course of the last five weeks. Granted, infant mortality is a scandal in this malevolent part of London, but surely, even given this low starting point, such a figure would raise the most implacable eyebrow?

"Dr. Carey is unavailable, is he now?" Mother Delaney cannot hide her disquiet at seeing the elderly physician's junior counterpart present himself on her doorstep.

The young doctor, lean and spare, with a moustache to complement his physique, is not in the least bit apologetic. "Indeed, he is. You have me today. Mrs. Delaney, isn't it? I am Dr. Greatorex."

Mother Delaney is clearly a little put out, but sweetens her initial sourness. "Pleased to make your acquaintance, to be sure." Of course, she is not. Dr. Carey proved himself so malleable—an old fool, in fact. He never questioned how so many infants could fall prey to some mystery disease, or suffer from an unexplained condition. He took her word on everything, even to the point where he'd stopped wanting to see the tiny corpses. But this fellow, with his sharp eyes and brusque manner, might prove a little more difficult to handle.

"May I see the infants?" he asks as soon as he is admitted into the hallway. "The message said two."

"Yes. This way, Doctor," says Mother, pointing to the stairs. Philomena has suddenly appeared to hover nervously in the background. Mother scowls at her and shoos her away so that she scurries back into the kitchen. "Shall I take your coat now, Doctor?"

He shakes his head. "I'll keep it on, thank you. It's a little chilly in here," he tells her. She notes his critical tone as she leads the way up the stairs, heaving her bulky frame up to the bedroom where the girls and women give birth. It's where she always lays out the dead babies, too. It's not a bad room, but not salubrious, either. The wallpaper peels in the corner, the thick velvet curtains are dull with dust, and the air smells damp. It is, however, infinitely better than the pantry and several degrees warmer, even without a fire in the grate. None has been lit this morning, however, and the distinct chill in the air matches the doctor's standoffish manner.

The babies are laid out in separate cots, each covered by a sin-

gle blanket. Dr. Greatorex looks at the first one, a girl. He lifts up the cover. She wears nothing but a napkin, so that he can instantly see her ribs. He estimates she is around four weeks old. She is, in fact, eight, but she has been starved for the last three. He throws Mother an inquiring look. "She is very thin," he remarks.

The old woman shrugs. "A sickly child, Doctor" is her lame excuse. It is usually enough to satisfy Dr. Carey, but she is not sure if it will work on this young blade.

"And the other?"

Mother guides the doctor to the adjacent cot; this time, she takes off the blanket herself. The child, a boy, wears a smock. She is glad of it, although Dr. Greatorex is clearly not satisfied with a cursory glance at the body. He lifts up the garment. Once again, the child is painfully thin—a clear case of marasmus—and what's this? He hones in on a greenish bruise on his ribs, suggesting to him that the boy might have been roughly handled. He frowns.

"Do you know how this happened?"

Mother thinks quickly. "It's an old one. His mother was a drunk, so she was. In a terrible state was the poor mite when he arrived. Bless him. Black and blue."

The explanation is plausible, even if, in the doctor's eyes, it is highly suspicious.

"Do you have any other nurse children at the moment, Mrs. Delaney?" he asks, turning away from the cot. "You do know that under the law you need a licence?"

The old woman lets out a nervous chuckle. She's worried he'll report her. He's clearly the sort who might. "Sure I know, Doctor, and I have the right papers. But I've no more babbies at present."

"Good," he replies sharply. "Then I shall give you some advice before you take in any more. Infants need food. If their mother's milk is unavailable, then cow's milk mixed with a little water will suffice, but it must be given regularly. Then when the

child reaches six weeks, pap may be introduced." Mother listens without expression. She takes the thinly veiled criticism in silence. "But I'm sure you knew all that, Mrs. Delaney," concludes the doctor.

"To be sure, I did," she tells him, forcing a smile.

"Good," he replies with a nod. "Then the next time I am called upon, I'm hoping it will be to prevent a death, not merely to issue another certificate." He opens his case and brings out a small folder containing documents. He moves over to a nearby chest of drawers and begins to write. She watches him, simmering, until her anger spills over.

"I treat the babbies as my own, you know," she growls.

The doctor signs the last certificate with a flourish and hands it to her. "I am pleased to hear it," he says with a forced smile. It is clear he does not believe her.

It's shortly before nine o'clock and the haberdasher's shop in Bull Court isn't yet open. The shopkeeper, clipboard in hand, ensuring his stock is all in order after his two-day Christmas break, is finding he is being hampered in his work by the fact that it is difficult to function properly with a bandaged hand. His irritation is compounded by the fact that despite being before the proper opening hour, it appears that a customer cannot read and has chosen to ring the bell. He glances at the door, then places his pencil behind his ear and puts down his inventory. Peering through the glass, he spies a man. A gentleman by the looks of him, *he thinks. It seems not to bother him that the sign says* CLOSED. *And who's that with him? He hesitates for a second. He has spotted the blue serge uniform of a police officer. Calm. He must remain calm. Unbolting the door, he greets the plainclothes policeman with a wide smile.*

"Good morning, sir. How may I help you?"

"I am Detective Sergeant Hawkins and this is Constable Semple. I'd like to ask you a few questions, if I may, sir?"

The shopkeeper makes a sweeping gesture to usher the men inside. Before he shuts the door behind them, he checks that the CLOSED *sign remains clearly visible. He does not want any of his customers to see that he is being questioned by the police.*

Hawkins does not waste time, but walks toward the glass counter. He brings out a slightly tatty paper bag and shows its contents to the shopkeeper.

"Do you sell this binding, sir?" he asks, scanning the colorful array of ribbons on display.

The shopkeeper looks closely and scratches his limp sideburns. "Yes, that's one of ours," he replies. "There it is." He points to a tray of ribbons under the detective's nose.

Hawkins nods. "Have you sold any recently?"

The shopkeeper shrugs and pulls at a straggling whisker. "Not that I can think of. It's not one of our most popular ranges, but I'm only the manager. I order what I'm told. It's not that fashionable, you see," he ventures, casting a professional eye at the spool. "Used mainly to edge infants' clothes. May I ask . . . ?"

"A baby was found dead in Petticoat Lane, with a length of this patterned binding secured round its neck," Hawkins replies without giving too much away.

"I heard," replies the shopkeeper, his forehead suddenly furrowed. "A grim to-do."

Hawkins agrees. "Grim, indeed," he says, taking out his card from his pocket and handing it to him. "But if you think of anything, you'll let me know, won't you, Mr. . . . um?"

"Cosgrove," volunteers the haberdasher. "Albert Cosgrove."

The detective nods; seemingly satisfied, he is making for the door, when he suddenly turns, as if remembering something. "Oh, and, Mr. Cosgrove," he says.

"Yes, sir?" replies the haberdasher.

Sergeant Hawkins points to his bandaged hand. "Make sure you look after your wound, won't you?"

CHAPTER 19

Friday, December 28, 1888

CONSTANCE

It's Holy Innocents today, the day that marks the killing of all those poor babes by King Herod. He ordered the slaughter of the male first-borns 'cos he'd heard the King of the Jews had been born and felt threatened. I was reminded of it as I passed St. Jude's on my way to Paddington Station. I'm here for Miss Louisa. She's arranged to meet this old Irishwoman, this baby farmer, today. She won't know I'm here. I'll just watch from the wings. I remember Miss Tindall used to say to me in that lovely voice of hers: "Chance is perhaps the pseudonym of God when He does not want to sign." She hasn't exactly written her name on what has happened with Miss Louisa finding me and that, but I know she's given me directions. It's like she put a thread in the governess's hand and following it led her to me.

As I wait for Miss Louisa, half-hidden by a trolley piled high with trunks and suitcases, a voice comes from nowhere.

"There's a queer place to sell your wares, my gal!" A City type's looking me up and down. He's giving his temple a scratch. He's right, of course. I may have a basket of buttonholes to shift, but I'm not touting for custom.

"Yes, sir" is all I manage to reply; then I add cheekily: "Will ya be 'avin' one, sir? Cheer the ladies up on a morning such as this." I pick the best rose and hold it up under his nose. He weakens at the scent.

"How much?"

"To you, sir, just tuppence."

He narrows his eyes. "I'll give you a penny and no more."

That's how it is. You ask for the world and they always give you a half of it. "Fair dos," says I, taking his coin and handing over the bloom.

Truth is, I don't want no—I mean *any*—punters. As the gent marches off, I spot Miss Louisa arrive under the station clock. She looks all fragile and wan. Part of me wants to tell her I'm here, but I mustn't. I'm praying that the Irishwoman who's been caring for her son will bring him along this time and hand him over with no trouble. I'll be able to see and hear everything that passes between the two of them to make sure that this old biddy doesn't try and pull one over on her. Speak of the devil, here she comes now.

EMILY

Shortly before ten o'clock, I spot Louisa taking up her position under the clock on Platform One, just as she did five days ago. They have been the worst five days of her life. She has neither eaten nor slept, and the toll of her torture is all too evident on her face. The freshness and hope she once exuded has dissolved into fear. As she waits, the nausea begins to rise in her stomach. She looks about her. A nanny passes by, pushing a perambulator. A governess walks, hand in hand, with her small charge. A party of schoolboys is shepherded toward a platform. Are these children sent to torment her? Every time she sees one, she longs to hold her own. It was heartbreaking enough to think that she would have to give up dear Bertie for adoption, but now to be unsure as to his whereabouts is to tighten the rack. Other questions flood her mind, too. What if Mother Delaney doesn't keep their appointment? She refused to disclose her address. How can she contact her if she doesn't show?

The station clock strikes ten, and with each chime, Louisa's taut nerves stiffen until, come the last, she thinks they will snap. Frantically she casts around for a small, plump woman carrying a bundle. She sees none. Her desolation is about to manifest itself in a pitiful sob, when she hears a voice behind her.

"A good morning to ya, dearie."

Louisa's heart stops. She pivots. Mother Delaney stands behind her, her cobweb hair controlled under a black bonnet. But she comes empty-handed. Louisa regards her, horrified. Her throat constricts, as if strong hands are clutching at it. Despite this, questions still manage to struggle free.

"Where's Bertie? What's happened!?"

Seemingly oblivious to the young woman's obvious distress, Mother Delaney smiles and shrugs her plaid-covered shoulders. "A misunderstanding."

"What?" screeches Louisa, suddenly released from her initial shock. "What do you mean? Where's Bertie?"

The old woman will not be ruffled. "He's with a lovely couple in Brighton. I took him to Mass on Christmas morn and they were up visiting relatives. They were so taken with him that . . ."

Louisa's face is the picture of incredulity. "You gave my son to strangers on a passing whim? What were you thinking?" She takes a step forward. I see her gloved fists are balled. It is requiring every ounce of self-restraint that she possesses not to shake the old crone. Yet, Mother Delaney stands her ground. In fact, she does more than that. Detecting that Louisa might cause a scene, she turns the tables on her. She clasps her hands across her sagging breasts and rounds her shoulders to make herself smaller.

"Now you'd not be threatening an old woman, would ya?"

The accusation pulls Louisa up short. She bites her tongue; she takes a deep breath, as if to try and compose herself. "May I remind you that you were the one who was going to adopt my son, not some strangers? It was part of our agreement."

Mother Delaney nods. "Sure, I remember." She's self-assured, even arrogant. Her gaze is direct without the slightest twinge of embarrassment or regret. Unabashed she continues: "But 'twas too good an opportunity to miss. Such a lovely couple, they were. Followers of the true faith an' all. Your Bertie'll be brought up a good Catholic, you can be assured of that." It's as if she's just completed a successful business transaction that benefits all parties.

Louisa remains poised on the edge of despair. She feels an urge to jump, but before she does, she has more questions. "Do you have the name and address of this couple? I've changed my mind. I want him back. I must go to them."

*Mother Delaney's eyes widen. "*Changed your mind? *We had an agreement—"*

"But I haven't paid you the final amount," Louisa interrupts. "He's not yours to give away." She pauses for breath. "I must find them, this couple."

The old woman plays with the fringes of her shawl as she considers the request for a moment. "Very well," she says after what seems to Louisa like an eternity. "I'll let you have their address. It's not with me, mind. I'll post it to you."

"No, you will not!" snaps Louisa. Then realizing she needs to temper her tone if she is to make any progress, she elucidates. "Let us meet here again." She has teaching obligations she must fulfil back in Cheltenham, but she cannot obtain this address soon enough. "Monday? The same time?"

Mother Delaney considers her proposal. This time, though, with an arched brow, as if she is the one with the upper hand in this despicable game of poker. She is, it seems, a formidable player. She raises poor Louisa. "I'll come," she replies, then adds cruelly: "But only if you pay me the five pounds you still owe as a gesture of goodwill."

The words sting like a whiplash. Louisa has the money, of course, but she was resolved not to hand it over until she saw her little Bertie with her own eyes. This outstanding amount is becoming the hook on which Mother Delaney is caught. She is wriggling, but she is not yet in the net. She can still escape. Another compromise presents itself. "I will pay you the rest of the money when I have the address."

For the first time in their conversation, the Irishwoman shows a chink of weakness. It manifests itself in a twitch of her lips. She is being forced to retreat, if only a short distance. She concedes. "Very well. Monday, it is." She takes her leave with a defiant nod of her bonnet.

Poor Louisa watches her disappear out of the station before she allows the tears to well up and cascade over her cheeks. Her world begins to roll, as if she is on board a ship. She clutches at a nearby lamppost to steady herself. Before the meeting, she thought she could not feel more anxious or angry. Now she knows she was wrong. I think perhaps her pain would be eased a little if she knew that the entire encounter with the Irishwoman had been observed—and heard—by a well-wisher. Constance has borne witness to the meeting, but it is how she acts upon it that will determine the course of events.

Constance

There's no time to waste. I've got to follow this old crone if there's to be any hope of helping poor Miss Louisa. I saw how that Irish witch played her like a fiddle. As if she hadn't suffered enough already. But I'm on her heels. Miss Louisa may have let her go for the moment, but she can't escape from me. I follow her outside the railway station and watch her heave her old carcass onto an omnibus. I see on its board that it's heading for Poplar. I think of the newspaper advertisement. I know I'm on the right track.

Luckily, the penny from the City gent pays the fare. I wedge myself next to a fat man in a brown suit, who reeks of tobacco, and a young man with bad spots. I'm sitting toward the back, as far away from the old woman as I can, but I don't let my eyes stray from that miserable face of hers. She was all false smiles with Miss Louisa when they met; then that grew into a "How can you be angry with a poor old woman?" face when she didn't have the babe. It's like she can change her look to suit the weather. All sunny one moment, then thunderclouds the next. But it's her eyes that tell me everything I need to know. They're cold and gray as the Irish Sea. Yet, there she sits on the omnibus bench, smoothing her skirts, all righteous and God-fearing. I wonder how many young mothers she's fleeced in her time. She's not the caring matron that Miss Louisa thought she was when she first went to her for help. She's a baby farmer. Nothing more and nothing less. I've heard about her sort and I know they have hearts of stone. I'm that fixed on the old woman that it's a jolt when the conductor calls out the next stop.

"Poplar!"

Mother grabs hold of the pole and rises. She's getting off. I'm at the back, but manage to fight my way to the front of the bus just in time to hop off. I look left. No sign of her, then right. She's crossed the road. She knows where she's going, sure enough. She's got a spring in her step for an old bird, but I'm on her tail.

Poplar looks different in daylight. Better. Cleaner. It's not the West End, mind you, but with more light between the houses, it's not as dark or as dingy as Whitechapel. I'm trailing the Irishwoman along the high street. Some of the shops are closed down, but it's busy enough with the comings and goings of carts and drays from the nearby docks as they clatter toward the warehouses in Houndsditch. There's something else going on, too. Down at the dock end of the street, there's a crowd gathering. It's mainly women. There are lots of them. Some are carrying placards and there's a stream of them heading toward the East India Dock gates. I manage to snatch a glimpse of what their banners are saying: DRINK IS POISON. It's the Temperance Movement lot, and by the looks of it, they've joined forces with some of the gas workers, too, who don't want to work on the Sabbath.

They start crossing the road, coming toward me. I try and sidestep, but it's too late. I'm lost in a press of people and I take my eye off the old crone. She's swallowed up by the approaching crowd, too. People are shouting and jostling all around and here comes Old Bill. I better get out of here as soon as I can. It's been a wasted journey. I can't wait to get home and I start to rush back along the high street, heading for Whitechapel.

I'm only a few paces into my journey when something makes me look to my left, I'm not sure why, and I see a sign at the mouth of an alleyway. The letters suddenly loom large in my vision: CLARKE'S YARD. It's where they found Cath. Maybe my bus ride was worth the fare, after all. Maybe I was meant to come here, anyway, to see the spot where she died.

I pick my way through the muddy ruts and puddles until the alley opens out into a courtyard. It's lined with workshops and you can't hear yourself think, for the clattering of hammers and the clank of chains. It don't half stink as well—a mixture of horse shit and sulfur. A couple of lads spot me. One of them catcalls me. It's a busy old place and I'm not sure where to turn to find where Cath fell. I try and recall what I read in the newspaper. From out of nowhere, a name pops into my head. A man named Braithwaite, I think it was. He was mentioned in a report, as I recall. It said he was a blacksmith, but he told the police he didn't see or hear nothing. There's a boy leading a nag. I'll ask him as he's passing.

"I'm looking for Mr. Braithwaite," I yell at the nipper over the racket.

"Braithwaite?" the lad answers. I nod and he lifts his arm to point to the nearby shed, where a smithy is hard at work shoeing an old cob. The coals of his furnace glow red in the gloom and the sparks from his hammer are flying bright red against the black of the inside. As soon as I look on them, something strange happens. It's like a firework's exploding and my brain fizzes at the sight. I already know that something bad happened in this place, that Cath was found dead here, but there's something else. I freeze and a sudden fear sweeps over me as images flash before my eyes. There's a woman—I think it's Cath—and a man. He's threatening her, pinning her against a wall. She's frightened. Then the vision shatters like the glass in a mirror and all the shards are catapulted into the air.

After a moment, I shake my head and everything is back to normal, even though I'm still trembling as I move toward the shed. As I draw closer, I feel the welcome heat of the furnace even from the doorway. It's another moment until I remember why I'm here. I shout out the blacksmith's name, but he can't hear me above the clinking of his hammer, forcing me to really belt it out. "*Mr. Braith-waite!*" This time he hears and looks round. He's wearing a peaked cap, but at the sound of my voice, he pushes it back to show his face. It's all black, like one of them musical hall minstrels, and he's wearing a patch, but his good eye is trained on me, all right.

I find my courage again. "Mr. Braithwaite?"

"Who wants to know?" he says in a voice that tells me he's not a Londoner. He loosens the kerchief round his neck and starts to wipe the sweat and coal dust from his face as he walks toward me. He carries his shovel by its heft, and I'm not sure if I should feel worried.

"I'm a friend . . ." I break off, remembering. "I *was* a friend," I correct myself, "of Cath Mylett's."

At the mention of her name, he pauses, like I've pressed on a sore place. He leans on his shovel, then he shakes his head.

"I told the coppers all I know. I didn't see 'owt," he says, his good eye all screwed up. I think he might be a Yorkshireman from the way he talks. I've heard they call a spade a spade up there, in the north. They like plain talking and I'm up for that. Even so, I can tell he's going to be a tricky customer. He'll need coaxing out of his shell.

"I've come to pay my respects," I tell him. I point to the blooms I've been carrying in my basket all the way from Paddington. "We were with her the night she died. Can you show me where they found her?"

He throws me a surly look, but lays his shovel against the doorpost. I can see my words have done the trick. He straightens himself again and flattens his cap.

"Follow me, lass," he says.

The yard is sheltered from the wind, but away from the furnace, it's still cold and I can barely feel my feet as he walks ahead of me. I almost have to break out into a trot to keep up. A moment later, he stops in a corner where two walls join. "Here," he says, pointing to a patch of mud that looks just the same as any other patch of mud in London, pitted and rutted with footprints and hoof marks. I don't know what I was expecting to find. I look up at Mr. Braithwaite, a little dazed, then at my flowers. I feel his eye bore into me from beneath the peak of his cap and catch a look about him, like he's sad, too.

"There," he repeats, and suddenly he whips off his hat as a mark of respect. Is that a tear on his black cheek? I wonder if it's the cold wind or something else that's making his eye water. I step forward and lay a single bloom—a pink rose like the one Cath had on her hankie—on the spot. I stand back, and am just about to bow my head to reflect, when the rose suddenly blackens before my very eyes, like it's got a terrible blight. I frown.

"What the . . . ?" I bend low to pick up the bloom and the petals fall away, so that I'm left holding only a stalk. I think it strange. "I ain't seen that happen to a flower before," I say. The smithy's puzzled, too.

I replace it with another one from my basket that seems healthy enough. I lay it on the ground and stand back once more.

"She didn't deserve to die like this," I say quietly. I ask Miss Tindall to look after her wherever she is now, then turn to see the blacksmith's head is also bowed, like he's praying, too.

"Perhaps I can come again, sometime, to lay more flowers?" I ask.

"Suit your sen," he says, slapping his cap back on his head. He wipes his cheeks with the cotton scarf around his neck. I can't quite make him out.

It's getting late by the time I arrive at Miss Louisa's hotel. I'd agreed I would meet her there as soon as I had anything to report, but when I ask to speak to the guest in room number four, the landlady shakes her greasy head and says she ain't seen her all day. I think of her face when the old crone told her she didn't have her Bertie. So I ask for a piece of paper to write her a note and tell her what happened and that I'm sure Mother Delaney lives in Poplar. I'm hoping that'll lift her spirits. Heaven knows she needs some good news. I just pray she hasn't done anything stupid. She's got to keep strong for Bertie's sake, and soon, God willing, the old witch should give her the address where the little mite's been taken.

CHAPTER 20

Saturday, December 29, 1888

EMILY

Constance is not the only one who has misgivings about this man Braithwaite. Detective Sergeant Hawkins is on his case, too. He may be young and relatively inexperienced, but he can tell when a man is not what he seems. That is why, despite orders from his commanding officer, he cannot let this matter rest. The press may have been briefed that Catherine Mylett was a drunken whore and that no one else was involved in her death, but inwardly, he refuses to believe it.

We're back at the Commercial Street Police Station. Hawkins has just returned from another fruitless foray trying to track down Montague Druitt. As he passes the duty desk, he spots the hirsute Sergeant Halfhide. The two men swap pleasantries.

"'Morning, Halfhide."

"Good morning, Hawkins." The policeman's bewhiskered face lifts into a smile.

"Mrs. Halfhide well?"

"Her rheumatism's playing up again. This weather..." He looks to the heavens and shrugs to signify the inescapable drudgery of late-December wind, rain, and sleet.

Halfhide is an H Division stalwart. He's been stationed in Whitechapel for the last twenty years. There isn't much that's happened over that period that he hasn't made it his business to know about. The veteran is held up to be a walking catalog of crime, and much more reliable than the vague and, quite frankly, shoddy record-keeping of the station these past two decades.

Hawkins is about to return to the mayhem of his large office, which he shares with his peers, when the thought strikes him midstride. He stops and turns.

"By the way."

"Yes?"

"Does the name Braithwaite *mean anything to you?"*

The older man narrows his eyes and scratches his hairy chin. "Braithwaite? Rings a bell. A Yorkshireman?" He lifts his forefinger in a gesture of promise, then lowers it to stroke his beard in thought.

"Might we have anything on him?"

"Let me see what I can find," he says, touching the tip of his nose. "Leave it with me."

CONSTANCE

I've slept bad, but then I do most nights. I'm up earlier than Flo and Ma. It's still dark and my head's all fuzzy, but I know it's no use trying to get more shut-eye, so I creep downstairs and light the fire in the stove. I fill the kettle from the pail and put it on the hob. I decide I may as well make a start on breakfast and fetch the loaf from the cupboard. It's three days old, so I scrape off the blue mold and, clamping one hand on the crusty top, begin to cut with the other. I'm so tired that as I slice, I drift off. I'm thinking about Cath and the dead baby and, of course, about poor Miss Louisa, and I'm telling myself it's no good leaving matters in the hands of the powers that be. Miss Tindall taught me that. She used to say if you want action, then you've got to get up off your own arse and do it yourself—only not in such words, of course, but that was the gist of it.

I know I can't trust the police to investigate Cath's death. Sergeant Hawkins means well, but I think he's stretching himself too thin. His boss is leaning on him to find Saucy Jack, and the police seem convinced that Cath wasn't murdered, anyway, even though a lot of them medical men say she was. My mind takes me back to that night in the George and I see Cath by my side, looking all forlorn and troubled. Grief was eating away at her, all right, like a dog gnaws a bone. But there was something else in them eyes of hers. There was . . . I picture her face: the set jaw, the resentment. There was anger—that was it. She was angry, as well as heartbroken, and that can be a dangerous mix. I look down at the blade I hold in my hand as it slices through the crust. It's then that I recall her bending down to show me the knife she carried in her boot. Just as the thought drops into my head, the kettle's whistle screams on the hob, startling me. The blade slips and cuts my finger.

"Ah!" I cry. My stinging finger shoots up to my mouth and I suck away the blood.

Next thing I know, Flo's shouting down from the top of the stairs. "You all right, Con?"

"Yes," I cry, grabbing a rag and binding my finger. "Just got to nip out for a mo!"

Snatching my shawl, I hurry through the front room and unbolt the door. I have to tell Sergeant Hawkins what I've just remembered.

I find him up a ladder in the big office. He's putting back a book on the top shelf and seems none too happy when he looks round to see me waiting for him. He wobbles a bit and clings onto the rungs for dear life as he climbs down. It dawns on me that he don't like heights. I can tell he's got no head for them.

"Ah, Miss Piper." He's all embarrassed. I've caught him in a bit of a pickle, but he manages to reach solid ground. Safely landed, he shoots me a smile; although as soon as he spies my bandaged finger, it turns to a frown.

"Have you met with an accident?" he asks, all stiff and concerned.

My eyes drop to the bloody rag round my digit and I shrug. " 'Tis nothing," I tell him, holding his gaze. "A cut, but it made me remember something."

"*Something?*" He motions to the chair in front of his desk.

I sit as he bids me. "Something about the night that Cath, that Miss Mylett, died."

I think he might turn me away, but rather he walks to his desk, sits himself down, reaches for a pencil, and holds it poised over that notebook of his. "Yes?"

"She had a knife." I've said it. I recalled the memory of it as it flashed into my head just before I cut myself with the bread knife.

"*A knife?*" repeats Sergeant Hawkins. "Why would Miss Mylett have a knife?"

"She said you couldn't be too careful out on the streets, and especially not with Jack about."

He writes something in his notebook then looks up. "And where did she keep this knife?"

"In her boot," I tell him. "It weren't"—I correct myself—"it wasn't very big, short with a wooden handle," I add. "But I know it made her feel safer."

"Yet, no knife was found on her person." The detective is frowning. He's puzzled. I am too. "That's interesting information," he says, reaching for one of those boxes of his. He takes out a little card. "Here's the inventory," he says. I'm not sure what he's on about, until he reads out loud a list of things that were found on Cath's body. " 'Brown and black outer clothes. Dark tweed jacket. Lilac apron. Red flannel petticoat. Red-and-blue–striped stockings. Cash: a ha'penny.'" He eyes me. "No mention of a knife."

"So maybe her killer took it?" I hear myself being all eager.

Sergeant Hawkins arches a brow. "If, indeed, the coroner finds your friend was murdered."

I know he's still to be convinced. He's wavering, but somehow I've got to turn him to my way of thinking. His knuckles are on his desk like he's just about to push himself up and bid me good day. It's then I recall my meeting with the blacksmith.

"There's something else, sir," I say before he has a chance to get rid of me.

"There is no need to call me 'sir,' Miss Piper."

I blush. Of course, he still believes me to be different from your average flower girl.

"So?" he says, settling himself again. "This information?" His head bobs to catch my attention once more.

I look at him straight and take a deep breath. "There's a man, in Clarke's Yard, where they found the body. A smithy. I reckon he knows something."

Sergeant Hawkins nods and I think he is almost smiling. "You'll be a detective yet, Miss Piper," he tells me.

I'm puzzled. "You know about him already?"

Another nod. "I visited Mr. Braithwaite last week. He is the man to whom you refer?"

"Do you think he could have killed Cath?" I ask.

"You know I can't say." He's taken aback by my boldness, that's for sure, but he softens a little. "If that had been my way of thinking he'd be behind bars by now, but he may be able to shed more light on the incident."

"*Shed more light?*" I repeat. That's how the quality say this Braithwaite is shifty. He seemed nervous, too, like all his feelings were bottled up inside. I pause as I dwell on my encounter, but Sergeant Hawkins's curiosity is already touched.

"And may I ask you what you were doing up in Clarke's Yard, Miss Piper?"

My face falls. I know I shouldn't have been there. I was meddling. Laying flowers on the spot where Cath was found was only a flimsy excuse, but it'll do. "I went to put fl . . ." But it's no use lying to a copper who can see straight through me. He eyes me like I'm a kid.

"I know how frustrating this must be for you, Miss Piper, but, believe me, we are doing all we can to find out what happened to your friend. I greatly appreciate your efforts on behalf of the dead infants, too, but when it comes to this sort of investigation, it would be helpful if you could leave it to the appointed authority."

It's like I've just held out my hand and had it slapped by my teacher. I feel like a naughty schoolgirl—no, worse, a stupid dunce. Part of me thinks Sergeant Hawkins trusts my intuition, while the other knows I should keep well out of police affairs.

"Of course. I'm sorry" is what I say.

EMILY

In the creeping gray of one of the coldest winter mornings of the year, Mother Delaney greets her brood. There are now four orange crates in the pantry. The contents of two of them are asleep. The third and fourth are awake but insouciant, courtesy of a good dose of tincture.

The old woman reaches into a box and scoops up one of the babies, a girl. "Let's be having ya," she says cheerfully.

There is no response. The child's head wobbles, then flops back, without even opening her eyes. "Come now, Ethel," she scolds. "You've to go to your new ma and da today." Still, she does not waken. Mother holds her aloft, closer to her lit candle—remember, there are no windows in the pantry. Steadying the child's lolling head with her palm, she squints at her lips. They are a strange shade of blue, but the color is familiar to her. "Come now, little Ethel. Stir yourself." She shakes the girl, gently at first, then harder, and harder still, until she shakes her like a terrier does a rabbit. "Curse you!" she cries finally.

Hearing her mother's entreaties, Philomena stands at the door. When she sees the old woman throw the baby back in the box like a bag of rags, she looks resigned.

"You want me to call Dr. Carey, Ma?" she asks.

The old woman, her frilly cap askew after her exertion, pauses. "Yes. Make sure it's him, mind, and not that other quack," she insists. Her encounter with Dr. Greatorex has clearly unsettled her. Such procedures had been a mere formality. Now she knows she'll have to take greater care. Dr. Carey had shown himself to be easily persuaded of the fragility of infant life in the neighborhood. She knew she could trust him to issue a death certificate without any questions asked. But she can't take any chances with little Ethel.

"There's another angel in heaven today," she says, gazing wistfully on the motionless child in the crate. "Take care of her, will you? There's a good girl," she tells her daughter, untying her apron strings.

Philomena walks into the pantry, bunching her shawl around her shoulders against the cold. She leans forward and looks with sad eyes at the dead babe. She has no desire to wrap yet another little corpse in a napkin for burial, although she is finding it much easier than it used to be.

"You off out, then, Ma?" she asks, bending low to pick up the babe.

Her mother twitches a smile as she fastens her jacket buttons. She should be on her way to an appointment at Paddington Station, to see Bertie's mother, but she will not keep it. Instead, she is meeting a nice young couple that wants to adopt one of her babies. She leans over the crate next to little Ethel's, where an unusually docile child, with wisps of reddish hair, appears to be waking from a torpor.

"Come now, Bertie, my dear," she coos. "You'll have to do, instead."

Chapter 21

Constance

It started to rain as I left the police station. By the time I reach home, it's lashing down, whipped up by an easterly. It's the sort of day you just want to sit by a fire and drink hot tea, but I need to be out there. I've told Ma and Flo I'm off to St. Paul's area today. Only, I'm not. I'm going to Paddington Station again, and I'm running late. In my note, I told Miss Louisa I'd be there again to support her when—and *if*—the baby farmer gives her the address of the couple that've got her Bertie.

Ma's having a lie-in. It wouldn't do her chest any good to be out in this weather, anyway, but I find Flo coming down the stairs looking white as a sheet.

"You all right?" I ask.

"I'll live," she replies, even though it's clear as a shift bell at the docks she's queasy. Next thing I know, she's all woozy, too, like she's been on the sauce, and she slams against the wall to stop herself from keeling over. I race over to catch her before she falls and help her into a nearby chair. Her eyes flicker up into her head and I realize she's out cold. I rub her hands, slap her cheeks, but it's no use. I think she's dead.

Oh, God! Oh no! Miss Tindall! What would Miss Tindall do? We've got no smelling salts, but I remember when Libby Lonergan fainted in class once, Miss Tindall sat her down and put her head between her legs so that the blood would flow back to her brain. So that's what I do. Gently I push Flo forward so that she's bent double and her head flops down. It does the trick. She starts to moan.

"Oh, my Gawd!" she groans like a grumpy bear.

"You gave me that much of a fright," I scold, clamping my hands around hers. "Just you take it easy today."

"But . . . ," she protests, jerking up.

I still her mouth with my finger. "No *but,* Flo. You've got to get yourself better." I ease her head down again, gentle like. I know I should call the doctor, but he'll charge a princely sum for his services and won't do any good, anyway. And besides, I know she don't want to make no fuss. I bring her a blanket from upstairs and see that she's comfy. I'd like to make a fire in the grate, but we don't have the coal. Instead, I go to the kitchen, where there's a fire in the stove, and brew us both a nice cup of tea. I give Flo an extra spoonful of sugar, too. I heard sweet tea is good after a faint.

We sit in silence for a while, just listening to the sound of the rain on the windowpane. It's like someone's throwing handfuls of pebbles at the glass. I think Flo might drop off to sleep. I wish I could, but it's not something that comes easy to me these days. But I'm mistaken, she was only catnapping and her voice suddenly breaks into the room.

"You're an angel, Con," she says to me after a while.

I shake my head. "I'm no angel," I say, knowing that I'm not keeping my promise to Miss Louisa. I'm supposed to be at Paddington in less than twenty minutes, but I'll not make it. Not now. If, as we dreaded, that old crone doesn't come up with the address of Bertie's new home, I'll tell Miss Louisa to go to the police. They'll set the Cruelty Men onto the old witch and soon put an end to her miserable trade.

"You'll be all right, won't ya?" I say to Flo. It's like I'm telling her she will. If I run and jump on the omnibus, I might just catch Miss Louisa before her train leaves for Cheltenham. From Flo, there's no reply. She's sleeping like a baby now.

This time, I don't bother with my hat. It's still chucking it down outside, but I can't waste a second. I put my shawl over my head and hurry out onto the street. There's not many about, and those that are hunch over like cripples, blinking the rain out of their eyes. Collars are upturned; hats are pulled down; shawls, like mine, are over their heads. Eyes to the ground, avoiding the deep puddles, I reach the end of our row. I'm just about to turn onto the main road and I hear a faint voice. I think someone's calling my name. Could it be Miss Tindall?

"Miss Piper!" There it is again.

I look up and blink away the rain to see a lady at my side. Soaked to the skin, she is, but she don't seem to care. She's not even wearing a hat. It's like she's a ghost.

"Miss Louisa!" I cry.

She's looking at me, all wan. Her hair hangs in straggles and I can't tell the raindrops from the tears. The despair on her face moves me so much that I open my arms to hold her, feeling her wet, shivering body shudder in a sob that seems to draw the life out of her. I know it's bad news.

"Let's get you inside," I say.

EMILY

Less than two miles away, where the River Lea meanders through Stepney and into the Thames, the ragged watermen of Bow Creek are complaining even more than usual. They're a surly lot at the best of times, carping about both the currents and their customers in the same breath. There's even talk of building a tunnel under the Thames to take traffic. That'll mean an end to their livelihoods for sure. Today, however, the driving rain is the object of their curses. Today no one in their right minds wants to be out on the river in a flimsy craft, unless they're desperate, or up to no good, or both. Even if they were keen to take such a passage, there's a fair chance they'd be swept farther up river, so strong is the prevailing easterly wind, so half a dozen of them are huddled around a brazier. With purple hands held out to catch the feeble heat that emanates into the chill air, they hotch from one foot to the other in an effort to trick their bodies into keeping their blood moving about their extremities. Of course, they'd rather be in the nearby Prospect of Whitby, drowning their sorrows and watching a cockfight, but they need to earn the money first.

Only the mudlarks are foolish enough to brave the weather today. There are at least a dozen of them strung along the shoreline on this wide bend of the Thames. Like vultures, they are picking over the carrion that the high tide has brought in. Unlike vultures, however, they are all secretly hoping they do not find any female body parts, as was the case last summer. No one cares to come cross a severed leg or arm, and, besides, there's no money in such a souvenir. The only reward is a good grilling from the police.

Already a little party of scavengers has progressed to one of the outfall pipes of the storm relief sewers that carry excess water when the normal system can't cope with the deluge. The incessant rain has meant there's more detritus than usual. The water has pummeled away at branches and cart wheels and barrels and sacks, which have stayed happily lodged since last winter, and has set them free. They've been carried along in the sudden torrent of rainwater and deposited in their temporary new home here at Bow Creek, opposite Blackwall Point. What riches will these industrious foragers find today? A tin trunk—who knows what might be inside? Surely, not more body parts?! A pewter fork. A pewter plate. A horse's harness and a wooden pail. These are some of the choicest finds. But there is more.

"What ya got there, then?" asks a gnarled old waterman.

He's broken away from his fellows, partly because he can't stand their whinging. He's approaching a huddle of youngsters as they gaze at something near a storm drain. Two of the boys are taking it in turns to nudge the object with their feet; then one appears with a long stick that emboldens him. Managing to roll the bundle over, he pokes gingerly at the wrappings; then, egged on by his fellows, he prods more aggressively. Soon the gruesome content is clear for all to see.

CONSTANCE

I guide Miss Louisa into the kitchen and sit her down by the stove. Carefully I ease off her woolen jacket, which reeks of old sheep, and hang it on the back of the chair. The water's gone right through it at the seams, darkening the shoulders. There's a big wet patch on her back, too. Worse still, her teeth have started to chatter.

By this time, Flo's stirred and shambles in to see what's going on, a blanket still draped around her shoulders. She looks shocked at the state of our unexpected guest. "Oh, my Gawd. Been swimming in the Thames, 'ave we?" she says unhelpfully.

"This is Miss Fortune," I reply. I'm kneeling on the floor, prizing off her boots. They've let in water and left her feet soaked.

"Miss Fortune?" Flo puts on that voice of hers when she mocks me for sounding like a toff. I can tell she's feeling better after her nap.

I look daggers at her. "She's a friend of Miss Tindall's."

"Oh!" Flo nods her head, like everything's clear to her now. She gives her a look that's a mixture of curiosity and respect, but I can't see much sympathy in her eyes.

One by one, I peel off Miss Louisa's wet stockings, then grab a tea towel, which is hanging by the stove, to dry her feet. I notice how dainty they are and how neat and clean her toenails.

Her soles are soft, too. I fear if I rub them with my coarse cloth, I'll make them sore, so I stroke them gently, letting the towel soak up the wet. The motion seems to make her relax a little, but the heavy hem of her dress is so sodden that the rainwater begins to drip down her legs in thin rivulets. I follow a little stream from the side of her calf to her ankle before I dab it away. I glance up to see that she is watching me with a childish curiosity.

"We'll soon get you sorted," I tell her, but she doesn't reply. She may be looking down at her own body, but it's like she's not really here. She's far away, and I can guess where that is.

I start to rub her toes gently, to get her blood flowing. "Mother Delaney didn't show, did she?" I say. It's not really a question. The look on her face tells me the answer.

She lowers her gaze, and for the first time, she's meeting my eyes. "Where is he?" she asks helplessly. "What has she done with my baby?"

There's such sorrow in her voice that it breaks my heart to hear it. I stop dabbing her toes and, still kneeling, put my hand on hers. I want her to understand that I care. I can't bear to see her suffer so. How could that Irish witch be so cruel? For now, there's no telling if Miss Louisa's little 'un is alive or dead. There's no proof. And how can she trust the say-so of a woman who makes her living out of farming babies? She has a right to know what's become of her own flesh and blood. That's what Miss Tindall would say.

The kettle wheezes into life and I make us all a brew. Miss Louisa cups the mug in her hands. She's stopped shivering, and for that, I'm grateful. I hang her stockings to dry on the mantel over the stove and put her sodden boots under the fireplate. I find some biscuits in a jar Ma keeps for visitors, but she refuses to take one.

"I shan't eat until I see him again," she tells me, staring into her cup; then suddenly her head jerks up. "You said in your note you know where Mother is now." She jumps up. "Where? Tell me, please. I shall go to her." She's on her feet. They're still bare on our earthen floor. "I'll make her tell me where Bertie is. I'll . . ." Her hands are raised and she clamps them onto the side of her wet head like she's going out of her mind.

"Calm yourself," I say, rising and tugging at her sleeve. "I think she lives in Poplar, but I don't know where exactly. But we will find her," I say, pressing her back onto the chair. "And when we do," I tell her, "the Cruelty Men will pay her a visit."

"What?" She darts me a shocked look.

Instead of being grateful, as I think she surely will be, she scowls at me. "No." She shakes her head, swishing her rats' tails at me. "Don't you see? The authorities can't be involved."

I frown. I don't take her meaning. "But what if they help you find your baby?"

She's up on her feet again and walks toward where the kitchen door would be, if we had one, then back again. The blankness in her expression is now filled with a kind of anger, or maybe it's more like worry. *Anxiety.* Yes, that's the word—"anxiety"—Miss Tindall would nail on it. She's very anxious.

"I told you," she blurts. "Bertie's father is the son of a very wealthy gentleman, you see. He is titled, with estates in Essex and in this part of London."

I feel like I'm stepping on eggshells. I understand she wants to keep her situation secret. If she were found out, a woman—or, should I say, a lady of her standing in society—would never recover from such a scandal. But there's something in her eyes that tells me that she still loves this man who has ruined her life. There was a flicker of light in them at the very thought of him. He's used her and abandoned her, but she still holds a candle for him.

"Is there any chance . . . ?" I know it's not my place to ask, but now I'm privy to her situation she seems easier with me.

She gleans what I want to know. "If it weren't for his father . . . ," she says with a shake of her head; then she turns and looks me straight in the eye. "Bertie's father loves me, you see. And I still love him."

I may only be young, but I've already seen enough in my short life to know that when a man says he loves you, he's usually only after one thing. I've many a friend who's found herself a fully paid-up member of the pudding club on the promise of a ring that never gets put on her finger.

"Does he know about the baby?"

She nods sheepishly and I wait for an explanation. "He knows of my pregnancy. He wanted to marry me," she says earnestly, and I know she believes it, "but his father told him that if he did, he would disinherit him."

I feel myself shaking my head. I don't want to judge, but the way I see it, this man of position is nothing but a spineless prick, and, like most men, only out for himself and damn whoever gets in the way.

As if she can read my thoughts, she speaks up for him. "We would have been penniless," she offers by way of an excuse.

And now, it's only you and the little 'un who won't have two farthings to rub together. Try as I might, I can't hold my tongue. "If you don't mind me saying, miss, it doesn't sound very honorable behavior to me." Her brows shoot up and I fear I've overstepped the mark. Perhaps she thinks it's rich that I talk about honor when I live in near-squalor in Whitechapel. Honor's in short supply in the nameless alleys and godless courts that pit the district like pock scars. Perhaps she thinks, like most members of the quality, that the poor wouldn't recognize honor if it hit them in the face. But, no, I'm mistaken. She's softening.

"You are right," she says with a nod, gazing into the fire. "But the fault lies with me. I persuaded him to leave me and our son. I thought it would be best for all of us. I'd find a loving home for Bertie, obtain another position for myself, and he, well, he could go on to marry the wealthy heiress his own father has chosen for him." She sniffs a little. "And life will go on."

Yes, life always goes on, but is it always worth living? And as if she's read my thoughts, a frown scuds across her forehead as she turns toward me.

"What if Bertie is dead?" she asks. She shocks me by suddenly grabbing hold of my hand and searching my face for an answer. "You can tell me, can't you, Constance? Miss Beaufroy said you had powers. She said you can speak to Emily. Will you? For me, please?"

As soon as she touched me, I sensed a charge shoot through my body. It's left me with this strange sensation, like I'm filled with an energy. It floods my brain with light, like the sun coming up over the horizon. My face almost lifts into a smile. Almost, but not quite.

"I cannot speak to the dead," I reply. "But if Miss Tindall wants to tell me something, then I may be able to help you."

I'm worried my answer might disappoint her, but once again, she clasps my hand like she never wants to let it go. She fixes me with imploring eyes, as if I'm some sort of saint or miracle worker. "Then you are my only hope," she says.

EMILY

The heavy rain continues to fall on east London throughout the day; however, the downpour is also causing further disruption elsewhere. Thirteen miles upriver from where the baby's body was found a few hours previous, Henry Winslade, a waterman, is plying his trade just off Thornycroft's Wharf, in Chiswick. It's more sheltered here than the Thames proper, but he's only taken four passengers this morning. The weather is foul and turning fouler by the hour. The rain is slanting and it's so cold that he swears snow must be on its way. He's dreaming of sitting by the blazing hearth, eating toast, when he spots what he thinks is a log in the water. Rowing closer, however, he sees that he was mistaken. Calling for help and a billhook, he inspects the floating object. Moments later, at around one o'clock, he heaves the bloated body of a man ashore.

CONSTANCE

By now, the winter light is growing weak. The rain still falls. I loosen Miss Louisa's fingers and rise to go from the kitchen to the front room. My eyes adjust to the gloom as I walk over to the window to draw the tatty drapes. In the corner, Flo stirs. She's been asleep the whole time that Miss Louisa and me have been talking. The trouble is, I don't want her to know what I'm about to do. She'll mock me, and that's for sure, so I'll do it on the quiet, in whispers, in the dark. I go back to the kitchen to find my visitor bent double, slipping on her stockings.

"If we're to do this, it must be now," I tell her in a low voice.

She nods. It's like I'm her teacher and she'll do anything I say. We sit at the upturned crate that serves as our kitchen table and I snuff out the candle. It's soot black. In the darkness, I find her hands. They're smooth, not calloused and rough, like mine. I take a deep breath to settle myself and clear my mind of all earthly thoughts, just how I do when I pray. I close my eyes and I imagine Miss Tindall, standing right in front of me, bathed in the light, just as she was that night on Brick Lane. I will her to come to us and appear to Miss Louisa, too.

"Miss Tindall," I whisper. "Miss Tindall, we are here. We are here and we need your help."

I feel Louisa's grip tighten. She is tense. "There's nothing to fear," I tell her as we wait.

The sounds of the street filter into the silence of the room, but I manage to block out the clatter of the carts and the church chimes. They recede into the distance as I focus on the image of Miss Tindall's face.

"Miss Louisa is here and she needs your help," I state. "Your friend needs to know if her son has joined you. Is he with you?"

I still see Miss Tindall's face glowing brightly out of the darkness, but something is not right. I do not feel her presence. Her image is only in my mind. The room remains cold and hard and empty. She is not here. There is no warmth, no power. It does not feel how it has felt before. My heart quickens. I try to steady my breath as l find myself becoming uneasy. "Is there a child in the room?" I ask once more. "A baby?" Again Louisa squeezes my hands. "Give us a sign," I plead.

For a moment, it's all quiet. We can barely see each other, let alone anything around us, when suddenly I spot a pinprick of light in the blackness of the front room. I hear Louisa gasp. She sees the light, too, traveling across the space like a sprite. It dances on the wall for a second, then comes to rest just above Flo's head as she sleeps.

"Bertie," whispers Miss Louisa. "Bertie, darling, is that you?" And before I know it, she's up from the table and out into the front room, blindly rushing toward the glow.

"No!" I cry, scrambling after her. She mustn't touch a spirit. I know she can't touch a spirit. "Leave it!" I yell as she approaches the window.

The next thing I know, she's letting out a terrible scream that shakes the room. Flo wakes and screams, too. It's then I see the man's face leering in at the window.

"What the f . . . !?" cries Flo, leaping up from her chair.

The light falls and disappears. My head's all of a spin. I don't know what to do. I fumble about in the gloom. It wasn't supposed to be like this. Have I unleashed the demons of hell? It's then there comes a loud banging on the door. I hold my breath, my heart bouncing in my chest.

"Miss Piper," booms a gruff voice. I glance through the window to see the light of a lantern. "Constance Piper." I freeze. "Open up. It's the police."

Emily

The police wagon transported Constance to the station. It parked at the end of the street, forcing her to brave the rain and the twitching curtains of White's Row. The neighbors will all be thinking that she's been done for thieving—or worse, after the incident with the infant in the market. She knows Flo will set them right; but for now, she is more concerned about the dead babe washed up on the shore. She's praying it's not little Bertie.

"I will spare you the sight of the child, Miss Piper." Detective Sergeant Hawkins is looking grave. Constance sits opposite him in what she now knows is the interview room, her clothes still soaking. The room is where they question suspects before letting them go or remanding them behind bars for trial. It's cramped and dingy. The solitary window is high up and the only furnishings are a table and two wooden chairs. Comfort has not been a consideration. It is, for all intents and purposes, a cell.

"Was it a boy or girl?" she asks anxiously. Wet straggles of hair hang limply from her bowed head. Her hands are in her lap.

"A girl," he replies, "but a few days old."

Relief floods through her veins, even though she knows it's not right. Bertie might still be alive. The dead child, wrapped in a napkin, was washed up at Bow Creek, near Blackwall.

"The heavy rain seems to have flushed the infant's hiding place, and brought it downriver. It may have been in the water for several weeks," Hawkins tells her.

There's an oblong box on the table, similar to the one Constance has seen before. She forces herself to look inside. There's a sheet of brown paper folded in four and a square of white muslin. But it's a sodden piece of ribbon, measuring no more than two feet in length, that interests the detective. She's seen the pattern before. Or so she thinks. Hawkins dangles it in front of her. "Around the child's neck was this binding. It was tied under her left ear."

Constance's jaw drops in astonishment as her gaze clamps onto the yellow ribbon. "But it's . . ."

". . . an exact match with the material found on the infant in Whitechapel. Yes."

Constance looks up, her pretty face crumpled in a frown. She's twisting the edge of her soaked apron.

"So the same person . . ."

"I fear so."

"Where was the child found?" she asks in a more measured way. I think her question shows reason.

"By mudlarks at Bow Creek."

"So she was washed down from somewhere else?"

"Yes. Down the River Lea. From Stepney way."

"Stepney," *she repeats. The mention of the place where Catherine Mylett once lived causes Constance to pause for a moment.*

Hawkins gazes at her intently. Something is happening in that mysterious mind of hers, *he thinks. He tents his fingers, but says nothing, choosing instead to wait for her to put her thoughts into words. They come soon enough.*

"There is something you should know, Sergeant," she says quite formally. "Cath Mylett put her little girl, Evie, with a minder, a baby farmer, last year, and she died. Cath was sure the old woman killed her."

I can tell he's not quite grasped the connection. He's not ready to cut her off, but Constance needs to explain herself quickly. "The night she died she was angry. Something had set her grief off again. She had this look in her eyes."

Hawkins listens intently. He reaches for his notebook. "And where did this baby farmer live?"

"In Stepney, where Cath was dossing at the time."

"So you're saying that Miss Mylett tracked down the baby farmer to her new abode in Poplar and was intent on avenging

the death of her daughter?" The tone of his voice betrays his doubt.

Constance grows frustrated. "It's possible, isn't it? You didn't see the look in her eyes. Mad, she was."

"I'm afraid I can't deal in conjecture, Miss Piper. Evidence is my currency, and as regards your theory, I can find none." He shakes his head as he speaks, but dips his eyes. He knows she will be angry.

Constance leans forward, scowling. "So that's it?"

Hawkins leans back, grasping the edge of the table. "As you know, I've been specifically drafted into this division to deal with the Ripper murders."

Constance is riled by his reply. "No!" She slaps her palms on the table. She's letting her old self get the better of her. She needs to control her temper.

"Miss Piper!" the detective upbraids her.

She pulls it back. "I'm sorry, Sergeant." She straightens herself. "Of course, you have your priorities." The comment carries a barb, but Hawkins ignores it.

"My inspector does not wish me to work on other cases, and until the coroner has given his verdict, your friend died of natural causes."

"And the babes?" she bites back. "You can't say they tied the ribbons round their own necks."

The detective leans forward once more, and when he speaks, it is in a more conciliatory tone. "The hunt for the Whitechapel fiend is taking up all of my time." Constance knows that to be true. The long hours are showing in his face, gathering in dark circles under his bloodshot eyes. "Would you have me neglect my duty in that respect?" The sergeant shows a flash of temper that Constance has not seen before. I will her to acknowledge the difficulty of his position. She pauses before she answers.

"Of course, Sergeant. I know you are most diligent in that respect," she replies in a voice tinged with humility.

He breathes deeply, as if to rein in his ire, before adding, more gently: "I appreciate that you are taking a special interest in the killing of these infants."

The remembrance of the dead baby found at the market flits across her face. "Yes, I am," she says. She pushes back the urge to cry; from his manner, she is aware that the sergeant is about to say something important. She braces herself.

Hawkins's words, when they come, are unanticipated, but welcome. "You should know, Miss Piper, I have ordered a post-mortem on the baby found today. I should have the report next week," he tells her.

Constance is surprised, but glad of this unexpected fillip. At least there will be some form of inquiry into yet another senseless slaughter of an innocent, by, it would seem, the same hand as the babe in the market. However, the detective has not yet finished. There is more encouraging news. He pins her with a mollifying look. "I was therefore wondering," he continues, "if you would like to make some inquiries yourself, Miss Piper."

The proposal lands with a thud in front of her. I can see she was not prepared for it. Nor, indeed, was I. It is an unorthodox suggestion: a lowly flower girl pursuing an investigation into at least two cases of murder. It would be unthinkable, had it not been for these testing times. Both Scotland Yard and the Metropolitan Police are at the end of their metaphorical tethers. Their amount of work has become unprecedented, unbearable. Moreover, they are both proving themselves totally incapable of dealing with the dire situation. Chaos reigns.

Constance's reaction does not come immediately, and Hawkins suddenly regrets asking her. "Forgive me," he says quickly, trying to read her face. "A foolish notion." He waves his hand, flapping away the very idea.

"No," Constance snaps back.

"Gently," *I whisper to her. She knows she has him in the palm of her hand, if she can but realize she will gain so much more by being sympathetic to his dilemma. I think she hears me. More calmly she adds: "No, not foolish at all, Sergeant. You are in a very difficult position."*

A smile slowly lifts Hawkins's lips. "So you might consider gathering information?" He detects a flicker of hope. "And, of course, you will have sight of the medical examiner's report, although"—he breaks off and sticks two fingers down his collar in a vain attempt to loosen it—"although that is strictly confidential, of course."

"Of course." Thoughtfully she nods. "And if I did uncover evidence, you would act on it?"

Hawkins places his hand on his breast. "You have my word that I will personally follow up any lead that you give me."

She digests the sergeant's offer as she studies his face. She knows him to be a good, honest man, even though he sometimes bows to outside pressure. She will trust him to follow through on his promise. "Then I shall make sure you honor it, Sergeant," Constance tells him, rising. She thrusts out her hand in the only way she knows to seal a deal, the way she has seen businessmen conclude their affairs.

The sergeant is a little surprised by her gesture. He looks down at the small, bare hand she offers. He is not used to shaking a woman's hand, let alone one that is not swathed in a glove. He feels a little awkward, but receives it into his grasp, nonetheless. It is cold and rough, but there is a comfort in it. He smiles at her and she at him. After a second, she feels it is polite to withdraw, but Hawkins suddenly tightens his grip a little.

"Please believe me when I say that I wish to see this case brought to a satisfactory resolution just as much as I'd like to see Jack hang, Miss Piper. It's only that . . ." His urgent voice trails off as if he has just recognized his own inadequacy. He lets go of her hand.

"I understand," replies Constance. She sympathizes with his position, she really does. Hawkins is not at fault. It is the way of

the world—the machinery that makes us all mere cogs in the wheel. She is only grateful that she has been given the chance to play a greater part in the apprehension of this monster that preys on helpless babies, and may even have killed Catherine. I can see the weight of responsibility has just dawned on her, but she hides her trepidation well. She regards the detective confidently.

"Thank you for this opportunity, Sergeant Hawkins," she adds. "I will do my very best."

CONSTANCE

We shan't stay up to see in the New Year festivities. There'll be many from round here who'll gather at St. Paul's for the midnight peals that ring in 1889. Flo was talking about going with Danny before they broke up, but she's in bed before eleven. And me? I can't think there's much to celebrate. Seven women is dead in this neck o' the woods alone, not to mention dear Miss Tindall, and now two babies have joined their number. The year 1888 will go down in the history books as the year of Jack the Ripper, I'm sure of that. It's a year I'd be happy to forget. The worst of it is, there may be more murders to come.

EMILY

As New Year's Eve draws on, the usual trail of drunk and disorderly rabble-rousers moves through Commercial Street Police Station. It's certainly a lively place to be tonight. Three revelers are already the worse for wear, and there've been two serious brawls, four reported incidents of personal theft, and a stabbing. And all before ten o'clock. Even by Whitechapel standards that is more than on most nights. But the general mayhem is about to seem as mere routine when Constable Tanner walks into the large detectives' office, heading for Hawkins's desk.

"Constable," greets Hawkins upon hearing the young man's light tread. He's already noted the piece of paper in his hand and fears, from the expression on the young policeman's face, that he is the bearer of bad news.

Without a word, Tanner hands him the note and Hawkins reads it immediately. After a short pause, as if he needs to process what he has just seen, his head drops and meets his raised hands. When he resurfaces, he sighs deeply. "Inspector Mc-Cullen won't be happy," he says, drumming his fingers on the paper.

Constable Tanner nods his head. It's not his place to comment. All the same, he can't help muttering under his breath: "That's an understatement."

The note reads: Body found decomposed in Thames at Thornycroft's Wharf. Male, around 30 years. Taken to Chiswick Deadhouse for postmortem and identification. Believed to be Montague Druitt.

Constance

The bells of St. Jude's are chiming ten as I start to ready myself for bed. Flo's already dozing as I slip my dress off and fill the ewer with water. In the candlelight, I lean over and start to splash my cheeks. It's like I want to wash the old year away. The surface ripples, then clears, so that I see my own face reflected back at me. Or at least I should, but the image on the water suddenly clouds and shifts so that it's no longer me I can see, but—God in heaven—Cath. It's her face, all right, not mine. She's looking angry. No, worse than angry . . . mad. Her eyes are wild and she's screaming at someone. Her arm is raised and . . . What's that? *The knife!* I see the knife she showed me in her hand. A second later, I see a shower of blood hit her face.

"No!" I gasp, and lurch backward in terror.

Over in the bed, Flo stirs. I steady myself on the bedstead, gripping it tightly with both hands. I shake my head, trying to banish the image, but I know what I saw was real. It wasn't a nightmare. It was what Miss Beaufroy would have called a "vision," just as I saw Miss Tindall lying sick in the bed the other time. It's what truly happened to Cath. I just know it.

Still reeling from the shock, I slip on my nightgown and creep beside Flo. I've just seen Cath. I've seen her with a knife and I've seen her face sprayed with blood. But how can that be? She was strangled, so it seems. She wasn't stabbed; leastways, they say there were no other injuries on her poor body, not even any signs of a struggle. It just don't make sense. And who's going to believe me, anyway? I doubt if even Sergeant Hawkins would pay heed to my unlikely tale.

EMILY

Inspector McCullen does not take kindly to having his Hogmanay celebrations disturbed, but on hearing the news of Druitt's death, he thunders into the station, demanding to see Detective Sergeant Hawkins.

"You were supposed to have this Druitt under surveillance." McCullen is jabbing a thick file in front of him on his desk. On the other side stands an embarrassed Hawkins. He can offer no excuse. The constable he'd tasked to watch Druitt on that shift hadn't taken a day off in a month and had fallen asleep on duty. "Now we'll never know," murmurs McCullen.

The young detective could, of course, contradict his commanding officer. If another murder were to occur where the victims displayed similar injuries, then Druitt's innocence would be proven. He thinks it politic to resist such an urge and remains silent.

The Scotsman rubs his chin. "You'll have to make a good account of yourself, laddie, to Assistant Commissioner Anderson. Druitt was his favorite, after all." He sniffs and loosens the ca-

tarrh at the back of his throat. "But, personally, I don't see why." He winks at Hawkins. "Between you and me, I think this schoolteacher, or whatever he was, was a red herring, eh?"

Hawkins is secretly delighted his superior is flexing and agrees with him that Druitt should never have been considered a suspect in the first instance. "It's not my place to say, sir," he replies tactfully, tugging his waistcoat.

"Humpphh!" McCullen blows through his nose and leans back in his chair, as if to draw a line under the matter, for the time being at least. "Now let's concentrate on finding the real villain, shall we?"

CHAPTER 22

Wednesday, January 2, 1889

EMILY

The inquest into Catherine Mylett's death reopens this afternoon at Poplar Town Hall. Constance and Florence manage to find seats near the back. Detective Sergeant Hawkins duly attends, too. Naturally, he is hoping Mr. Wynne Baxter, the coroner, will favor the police's view that the deceased died from natural causes. His life would be so much easier if that were the case, but despite Inspector McCullen's insistence, I know he is having serious doubts about the nature of Catherine's demise.

In the gallery, the detective spots the sisters. He delivers a shallow bow; Florence does not notice, but Constance acknowledges it with a nod of her head. That is all. There is no attempt at conversation. After all, in this matter, she regards Sergeant Hawkins as being in the enemy camp.

Those assembled are called to rise as the coroner enters the room. Silence falls. Mr. Wynne Baxter is respected in these parts.

He's not one to kowtow to authority. Nor is he in the pay of the police; so when he states plainly at the outset that he wants nothing to do with this "nonsense" of "death by natural causes," a few constabulary eyebrows are raised. The Commissioner, James Monro, has sent his representatives. It's clear they believe the verdict is a foregone conclusion. Granted, since the opening of the inquest, more questions have been raised as to the manner of the unfortunate's death, but the police are confident that the coroner will accept their version of events. Those in the gallery, however, are of a generally different persuasion. They are heartened to know that Mr. Wynne Baxter will not allow himself to be swayed by pressure from the powers above.

One of the key witnesses today is Catherine's mother, Margaret Mylett. She's a frail woman and vague, too. It appears that she can do little more than state her daughter's age. The barrister sent to cross-examine the poor widow on behalf of the police is sterner with her than the coroner. He wants to know how she earns her living, but little headway is made until Mr. Wynne Baxter steps in.

"You say your son, William, allows you so much a week, Mrs. Mylett. Where does he live?"

At this seemingly simple question, the witness becomes even more agitated. "I cannot say."

Mr. Wynne Baxter's lips twitch in an ironic smile. "Come, now. He allows you so much a week. How do you get it?"

The old woman licks her lips and scans the courtroom nervously. "I went for it a week or two ago." Then, more confidently, she adds: "My son is in a government office."

The coroner remains unimpressed by this new information and repeats his original question twice more, but when no credible answer is forthcoming, he realizes there is little point in questioning the hapless woman further. He allows her to step down to make way for what he hopes will be more enlightening testimony from the medical examiners.

CONSTANCE

The coppers are looking smug. There's four of them, counting Sergeant Hawkins. He just seems a bit awkward, to be honest. It's like he doesn't really want to be here, or rather he doesn't want to sit next to his bosses. They are stuck in the mud and won't budge at the moment. Catherine was drunk and accidentally strangled herself, that's what they're saying, but I'm hoping what Mr. Harris, the surgeon, and Doctors Brownfield and Hibbard are about to say will wipe the smiles off their smarmy faces. And it does.

You can hear a pin drop as they give their evidence. They all say Cath died by another's hand. It's not what Old Bill wants to hear. But then, Dr. Bond takes the stand and it's all changed. He agrees that Cath died by strangulation, but that she wasn't murdered. All hoity he is when he says that in his opinion Cath fell down in what he called "a state of drunkenness," and that the neck of her jacket pressed against her windpipe, so as she couldn't breathe. The memory of her touching her collar, just before she left the pub, reappears in front of my eyes, but I dismiss the notion that it could've killed her. I've never heard such a load of tosh in my life. At my side, Flo's fuming. I can tell she's a mind to stand up and give this Bond a mouthful, but I clamp my arm on hers to stop any such rashness. She'll only be given the boot from the court, and that won't do any good at all.

The day hasn't turned out like we hoped it would. As we rise to leave, I glance over to where Sergeant Hawkins sat. He's on his way out, trailing behind that Scottish inspector of his, like one of them bloodhounds they planned to set a-sniffing on Saucy Jack's trail. He doesn't bother to look my way. Flo's still on edge.

"Any fool will tell ya she was murdered," she mutters to herself as we slowly make our way out of the main door. There's bodies pressed all around us. It's like half of Poplar's turned out for the inquest, so it takes a while for us to reach outside. When we do, who should we see but Sergeant Hawkins's boss speechifying to a pack of pressmen?

"So, in conclusion, gentlemen, we are still holding to the theory that no murder has been committed."

The little cluster of men with notebooks erupts around him. There's a flash and the sound of breaking glass as a photographer's bulb hits the ground; but undeterred, Inspector McCullen plows on through them toward his waiting carriage. Behind him follows Sergeant Hawkins. We stop to watch the police's top brass as they pile in.

Flo nudges me. " 'Ere, look there's your man again."

We watch as he's about to climb in the carriage, when he turns and catches sight of me. I can't be certain, but I think there's almost a look of an apology on his face.

"He's no man of mine" is all I say to Flo.

CHAPTER 23

Thursday, January 3, 1889

CONSTANCE

We're off to pay our respects to Cath's mother, Margaret, in Pelham Street. Ma's already been round to offer her sympathies, but seeing her yesterday at the inquest, all lost and frail, made us feel that sorry for her. It also got me thinking. The answers she gave the coroner were so woolly that, at the end of the day, no one took her serious. Only there was something she said that made me sit up and pay notice. Cath never mentioned she had a brother.

"Did you ever meet William?" I ask Flo before we reach the end of our row.

"Na," she replies. "Bit of a black sheep, he is."

"How d'ya mean?"

"Done time, he has."

"What for?" I ask.

"He's a docker, down at East India. Done for pilfering. Got hard labor."

"That's enough," Ma suddenly snaps. It's not like her, but the mention of William Mylett's name seems to have rubbed her the wrong way. "As if poor Maggie ain't got enough on her plate, as it is."

So that's where our conversation ended, but I must confess it's one of the reasons I'm so keen to visit Mrs. Mylett. I need to find out more about her son. It wouldn't surprise me if when she said he worked for the government, she really meant he was toiling at Her Majesty's pleasure, if you get my drift.

Anyway, Mrs. Mylett has told Ma she don't want no one going to Cath's funeral. Just a quiet affair, she says. We have to understand that each of us grieves in our own ways. Some want show, or support, and others just want to spend a quiet time before the burial. But we put our mourning clothes on; the ones were wore for Catherine Eddowes's funeral back in September, just to show willing. We're armed with a quarter of tea, half a Dundee cake from Mr. B's last visit, and a bunch of winter roses, in the hope that we'll lighten poor Mrs. Mylett's dark day. It's like Flo and me are trying to make it up to her for us leaving her daughter to fend for herself. That feeling of guilt is still festering inside me. What if we'd walked a way down the road with her? What if we'd stayed and seen her to her doss house?

I'm dreading Mrs. Mylett will ask us how it was that we left Cath late at night. Never mind that she worked on the streets. She needed protection like any other woman—more than any other woman—in the East End. She was vulnerable and sick. And Flo and me let her down.

The three of us link arms, Ma in the middle and Flo and me on either side, as we walk down Brick Lane. What a sight for sore eyes we must look, but we're together and that's what counts. Soon we turn down Pelham Street and knock. The door is answered by a woman the image of Cath, only plumper and with fair hair. It turns out she's her cousin Fanny, but she don't live round here. She's just come to stay with her aunt. She don't know us from Eve; but when Mrs. Mylett hears Ma's voice, the old lady shuffles through.

"Patience?" she says, like she's surprised to see Ma, even though we'd arranged everything beforehand.

"Yes, Maggie. Had you forgotten we was popping round? We said yesterday, at the . . ."

Mrs. Mylett touches her temple. I notice her fingers are like claws with the arthritis. "So you did. My memory's not what it was," she replies, managing a smile. "And you've brought your girls! 'Tis good to see you all, again."

We're ushered into the parlor, where there's a fire in the grate, and Fanny fetches two chairs from the kitchen so we can all sit down. Mr. Mylett used to labor at the starch works before he passed over. Ma once said he had a bit of a roving eye, and I know life's always been hard for them, but no worse than ours. And at least William seems to be giving his ma a helping hand, although I bet she never asks where he gets his money.

Looking round the room, I see there's a photograph on the dresser. I assume it's of Will—taken with Cath. It's an old one, because she looks much younger. She was so carefree in them days, and he had wild curls that framed a cheeky face. Fanny disappears into the kitchen to make us all a brew and I offer Mrs. M the cake.

"Plate's on the dresser, love," she says, pointing with her hooked finger.

It looks a nice bit of porcelain, painted all fancy with gold edging. I can see Ma and Flo eyeing it, too, before our halved Dundee cake lands on it. Mrs. Mylett cuts it into five small slices with a shaky hand.

"Help yourselves, do," she says. So I do the honors.

Fanny comes back soon after with the tea. Once we've got our cups filled, it's difficult to know where to begin. The pouring and the fussing was a sort of ritual, like a service in church when everyone knows how to behave, but now that it's done, we're a bit stuck as to what we should do next. Fanny's all settled, but quiet, and Flo and me are hoping Mrs. Mylett will lead us. And she does; but when she does speak, it's not what we want to be reminded of.

"The police told me you were out with our Rose the night she . . . that night," she manages. Rose was her name for Cath.

Flo darts me an uneasy look and nods. "We went for a drink," she volunteers. "She seemed down, so we thought we'd cheer her up."

Fanny smiles and pats her aunt's shoulder. Mrs. Mylett shakes her head. "She'd not been well for a while. Troubled, she was." Her voice quavers. "Little Evie dying . . ." Her tired eyes brim with tears. "I said I'd have her, you see, that I'd look after the mite. Rose was that excited to think I'd be minding her, instead of that woman. But the good Lord saw fit to take her before I could."

That woman. The second I hear her say "that woman," I feel my hackles rise. I think of the haunted look in Cath's eyes when she spoke of her lost little one.

"That woman?" I say out loud this time.

Mrs. Mylett nods. "Little Evie's minder. Rose was going to put her up for adoption, so when I said I'd look after her, well, she was that pleased."

I want to know more. I *need* to know more. My mind flashes back to that last night in the George and to Cath's fiery words: *"It's not right. The babes, dying so young."* I think of the dead baby in the marketplace, too, and the one washed up on the riverbank. Then I'm minded of Miss Louisa's Bertie. There's a link. *There has to be.* Miss Tindall's brought them all together in front of me. I just need proof that the same woman is the one behind all three deaths.

My mind's all in a whirl when something Ma says brings me back to the moment. "I'm sure William's being a comfort to you," she says as Fanny pours us all some more tea. But the mention of his name doesn't seem to go down that well with

Mrs. Mylett, nor with Fanny. Ma searches her friend's face for an explanation.

"Does as he pleases, 'e does," replies Fanny, shaking her head. "We've not seen him since . . ." Her voice trails off.

"I'm sure he'll be round soon," says Ma. She always sees the good in everyone.

Mrs. Mylett dusts talk of her son under the rug and switches to me and Flo. She says: "There's a few bits and bobs that our Rose left in her old room. Just nicknacks. I'd like you girls to help yourselves to a keepsake of her. I can't manage the stairs no more. Fanny's things are in there at the moment, but there's a tin. You'll see it. Will ya do that for me, now?" She's tilting her head and managing to smile. "Up the stairs and to the right. Off you go."

I look at Ma. She nods her head as if to say: *"It's what Cath would've wanted."* So we both rise and take our leave, climbing the steep stairs up to a small room. I'm ahead of Flo, and as I cross the threshold, I suddenly feel peculiar again.

"You all right?" Flo asks me sudden, peering at me like she's worried for me. Of course, I can't tell her that I'm not; I'm feeling how I felt just before Miss Tindall came to me.

"Yes," I answer.

On top of the chest of drawers is a biscuit tin with a picture of a pretty cottage on it. Me and Flo swap wary glances. We're both pulled to it, even though it seems all wrong doing this; it's like we're crows picking over carrion.

"Go on," says Flo to me as we eye the tin. "Open it."

"Why me?" I protest.

She comes back: "You're the one who's good with death. You're more comfortable with it than me." I think it an odd thing to say, but I suppose it's true. It certainly feels strange going into someone's room when they're no longer among us, but there's something almost comforting about it, like they're next door. I look about at the single bed and the chest of drawers, only I don't just clock them. Suddenly I see what they're made of, every detail: the knots and grains in the wood, the stitches and weave of the coverlet on the bed. Everything's drawn into sharp focus, clear and crisp as a frosty morning.

The tin looms up into my vision, then settles down again. I know I'm meant to open the lid, so I do. There's not much inside. A lock of blond hair—Evie's, I guess—tied with a pink ribbon, a needle case, a sprig of dried hop flowers—a souvenir of when she went picking in Kent—a large whelk shell, a few odd buttons, and another faded photograph of Cath, taken when she was much younger. The smell of the hops fills the room. It reminds me of tea leaves and hay. Flo picks up the needle case. It's made of cream felt. There's a pink rose embroidered on the front. I recall there was one like it on her hankie.

"Why does Cath's ma call her Rose?" I ask.

Flo's lips twitch. "She used to say she were her rosebud when she was little. It just stuck, I s'pose." She opens the flap on the needle case.

Inside there are three needles and a few pins.

"You have it," I say.

My own eyes stray back to the photograph. I lift it up from the tin and study Cath's girlish face. Her look seems so eager and full of hope, and her lips are shaped in a smile. I don't remember seeing her smile of late, except when she talked of her Evie. Come to think of it, she didn't have much to smile about at all. How did her life go so wrong? I wonder. How did it go from this pretty, happy girl to . . . ?

And just as the question is flitting through my mind, just as I'm pondering on her misfortune, I think I notice her image change in front of me. As I hold the photograph in my hand, Cath starts to age. The skin on her face is scraped back and pulled tight over her cheekbones. Her eyes narrow and there's a fear in them. Lines appear on her forehead and around her mouth. Her expression is suddenly pained and the lips, which have lost all their plumpness, begin to move. I watch transfixed as I realize she's trying to say something to me. I want to scream. This isn't real. I want to be rid of the photograph, but my hands are locked on it, just as they were locked that night at the Egyptian Hall. And then I hear her voice. Distant at first, like a whisper, until it grows louder and louder and I can hear what she's saying. "She killed her!" she cries. "She killed her."

A heavy weight presses on my shoulders and chest. Panic seizes me, but I can't shake it off. I feel my tongue thrashing inside my mouth, and the words are fighting to break free. "Who?" I choke back. "Who killed who?"

"What?" asks Flo, swirling round, the needle case still in her hand. "What you on about?"

As she turns, I see a scrap of paper fall out of the case and float down to the floor; and suddenly I'm released from whatever had a grip on me. I look at Flo, then glance back at the photograph. Cath is a young girl again. My eyes drop to the floor and I know I need to reach down and pick up the paper because it is not just a loose scrap. It's a fragment that's been torn from a newspaper.

"What you got there?" asks Flo, craning her neck to get a view.

"Nothing," I say. "Just a bit of old scrap," I tell her. I pretend to turn my attention to the rest of the tin's contents as I study the cutting before dropping it into my apron pocket. It's caught my eye, you see. It's an advertisement and the sight of it has slammed into my brain and sent my heart racing. It reads: *Respectable woman and her doctor husband seek up to four children to call their own. Good food and sound education guaranteed. Terms from £10. Address: Mother, Post Office, Poplar.*

The woman who minded little Evie must be the same woman who's stolen Miss Louisa's Bertie. She must be Mother Delaney. This torn piece of paper might be the proof I'm looking for. It may even hold the key to at least one murder. It's up to me to follow the lead.

Chapter 24

Emily

In a shabby boardinghouse in Cheltenham, Louisa Fortune is writing a letter. It is to the father of her child, the man who seduced her and then who, because of his family's disapproval, abandoned her when he discovered she was pregnant. Most men would sympathize with him, no doubt. He stood to lose his inheritance, after all. Most women, however, would call him a lily-livered coward, incapable of facing up to his responsibilities. But I am not here to judge. I am merely reporting what I see.

The room is ill lit. There's a rush lamp on the table, which serves as a writing desk. A small fire has long burned itself out. Its residual heat is fast ebbing away and Louisa twitches her shawl around her shoulders as she re-reads the letter she has just penned. It is her fifth draft. She began very stiffly—Dear Robert—*but her tone has softened with each version, for she remembers how much she loved him, and he her. Her fourth draft was ruined by her inconvenient tears, which caused the ink to run. For the fifth, she kept her handkerchief in plain sight and managed to sign her name before she began to cry once more. The letter now reads thus:*

My dearest Robert,

Believe me I have no wish to burden you with my woes. We agreed that it would be best for all our sakes to go our separate ways. I can now tell you I was safely delivered of a beautiful, healthy boy in October. I named him Robert in your honor. Although it broke my heart, I left him, as we previously discussed, in the care of a woman who assured me she would love him as her own. I, however, found it harder than I could have imagined to part with our dearest little boy.

Before I paid her the last installment of her adoption fee, I confess I succumbed to my maternal weakness and would have asked her to board our son on a weekly basis. However, this minder, a woman of previously good character who supplied excellent references, has betrayed my trust. Twice she has failed to produce him at our appointments, on very flimsy pretexts, so now I am distraught beyond words. At our second meeting she told me she had already placed him with adoptive parents. Worse still, she will not tell me where they live, or indeed anything about our child's welfare or whereabouts. She is taking advantage of my sex and my vulnerability by treating me so contemptuously.

Dearest Robert, I know that our circumstances will forever keep us apart, but I would ask one last thing of you—that you support me as I approach this woman a final time so that Bertie and I can be reunited.

I will be forever in your debt.

Yours most truly,

Louisa

Meanwhile, several miles away in a room that is even shabbier and colder than Louisa Fortune's, Constance is also writing a letter. Her hand is rather more labored than the governess's. There are few curlicues and loops. Hers is the sort of script copied on a slate in the ragged school, but she learned her lessons well, and the hours of replication she has completed are evident in the even spacing, neat formation, and accurate crossing of t's *that I, as her former teacher, would have expected of her. Her spelling and punctuation are also remarkably good. I spot just two mistakes. I will her to rectify them, but she takes no notice of me. This evening, she does not heed my presence. However, on this occasion, it is of no consequence. Her letter is in reply to the advertisement that was secreted in the biscuit tin in Catherine's room.*

Of course, I directed her there, and she has acted upon its discovery, as I hoped she would. It is no coincidence that the address given in the cutting is in Poplar, nor that the wording is exactly the same as the advertisement Louisa answered, too.

Constance wisely chooses to write under my name. Her response reads thus:

> Dear "Mother,"
>
> Seeing your advertisement in the East London News the other day, I pray you can help me. I find myself in a very difficult posishion and have no one in the world I can turn to. I fear that I can no longer hide my condishion and would therefore seek your help in this delicate matter. I beg you to consider taking me in for my delivery any time now.
>
> My circumstances mean that I cannot keep the child and, to avoid shame on my own family, I would seek its full adoption. I would like the child to go to a loving and Christian family and would ask that you consider it.

If you are interested, perhaps you could kindly send a line to let me know where and when we might meet.

Please address your reply to 29 White's Row, Whitechapel, London.

I am your servant, madam,

Emily Tindall (Miss)

CHAPTER 25

Friday, January 4, 1889

EMILY

Today it is the turn of little Nellie. "Well, what a bonnie thing you are, to be sure," says Mother, inspecting the infant as she lies on the kitchen table. "That dress has come up nice, so it has," she tells Philomena, examining the flounce on a garment that once belonged to another child, now deceased.

Her daughter nods. It wasn't easy putting the creases back into the gown. Lotte proved completely incapable of the work. Moreover, in this weather, even a crimping iron feels the cold, but she'd managed it and was pleased with her efforts.

"I'm off to Paddington," Mother announces, tying the child's bonnet. She's rough and takes no care. She sets the little girl crying.

Philomena picks up Isabel, who's standing nearby. She's worried the babe's whimpering will set her off, too. She hugs her and strokes her golden hair.

"A couple from Bath," Mother continues, scooping the baby into her fat arms. "They're paying handsome for this one, so

she's got to look her best." But wait, something snags on her shawl. The matron looks down to see the child still wears a silver christening bracelet. "Well, I'll be," she says with a tut. "We'll be having that, won't we now." She scowls at her daughter from under her bonnet. Philomena steps forward quickly and unfastens the bracelet. It'll be added to the stash they have amassed since Christmas.

CONSTANCE

The day has seemed even longer than usual, but until I've had a reply to my letter, there is not much more I can do. I can't say I'm sorry when it's time for bed, but even then, sleep brings little relief. I finally drift off, thinking about the photograph I saw on Mrs. Mylett's dresser, the one of Cath and her brother. But it's not them I dream about.

Tonight I'm looking at a young woman on a bed. She's in the pangs of labor. Her hair's wet with sweat and plastered round her head. Her red face is all screwed up with pain. She fills the room with noises that come from somewhere deep inside her. They don't sound human. At her shoulder stands another woman, about the same age, who's trying to comfort her. Wait! It's Miss Tindall—her hair, the way she carries herself. Yes, it's Miss Tindall. She's been sponging the other woman's forehead, whispering to her, saying it won't be long now. But a shadow is suddenly cast across the bed and her head lifts to see a man standing at the foot.

His back is to me, but I see he is a gentleman—tall and broad in a well-cut frock coat. The next thing I know, a baby is crying lustily, filling its lungs with the air of this strange, new world. The gentleman moves aside so that I see for the first time that the woman who cradles her newborn in a shawl is Miss Louisa. She draws back the swaddling so the man can see the child; but instead of showing any interest, he backs away.

Miss Tindall looks at him and starts to plead with him, but, ignoring her entreaties, he moves toward the door. All the while, he is shaking his head and lifting his hands, as if to push something away.

"No!" I scream as I jerk up from my pillow.

"What the . . . ?" Flo's up, too, her hand clamped on her chest to still her thumping heart. She blinks away her sleep, trying to make sense of what's just happened before flopping back down. "Gawd save us from your bleeding nightmares!" she cries.

I don't make a fuss. "Sorry" is all I say in a breathless whisper as my own heart calms itself. I lie down again, only this time I know there's no use trying to sleep. I think on the dream and on what I've just realized. The gentleman I saw in my vision is not just Miss Louisa's lover and the father of her baby—he's also the man who betrayed Miss Tindall. He's the one who helped send her to her death. He may look handsome and charming on the outside, but inside he's a coward without a backbone. He's the one who wouldn't speak up for what he knew to be right. He even kept silent about a murder, because he was so afraid of his powerful father.

I feel as though I know him already, and yet we've never met. But I have a notion that's all about to change. I'm not sure how or where, but I'm convinced I shall soon be making the acquaintance of Mr. Robert Sampson.

CHAPTER 26

Saturday, January 5, 1889

CONSTANCE

East India Docks is no place for a woman who wants to keep herself in tact, if you get my meaning. It's no place for a woman at all, in fact. Life is hard here, even harder than in Whitechapel. Brutal, you might say. That's the word. The minute you cross under these massive gates, topped off with the great stone arch, it's like you're going into another world.

For a start, there's men with turbans or funny upside-down flowerpots on their heads. There's lascars from India and Chinamen, too. The air's different, and all. There's the pong and the salty tang of the Thames, but there's spices as well: cinnamon and ground ginger. There's colors that shock the eye and lift the heart, bales of silk in blue, green, and gold. They come in on the great ships that sail the seven seas and all the cargoes need unloading. That's where the dockers figure. It's tough for them. The work's not regular, see. When a ship arrives, the men are chosen by the foreman, who looks them up and down, like they were cattle. He'll only takes the strongest, or the ones who'll do him favors. They're all so eager to get work that they sometimes trample each other underfoot or fight for the chance of a day's graft.

And somewhere in among this teeming mass of men, horses, carts, and wagons, I'm hoping to find Cath's brother, Will. I'm wondering why he hasn't called to see his ma to comfort her, or why he'll not be at the funeral, and I'm wondering if he can tell me anything about the company his sister kept that might help track down her killer.

My first stop's the foreman's office. It's crammed with men, milling around, waiting to be called when a ship comes into dock. The stink's nearly as bad as a backyard privy, but I take my courage in both hands and push and shove my way to the front. It's not easy. I'm grabbed and groped as I go, but I manage to fight off the dirty hands and arrive breathless in front of a man who seems to be in charge.

"Sir!" I yell above the palaver. "Sir, I'm looking for William Mylett."

"What?" The foreman's pockmarked face leers down at me for a moment. He's got other things on his mind and is shocked to see a woman among the rabble. "Be off with ya!" he scowls.

"William Mylett!" I yell louder, like my life depends upon it. "His sister's dead!"

"What?" He's taking notice now.

"William Mylett. I need to find him. His sister's dead and his poor mother needs him."

For a moment, I think he might help me. For a second, I think he has words in his throat, but the right ones don't come out. "No. Can't help. Now get out, will ya, before you cause a riot." He's pointing back toward the entrance.

I turn toward the gaggle of men. They jostle me and grab at my breasts, then one pushes me forward, knocking my bonnet over my eyes, and I fall into the arms of another. Pulling back my hat, I look up and am blasted in the face with the stench of stale breath and see a row of rotting teeth above me. I manage to push away and struggle through more grasping hands, until at last I find the door. I stumble out, straighten my bonnet, and smooth my skirts. There's a tear in the hem. I'm just inspecting it, when I hear a voice behind me.

"You need a hand, miss?"

I switch round to see a scrawny little boy with a freckled face. He can't be more than ten. I think he's looking to scam me and I press my hand over my apron pocket, where I keep a couple of farthings.

"I'll manage," I say, looking at him all wary. I straighten up and point myself in the direction of the big gates, but he scoots in front of me. He's going to rob me, I'm sure of it, but no.

"You looking for Will Mylett?" he asks, his head tilted to one side.

I stop in my tracks. "You know him?"

"I knows him, all right, but what's it worth to you?"

You don't get something for nothing in this neck o' the woods, so I delve into my pocket and bring out a coin. I hold it in front of him. "Spill the beans, then. Where is he?"

Freckles shakes his matted head. "Ain't seen him since afore Christmas," he tells me. "We was mates, but then he scarpered." He lunges for the farthing, thinking he's earned his money. I think otherwise, so I lift it up in the air out of easy reach.

"Where's he gone?"

"Dunno," he says with a shrug, then reaches again for the coin.

"Where's he gone?" I repeat, holding the farthing even higher.

"They say he's jumped ship."

"*Jumped ship?* Where's he gone?"

"Dunno. I swear. All I know is, he's been gone nigh on three weeks."

"Three weeks," I repeat. Around the time of Cath's murder, I think. "His sister's dead. Does he know?"

The boy shrugs his shoulders and raises his grubby palms to the sky. "Search me."

I think he's telling the truth, so I hand over his reward. "You hear anything and there'll be another farthing in it for you," I tell him. "Just leave word at the George in Poplar. Constance is my name. Constance Piper."

The boy nods as he bites my coin. "Will do," he tells me, lifting his hand to his temple in a little salute before he turns tail and runs off.

I can't leave the dockside soon enough, but I'm taking my troubles with me. If Will Mylett has done a runner, why would that be, unless he's got something to hide, or unless he's hiding from someone? I'm more confused than ever, and certainly no nearer to finding out the truth.

Emily

The postboys of London are very busy at the moment. Louisa Fortune did not have to wait long for a reply to her letter. It was sent by return.

> Dearest Louisa,
>
> Your news came as a terrible shock to me. I thank God for your safe delivery and accept that I have hitherto been a neglectful father, but you should not have to go through this difficult time alone. It pains me to think of the deep anxiety this woman is causing you.
>
> I therefore suggest we meet tomorrow at three o'clock at the tearooms we regularly favored to dis-

cuss the matter. Together we will see our way through this problem.

Yours truly,
Robert

It is much later in the day when Albert Cosgrove receives a letter; evening to be precise. In the relaxing parlor of his rented Poplar home, he is making up a well-deserved pipe. He'll soon enjoy a glass of sherry and peruse his newspaper before Lotte calls him through for dinner. For all intents and purposes he is a man of means, self-made and comfortable. That is what he would like us all to believe. Today and for the foreseeable future, he will be Albert Cosgrove. That is until there comes such as time, as there inevitably will, when he is obliged to become Austen Richards, Walter Collins, Edmund Blunt or one of a half dozen soubriquets at his disposal. He hopes he can reside at least a few more weeks in Poplar. If they play their cards right and attract no more suspicion, they won't have to up sticks for pastures new, as they have so often in the past. Two months here, six months there - as if it isn't hard enough to find work in the drapery business without such interruptions. Then there's always the matter of forging references. Yes, he thinks. He could get used to this life of a comfortably-off haberdasher. Settling himself in his favorite arm chair by a blazing fire, he opens his pouch and packs down the tobacco into the bowl of his favorite pipe and sucks.

A copy of the evening newspaper lies folded on the console table by his side. He reaches for it just as Lotte scampers in with his aperitif on a silver-plated tray, together with a fistful of letters she's collected from the post office.

"Ah, good," he says, addressing the housemaid. "I was wondering about today's post."

Lotte sets down the tray, bobs a curtsey and leaves.

Philomena looks up from her sewing. "More letters, Albert?"

She emphasis the word 'more' as if to draw his attention to the fact that each one means more work for her, since she is the one who has to reply to most of them.

Albert seizes upon the stash with glee, just as Mother waddles into the room. "The dear child's all tucked up, to be sure," she informs the 'dear child's' parents. Isabel is always so well-behaved for her grandmother, especially compared with the other wretches. Philomena looks at her mother gratefully. Cosgrove, however, is preoccupied with the post.

"Another crop of desperates," he mutters, leafing through the envelopes. It's his custom to study how the address is written. He's become something of an expert at judging the class of the writer. He always opens the ones from the most-educated first. He knows they can be charged higher fees because they have their reputations to lose as well as everything else. "There are more out there than we dreamed!" he remarks. He's in a merry mood even before he takes his first sip of sherry.

Mother seats herself on a winged chair beside her son-in-law. It was she who recommended the wording of the advertisement. Posing as a woman married to a doctor has always worked well in her experience. It gives that extra cache and, of course, it attracts the quality, too. Yes, it was a penny well spent, the day she paid for that advertisement. All they'd had to do was wait for the losers, the nay-sayers and the nowhere-else-to-goers to come flocking to their door. They did not have to wait long. They must have had more than a dozen replies since settling in Poplar. Some of the leads have, of course, fallen by the wayside when a statement of charges was returned to enquirers by post. It seems that a handful were not prepared to pay extra for doctors' visits and medicaments.

After all, they are entering into a business transaction. There can be no room for sentimentality. Others enquiries have, however, borne fruit. The first two to arrive at this address were from genteel persons; one a mother enquiring on behalf of her wayward daughter, the other a lady of means. There were two shop girls who'd succumbed to their managers and a bar maid—there are always bar maids.

Today's batch of post has produced three more letters of potential interest. One of them stands out. Albert Cosgrove considers the hand to be reasonably educated, but not a lady's. It's far too labored for that. And the loops on those g's *and* y's *are way too fat. He removes his pipe from between his lips and slits the seal with a paper knife he has nearby.*

"Now here's an interesting one," he proclaims, examining the script. He reads aloud: "'Dear "Mother," I find myself in a very difficult posishion and have no one in the world I can turn to.'" He looks up and smiles broadly. "Violins, please, ladies!" He carries on: "'I fear that I can no longer hide my condishion and would therefore seek your help in this delicate matter.'" He looks over to Mother. "Worth a pretty penny to us, I'd say."

Mother nods, then counting on her chubby fingers, tots up the sums. "Delivery, board, and adoption. Good for fifteen quid at least, to be sure."

Both of them are so pleased with the prospect of such riches that are surely about to come their way that the newspaper remains neglected on the console table. Tomorrow its sheets will be separated and laid on the upstairs bed to be used for the next woman to birth. Had Albert Cosgrove but read it, however, he would have seen a small insertion at the bottom of the third page whose headline reads: SECOND BABY FOUND STRANGLED.

CHAPTER 27

Sunday, January 6, 1889

EMILY

They have agreed to rendezvous at the tearooms off Fleet Street, where they had met before under less stressful circumstances; it is a public place, true, but the establishment has an intimate corner that is screened from the other tables. It is here that Louisa heads, and here that she finds Robert Sampson already waiting. He rises quickly. She thinks him even more handsome than she remembered him: lush, dark hair and those eyes that are so piercing that she knows there is no point in having any secrets.

It's been six months since they parted. She remembers the date very well, the sixteenth day of July. In the evening, she'd contemplated taking her own life. She'd even trudged to Waterloo Bridge and pondered on joining the many who throw themselves off its parapets most weeks. And then . . . she'd remembered that she would have been taking not just her own life, but another's, too. So, forlornly she'd turned and walked away from the water.

Of course, she's explained everything, albeit briefly, to Robert in the fifth draft of her letter. She'd contemplated tearing that one up, too, and starting again, but then she'd thought better of it. There was no harm in revealing her anguish. She was already vulnerable and she lacked the will to hide it. It seems to have achieved the desired effect.

Robert watches her as she appears. The flame inside him flickers, but he must douse it, in public at least. She proffers her hand by way of formal greeting and slides gracefully onto the banquette. He thinks she has lost weight since he last saw her, but it only adds to her fragility. How delicate she looks to him. How he longs to protect her. He hopes she will allow him. They sit opposite each other. He orders tea for two. Lapsang souchong—their favorite—and a plate of langues de chat *for her.*

As soon as they are alone, they both begin talking simultaneously.

"Louisa." "Robert." "My dear." "My love." "Forgive me. I . . ."

Their words buff against each other. They are united in their concern. Robert reaches across the table and Louisa puts both her small hands in his. "I cannot tell you how . . ."

"No. No, you must not blame yourself."

"But I do."

"We agreed that he should be adopted."

"Only because I didn't have the courage to stand up to my father."

She knows what Robert Sampson says is true. He had been forced to make a choice, and he had chosen his father over her. Part of her thought it understandable, but the other thought it unforgivable. Her heart is so full of feelings that she thinks it might burst. And yet, despite this, despite the hardship and the unbearable suffering he has caused her, I still see love for him in her eyes. It is such a strange thing; this candle that burns so brightly inside some of us who have been wronged, as if we are moths drawn to a flame. And yet, wait . . . there is something in

Robert's eyes, too. He has admitted his own weakness. Perhaps there is hope that this flame may also be rekindled.

It was, indeed, his weakness that contributed to my own passing. I shall never forget that fateful night. I knew great evil was being perpetrated against some of the girls who were my pupils at Sunday school. I suspected a regular visitor to my class. Dr. Melksham claimed to be the agent of a benefactor, but I discovered he was abducting the girls and delivering them into prostitution. That is why I followed the doctor's carriage one afternoon, when I knew he had one of my girls on board. To my horror, I found she had been drugged and taken to some sort of vile quasi-Masonic ceremony to initiate new members. Robert was one such.

I came from out of the shadows to save an innocent child from being so cruelly abused, but he did nothing to protect me. He betrayed me to his domineering father and his vile cohorts. He could have defended me, but he chose not to. The stain will be on his character for the rest of his life, unless he repents and atones for his grievous sin against me. Facing up to his responsibilities for Louisa and his son would go some way, and I am beginning to think he may be on the verge of making amends.

Louisa stirs sugar into her tea, contemplating the vortex her spoon is creating in the muddy liquid. After a moment, she lifts her face. "What shall we do, Robert?"

He juts out his chin in a show of defiance. "We shall find him." He takes her hands. "We shall find our son."

"But how? The woman will tell me nothing. I don't even know where she is living now. She was in Stepney, but has since moved and could be somewhere in Poplar, although I have no idea where." The words tumble out breathlessly before she pauses to say: "And going to the police is out of the question."

Relief floods Robert's face. He is grateful that she has ruled out the police. It could be very awkward for him. He thinks for a moment, stirring his own tea. Eventually he says: "I shall hire a private investigator."

At this, I see Louisa's breast heave as she takes a deep breath. Robert is throwing her a lifeline. "You would do that?"

"Yes, of course," he tells her, as if it is the only course of action to be taken, as if it is the most natural thing in the world. "Yes," he continues. "Someone discreet."

"Oh, Robert, thank you," she says more calmly. She regards him as he contemplates. "Someone discreet," *she repeats, joining in with his thoughts. Of course, I cannot speak to her directly, as I can to Constance; but before long, I see her eyes widen. An idea has come to her rescue. "I know just the person," she tells him.*

CHAPTER 28

Monday, January 7, 1889

EMILY

They buried Catherine Mylett today. In accordance with her mother's wishes, it was a very quiet affair. So quiet, in fact, that there were only two mourners: Margaret and cousin Fanny. Of Catherine's brother, William, there was no sign, even though he was, in fact, less than three miles away. That's because he's in hiding in the attic of a tumbledown tenement, not fit for human habitation, let alone for the rats that live there in their dozens.

Under cover of darkness, I watch the young boy with freckles scamper up the stairs. He's the one whom Constance encountered at the East India Docks the other day. Unbeknownst to her, she was followed and has inadvertently put the boy in harm's way. It remains to be seen whether he can escape his perilous predicament, although his past form suggests there is a chance. Orphaned at age five, he's as cunning as a fox cub, living by his wits. So when he was offered money to help out a man known to him who's in a tight spot, he was only too happy to oblige. There are others who live in the building, of course: mainly lascars from the docks, who light fires in buckets and cook with strange and exotic spices, the aroma of which masks the stench of damp and urine that normally pervades. There's a bag slung over the boy's shoulder. Half a loaf of bread, a piece of cheese, and a worm-eaten apple are all he could scavenge today, but it's better than nothing.

Up ahead of him are the stairs. The treads are rotting and in the dark it would be easy to let a foot slip through, but he's come prepared. A lantern lights his way. Despite its beam, on the first landing, he almost stumbles over a ragged child. On the next, there's a crying woman, with a cut to her face, while all the time the sounds of bawling babies and angry men rise and echo in the stairwell. He edges on regardless, up another flight, until he reaches the top floor. He knows he's at the top because he can see a patch of smoky sky through a large square in the roof, where the cold air blasts in.

It's his head, not his feet, he has to mind now. The rafters are so low that he's forced to duck, even though he's no more than four feet tall himself. The beams are festooned with so many cobwebs, they tickle his face. He doesn't like it up here. It's cold and it's dark, but at least Mr. Will is safe.

At the top of the stairs, he turns right and crouches below a thick plank above a low door. He taps three times and, after a moment, an unseen hand opens it.

"I thought you wasn't coming," complains Will Mylett, snatching the bag from the boy. He moves like an animal. He looks like an animal. It's almost three weeks since his sister's murder—three weeks he's spent in hiding, but already his dirty face is covered by a full beard and his fingernails are long and black. Rifling through the bag, he helps himself to the apple and bites into it like a rabid dog into meat.

The freckled boy watches with amusement rather than horror.

He's been just as hungry himself. He understands that hollow feeling in the pit of your stomach when you think you've been scooped out and the only thing left inside is a constant, gnawing ache. He waits until Mylett has finished attacking the bread and cheese. There are stale crumbs caught on his beard.

"Well?" the fugitive asks finally. "What news do you bring?" It's been two days since the boy's last visit. "What's said at the coroner's court?"

Freckles perches on a beam and tilts his head. "That she died of the drink, but it's not finished yet. They reckon it'll be Wednesday afore the coroner will say," he tells him.

"Wednesday," repeats Mylett. He'll lie low until then. If the verdict's murder, the gallows will loom. But if it's recorded his sister died of "natural causes," he'll be in the clear. Only then will he be free—free to wreak his revenge for Catherine's death.

CONSTANCE

A postboy's not a regular sight down White's Row. Luckily, Ma and Flo are out running errands, so I know I've a few minutes alone to read my letter. I can guess who it's from. I'm right.

> *Dear Miss Tindall,*
>
> *Thank you for your letter. My husband and I should be glad to meet with you to discuss your situation at our home in Poplar, this coming Friday. Although money is not our primary consideration, you might also wish to bring with you a deposit to secure your bed during your confinement, should the arrangement be mutually agreeable.*
>
> *We look forward to meeting you at 9 Woodstock Terrace, Poplar, on Friday at 11 o'clock.*
>
> *Yours sincerely,*
> *Edith Blunt (Mrs.)*

I've laid a trap for this Mrs. Blunt and she's taken the bait. I'd sent the letter care of a post office, but now I have a proper address to give to Miss Louisa. She can do with it what she will. She may even wish me to accompany her to confront this fake. A message came yesterday from her and we've finally arranged to meet again tomorrow morning at St. Jude's. We're nearer to finding what's happened to little Bertie. So why have I suddenly started to shake?

EMILY

That evening at dinner, Albert Cosgrove is in a somber mood. He's little appetite for his meal because his stomach was already so full of spite. Now he pushes away his plate to make an announcement. "From now on, we shall take in more weeklies."

Earlier in the day, at his shop, he'd heard two of his customers talking about the discovery of a strangled baby in the river at Bow Creek. They were speculating on a connection with the infant found dead in the market at Petticoat Lane just before Christmas. This, coupled with the fact that Philomena had mentioned the overzealous physician who'd replaced Dr. Carey on a recent visit, had made him rethink their strategy.

Mother Delaney's suspicious eyes dart across the table to her daughter. "What you been saying, my girl?"

"I know about the new doctor," snaps Albert, protecting his wife from her mother's tongue-lashing.

Mother's mouth droops in a show of contempt. "Too clever for his own good," she snarls under her breath, shifting angrily on her chair.

Albert starts to play with the knife on the plate in front of him. "We've got to be careful. We can't have the same thing as happened in Stepney. We've not been here three months." He can tell that Mother Delaney is simmering with rage as she eyes her daughter. She needs bringing to heel. He jabs the handle of the knife down hard on the table like a gavel, sending the other cutlery clattering. It does the trick. He knows he has their undivided attention.

"We need more nurse children," he announces. "Granted, the return's not as good, but it means that if the Cruelty Men come knocking, we can show them a couple of healthy ones."

Mother Delaney stares ahead of her. She remains angry.

"What happened to that redhead?" asks Albert.

"Bertie?" says Philly helpfully.

Her husband nods.

"The couple wanted a girl," replies the matron.

He switches to her. "Did you bring him back?" She has, after all, been known to dispose of children under such circumstances.

"That I did." She's softening, and adds: "But I've another interested couple tomorrow."

"Keep him," barks Albert.

"What?"

"Keep him, I say." He brings out a letter from his breast pocket. "That way, we'll have him, and this . . ." He glances at the missive.

". . . Miss Tindall's brat when it's born, and that should satisfy any prying crusaders." He leans back in his chair, fixing Mother with a stern glare. "And no more dumping. Not for the time being at least."

Mother shakes her head. "But if we can't get a death certificate, what are we supposed to do?"

In reply, Albert raises a brow and looks her in the eye before he tells her calmly: "That's why we got a garden, ain't it?"

CHAPTER 29

Tuesday, January 8, 1889

CONSTANCE

I sit at the back of St. Jude's. I arrived early so I could change into my smart clothes, the ones that Miss Beaufroy bought for me. I was worried the moths might've feasted on the wool jacket, but it seems to have escaped the little blighters, even if it does smell a mite damp. The hat's a bit out of shape, too, but the skirt and boots are good as new. The outfit makes me feel different again. I keep my back straight and my chin up. I'm a lady.

The church is almost empty apart from a couple of old biddies kneeling in prayer at the front. I like it when it's quiet. You'd never know we're on a busy road in London. The big, heavy doors shut out all the noise and bustle, so you can hear yourself think. I'm still a little early, so I kneel in prayer. I ask God to protect the people I love, both the living and those who've passed: Ma, Flo, Pa, and, of course, Miss Tindall.

I look about me at the big columns and at the stained-glass windows and I half expect to see her somewhere among them. I'm half expecting her to join me in the shadows. I close my eyes and empty my mind of thoughts. My breathing slows and I start to feel her presence. It comes like the dawn. There is a soft glow at first, until the light grows stronger; when I hear the doors open and turn to see Miss Louisa arrive, I know Miss Tindall is nearby.

Miss Louisa is not alone, either. There's a man with her. He whips off his hat as soon as he enters the church and follows slowly behind her. She pauses, then catches sight of me and comes closer.

"Miss Piper," she greets me in a half whisper. I stand and unthinkingly bob a curtsy. When I look up, I see she still bears the strain of her ordeal on her face.

She begins: "I'm so glad you're here. This is . . ." She turns to introduce her gentleman companion, but there's no need for introductions. As soon as I set eyes on him, I realize I know him already.

"Robert Sampson," I mouth.

Luckily, she doesn't see me. "My companion," she says, trying to be discreet. He remains solemn. I notice he's staring at me like he's just been reminded of something, or someone he'd rather forget. It's like he's just seen a ghost. Miss Louisa catches his stunned gaze. "You already know each other?" Her lips twitch, like she's not sure whether she's made a terrible mistake bringing him with her.

Mr. Sampson pauses for a moment. I see him swallow, like his mouth has gone dry. "No," he replies quickly. "I don't believe so."

I have turned my face toward his and away from Miss Louisa. I simply look unblinking at him for a moment, allowing him to take in all my features. I know what Miss Tindall has done, you see. I know she is playing games with this Mr. Sampson. She can't let him escape the consequences of his betrayal and his cowardice. The cock crowed three times in that Masonic hall when he didn't lift a finger to help her. He needs to suffer for what he did—or didn't do. If I was to look in the mirror right now, I wager I'd not see myself. I'd see a reflection of her, just as I have before.

"Perhaps we can take tea somewhere?" Miss Louisa suggests after an uneasy moment. She senses the awkwardness between us that's chafing like horsehair against both our skins.

"Yes. Yes, let's," agrees Mr. Sampson. He rubs his gloved hands together, eager to leave the church. It's as if he's keen to see my face in daylight, to satisfy himself that his mind is playing tricks on him. It's a wise move on his part, I think, because as soon as I walk out of the church, I feel Miss Tindall leave me. It's like I'm stepping out of her dress. She's gone from me and I turn to face Robert Sampson, knowing that he'll be seeing Constance Piper, the flower girl.

We soon find a small, quiet tearoom, just off the main street. Mr. Sampson orders a pot. Nothing else. This is a business meeting, not a social call; yet from Miss Louisa's expression, it's clear she's got something up her sleeve. She's looking less fretful, and it's not long before she's telling me the reason. Barely has she taken off her gloves, when she blurts: "Dear Constance, we have news!" She's almost smiling as she speaks.

"News?" I reply. From the way she's looking at me, I guess it must be good.

She regards Mr. Sampson, like she's asking for permission to speak, then moves closer so that their sleeves touch. "We are wed," she says softly. By way of proof, she dangles her left hand under my nose. There is a shiny gold band on the third finger.

My eyes focus on it for a second, then lift first to her face and onto his. Suddenly they are both smiling. "But that's wonderful news," I say, and I mean it.

"You're the only person we've told so far!" She squeals like a little girl. But she's so relieved to get it off her chest that the emotion of it all suddenly overcomes her. I see her well up and soon her face is pink and her handkerchief comes out.

"I'm very happy for you," I say. Mr. Sampson smiles awkwardly, but Miss Louisa's floodgates have opened and she's in danger of making a spectacle of herself, so she offers her excuses. "I must go to the ladies' room," she tells me.

Mr. Sampson rises as she leaves the table, then sits back down again; yet there's no sign of the smile of a few seconds ago. It's like a shadow has passed over his face and suddenly he seems fearful. He cranes his neck to make sure no one can hear our conversation, as if he's looking for spies. He leans forward, all cloak and dagger, and says to me in a half whisper: "What do you want? If it's money . . . ?" He reaches for his wallet, but he's all fingers and thumbs.

I don't mind telling you I'm shocked. "Beg your pardon, sir" is all I manage.

"Please, we have little time before she . . . ," he corrects himself, "before my wife returns. I know you knew Miss Tindall. Louisa told me you had some sort of 'special bond.' I'm assuming you want payment to keep quiet about what happened? And now you're playing tricks, trying to look like her."

The insult forces me to slump back in my chair, like he's punched me in the stomach. I'm used to being shouted at and called names, but he's just accused me of blackmail. I put on my wounded face, but then I think that perhaps I shouldn't be offended at all. Perhaps I should savor this moment. It's like he's saying I've got the upper hand. I'm not a downtrodden flower girl in his eyes, but—what do Frenchies say?—a *femme fatale.*

I wonder how Miss Tindall would handle him. I find myself raising my gaze and looking about me to see if Miss Tindall is nearby. Sadly, I can't see her, but I think she may have heard. I hope so, but I know she wouldn't be tempted to gloat, not like me. All the same, I trust she's been watching what's as good as a confession of Robert Sampson's own guilt and the part he played in her death.

All of a sudden, I feel my head begin to shake. "*You have already started to pay, Mr. Sampson,*" I hear myself say. Only it's not my voice that's launching off my tongue. It's Miss Tindall's. "*By marrying Louisa, you have begun to atone for your grievous mistakes. You have done the right thing.*"

As he regards me across the table, I think his eyes might pop out of his head. My voice sounds like hers, I can tell. The color is leaving his cheeks. He reaches for his handkerchief to wipe away the droplets of sweat that prick his brow.

"I . . . I don't . . . ," he stammers, but before he can say any more, Miss Louisa returns.

"I apologize for my little show," she says, managing a weak smile. She smooths her skirts as she slides toward her new husband. The waitress appears with a tray of tea and sets it all down in front of us on a crisp white cloth. "Shall I be mother?" asks Miss Louisa with a giggle, which sounds odd coming from her lips. I'm seeing a new side of her; it's as if the strong, independent woman is allowing herself to dissolve into her new husband, just like the sugar lump held in tongs poised above my cup.

"One or two, Miss Piper?"

"Thank you. Two lumps, please."

"Of course, our marriage means that we want Bertie back with us," she tells me eagerly. "Doesn't it, my dear?" she demurs to her new husband, before returning to me. "Milk?" I give an awkward smile and nod.

"Naturally," he replies gruffly. "My wife did not pay the full adoption premium, so he is legally still ours."

Miss Louisa nods. "So we shall be renewing our efforts to find him." She reaches for the tea strainer and places it over the rim of my cup.

"We want to raise him ourselves," says Mr. Sampson. He's forcing himself to act natural with me.

"Of course," I agree. I'm playing along, so I'm half expecting what comes next.

The teapot is lifted to pour, but Miss Louisa puts it back down onto the table, as if what she is about to say is too important to be delivered while doing anything else. "But first we need to know where he is and that's where we hope you can help us."

My eyes flash from hers to the teapot. I knew it would come to this. I am prepared. I open the small reticule that Miss Beaufroy bought me and bring out the letter I received yesterday in reply to the advertisement.

"Yes. I think I can," I tell her, trying not to sound smug. I unfold it and push it over to them. "You see, I saw an advertisement in the local paper. The wording was the same as the one you showed me, only the address was different. So I replied to it."

Louisa lets out a little gasp as she examines it. "The writing! Yes. I recognize it. The name may be different, but it's Mother Delaney's daughter's hand. I'm sure of it!"

She passes it to her husband, only I'm not expecting how he reacts.

"Woodstock Terrace!" he exclaims, slapping the letter. He says it so loud, two ladies at a nearby table stop to look at him.

"What is it, dearest?" asks Louisa, laying a steadying hand on her husband's arm.

"The address." He points to the letterhead. "That's one of my father's properties."

It doesn't surprise me. Sir William Sampson, Robert's father, owns half the houses in Whitechapel and almost as many in Poplar.

"What does that mean?" asks Louisa.

The thought pops into my head and I know immediately, but it's not my place to say.

"It means we can threaten this woman with eviction if she refuses to tell us where Bertie is." He's excited by the prospect. He's just realized he's been dealt a better hand in this game of poker, where the stakes are his baby son. Now he must keep a cool head. He turns to his new wife, his piercing eyes sharper than ever. "We must go there this morning," he tells her. "There's no time to lose."

EMILY

So Robert Sampson is turning over a new leaf. I am glad he has done the right thing by Louisa. It seems that since my unfortunate demise, he has been questioning his own values, his own morality. It appears that now he is even prepared to distance himself from his father. It could prove an astute move in the scheme of things. But I am getting ahead of myself. For now, I am in Poplar High Street watching a newly married couple stride, arm in arm, toward Number 9, Woodstock Terrace. Their steady pace belies the maelstrom inside both their bodies, but Louisa's in particular.

The house is not what Robert Sampson expected, even though he knew it to be one of the higher-yielding investments in his father's portfolio. His business has never brought him to Poplar before, but he is pleasantly surprised. It seems a respectable residential street. There are no families living in a single room here. There's no standpipe at the end of the row. It's all clean and neat and civilized.

Louisa, too, is oddly gratified that no squalor is evident. Indeed, this neat row of brick-built homes with pleasant bay windows reminds her of the place where she stayed in Stepney with Mother Delaney, where she was delivered of Bertie and where she and her baby son spent their first few days together. They stop outside the property and look up at it from the foot of the steps.

Robert regards Louisa. "Are you ready?" he asks softly.

She takes a deep breath. "Yes," she says, although she remains on tenterhooks.

They uncouple their arms and he strides up the steps first. She stays a few paces behind on the pavement. The nausea is rising in her stomach as she hears her husband's fist pounds on the door. A moment later, it opens. A young woman stands on the threshold. Louisa climbs the steps to see that it is Philomena. Little Isabel is perched on her hip.

"Is your mother in?" Louisa asks curtly, suddenly experiencing a surge of courage with her husband at her side.

Robert removes his top hat. "We would speak with Mrs. Delaney, urgently, if you please."

Philomena works her jaw. She's been taken off guard and she never did like Miss Louisa, anyway. There is little room for civilities in this encounter. Even Isabel is aware of the atmosphere. She starts to grizzle as Philomena retreats and goes in search of her mother. A tense few seconds follow. Neither Robert nor Louisa can be sure that the old Irishwoman will appear to face their wrath. Yet, a moment later she does.

Sidling up to the threshold, she crosses her arms in a gesture of defiance. "What is it that you want?" she asks brazenly.

Robert can barely believe her effrontery. Louisa clasps hold of her husband's arm. "You know very well what we want," replies Robert. "We want our son. What have you done with him?"

Gone is the kindly old woman who first took Louisa in and cut little Bertie's birth cord. That benign nursemaid has been replaced by a harridan, a harpy of the first order. Her mouth barely moves as she delivers her riposte. "I told you he is gone." Her glare is fixed on Louisa, as if she should not dare to question her son's fate.

Robert takes a step forward. "Gone where?"

Mother Delaney stands her ground. "And who might you be?" she asks, regarding Robert with contempt.

Louisa intervenes. "This gentleman is my husband. We want Bertie back and we will pay you for him." She fumbles in her reticule and brandishes a crumpled banknote. "Here's fifteen pounds."

The old woman doesn't even give the note a glance. "He's gone, I tell ya." She's about to shut the door, when Robert takes another step forward and wedges his foot across the threshold.

"How dare you?!" he cries. His voice is boiling with rage. "Do you know who I am?"

The old woman throws him a contemptuous snarl and presses even harder against the door.

He counters with his own weight. He never intended to reveal his own identity, but now he feels compelled. "I am Robert Sampson, the son of Sir William—the owner of this house," he shrieks. "I can have you evicted in an instant!" He is virtually screaming at her, but she suddenly kicks him sharply on the shins and sends him reeling backward.

"No!" cries Louisa as her husband bends to clutch his leg in pain. In that second, the door is slammed shut. The sound of the key turning in the lock is the last they hear from inside.

"You'll pay for this. Damn you!" yells Robert, his fists hammering vainly on the door. Yet within, all remains quiet. I watch the couple stand in shocked silence for a moment longer before Louisa plunges into Robert's arms, sobbing as loudly as any bereaved young mother.

"Let's get away from here," he tells her, and he takes her arm and leads her, still crying, down the steps. "We're not finished yet!" he shouts for all to hear. "They'll rue the day!"

CONSTANCE

I've been praying in St. Jude's for the past hour, waiting for the Sampsons to return. I've asked the good Lord to make Mother Delaney see the error of her ways and come clean. But as soon as I see only Miss Louisa arrive, I know my prayers have gone unheeded.

"Oh no! What happened?" I rise and hurry to her. I take her hand and we sit down beside each other in the gloom of the empty church.

In the candle glow, I see Miss Louisa's eyes glisten. The handkerchief she clutches in her hand is limp with her tears. She shakes her head. "She just refused. She just refused to tell us anything." Her voice breaks like a wave and tears wash over her cheeks once more.

I put my arm around her, even though it is probably not my place to do so. She doesn't flinch and I'm glad of it.

"What are we to do?" she sobs. "I just want my baby back! My Bertie!"

From behind one of the columns, a solitary woman suddenly appears and lifts her finger to her lips to tell us to be quiet. "This is a place of worship," she scolds. I raise my hand like I'm surrendering and she disappears again.

"My husband has gone to visit his father, to see if he can have the family evicted." She looks heavenward, as if asking the Lord how he could be so cruel. "Will you pray with me?" she asks.

I don't know why, but her question surprises me. "Of course," I say. We kneel together, side by side, and bow our heads. I know I'm expected to lead, so I do. I wonder if Miss Tindall is near. I can't sense her, but I think Miss Louisa wants me to call her. So I do.

"Dear Lord, we pray for little Bertie Sampson. We are looking for him, Lord. We beg you to let your servant, Emily Tindall, lead us to him, so that he may be reunited with his stricken mother. We ask this through Jesus Christ, Our Lord. Amen."

"Amen," Miss Louisa replies meekly.

There is silence for a few seconds. I'm holding my breath, like I'm waiting for Miss Tindall to show. I think she might, but another minute passes and nothing happens—until, that is, a thought crawls out from somewhere deep in my brain.

"We must go to the Cruelty Men," I blurt suddenly.

Miss Louisa stops sniveling and lifts her face. I'm expecting her to disagree. "The men you told me about before?"

I nod. "They'll visit the house. They can search it, but they're not the police."

She's softening. "If you think they can find . . ."

Again I raise my hand. "Let's go outside," I say. And so we do. I guide her into the daylight and sit her on a nearby bench in the churchyard.

"Robert," she begins, before remembering she ought to be more formal. "My husband says his father can send the bailiffs round to the house where Mother Delaney lives."

"But if they're evicted, they'll go goodness knows where," I point out. "They'll just disappear and then you could lose all hope of ever seeing . . ." I stop myself midsentence.

My words bring on more tears and I'm sorry for it, but, after a moment, Miss Louisa says: "These Cruelty Men." She's reminded me of the thread of our talk in the church. "You say they can search the house?"

I nod. "Yes, they can. If they find any . . ." I pull myself up sharpish. I want to say "cruelty," but it's such a harsh word to use to someone as fragile as Miss Louisa. "If they find anything wrong," I continue, "they can have Mother Delaney and the others arrested."

Suddenly she's frowning again. She's balked at the idea. "Does that mean I would have to give evidence against them?"

I think quick. "I'm sure if you do, you won't have to say your name in court," I lie. I really have no idea. All I do know is that Mother Delaney needs to be brought to justice, and fast, before more babies go missing. I think of the dead ones, too. If the Cruelty Men do manage to search the house, I'm fearful what they might find.

Shortly Miss Louisa lets out a deep sigh, which sounds more like a shudder. “I have an alternative suggestion,” she says. I can’t think what it’ll be, short of going straight to the police, but obviously I’ll listen. I nod and then she lobs a big, fat shock at me. “Will you keep a watch over Mother Delaney’s house for us?” I know my eyes betray my surprise, but she carries on. “We’d need you to follow her when she leaves the house, too, to keep her under surveillance.” I’ve not heard that last long word she’s just used before, but I’ve got the gist of what she’s proposing, all right. And there’s more. “Of course, we’d pay you for your time,” she adds. She’s trying to sweeten the bitter pill she’s asking me to swallow.

“Well,” says I, after a moment. “I—”

“We’d like you to keep a record of all the places Mother visits and what she does,” she breaks in. “It’s the only way we’ll find out where she’s keeping our Bertie.”

“I . . . don’t.”

“Please,” she pleads. I look down and she’s grabbed hold of my hands. “I implore you, Constance. You’re my only hope.”

That phrase! It’s the one that jabbed at my heart before, and it’s doing it again. Miss Louisa is welling up once more and I feel my reason melt like candle wax. I’m no detective. I’m no—what’s the word?—private investigator. I’m a flower girl who’s been given a strange gift. I’m being asked to sneak around after this wicked old crone, who’ll do God knows what to me if she thinks I’m on her case. If she is the one who’s killed those poor mites, then what’s to stop her killing an adult? And then, of course, there’s Jack. He’s still out there, on the streets. It may even be that he murdered our own Cath.

“I’m sorry, I can’t,” I’ve said it. I shake my head and turn away from her tormented face. I can’t bear the look of despair she wears.

“Very well,” I’m surprised to hear her say after a moment. “I understand. My husband and I will have to engage someone else.”

I can't believe she's not putting up more of a fight. "It's just that . . . well . . ." I start to blather like a child. I turn to see her nodding.

"We have asked too much of you. When one is desperate to find the answer, one is forced to seek unconventional solutions." The way she puts it makes me realize that there is still a big divide between our classes. Maybe she doesn't understand the terrible risk I'd run if I was to agree to such an undertaking. Part of me is still an ordinary flower girl and I'm scared.

"I'm sorry, miss," I say, for a moment forgetting that she is now married.

"Don't be," she replies. "I just thought because of your special talents . . ."

I think she's being cruel, but she is, of course, right. If I could be sure that Miss Tindall would be by my side, then I'd have the courage I need to do what she asks. I listen as the silence grows between us. I listen for Miss Tindall's distant voice to tell me what to do. A whisper is all I ask, but the only sound I hear is the clatter of horses' hooves and carts as they pass by on the main road. No voice comes.

I feel so wretched, I can't even bring myself to look at Miss Louisa when I say: "I'm sorry."

CHAPTER 30

Wednesday, January 9, 1889

EMILY

It's the morning of the summing up at the inquest at Poplar Town Hall. Detective Sergeant Hawkins arrives even earlier than usual for work to collect his papers before heading to the hearing. As soon as he sets foot in the Commercial Street Police Station, however, he's accosted by Sergeant Halfhide. The veteran officer is on the desk and calls to him in a hoarse, almost conspiratorial whisper as he passes.

"Hawkins! A word, if I may."

The detective moves toward him, slightly puzzled at first, until he remembers the sergeant was tasked to make an unauthorized line of inquiry.

"You've found something on Braithwaite?" He leans in and speaks in a low voice.

"Indeed, I did." There's a glint in the older man's eye as he opens the large ledger, which is lying on the desk, at a page he

has marked with a folded sheet of paper. "I told you the name rang a bell and here it is." He points to a few lines in the charge record. "Late spring, it was. About eighteen months back."

Hawkins reads the entry for himself: May 28, 1887: Adam Braithwaite charged with affray, together with Joseph Litvinoff and Catherine Mylett. Braithwaite and Litvinoff found guilty at Bow Street Magistrates and fined one shilling each. Charges against Mylett dropped. *Hawkins looks up. "So Adam Braithwaite knew the deceased."*

Of course, he has always had his doubts about the case and secretly sided with Brownfield and the other knife men of the same persuasion. In his mind, there has never been any real doubt that Catherine was murdered; but, of course, he can do nothing until the coroner gives his verdict. But if he does conclude that Catherine Mylett was, indeed, strangled, then Hawkins can imagine McCullen will want to move swiftly to make an arrest. And if that happens, then he just might have an ace up his sleeve.

CONSTANCE

Flo, Ma, and me make it to Poplar Town Hall for Mr. Wynne Baxter's summing up at Cath's inquest. It's a struggle to find a seat. I spy some familiar faces from Whitechapel who've made the journey over here just so they can stand at street corners and gossip about a dead gal who never did no one no harm. There's Widow Gipps and that son of hers, who leers at every woman under thirty he sees, and Mrs. Puddiphatt from down our way. Got herself a seat in the front row, she has. She must have been outside when the doors opened.

I'm not sure how Cath would feel, seeing all these mawkish people here, curious to know what happened to her. She'd probably say that no one gave a fig for her in life, so why now, in death, do they take such an interest?

Ma sits next to Mrs. Mylett. She's in a right state, poor woman. It's hard for her, hearing all these things about a daughter who must seem like a stranger to her.

We've just settled ourselves down in seats at the back row, when who should walk in but Detective Sergeant Hawkins? I pretend not to notice him, but Flo nudges me.

"There's your fancy detective," she says, knowing how it'll annoy me. He's wearing a dark blue long coat with the collar turned up against the cold. Under his arm, he carries a large leather wallet. I have to confess, he looks quite the gentleman.

"He's not half bad-looking," quips Flo.

I feel the color rise in my cheeks and hope that he hasn't seen me just a few feet away. He's having a word with one of the constables stationed at the door when he spots me and dips a shallow bow. I feel Flo's elbow dig into my ribs once more.

"I reckon he fancies you, too," she whispers.

We all rise for the coroner and it's not long before he starts on his summing up. That's what everyone's come for, and this Mr. Wynne Baxter knows it, so he's quick to cut to the chase. He's no mug and he tells the jury what's what. It seems he don't—sorry, *doesn't*—have much time for Old Bill. He tells them that despite the two policemen's initial thoughts on the matter, the first medical men to see poor Cath thought it was—what did he call it?—"a case of homicidal strangulation."

Well, once foul play was suspected, doctor after doctor went down to view the body without his say-so, and he weren't happy about it. "I had never received such treatment before," says he. So, of the five doctors who saw the body, Dr. Bond was the only one who said it weren't murder. But he didn't see Cath's body until five days after she died. Old Bond said if she'd been strangled, he should have expected to find the skin broken round her neck, but Mr. Wynne Baxter—well, he argued that there were some Indian doctors who've shown there are ways of strangling someone without leaving any marks at all.

So the gents of the jury agree with what me and Flo knew all along: Poor Cath didn't die because her collar was caught, or from drink. She was strangled by another. A verdict of "unlawful killing" goes down in the books. At least now the police will have to start looking seriously for her killer.

On the way out of the hall, our paths cross with Sergeant Hawkins's. We're all filing out together and it's a right scramble for the door. Ma's latched onto Mrs. Mylett and manages to get out pretty quick. I think the sergeant might be trying to avoid me, and I understand. The police have been proved wrong, but Flo catches his eye and drags me with her toward him. She wears her feelings on her sleeve, does Flo. She can't hide her smugness. I know the verdict's added to the police's duties, for sure, but Flo just rubs salt in the wound.

"So you'll just have to look for Cath's killer now, won't you, Detective Sergeant?" She's all flirty and cocky at once.

I think she'll annoy him, but he don't seem that troubled.

"I've just instructed my men to make an arrest, Miss Piper," he comes back at her.

That takes the wind out of her sails, I can tell you. You could blow her down with a feather. Sergeant Hawkins looks at me in a knowing way. If he weren't such a gent, he'd tip me a wink, for sure.

"Who is it then?" Flo asks. It hasn't taken her long to get her courage back.

The sergeant fingers the brim of his hat, then looks at us direct. "I'm sure you'll be reading about it in the newspapers ere too long. Good day to you both, ladies," he tells us with a full-of-himself smile. With that, he drops his hat on his head, pats it down, and he's away.

I'd say he's got a rabbit in that hat, and I'm not sure when he's going to bring it out. Old Bill's been left on the back foot; and now that the verdict is accepted, the question hanging in the air—and on the minds of most of us present—is not whether or not Cath was murdered, but was it by Jack the Ripper's hand?

Emily

News of the coroner's verdict travels fast. So fast, in fact, that within an hour of its delivery, a young, freckled urchin is knocking on the door in an attic of a tenement building near East India Docks.

Will Mylett unlocks the door. There's a look of expectancy gripping his face. His eyes are wide and glaring from out of their grimy sockets.

"Well? What did 'e say?"

The boy darts over the threshold and Mylett shuts the door behind him. "Murder. She were unlaw . . . unlaw . . ."

"Unlawfully killed."

"That's it," says the boy, nodding his small head.

Mylett lets out a long, hard sigh that grates against his lungs, before grinding his teeth. "That bastard," he says. He punches a nearby beam, then cradles his knuckle as the pain spreads throughout his hand.

The boy watches, seemingly unperturbed. He's only one thing on his mind. "You got my money?" he asks, holding out his palm.

Mylett takes a silver shilling out of his pocket and lays it in the child's grubby hand. "Be off with ya now," he growls, returning to his throbbing fist.

The boy takes the coin gleefully. His work here is done and now he is thinking about the eel pie he will buy with his well-earned gains. He trots off contentedly.

Will Mylett has barely shut the door behind him, let alone bolted it, when he hears a scuffle on the stairs. Puzzled, he opens the door, just a little, to see what's going on. The stupid boy has taken a tumble, *he tells himself as he peers through the crack. He'd call to him, only he doesn't want to alert anyone else to his presence. Instead, he shrugs and starts to close the door once more. He has plans to make and he doesn't intend to stay in this squalid hellhole any longer than he has to.*

But just as he's about to slide the bolt across the door, it's pushed toward him with such force that he staggers back into the attic and crashes into one of the upright beams. He's still on his feet, but reeling from the shock. Then, from the shadowy landing, appears someone he was not expecting. Someone he most feared seeing.

"You!" he cries.

CONSTANCE

I suppose I should be relieved that common sense has won the day. Everyone knew Cath was murdered—everyone but Old Bill—and now they're forced to open a proper investigation. So why am I not jumping up and down? As Flo and Ma and me leave the town hall and start our walk home down Poplar High Street, none of us is. Maybe it's because we don't have much faith in the police. I know Sergeant Hawkins will do his best, but he's just one man. And there are only so many hours in the day, but at least there'll be blues working on finding her killer.

Little Bertie gets no such treatment. His parents are the only ones trying to track him down. The whole sorry business sets me thinking that I was wrong to refuse Miss Louisa. I am special. I have been given a certain gift. It's my duty to use it for the good of others. If I can help her, what right do I have to turn her away? What sort of a person does that make me? The Bible story of the Good Samaritan springs into my mind. I don't want to be the one who'd pass by on the other side when there's someone in such desperate need.

I can only imagine Miss Louisa's pain. I'm angry for her, just as I'm angry for Cath, and all the other mothers who've suffered at the hands of that evil woman and her family. But most of all, I'm angry for the children who have been neglected and, worse still, even murdered. Suddenly it's my own inner voice that tells me I have no choice. I have to help and, what's more, I know I have the power.

"I'll do it," I blurt out just as we skirt Poplar Infirmary.

"Do what?" asks Flo, taken by surprise by my exclamation.

I shrug. "Something I know I'm meant to do" is all I say.

Chapter 31

Thursday, January 10, 1889

Emily

It is early morning and barely light as a well-dressed young woman is pushing a baby carriage down the road, accompanied by her husband. People are about their business. Many are heading toward the dock gates. To all the world, they are an ordinary, respectable couple: he, of middling height, with unruly sideburns, but smart in his coat and billycock; she is thin, with a sallow face, which is hidden by her fetching wide-brimmed hat, and polished boots. When they come to the main junction, they engage in a perfunctory kiss before parting.

"You won't forget to settle up with the poulterer's now, will you?" the wife reminds her husband.

He nods and looks toward the baby carriage. "That extra cash'll come in handy," he says.

She turns off down a side street. He carries straight on, headed toward Whitechapel.

Not far behind this couple trails Constance. At first light, she stationed herself at the junction of Woodstock Terrace and Poplar High Street. Her mission is, of course, to gather evidence to be used against the inhabitants of Number 9 who have treated Miss Louisa so cruelly. Once she can prove, as she suspects, that this house is actually a baby farm, where children are effectively bought and sold, then she can report Mother Delaney and these two other accomplices to the Cruelty Men.

Her basket of flowers has masked the true purpose of her visit to Poplar. It acts as a plausible cover. She has until her interview with the prospective adopting parents on Friday to investigate. She is hoping she will not have to go through with her meeting, so she is doubly keen to uncover any evidence that may lead to their conviction. She will follow the woman with the perambulator.

CONSTANCE

So that was the man from the advert, the one who's supposed to be a doctor. He don't look much like one to me. From his bearing and his dress, I'd say he was more a clerk or a shopkeeper. Hang about! He looks familiar. He's the haberdasher from Whitechapel. Surely he can't be married to Mother? He must be the son-in-law Miss Louisa was on about. As for the woman, well, she's dressed like she belongs in the West End. She must be the old crone's daughter.

She keeps her head down under that hat of hers, like she don't want no one to notice her. I've seen a few young mothers pushing their babies in parks and they've all got this certain look about them. When an admirer peers under the hood into their baby carriage, they welcome them and smile and accept any compliments that come their way. But I can't imagine this one fussing with coverlets or nodding at old ladies who bill and coo. It's as if she's on business. She's striding so fast down the road I can barely keep up with her. She's not minding the ruts and bumps, neither, so that the poor child inside that perambulator will be getting bounced around like a football. It's not long before I understand why.

Toward the end of this dark side street, I can make out a shop. The woman parks her baby carriage outside. I follow close behind and station myself by some chapel railings just in time to see her reach down to fetch up her baby—only there isn't one. It's a sack she lifts out of the perambulator and my jaw drops open at the sight. My eyes follow her into the shop with her booty.

EMILY

As you know, in nearby Commercial Street Station, the police have at last come to their senses and launched a murder investigation. The hunt for Catherine Mylett's killer is finally on, and Detective Sergeant Hawkins has acted upon the information supplied by Sergeant Halfhide. He has brought in Adam Braithwaite for questioning. The prisoner now sits before him in the interview room.

"Do we really need to play games, Braithwaite?" asks the detective, shaking his head. "I know you and Catherine Mylett were charged with affray last year. Why didn't you tell me you knew her?"

The blacksmith, his face still smeared with soot, fiddles nervously with his eye patch. He came quietly to the station, as if he half expected he would be found out. He accepts that he has not been entirely honest with the police.

"I knew, Cath, yes," he admits with little prompting. "But I didn't see her that night." The grime on his forehead glistens with sweat.

"Why didn't you tell me before?" asks Hawkins, even though

he knows the answer. "Why didn't you say you knew the woman?"

Braithwaite looks wounded. "Because until yesterday, you coppers thought she fell down drunk and died, and so did I."

The coroner's verdict is undoubtedly an embarrassment to the Metropolitan Police, but Superintendent Arnold has since accepted the findings. Hawkins winces at the reminder of the collective incompetence of the force. "But now we have admitted our"—he searches for the right word—"error of judgment, you will tell us all you know. Yes?" There's a note of exasperation in his voice.

Braithwaite sighs, as if he knows the game is up. "Cath and me, well, we were more than friends once."

"Once?"

"Last year," he replies with a nod. "But then I met my wife and . . ."

Hawkins nods. "I see. Then Miss Mylett became a problem. Is that so?"

The smithy shakes his head. "No." He pauses, confused. "Yes. I didn't want my wife to know about her, because, well, I . . ."

"Because Catherine Mylett walked the streets and your wife is a decent, God-fearing woman who isn't forced to sell her services to other men?" Hawkins has done his homework and made inquiries in the neighborhood yesterday afternoon. The blacksmith married only four months ago.

Braithwaite is surprised by the detective's insight, but after a moment he nods. "Exactly so, sir," he replies, showing a vestige of humility for the first time.

Hawkins gives a triumphant nod. He is making progress. It is time to hand the suspect over to Inspector McCullen for more questioning. He wonders if his commanding officer will be so understanding.

CONSTANCE

Mother Delaney's daughter doesn't spend long in the shop. It's five minutes at the most before she's out again carrying an empty sack. She looks up and down the street, then turns and sets off in the direction of her home. I stay put and wait until she's turned the corner before I pay my visit to the shop. Not a word has to pass my lips before I see my worst fear with my own eyes. The assistant, an elderly lady with spectacles, is sorting through a large pile of clothes on the counter. As soon as she sees me, she looks up.

"Yes," she says, peering over the rim of her glasses, without a smile. It's rare my sort's ever shown one in shops.

"I'd like to look at some baby clothes," I hear myself say, staring at the pretty little smock edged in blue on the counter. "For a friend," I add quickly, in case she thinks I'm in the family way.

The woman gives me a sort of hoity look, as if I'm fortunate to be allowed in the store. "You're in luck, young lady," she says. "We've just had some in. Good quality, they are."

The assistant picks up a little dress, a white one. It's followed by a boy's smock, made of fine linen and stitched in blue thread, with a monogram on the front. The letters are all curly, but they suddenly grow larger before my eyes until I can read them clearly. "RLF," I suddenly say out loud. I'm not sure what the *L* stands for, but I'll wager the *R* and *F* are for Robert and Fortune—little Bertie's initials, the same initials that are on the silver cup that Mr. B palmed off on me at Christmas.

"What?" snaps the woman.

"The initials," I explain.

She peers at the embroidery. "Very fine," she remarks, followed by "Boy or girl?" She reaches for a length of brown paper from the large roll attached to the counter.

"Sorry?"

"Are you looking for clothes for a boy or a girl?"

"A boy," I manage. I pick up the little smock with the initials. "I'll take this one," I tell her.

"A good choice, if I may say so," she says. "And you can always unpick the initials." She's changed her tune, now she knows I'm a serious buyer. "I'll take a shilling for it."

I think she expects me to haggle, but I don't. Miss Louisa has given me some money up front. "Here." I slide over a coin and I watch her parcel up the smock in the brown paper.

When she hands it to me, she must wonder at the look of disgust on my face that I find difficult to hide. The truth is, I dread to think of what has become of the baby boy who once wore this fine smock. I dread to think of what has become of little Bertie.

Emily

We shall leave Constance for the moment as she awaits the reappearance of the young mother she is surveilling. In the meantime, return with me, if you will, to Whitechapel to follow Florence. Her mother has given her a shilling to buy a capon for tonight's meal with Mr. Bartleby. She's said they'll eat it in honor of Catherine, in the hope that now, at last, she will get justice. Florence—always glad for an excuse to celebrate—agrees it's a thoughtful gesture, although she's a little reluctant about a visit to the poulterer's.

Greenland's is, you'll remember, where Mick Donovan, otherwise known as Irish Mick, works. She recalls very little about their last encounter that night in the George, but she does know she made a fool of herself in front of him. Nevertheless, she forces herself to swallow her pride for her mother's sake. That is what brings her to the poulterer's shop, a basket over her arm, on this chilly morning.

It's as she feared. Donovan stands in the corner of the shop, a ball of twine in one hand and a pair of scissors in the other, trussing plucked fowl. Florence pretends not to notice him.

"Good day to you, Miss Florence," says Mr. Greenland, tipping his boater to her. "What can I do for you?"

She tells him she'd like a nice plump bird. She flashes her eyelashes at him as she speaks. Mr. Greenland easily succumbs to her charms and offers her one that's already plucked at no extra charge.

"Mick here's got some ready." He bobs his head at Donovan. "We don't want you spoiling them pretty hands now, do we?" he tells her. He turns toward the Irishman. "Let's be having a good one here."

So Donovan cuts a length of twine and ties the bird's legs together at the back. He walks over to the counter and hands it to Mr. Greenland for wrapping; but just before he makes to return to his corner, he leans toward Florence. "I've heard you like it nice 'n' tight," he whispers.

It takes a good deal to make Florence blush, but his words cause her to color.

"Here you are," says Mr. Greenland, placing the wrapped bird in her basket.

Florence fumbles in her purse and hands over a few coins. She's flustered and can't leave the shop too soon. As she heads for the door, however, she bumps into a man in a billycock hat with limp sideburns. An expletive escapes from her lips and the impact causes her to drop her basket. As Florence stoops to pick it up, Mick Donovan springs to her rescue. So, too, does the man with the sideburns.

"Leave it to Mick, now, Mr. Cosgrove," urges Mr. Greenland, clearly upset that a good customer should be inconvenienced in his shop.

Just as Donovan delivers the dropped capon back into Florence's basket, he becomes aware that this Mr. Cosgrove is staring at him. Donovan stares back, and in that moment, an unsolicited memory returns. He glances down at the man's hand, noting it bears a recent wound, and his expression betrays him. He turns back to his trussing, but it is too late.

"Come to settle up, have you, sir?" asks Mr. Greenland of his customer, just as Florence slips out of the shop. "Good day, miss," the poulterer calls after her as, with the trussed capon in her basket, she begins her exit in all haste for the second time. It is what she has unknowingly left in her wake that will concern us later.

Meanwhile, Florence cannot return home quickly enough and hurries past an alley at the side of the shop. It leads to a courtyard at the back, where much of the slaughtering of the fowl is done. The alley is wide enough to park the delivery cart and it's where we find a puzzled Gilbert Johns scratching his head in thought. He works for Mr. Greenland, alongside Mick Donovan, and he'd swear that someone has moved the cart overnight. It's not where he parked it. Someone must have taken it out last night.

Pulling down the tailgate, he climbs on board. What's this? Dried blood? *he thinks. There's far too much of it to have come from a bird, and he swears it wasn't there when he parked up the cart yesterday.*

"Gilbert!" calls Mr. Greenland from inside the shop. "Where's that brace of pheasants?"

Gilbert looks up. The discovery of the cart had led to him forgetting he was meant to fetch the birds from the hanging shed. "Coming Mr. Greenland," he replies. The errant trailer is soon removed from his thoughts.

Constance

I return to the corner of Woodstock Terrace. The woman with the baby carriage has arrived just in time to catch a girl—about my age, I'd say—waddling up to the house. The two of them talk a little at the foot of the steps; then the one that's expecting is shown inside. Close to her time, she is, and I'm guessing she'll birth there, then give up her baby for adoption. That's the scheme of these things.

A couple of hours later, there's another woman, older this time. She hands over a bundle on the doorstep before she walks away sobbing so loud they could hear her at St. Paul's. But it's the old crone I need to catch. I need to see her leave the house with a baby in tow. If she does, I'll follow her and try to nab her in the act of handing it over for money. Don't ask me what I'll do then. She might not be breaking the law, but then again, she might. I'm not sure I'll have the courage to confront her. I'll just have to pray that Miss Tindall will tell me what to do when the time comes—if it ever does.

EMILY

It's the turn of Inspector McCullen to interrogate Adam Braithwaite. He prefers his interviewees to be malleable—that's why he tasked Hawkins to soften him a little—but this blacksmith is proving reticent, to say the least. He's as stubborn as a brewer's dray horse when it decides its cart is too heavy to pull. Despite McCullen's years of experience, his detainee will not shift.

"And again, if you please." There is exasperation in the Scotsman's voice. "Account for your movements from ten o'clock on the evening of December nineteenth." One of Braithwaite's fellow artisans, a cooper, had vouched that he'd left him working in the yard at around ten o'clock that night. "What were you doing between just after ten o'clock and three in the morning when they found her?" repeats McCullen, thrusting his face close to his prisoner's.

Braithwaite remains sullen. A bruise is blooming on his right cheek. Detective Sergeant Leach was a little too enthusiastic earlier on today. He lost his temper when he received a discour-

teous riposte to one of his questions. The detective punched him in the jaw and the blow has left its mark.

"I was catching up on orders until midnight, I tell ya," he growls.

"And nobody saw you."

"I can't say." He bites his lip, then adds: "I was home by half past twelve."

"Ah, yes. Home,*" repeats Cullen. "Can you tell us where your wife is? We called on her, but were told she's not been seen for a few days."*

Braithwaite rolls his eyes. "She's looking after her old aunt. Staying with her for a week or two, she is."

The inspector's lips suddenly twitch into a rather cruel smile. "How very convenient," he says.

Constance

Mr. B's eating with us this evening. No doubt, he'll be baiting Flo and me again; rubbing us the wrong way for his own amusement. I try to tell myself I mustn't take him so serious; but as soon as I open the door, I can tell something's up. Flo rushes over to me, waving a copy of the late edition of the newspaper.

"They've got someone," she says breathlessly. She thrusts the rag into my hand as I cross the threshold.

"For Cath?" I ask.

Ma's hovering behind Flo. "Read it to us, will ya, love?" she pleads, all anxious.

Not even bothering to take off my hat, I walk toward the light of the candle that burns on the mantelshelf. The glare pools over the front page and a headline that reads: MYLETT MURDER: BLACKSMITH ARRESTED. Then, underneath, in italics was written: *Could he be Jack?*

I read the headline out loud, then look up. "Mr. Braithwaite," I say with a frown.

"Ain't he the one you spoke to? The smithy that works in Clarke's Yard?" asks Flo. I told her all about my visit and how I'd laid flowers on the spot where Cath was killed.

"Yes," I reply.

She nods her head. "I knew it," she says, slumping down into the nearby chair. "Didn't I tell ya she was seeing someone there? Didn't I say?"

It's true, she did, in the George just before Cath joined us that night. I wonder if Braithwaite was the suspect Sergeant Hawkins had in mind when he spoke to us after the inquest. But deep inside me, I know that something's not right. It's been too easy. There's a niggling doubt in my head and a feeling in my heart that tells me there's more to this situation than meets the eye.

"Hold up. Here comes Mr. B," says Ma, glancing out of the window.

I know Ma's hoping to celebrate, what with the capon and all. A lot's happened in the last two days: not only have the coppers come to their senses, they think they've nabbed Cath's killer, too.

"'Evening, ladies. I expect you 'eard about the arrest," greets Mr. B, all full of glee as soon as he crosses the threshold. "Looks like Old Bill's finally nailed him what did for your friend, gals."

Flo sighs and manages a nod. "S'pose that's somefink."

Me? I just stay quiet. It's only when I'm in the kitchen, leaning over the big pan and looking at the bird being boiled, that it hits me. The capon's legs are still trussed together and I notice that the twine that binds them is a four-thread cord. A muffled gasp escapes my lips.

"You all right, Con?" asks Flo as she mashes the potatoes.

"Scolded my finger, that's all," I lie. I wonder if Cath was strangled with twine from Greenland's.

CHAPTER 32

Friday, January 11, 1889

EMILY

Meanwhile, in Commercial Street Police Station, Adam Braithwaite has spent the night in custody. Of course, he has slept very little, and not only because he has been deprived of a blanket. He is beginning to feel increasingly damned. His story about his whereabouts the night of Catherine's murder is, he is forced to admit, rather nebulous, to say the least. There are as many holes in it as a chestnut seller's brazier; and without an alibi, he knows the noose is as good as round his neck. It is therefore with trepidation that he hears the key turn in the outer door and sees Sergeant Hawkins stride toward his cell. The detective is not alone. As well as with a constable, he is accompanied this time by an attractive blond woman, in her late twenties, wearing a waspish expression.

"Mr. Braithwaite," calls the detective.

The prisoner's head is in his hands, but he raises it and his face instantaneously breaks into a smile. "Thank God you're here."

He leaps up and rushes forward to embrace the woman, but Hawkins sidesteps and stands between them.

"Adam, it's all right," she assures him, craning her neck over Hawkins's shoulder.

"Sit down," the detective orders Braithwaite. He complies.

"This man is your husband?" he asks the woman.

"He is, and you've got no right to keep him behind bars," she snarls like an angry lioness.

Braithwaite is relieved. "Tell him, love. Tell him I were home by one."

"Course you were, but the coppers don't need to take my word for it," she sneers, looking pointedly at Hawkins. "Isn't that right, Sergeant?"

It's true. Mick Donovan, making deliveries of poultry to homes in Poplar, came forward earlier to testify he saw Braithwaite leaving Clarke's Yard shortly after midnight on the night in question. The detective nods.

"The Irish lad you know from the George," his wife informs him.

"Does that mean . . . ?" Braithwaite searches Hawkins's face.

"You are free to go, Mr. Braithwaite," the detective says, and he directs a constable to open wide the grille to allow the prisoner's release.

Hawkins is inscrutable. As I watch the blacksmith leave, I see the detective's frustration, but he has not given up. He simply needs more time to pry deeper. The sudden appearance of Mrs. Braithwaite to corroborate her husband's whereabouts and the production of an alibi, who just happened to be driving a delivery cart when he spotted the suspect, is all very convenient. His instinct tells him Braithwaite knows a lot more than he is letting on. And now, of course, he must face the wrath of Inspector McCullen who is not yet privy to the news. He is effectively back to where he started.

Detective Sergeant Hawkins is not the only man experiencing difficulties. In Poplar, Albert Cosgrove is preparing for the worst. News of the visit from the desperate couple inquiring about one of Mother's charges has only just reached him via Philomena. The old matron had made her daughter swear she wouldn't say anything about the unpleasant scene to her husband, but she'd accidentally let it slip over breakfast. Philomena had been up most of the night attending a breech birth. It was lucky the girl didn't die, as well as her baby. The mother's body would have been harder to explain away, even if it was Dr. Carey who'd attended. So, when Isabel had started bawling for her porridge, Philomena snapped at the child, telling her she'd enough with which to contend without having to put up with her daughter's tantrums.

"What do you mean by that, Philly?" Albert had asked, lowering his newspaper. Reading the look that his wife gave her mother, he recognized something was afoot. "It's one of the babes, ain't it? There's trouble."

Mother, eating a plate of ham and eggs, had shaken her head. "'Tis nothing we can't handle," she'd mumbled, ejecting a gob of yolk as she spoke. "I'll just lie low for a few days. 'Tis all." But, of course, Albert could tell from his wife's expression that perhaps the pair of them had bitten off more than they could chew. Philly was forced to come clean and tell her spouse that Bertie's father just happened to be the son of their landlord and had threatened them with eviction.

So now, Albert is well and truly riled. He's pacing up and down the dining room's floor, his hands clasped behind his back. Mother is still eating toast, seemingly unperturbed, and Philomena is jiggling Isabel on her knee, trying to get her to be quiet, and looking most agitated herself.

"I feared it would come to this," growls Albert, his whiskers seemingly drooping under the pressure of his woes.

"He can't turn us out. We've paid the rent regular," Mother chimes in. She's wearing a sour expression, as if she's just sucked a lemon.

Albert pivots on his heel and leans close to her, wagging his finger as he does so. "He can and he will, and we'll have to do a runner again, just like in Stepney when you was spotted throwing that parcel in the river, you silly cow," he berates. He turns his back on her, biting his knuckles, then switches back so suddenly that he makes the old woman jump. "That girl!" he cries.

"What girl?" snarls Mother.

"The flower seller. Remember?" He's fixed on his wife.

Philomena frowns. "The one at the end of the street yesterday?"

His head seems to go into a spasm as he nods vigorously. "That's the one. There was something about her. She was following us. I'm sure of it."

Mother coughs out a laugh. "Will ya listen to yourself, Albert?" she tells him, not bothered at all. "You'll next be telling us the Devil Incarnate is after us." She chuckles to herself.

He'd like to wipe the smile off her face with the back of his hand. Instead, he punches his own palm. "You mark my words, Mother, you've done it too brown again. We'd best make plans to leave."

CONSTANCE

I'm back by the junction of Woodstock Terrace and Poplar High Street, where I was yesterday, and I've just spotted Mother coming out of the house. I've already seen the haberdasher with the billycock leave like he did before, only there's been no sign of his wife. But Mother's the one I'm really after and she's just shut the front door behind her. I'm on her case.

With a plaid shawl around her shoulders and a black bonnet tied under her chin, she teeters down her front steps with a bundle in one arm and a carpetbag, with a handle, slung over the other. It's a baby she's carrying, all right. I can hear the poor mite bawling as she waddles along toward me. My eyes dip to the pavement as she crosses to the other side of the lane in the direction of the high street. I follow her to the junction, where she turns right. She's headed for an omnibus stop, I'll wager.

I'm keeping my distance, a good few yards behind. I'm nervous. Being a spy don't come natural to me. I feel all shifty and sly as I go by a row of barrows. There's not many people about, but my eyes are swiveling on their stalks: up, down, left, and right. I keep having to remind myself I'm doing this for Miss Louisa.

Mother's still in my sights as I hurry along the street, and I'm passing a narrow alley, when suddenly I feel something heavy clamp my shoulder. I open my mouth to gasp, but no sound comes out. Suddenly I'm being dragged backward toward the darkness. My basket tumbles to the ground and the few blooms I have are spilled into the mud. I manage to let out a sort of squeal as I'm pulled back roughly, but any noise I make is muffled by a gloved hand over my mouth.

It's a moment before my eyes adjust to what little light there is in the alley, and I feel two hands grip both my arms and turn me round. I'm facing my attacker. His hands are off my mouth now so that if I'd a mind to scream, I could. But I don't, because I recognize him. And, what's more, he recognizes me.

"You!" he cries. There's shock and there's anger in his voice, all melded into one. It's the haberdasher from Number 9 I saw yesterday, the one from Whitechapel, the one with the baby's ribbon. He's come up so close that I can smell his stale breath.

"What was you doing following that old woman?" He jerks his head toward the main road. "I saw you yesterday, too. Who you working for?" he hisses. When I don't reply straightaway, he grabs hold of the lapels of my jacket and shakes me. "Well?"

"No one," I manage, but I'm so terrified that I can barely think right.

"Who's paying you to spy on us?" He tugs at my jacket again. "It's that governess, ain't it? She put you up to this."

"I . . . I'm a flower girl, sir," I bleat, barely able to breathe.

He lets go of me and I stand for a moment, frozen to the spot with fear. He hones in on me again, so that his angry face is so close to mine that we're almost touching.

"If I see you around here again, I'll crush you like one of your flowers," he says with a sneer, pointing to the slippery ground below. And he stamps on one of my winter roses with the heel of his boot and grinds it into the filth of the alley to make his point. "You hear me?"

"Yes, sir," I reply. I take a couple of steps away from him before I bend low and manage to pick up my basket; then I turn and break into a trot back down the passage. The blood's pounding in my ears, but still, over the thrumming sound in my head, I can hear him shout: "Tell her that her boy's gone! She'll never see him again!"

His words cut like a knife; for a second, the stab of them makes me want to stop. Somehow I manage to carry on and in another moment I'm back on the high street, where the world goes about its business as usual. I need to make sense of what's just happened, but I'm still so shocked. It's like I'm in a vise and it's hard to let the fear loose. Through a blur of tears, I glance to my right and I see the omnibus has just pulled up at the stop. Mother is boarding, but it's no good me following her anymore. I've been unmasked and poor Miss Louisa has lost her little Bertie forever. I feel so wretched I almost want to step out in front of the horses that are pulling the omnibus. There's no point carrying on.

EMILY

How I feel for my poor Constance! Weary and in despair, she starts to wend her way back along the high street in the direction of Whitechapel. Her feet drag, and despite her basket being empty, it only adds to the weight she feels on her young shoulders. She is deep in thought, and, as so often happens when she is disconsolate, her mind turns to me. I can see her energy is ebbing away, and with it, her hope. I know I have to do something to inspire her in her fight, but before I can act, someone else does. So careless of her surroundings is she that she does not look where she is going. Nor does she have any idea that she is being watched. Her shoulder skims a passerby. Or rather his skims hers. I know his action is engineered.

"Sorry," blurts Constance, glancing round apologetically.

"Will you look . . . ?" The man with the eye patch appears angry, but he is feigning his mood. He stops. "You're . . ." He's pointing at her, pretending he's not quite able to place her.

"Cath's friend." She's recognized him now: the blacksmith at Clarke's Yard. "But I thought—"

"That I was in jail," he butts in. "They released me."

She's not sure how to react. "Good," she replies halfheartedly, as if that is what she thinks she is expected to say. There's something that she doesn't trust about this man. She knows he is holding something back.

"Good?" *He works his jaw as he studies her uncertain expression, then after a moment says: "You think I killed her?"*

"No!" *Her riposte comes a little too quickly to be convincing. "No," she repeats, more gently.*

He shakes his head and shoots her an odd look that makes her feel guilty for suspecting him. "I can explain," he tells her. "You got time for a drink?"

Constance

He suggests we go to the George. I'm not comfortable with it. I hardly know the bloke, but it's clear he wants to get something off his chest. So I agree to a quick bevy and we return to the place where Cath spent her last evening on this earth. He buys me a lemonade and it's a pint of ale for him. We sit in a quiet corner and he takes out his papers and tobacco from a tin in his pocket and rolls a cigarette.

"You want one?" he asks me, shoving the rolled-up cig under my nose.

I shake my head in reply.

He shrugs, strikes a lucifer, and lights up. I watch him in silence as he takes a long drag, then blows out the smoke. I lean back and cough a little. I'm not sure if he meant to puff it out in my face, but it's like he wants me to know who's in charge, that he has a certain power over me. I know a lot of men like to do that with women, so I don't read too much into his arrogance.

Suddenly he leans forward, all jumpy. He plants his elbows on the little table between us and his voice is urgent. "If I tell thee what happened that night, you'll not tell it to police. Things is best left. I don't want no one else to get hurt, you understand me, lass?" He's not asking me, he's telling me.

"I shan't tell," I reply, even though I know I can't promise.

He takes a gulp of his ale, as if it'll give him courage. "I did see Cath that night," he says. "The night she died."

It's no big surprise to me, but I think it best to play all innocent. "So you knew her?" I can tell by his expression they were more than just friends, too.

He nods. "Aye. We met afore she took sick and ended up in the asylum." I suddenly wonder if little Evie might have been his child; but for now, it don't matter. I let him carry on. "While she were away, I got wed, but when Cath were better, she still came to see me now and again." He shakes his head and gazes into his tankard. "She were an unhappy lass, especially after the little girl . . ."

"Evie," I say.

His expression hardens. "Evie, aye," he replies. "She were sure the minder killed her, you know. She were sure there were others, too."

His words make my memory flash back to Cath's ramblings: "*The babes, dying so young.*" And the specter of Mother Delaney rises before my eyes. He's opening up. I need to pry deeper. "So what happened?" I ask. I need him to focus.

"That night, I were locking up, when she came to me. In a terrible state, she were, crying and trembling and talking so fast. I couldn't make sense of it." He shakes his head and drags on his cigarette. "Blood on her face, there was, and on her hands."

"Blood?" I'm confused. "But Cath was strangled," says I, but then I remember my vision. There was blood on her face.

He nods and goes on: "You're right. At first, I thought she'd been roughed up, but as I wiped her cheek, I realized the blood weren't hers. I tried to calm her. I sat her down in my workshop. I gave her a blanket and some gin."

He takes a gulp of his own beer. "We sat for a while until she'd calmed down and then I asked her what happened." He pauses. There's a faraway look in his eye.

"And?"

"She said she'd found out where Evie's minder was living. She was sure she'd killed the mite and so she'd taken a knife with her, to threaten her, just in case."

"In case of what?"

He sighs heavily. "In case, she wouldn't pay up."

"*Pay up?*" I'm not sure where all this is leading.

"She were going to ask for money to keep quiet about the little 'uns dying."

I'm shocked. I never took Cath for a blackmailer.

"She knew the son-in-law was in on it, too. He opened the door that night, and she told him if he didn't cough up, she'd go to the law."

I'm on the edge of my seat. What I'm hearing just doesn't make sense to me. "She didn't go at him?"

"He tried to get the knife off her and there was a scuffle. He got hurt."

"I can't believe Cath would do such a thing. Why didn't she go straight to the coppers?"

Adam Braithwaite shakes his head. "You think they'd believe her sort? To the coppers, she was now't but a dog turd."

I can't argue with him on that score, but I still can't believe Cath could hatch such a plot. Blackmail is an ugly thing. It takes cunning, too. Surely, it wasn't in her nature? But the answer to my unasked question comes quick enough.

The blacksmith casts a glance over his shoulder to check we're not being overheard and lowers his voice. "The thing is, the money weren't her idea. It were that no-good brother of hers."

"Will?" I say. The old photograph of the young William Mylett pops into my head.

"Aye, he's the one." He spits on the floor. "Bastard. He made her do it, see. The minder bloke coughed up thirty quid for her silence."

"Thirty quid!" I repeat.

He nods. "That's when she came to me."

I picture the scene: Cath's face spattered in blood, Braithwaite calming her down. "She must have been beside herself," I say.

"That she was," he agrees, taking another sip of his ale.

But then another thought drops into my head. I'm not sure if Miss Tindall has put it there, but I remember that Cath was found with only half a penny in her apron pocket.

"So what about the money?" I ask. "The thirty quid."

"I'd never seen that much money. She said she had to split it with that brother of hers, otherwise he'd be after her. And then . . ."

"Yes?" I press him, seeing that he's welling up at the recollection of something important. "Then she says to me that she wanted us to run away together, to make a fresh start." He sniffs. "Part of me wanted to, of course, but I'd my wife to consider and my business. I couldn't just up and leave, as much as I wanted to." He wipes his nose with the back of his grimy hand. "She said she were meeting Will to give him his share of the cash. I said I'd stay with her till he showed, but she told me to go. I could see she were afraid of him. That's when we started to row. I told her she were making a big mistake, that she should take the money and run, but she wouldn't have it. I left her alone and she stayed put at the yard entrance."

"And that was the last you saw of her?"

"It were." He takes another drag of his roll-up. "Course the next thing I know is I get to work and there's coppers in t' yard, saying they found a dead woman. When I heard it were Cath, I couldn't say 'owt. They'd never believe me."

For a moment, I'm speechless; then the words crawl out. "So you think Cath was killed by her own brother?"

"That I do."

It's hard for me to swallow. I recall the photograph of the pair of them, looking so happy. "And where is Will now?" No one, it seems, has heard from him since the murder. He's vanished.

"Rumor is, he stowed away and sailed to America with all t' cash. He could be anywhere." He drains his glass.

He's shocked me.

"But you can't let it rest like that?" I say bitterly. "Why didn't you tell the police all this?"

He shrugs, takes one last drag, then stubs out his cigarette on the floor. "As I said, they wouldn't believe the likes of me. I'm the one they thought as did it. They wouldn't believe my wife when she told them I were at home, but I was lucky a cartman spotted me coming out o' Clarke's Yard when he did, elst I could've had an appointment with t' gallows soon."

"So that's why you were released. You had an alibi?" I can't let this story rest.

"That's a fancy word, lass, but yes. Someone saw me, so they let me go."

"And meantime, Will Mylett is free."

"Right again." He frowns, then leans closer, so we're not overheard. "But you can't tell Cath's old mum, eh? Kill her, it would. You hear?" His gaze is intense, and I know what he says is true. It would be the death of poor Ma Mylett. "Besides, Will's long gone. He'll not kill again. Leastways, not round these parts."

Chapter 33

Emily

Gilbert Johns flaps away a persistent bluebottle. He's gathering up the entrails of the chickens he's just dressed in Greenland's yard. It's the end of the day and he's dumping them into a barrow to take to Mrs. Hardiman's Cat Meat Shop. He's scooping up another batch of slippery innards when he sees Mick Donovan loping toward the hanging shed.

"Oi!" he calls. He wipes his bloody hands on his apron. The Irishman turns. Gilbert casts a look inside the shop to make sure Mr. Greenland isn't watching. "Here." He beckons to him.

Donovan narrows his eye and draws closer.

"Why d'ya take the cart out the other night?" asks Gilbert. He's been meaning to ask him before, but the time hadn't been right.

The Irishman's slouched shoulders suddenly straighten, but he does not reply. Instead, he frowns and carries on his way.

"Why? You know you're not allowed." Gilbert hears his own voice rising in anger and follows him. "Why?" He grabs him by the arm. "You're one of them Fenians, ain't ya? Wanting Home Rule and not caring who you blow up while you're about it?"

Donovan fingers his measly moustache. "Leave it, will ya?" he pleads, eyeing Gilbert's hand on his sleeve. "I was just running an errand. You know I need the cash. Up to my ears, I am," he says, lifting his bloody hand to his head.

As if the sight of the blood reminds Gilbert, he says pointedly: "There was blood. Blood in the cart, and it weren't from no birds."

Donovan shakes his head. "I didn't ask no questions," he tells him in the hope that he will be asked no more himself. He turns and begins walking toward the hanging shed. But a second later, he feels Gilbert grab his collar. He twists round to see him towering over him. He's been lifted almost off the ground.

"What was you up to?" barks Gilbert.

"Nothing!" comes the muffled reply.

Gilbert's grip tightens. "Tell me!"

"A sack. I delivered a sack from the docks up to Poplar."

"What was in it?"

"I don't know, I swear!"

Gilbert is prepared to give the younger man the benefit of the doubt, but he knows his love of horse racing will be his downfall. "Debt" is a word that sounds so like "death," and in Whitechapel, the one can so easily lead to the other.

Constance

As I return home to Whitechapel, I have the feeling me and Adam Braithwaite didn't meet by chance. I'm not sure if Miss Tindall had a hand in it, but I think she's trying to tell me something. Nor am I sure I can believe the blacksmith's story about Will Mylett, but it stacks up. I swore I'd tell no one what I've just learned, but maybe I should. Maybe, sometimes, God allows us to break an oath if it might save the lives of others. William Mylett is still at large. Surely, if he is prepared to do in his own sister, then he will be prepared to kill again. I've a duty to tell Sergeant Hawkins what I've just uncovered. I make up my mind to go and see him on the morrow.

A few minutes later, I arrive home to find there's an unexpected visitor in our front room. He's filling our best chair with his enormous frame, taking tea with Ma.

"Miss Constance," Gilbert Johns greets me, leaping to his feet so suddenly that his tea sloshes in his saucer.

"Gilbert here's calling to see how you and Flo are faring, after Cath's inquest and all that," says Ma, beaming. "Ain't that kind of him?"

I nod and manage a flat smile. "Very," I reply, unpinning my hat. I take it off, together with my jacket, and hang them on the peg by the door. "We're much obliged to you, I'm sure," I say awkwardly. I smooth down my skirts and walk toward the fire. I'm so flustered to find Gilbert in our house that I even dip a little curtsy to him. Ma says he'd be a good catch for me and she's already hearing wedding bells. I'm not so sure.

"I just thought I'd see how you was," he says, taking his seat again. He's spilled tea on his trousers and is trying to hide the damp patch with his big hand.

"That's kind." I sit myself on the chair with the wonky leg and clench my buttocks to hold it still and stop it from rocking. I'm that tense, anyway, that it's really no bother. I don't want to see Gilbert Johns; and the sooner he knows he's not welcome, the better. There's an awkward silence between us. Ma fills it by asking me if I'd like a tea, too. I don't, but I say I do, just to get her out of the room.

Once she's in the kitchen, and I've got Gilbert to myself, I think I'll tell him straight that I've no time for courting. I shan't mince my words. It's not right to lead him on, so I'm just about to break it to him, but he bends his big head down low toward me and says: "I've heard something I think you should know." He takes me aback with his seriousness.

"About Cath?"

He nods. "You heard they let the blacksmith go?"

News travels fast as fleas in Whitechapel. I crane my neck toward the kitchen to see Ma's not loitering. "You weren't his alibi, were you? You weren't the cartman who vouched for him."

He frowns. "How . . . ?" He shakes his head, but is wondering how I know. "Not me," he protests. "Mick Donovan."

"Mick Donovan," I repeat. "Of course." Suddenly I'm back in the smoky pub that night and the bar's crowded, but I can see the Irish creep talking to some man sitting on a stool before he came over to join us. The other bloke had his back to us, but I remember he turned a little so that I saw the side of his face. I remember now he wore a patch over one eye. "How do you know?" I ask.

Just then, Ma brings in a tray with a fresh pot on it. "Here we are," she announces, all cheerful like. "And there's biscuits, too, Gilbert," she says with a smile, offering him the pick of the plate.

"That's very kind," says Gilbert, playing the charmer as he takes one.

Ma puts down the plate on the table and clasps her hand as she watches Gilbert take a bite. He keeps his mouth shut while he chews, prompting an admiring look from her. She turns her face toward me and mouths: "Such a gent."

I catch him coloring. His beefy neck is red and the flush is spreading to his cheeks. Gent or no, what Gilbert's just told me just threw a whole new light on things. If Mick Donovan did see Adam Braithwaite leave the yard for his home at that time, then the blacksmith must be telling me the truth. Even though the very thought of seeing him sickens me, I need to go and have it out with Mick.

"Con. Connie, love." Ma's voice breaks into my thoughts. I look down to see I've not touched my tea. It's gone cold. I've been so caught in the net of my own musings that I've paid little attention to our guest. "Gilbert's going now."

I turn to see him standing by the door, running his big hands around the brim of his hat. His jacket's too small for him and he reminds me of a schoolboy grown out of his clothes. He gives a shallow bow to Ma, then turns to me.

"Thank you for coming," says I, forcing my lips into a smile.

He flashes a shy one back at me. "See you again," says he.

Chapter 34

Emily

Mick Donovan is working late tonight. Mr. Greenland has asked him to sort an order for a society wedding. So, while his boss cleans up in the shop, Donovan is plucking a guinea fowl by the light of an oil lamp at the far end of the hanging shed. He sits on a stool surrounded by the carcasses of two dozen or more dead birds—mainly chickens, but there are geese and pheasant, too. They dangle forlornly from hooks on the roof rafters and even in winter are serenaded by the constant drone of the ubiquitous flies. It's quite late and he's only two more birds to pluck, when he hears the door creak open.

"Nearly done, sir," he calls over, thinking Mr. Greenland has come to check on him. One by one, he carries on plucking the fowl's fine feathers to reveal its purple, pitted flesh beneath. He hears footsteps approach, but thinks little of them. When, however, the footsteps come to a halt in front of him and he finally looks up, it's not Mr. Greenland standing before him.

Donovan jumps up in such a hurry. He knocks over his stool. "Mr. Braithwaite!"

"I've come to thank you," says the blacksmith, straight-faced.

Donovan can't quite read his expression, but he's on edge. "I only told the coppers the truth. Your wife asked me. It's what I saw—you leaving the yard way before they found the lass."

Braithwaite leans his stocky frame against the wall. "Aye, lad, but there's good truth and bad truth, ain't there?"

Donovan frowns as he follows the blacksmith's only eye as it travels the length of a dead goose, from beak to feet, a few inches away. He lifts his hand to stroke the snowy white breast feathers. "You see, it's good that you said I couldn't have killed Cath Mylett that night, but bad if you tell anyone about that delivery you did for me." He switches his gaze to Donovan. "Do we understand each other?"

The Irishman's mouth has gone dry; when he tries to answer, he finds his words have shriveled. Instead, he nods his reply.

"Good," says Braithwaite. "Because I'd hate anything bad to happen to you," he tells him, his eye back firmly on the dead goose.

CONSTANCE

Later that evening, Flo and me are alone by the fire and Ma's taken to her bed. I'm quiet and my big sister knows something's amiss.

"Come on, out with it, then," she goads me.

"Out with what?"

"Get it off your chest, will ya? What happened today in Poplar?"

She knows I need to unburden myself. You can't share a bed with a person for nigh on nineteen years and not know them as well as they know themselves. So I spill the beans about what I uncovered. I tell her about following the old woman and how I was jumped on and threatened by the haberdasher, who, it turns out, is in on the whole dirty business.

"So he's in it, and all," she says.

I nod. "The three of them. They're up to their necks in it.

The same ribbon, the selling of the clothes, Miss Louisa's Bertie—"

She breaks me off. "And Cath's Evie?"

"Maybe," I say. I hold back on telling her about my meeting with Adam Braithwaite. She'll need to know soon, but I'm not sure she's ready to face the truth about what happened to Cath yet. I can't take it in myself. I shake my head. "But it's going to be hard to prove what they're up to without getting into that house and seeing for myself."

Flo sucks in a breath between her teeth. "But now, you've blown your chances."

I sigh and reach inside my apron pocket. "Here," I say, waving the letter from Albert Cosgrove in front of her. "I answered an advertisement they placed in the newspaper."

Her eyes widen. "You what?"

"I needed to find out where these baby farmers lived, for Miss Louisa's sake. It's just up in Poplar, in Woodstock Terrace, off the high street." I tuck the letter back into my pocket. "I'm supposed to call tomorrow afternoon. I'd told them I'm near my time and want the baby adopted, but now I can't go." I shake my head as I gaze at the fire. "I've messed up, ain't I?"

I glance up to see Flo's looking at me all strange. "So you reckon these is the same bloody beggars that Cath put little Evie with?"

"I do," I say, feeling the weight lift off my chest as the words leave my mouth. I suppose I should've shared my fears before, only I thought she had enough to deal with, what with Danny and then her being ill.

It turns out I was right. Her face darkens like thunder with the news. "So why haven't you gone to the coppers?" she cries. "That Sergeant Hawkins. Can't he do somefink?"

I fear she'll wake Ma, so I put my forefinger to my lips. "That's why I wanted to go to the house with a cushion under my jacket. I'd pretend I needed them to take my baby, so I could get proof of just what they're up to," I plead.

It's like the thought has only just dawned on her that there's a connection between the death of Cath's daughter and the two babies found murdered recently, too. "So you think they killed little Evie?" The horror is spreading across her face so fast that I'm not sure she'll be able to take my next piece of news.

"I know Cath believed they did. That's why she was trying to blackmail them." I've said it. It's out. I need to tell her the whole truth.

"*What?*"

"I was with Adam Braithwaite."

"The blacksmith? The one they nabbed and then let go?"

"Yes. He told me he reckons he knows who killed Cath."

"Oh, my God!" She lurches forward and grabs both my hands. "Who? For God's sake, Con, who?"

I'm looking deep into her eyes. I'm not sure if she's ready for the truth. "Her brother."

She lets out a strange sound that's halfway between a gasp and a moan. "Will?"

I nod and she lets her hands fall. Her eyes are downcast and despite the warmth of the fire that's flushed her cheeks, she suddenly turns ashen.

I try to explain what happened. "He put her up to blackmailing the baby farmers. They handed over money. She wanted a share of it, but Will wanted more. Seems like he lost his temper and . . ."

Suddenly she bends double in her chair and retches. Her hand flies up to her mouth, but she manages to hold it together. "I can't . . . No!" She's shaking her head. "How could he? His own sister!"

"I'm sorry," I say, standing and bending low to put a comforting arm around her.

"Where is he now?" she asks as tears mist her eyes.

"In America, so the blacksmith thinks. He reckons he stowed away on the first ship to New York."

She slumps back into her chair again and I return to my seat. "So that's why he didn't go to the funeral, or even see his mother." She's shaking her head; then she looks at me directly, thinking of the frail old woman. "The shock would kill her. You mustn't . . ."

"Not a word," I agree.

"It's probably best that no one knows," she says after a moment. She points to the ceiling, where Ma lies abed. "And that means her, too."

Of course, that's what Adam Braithwaite said. But I can't be certain. I think I should go to the police, even though I promised to seal my lips. It's a notion that sits uneasy on my conscience; the secret will fester and the poison will grow and corrupt. But I say nothing, and the silence between Flo and me stagnates as we become sucked down into our own dark thoughts.

That night, I make up my mind. I have to report Mother Delaney and her family to the Cruelty Men, even though I've very little evidence. Now that the haberdasher has recognized me, I won't be able to get inside the house myself. All hope of seeing just how many little souls there are, and how they're kept, has gone. The Cruelty Men are my only hope, but it's not going to be easy.

Chapter 35

Saturday, January 12, 1889

Constance

I break the news to Flo as we eat our breakfast, but my words don't slip down as easy as the gruel. She slams her bowl onto the table.

"And you think the Cruelty Men will listen to you?" she sneers crossly. There's a flash of anger in her eyes.

"I'll show them Bertie's smock that the baby farmers sold," I tell her. I know it'll be hard convincing them that an old dear, whose toothless mouth couldn't melt butter, is a murderer. I can imagine Mother Delaney now, the very model of Christian virtue, offering the inspectors tea and scones from her best china plates. But Flo's having none of it.

"The old witch can say he's growed out of it," she hisses, looking at the little smock. "It's not against the law to sell baby clothes that are too small, you know."

I don't anger easy, but my frustration is welling up by the second. "We've got to do something," I wail.

Upstairs, Ma stirs, so Flo leans over the table and keeps her voice low, but firm. "Think about it, Con. This old woman and her family ain't going to take notice of no gospel grinders when they're willing to kill babies, are they?"

I can tell she's still reeling from learning that Cath was most like killed by her own brother. The world is an even darker and more wicked place than it was this time yesterday, before I told her who strangled our friend. I know how she feels. No one can be trusted any longer. We are on our own, with no one to look out for us. She feels as though her heart has been ripped out of her and trampled underfoot. I understand, because I feel the same.

I push away my bowl of gruel. "I don't know what else to do, Flo. Miss Louisa and her husband will be mad with me if I tell the blues," I protest.

"Like we can't tell them about what really happened to Cath, neither?"

This last remark makes me wonder if she might be changing her ideas over going to the police about Will Mylett. It's time I reminded her of something.

"Remember, the same woman who's taken Bertie Sampson killed little Evie, most like," I say.

Flo's head shoots up. "You think I'd forgotten that?" she snarls. "I may not be well-learned like you, but I ain't stupid."

She puts me back in my box for a moment. I never meant to offend, but I see she's hurting, so I wait awhile before I tell her. I pour her another tea, then say: "If the Cruelty Men find evidence against this baby farmer, then the coppers will have to look into the case."

Slowly she nods as she stirs in the sugar, and I see the thought of revenge take root in her brain and spread into her features. She's stewing just like the leaves in the pot. "They'd 'ave 'er, all right," she says in a hoarse whisper, still stirring her tea. "And then she'd swing."

It's like someone needs to suffer for Cath's death. If it can't be her brother, then it should be the woman who Cath was convinced killed her baby, and perhaps even Bertie Sampson. Flo frightens me when she's like this, but before I can say anything to soothe her, Ma appears at the foot of the stairs, wheezing like a steam train.

"Where you off to today, gals?" she asks cheerily.

Flo and me swap guilty looks. "I'm going to stay around Whitechapel today, Ma," I reply. "I've got a couple of errands to run." I'm relieved when she doesn't ask me what sort.

Flo tells her she's off to St. Paul's. "There's some service on," she says. "There'll be a lot of toffs and big wigs." She rubs her fingers against her thumb, picturing rich pickings.

Ma sits down and I pour her tea from the pot. "Just as long as you both take care, me darlin's," she says, reaching for the milk.

"We will," we both reply at exactly the same time.

EMILY

As you've probably already guessed, Constance does not stay in Whitechapel today, but hurries to the office of the London Society for the Protection of Cruelty to Children in elegant Bloomsbury. It's a busy time of year for the worthy men and women who toil for this august body. In this inclement winter weather, so many infants are smothered when they share a bed with their siblings and parents, especially on a Friday or Saturday night when liquor is consumed. Add to this increasing toll the more straightforward cases of cruelty: the apprentice kept in a coal cellar, the young daughter pregnant by her predatory father, and the little boy beaten to within an inch of his life by his drunken mother. Surely, you must agree that the well-meaning members of this society have more than enough to occupy them. Constance intends to add to their work.

CONSTANCE

"I've come about a stolen baby, sir," I say when I'm finally shown into an office to see someone in charge. I've been passed from pillar to post until now, and I'm in no mood to be moved on again.

A short, dapper man, with wings of gray hair and a frock coat that's too large for him, is sizing me up. I've seen him before; in the congregation at St. Jude's, perhaps? I think I know him from church.

He squints at me. "Your face is familiar, Miss . . ."

"Piper," I say. "Constance Piper." He smiles, then looks at the brown paper parcel with Bertie's smock in it, which I'm clutching under my arm. "And you say someone has stolen a baby. I'm assuming it's not yours, *Miss* Piper." He says "Miss" all hard, like he hopes I've not had a child out of wedlock. The gentleman, Mr. Treadway, as I recall, asks me to take a seat.

I don't know why, but I keep my voice low. "I'm here to report someone who's a baby farmer, sir."

His expression suddenly changes and he shakes his head. "You know there's nothing illegal about such an operation, although it has to be licensed, of course."

I'm worried he's trying to get rid of me. "Yes, I know," I reply. Perhaps he thinks me cheeky, but I don't care. I need someone to take me serious. "The mother wants her baby back, but he's gone missing," I tell him. I think I've got his attention. "He's the son of a gentleman and he may have been kidnapped," I say.

I'm in a big office and from the walls the framed faces of children stare down at me. They're all thin and mangy. Some are naked; others are plain filthy. The sight sickens me, but it makes me more resolved.

Mr. Treadway leans toward me, dips his quill nib into his ink pot, and says: "So, Miss Piper, I will need details."

As much as I want to tell him about the murders of the babies in the market and at Bow Creek, I know he'll say they're police matters, so I concentrate on telling him Bertie's sad tale. Without mentioning his parents' names, I do say they are from the quality, knowing that will make a difference. Toward the end of my account, I place the parcel on the desk and open it up to show the gentleman the little smock with the embroidered initials. He notes down the letters, *RLF.*

When I've finished my sad account, Mr. Treadway puts down his quill and shakes his head. "This is a most distressing state of affairs, Miss Piper." But then he frowns. "However, may I ask why the parents are not making inquiries themselves?"

I knew he would stick his oar in, so I try to explain as best I can. "It's a delicate situation, sir. I am acting as their agent, as they wish to remain anonymous for the time being. The scandal—"

"Of course." He breaks me off. Scandal is to the quality, what hunger is to us poor—a thing feared before all else. I think him very helpful and ready to act, until he tells me: "We can send someone round next week."

My heart sinks. "*Next week?*" I repeat. "Not today, or tomorrow?"

Mr. Treadway shakes his gray head, making his wings flap. "This is one of dozens of requests we receive each month and every case has to be investigated. Of course, because it involves genteel persons, discretion will be our watchword, but please assure them that if there is any wrongdoing, then this woman"—he glances down at his notes—"this Mother Delaney, will be chastised."

"*Chastised?*" I blurt. It's like she's been naughty in school and needs a rap on the knuckles to keep her in line, not a kidnapper, or worse.

He offers me a fatherly smile and pushes the notebook away from him. "I can assure you, Miss Piper, most often it is enough for such people to see the error of their ways."

As I walk back down the stairs and out onto the street, I'm feeling more dejected than ever, like I've run up a blind alley. If the Cruelty Men don't act soon to stop Mother Delaney, and if Will Mylett has gone to America, it means they've both got away with murder.

It seems there's no justice in this world. I really should tell the police about Bertie, but I can't go behind Miss Louisa's back, can I? If the story got into the newspapers, her reputation would be torn to shreds. As for Sergeant Hawkins, he's up to his eyes in it with Jack. I've nowhere to turn. Miss Tindall, what must I do?

CHAPTER 36

EMILY

As much as I want to help dear Constance, I am needed urgently elsewhere. I am called upon to watch over Florence. She is a deeply troubled young woman; and unbeknownst to anyone else, she has traveled to Poplar. There she grasps the knocker on the door of Number 9, Woodstock Terrace, and raps three times. She stands back and waits. There is no reply. She knocks again, only louder this time. Still no reply. She spies a bell. She rings that, too, but in vain.

Anger is rising inside her. On her journey here, she had rehearsed just what she would do. At first, she would play the game; and, as Constance had intended, she would pose as a pregnant young woman with an unborn infant to offer for adoption. The trouble is, she doubts her own capacity to remain calm. She accepts she's not like Constance. Her tongue's made of pig iron, not silver, and just how long she can keep up a charade is anyone's guess. Even she worries that she is like a powder keg. Her emotions lurch from joy to rage in the blink of an eyelid.

Her rapping is met with more silence. That is when her wrath boils over. Convinced there must be someone at home, she be-

gins to hammer on the door, and her hammering rouses a maid in the adjoining house. The girl lifts the sash window and sticks out her head. She's obviously decided from Florence's dress and demeanor that she isn't a desirable sort, so she makes no attempt to stand on ceremony.

"You won't find no one in," she yells.

Florence takes a step back and regards the irritable maid.

"Do ya know when they'll be back?" There's no need for her to mind her manners.

The maid shakes her head and lets out a brittle laugh. "Don't reckon as they'll be coming back."

Florence's heart leaps in her chest. "What do ya mean?"

The maid is sanguine. "A carriage came for all their belongings, night before last. Reckon they've done a runner."

From somewhere inside the next-door house, a disembodied voice can be heard calling, "Daisy? Daisy, is that you shouting?"

The maid's head withdraws and the window is promptly shut.

Florence is left bereft on the doorstep, trying to take in what she has just heard. Her breathing suddenly starts to become labored as she feels the panic rise. She balls her fists and begins to hammer on the door again, even though she knows it's a futile gesture.

"You bastards!" she shouts. "You bleedin' bastards!" She wheels round and storms down the steps, then turns again to look up at the front door. "Curse you. Curse you!" she screams through scalding tears. "Murderers!"

Up and down the street, faces appear at windows. A sash is lifted. "Clear off," shouts an angry elderly man.

A front door opens and a woman wielding a broom shakes it threateningly. "Get away with ya!"

Florence's shouts and curses suddenly subside and give way to a terrible rasping sob that seems to mark time with each step she takes along the street. She's thinking of Cath and how she must've felt when her little Evie died. Glancing down at her skirt, she clutches at her waistband, as if to make sure that what is inside her is safe.

She knows her own baby is probably only the size of a walnut, and yet she's already got feelings for it. She's no longer sad that the pennyroyal didn't work. All around it, she can feel her innards roiling and churning in anguish, and yet she can imagine this tiny thing, this little being, tucked up cozily on its own little island, safe from the outside world's iniquity.

"Cath," she mouths silently as she stops for a moment to catch her breath. She looks about her. Up ahead lies Poplar High Street. Clarke's Yard can't be far away. She'd like to pay her respects. The thought of seeing where her friend was slain has been too much for her before, but she knows she cannot possibly plummet much lower than she's feeling at the moment. Perhaps seeing where she was felled might even bring her some comfort, some closure. She thinks the yard won't be that hard to find. With a new resolve, she blows her nose with a stolen handkerchief and sets off.

By now, the light is fading, but Florence is sure that if she keeps to the main road, she'll come to the yard. Past some ramshackle stalls she trudges, and carries on for a few more paces until, across the street, she sees an alleyway. There's no sign at its entrance, but she thinks she'll take a look, anyway. She crosses the road and ventures down the passage that lies between two boarded-up shops. Up ahead, she can hear the clank of metal on metal, so it's clear there are workmen about. It's safe enough, isn't it? *I know what she's thinking. She's trying to convince herself that Jack won't strike when there are others so close by. But then the doubts crowd in.*

Lifting up her skirts, she teeters round a large pothole and negotiates a pile of splintered wood that's been dumped against a wall. She can see the alley narrows, although there is light at the end of it. Still, the fear nibbles at her thoughts. Perhaps she should turn around and head back to the high street. Yes, she should. After all, she's got her baby to consider, too. And so she wheels round to face the entrance. At the same moment, in front of her, she sees something move in the shadows. It's a man. She must've passed him and not noticed him before. A knot of fear grips her throat. He's coming toward her. She backs away, but he starts to cough out an odd laugh as he draws closer.

"Don't tell me you came down 'ere to take in the scenery, your ladyship." His voice is gruff and husky and he wears a peaked cap, so that his eyes are hidden. He makes an exaggerated bow and flourishes his hand, so that his palm comes to rest on his breast. On this hand, Florence can see clearly the inked outline of a naked woman. Her eyes widen and he barks out another laugh.

"Recognize me now, don't ya?" he smirks.

Florence swallows hard. "Keep away from me," she tells him, trying to sidestep. "Keep away!" But he jerks in front of her and grabs her by the arm. He brings his face close to hers. "Your friend never made such a fuss," he growls into her ear.

"My friend?" she bleats.

He pulls her arm back behind her waist. "The one you was with in the George before Christmas."

Cath, *she thinks.* He killed her and now he's going to kill me. *Fear crawls across her skin like a thousand spiders. In a moment, she knows she'll feel his hands at her throat, and he'll push his thumbs against her windpipe and she'll be fighting for breath. He'll show no mercy, pressing harder and harder until there'll be nothing but darkness and she'll fall. Just like Catherine. Then she remembers her baby. She must not give in, for the child's sake. A great surge of energy floods her body.*

"No!" she screams, and with all her might, she lunges back and breaks free of the brute's grasp. Wasting not a second, she skirts around the pothole and down the alley, but her freedom is short-lived. He's back behind her, clawing at her shoulders, but this time she manages to dive forward. With her free hand, she

grabs a broken plank. Brandishing it above her own head, she flails blindly behind her until it jars in her hand. She's hit something hard and the tugging stops. He reels back. She spins round to see him right himself; and this time, he lurches toward her with a clenched fist that slams into her belly. His knuckles rob her of her breath and she doubles over. Pain shoots through her like a red-hot poker. He sees her winded, so he strikes again. She feels his hands about her throat once more. There's no fight left in her. This is it.

"What goes on?" A voice comes loud and clear. There's someone calling from the entrance to the passage.

Florence feels the brute's hands slacken suddenly. He pivots and sprints the other way. There's no time to lose. She recovers herself and, despite her pain, staggers out of the passage, not daring to look behind. She pauses only to catch her ragged breath once she has reached the safety of the high street. Her savior, a balding shopkeeper, stands anxiously waiting.

"You all right, love?" he asks as Florence doubles up, gasping for air. After a moment, she manages to straighten herself. Her nerves are like bedsprings, flexing all over her body.

"Yes," she says. "Thank you," she mumbles.

"Can't be too careful, with Jack and all at the moment," the shopkeeper warns, as if she didn't know. She also knows that she has just been attacked by Cath's killer. She needs to tell the police, but first she has to find refuge and a sympathetic ear. "I'm looking for Clarke's Yard," she tells the shopkeeper. "It's near, ain't it?"

"Up yonder," he says, pointing across the road to the mouth of another passageway.

"I'm much obliged," Florence pants with a nod. She starts back across the street.

"Take care now!" the shopkeeper calls after her. But Florence doesn't hear him. She's already halfway over the road and the pain is growing with each step she takes.

Constance

I know what I heard. The blacksmith told me William Mylett jumped a ship to New York the day after he killed Cath. He seemed quite sure of himself, but I don't know how he can be. I've been so deep in thought since I started back home from the Cruelty Men's office, I've not been paying attention to where I'm heading. I find myself stepping off the pavement on Commercial Street and into the path of a cart.

My head jerks up to see a fist balled and raised at me. "Will you mind where you're bleedin' going?" shouts the driver as he brushes past me, missing me by one or two inches. His rant wakes me up. I look about me. I'm a couple of turnings away from Pelham Street. I'll go and pay a visit on old Mrs. Mylett, to see if she might have any idea about where her wayward son may be. I'll still be subtle, mind. I can't go in there with a sledgehammer if I'm going to keep the truth from hurting her. But I need to track him down.

In less than two minutes, I've got the house in my sights. I'm walking toward it, when I see the door open and a man coming out. I stop and turn away, but then turn back to see it's someone I know. Mick Donovan, the Irish creep. He pulls his cap down and lifts his collar, but it's him, all right. I'd recognize that walk of his anywhere. But what business would he have with Mrs. Mylett?

I wait awhile before I knock. Fanny answers the door, but she greets me with a flinty face. I thought she'd manage a smile, but she's as cold as Christmas toward me. Her features are all pinched and sour, like she's been sucking sherbet.

"Yes?" She greets me in such a surly manner that I think perhaps she hasn't recognized me.

"It's Constance. Constance Piper," I tell her with a smile. "Cath's friend."

She leans against the doorjamb, one hand on the lintel, blocking the entrance. "I know who you are," she replies. "If it's Mrs. Mylett you're after, she's not here." She keeps her voice low, but it's no use. The old dear has heard her and calls through.

"Who's that, Fanny?" she asks.

Fanny rolls her eyes and is mightily annoyed that she's been found out. I almost think she's about to lie to her aunt and tell her I'm a hawker or some such. She shoots me the blackest of looks, but then she flings open the door. "I s'pose you'd best come in, then, but don't be long. She's tired," she tells me grudgingly.

Fanny leads me into the front room, but I'm quite shocked by what I find. Mrs. Mylett is slumped in an armchair, swathed in blankets. Her hair has broken loose from her bun; and her face is so gaunt, you could cut butter with her cheekbones.

Fanny can see the shock on my face as she hovers by the door. "'Afternoon, Mrs. Mylett," I say. "How are you doing?"

The old woman manages a smile when she sees me, but shakes her head. She lifts a forlorn hand, her fingers all crabby and stiff, but I can tell she's as weak as small beer. "I'm managing, thanks to Fanny," she mumbles, glancing at the door. "But I've lost my appetite, my dear."

She smiles, but she seems not to have the strength to shake her tousled head. I glance across at Fanny.

"Can't you see she's had enough?" she snarls. She's angry with me for disturbing the old lady. I think I've seen all I need. I can tell why I wasn't welcome.

I bend low. "I'll ask Ma to call round," I tell her, patting her icy hand.

"Don't trouble yourself," comes Fanny's snipe. "She don't need no visitors, just peace and quiet."

I straighten myself and walk toward where Fanny stands, all sullen with her arms crossed, by the front door. But it's what I see on the floor behind her that makes me take notice. There's a pair of dirty men's boots by the skirting. There's no mistaking she's got male company. She's seen my look worm its way to the hobnails and her face hardens. She's clocked I know there's a man in the house. I've nothing to lose, so I ask her.

"Still no sign of Will?" I say, all cheeky, tilting my head at her.

My question riles her and she unfolds her arms and comes for me.

"You're nothing but a mischief maker, you," she hisses, pointing her finger at me and narrowing her eyes. "You'd best be getting out, if you know what's good for you." She flings her arm toward the front door. I think she'll explode with rage in front of my eyes. Instead, she reaches across, grabs the door handle, and almost bundles me out the open door. "And don't you come back here again!" she shouts after me, as I move sharpish into the street.

She needn't worry. I won't be visiting in a hurry. But I think Sergeant Hawkins ought to.

Shocked by what I've just uncovered, I start to make my way home. Will Mylett may be Fanny's cousin, but he's also his sister's killer and he's being sheltered. I need to warn Adam Braithwaite. He already knows too much. He's in real danger. I have to get to Clarke's Yard to raise the alarm before Will Mylett silences him for good.

Emily

The door shut on her unwelcome visitor, Fanny returns to the front room. She's worried, but she's not sure what to do, so she decides to plump up her aunt's pillows.

"She'll not trouble you again," she tells the old woman, smoothing her blanket. "The neck of it, calling round here, waltzing in like she owns the place."

Margaret Mylett isn't, however, paying attention to her tetchy niece. She's too occupied with her own troubles. From out of the blue, she announces: "I know he's upstairs."

Fanny stops fussing with the blanket. "Beg pardon, Auntie?" she says, feigning a smile.

"I hears 'im," mumbles the old woman, lifting her eyes toward the ceiling. It's been months since she could manage the stairs. Her arthritic hips put paid to that, but she's adamant. "I may forget things, but I'm not deaf. I know he's up there. I hears 'im with his big boots."

Fanny's eyes widen, but she tries to stay calm. "You're mistaken, Aunt Maggie. There's rustling, for sure, on account of the mice, but no one else. Just you and me."

The old woman is unconvinced, or is it perhaps that she hasn't understood a word her niece has said. Either way, she shakes her head.

"Why can't I see him?" she whines. "It's because he don't trust me, ain't it?" Her face suddenly crumples into a scowl. She thought she could rely on Will, but he's turned out to be more like his father, a fly-by-night, than she'd originally supposed. "Whatever he's done, I'm still his mum, and if you can't trust your own mother, then there's no hope left in this world." The old woman begins to weep.

CONSTANCE

Darkness is closing in by the time I reach home. Ma's got a candle burning in the window. I'll just reassure her that I'm safe before I set off for Poplar to see Adam Braithwaite. I'm counting on Flo coming with me. I find Ma in the kitchen, slicing a loaf.

"Flo not back?" I ask. I don't want to go to Clarke's Yard alone.

Ma puts down the knife. "No," she replies, like she's surprised at my asking. "She told me she was going to meet you."

I frown. "I ain't . . . ," I start to say, and then I trail off as I remember the conversation Flo and me had last night, about me not being able to visit Mother Delaney's house. The idea suddenly blooms inside my brain, like spilt ink on blotting paper. "Oh, my God!" I cry.

"What is it, love?" Ma frets. "Tell me, Con?"

I feel my stomach start to knot as I think of Flo taking on Mother Delaney single-handedly. "I know where she's gone!" I cry.

Emily

The men who work in Clarke's Yard are already beginning to pack up for the day. It's almost dark as Florence edges her way along the dank passage toward the workshops that stand lopsidedly against each other. Her heart has steadied a little, and the fear is subsiding, but the pain in her belly is worsening. She's no idea how she'll make it back to Whitechapel alone. The thought of the long walk terrifies her. That's another reason why she's seeking out this Adam Braithwaite, the blacksmith who was Catherine's man. He'll help her, she's sure of that.

A brazier offers a little light in the courtyard and some of the men carry lanterns as they file out. One barges against her shoulder as he passes. Already on edge, she expels a cry. The laborer simply peers at her in the semidarkness, then laughs.

"Lookin' for business, love?" he gibes, and his friend roars with laughter.

Florence bites her lip. She feels like crying, but she's made of sterner stuff. She presses on, squinting into the gloom. Ahead of her in the blackness, she can make out a red glow. She thinks it must be the forge. She quickens her pace toward it.

"Hello," she calls nervously, ducking down below a beam at the entrance. The heat from the furnace makes the forge warm, but the fire's long gone out. Yet there's an odd smell. She sniffs. It reminds her of Greenland's, when they singe the fowls' feathers to dress them.

It seems there's no one about and her heart sinks. Perhaps the blacksmith has left for the day. She may even have passed him on his way out. As her eyes adjust to the gloomy light, all the paraphernalia of a farrier is before her. From a beam on the roof, there hangs an intimidating array of tools that, if she didn't know better, she'd think were instruments of torture. There are chains and tongs and long-handled pincers that could rip out a tooth or tear off a finger, just as soon as they could remove a nail from a horseshoe.

"Mr. Braithwaite," she calls, only a little louder this time. There's no one here. She ventures farther into the workshop. She thinks she can make out another door in the wall. Gingerly she steps toward it, just in case he's working out the back. It's many a long year since she's prayed, but she's praying now. She mumbles under her breath, "Where are you? Please be here." She's hoping that he'll soon emerge and take care of her. Constance said he seemed a caring man. He'll look after her and protect her from the brute with the tattoo. He may even see her safely back to Whitechapel.

She's edging forward, when suddenly another terrible pain shoots through her, cutting her in half. It takes a few seconds to pass. Just as soon as it does, she retches and her whole body convulses. As she tries to straighten herself, she realizes she's just by the back door. She moves toward it. It's slightly ajar, and her heart misses a beat. If he is there, then she is saved. Supporting herself on the workbench, she steps forward to reach for the handle. As she does so, she feels her right foot collide with something on the ground. Looking down, she sees the body of a man . . . a man without a head.

In the yard, the few men who remain are alerted by a scream that shreds the air. The next second, a distressed young woman stumbles from out of the forge. She's whirling round in a circle as if she's looking for someone, anyone, to rescue her from a nightmare.

"Someone. Please! No!"

"What's up, my gal?" asks an old cooper hobbling over to her. He stretches out an arm, but she suddenly bends double again. The pain lances into her womb. She staggers toward the entrance, one arm clutching her belly, the other groping for the wall.

"You ill?" asks the cooper. He turns and calls to his workmates. "Over 'ere. Bring a light!" He stays with her as she tries to steady herself, leaning against a gatepost for support.

An apprentice sprints up with a lantern and holds it up to Florence's face. He realizes that it's creased in agony. Her whole body is heaving.

"Best call a doc!" yells the cooper.

Florence screams again and suddenly her torment turns to terror as she looks down to the ground. "No!" she cries. "No!" The lad with the lantern follows her gaze and lowers the light to reveal a rivulet of blood running from beneath her skirts. At the sight, Florence's eyes roll back into her head and she slides down the side of the wall.

"Oh, God!" cries the apprentice in panic. "Is she dead?"

The cooper hollers for more help. "Police! Call the police!"

Constance

There's a knock at the door. My heart jumps. It can't be Flo. She has her own key.

"Never fear, ladies." For once, I'm glad to hear Mr. B's voice.

"You seen Flo?" I ask him, flinging wide the door.

He tenses and flicks a look at Ma, who's by my side, her face all puckered with worry. "What's up? She in trouble?"

"She could be," says I. "She went up to Poplar and should've been home a while back."

"Poplar?" he says sharpish. "But that's where . . ." He can see I'm fretting, even though he doesn't know the real reason why.

"Oh, Harold, she's not been well lately. What if . . ." Ma dissolves into tears.

Mr. B puts his arm around her. "Calm yourself, Patience." I can see he's thinking to himself as Ma weeps. A moment later, he knows what to do. "We'll get the committee lads on the case," he says, clicking his fingers. "We'll have her back safe in no time," he tells Ma.

EMILY

Up in Poplar, the word is out. Windows are thrown open. Heads appear from upper floors. Someone spots two flaming torches progressing along the high street. Something's afoot. People start to gather. In the distance, they hear two blasts, then two more, closer this time. The police arrive at the scene to find a young woman whose blood is pooling around her.

"Keep back!" cries a constable, trying to control the growing crowd. His colleague has gone to see what's amiss. "Keep back!" he shouts again. Another officer, just arrived, wields his truncheon threateningly, but it's too late. One of the Whitechapel lads who's been mustered by Mr. Bartleby—one with a torch—careens down the alley.

Panic breaks out and the police cordon crumples. The crowd surges forward, spilling into the alley. Once again, the cry that's become so familiar in Whitechapel goes up in Poplar: "Murder! Murder!"

CONSTANCE

"Let me through! Let me through!" I scream.

We've made it to Poplar in good time. Thanks to Mr. B's quick thinking, he managed to marshal a few lads from the Vigilance Committee. Gilbert Johns is one of them and now I feel his heavy hand on my shoulder, trying to calm me, but it's no use. I've the strength of a thousand men as I barge my way past a copper.

"Get back!" yells another policeman. "Get back!" Someone knocks off his helmet.

"I need to see. I need to see. My sister . . . !" I'm screaming like a madwoman.

Squeezing through a gap, I see a handful of men gathered around something by the wall. More men are milling outside the forge.

"Please," I yell, tugging at sleeves. "Please, let me see. My sister . . ." One of the blokes spins round and clocking the state I'm in, he steps to the side. It's then that I see her slumped against the wall, her white stockings turned scarlet by her own blood.

"Flo!" I scream, throwing myself at her. "Flo! She's not dead. Tell me she's not dead!" Crouching low, I put my shaking hand up to her neck. By the light of the copper's lantern, I can see the blue bruises blooming on her milk-white skin. At first, God help me, I think she's been strangled. I feel for a pulse. There is nothing. My hand drifts to Flo's parted lips—there is no breath—then I go back to her neck, and there, under my trembling fingertips, I sense a slow, faint thud like a summer raindrop falling to the ground. She's still alive.

"Clear the way. Clear the way!" I glance up to see a copper waving at two ambulance men with a stretcher. "Move away!"

I'm barely able to breathe as they approach. "She's alive!" I scream. One of the men bends low and feels Flo's neck. He pauses for a moment, then nods to the other before he, too, utters the sweet words.

"She's alive!"

I cradle Flo's head in my arms until the ambulance men are ready to lift her. They move quickly, but carefully: one slipping his arms under hers, while the other takes her legs and together they lower her onto the stretcher. I reach for her hand. It's stone cold. I know she's senseless, but still I lean to her ear and tell her: "I'm here, my love. It's going to be all right, Flo. I'm here."

EMILY

It will be all right. For the moment at least. Florence will be taken care of and her life saved, and for that, she has, in part, to thank her sister. I was with them both tonight. I know that as soon as she saw Florence lying senseless, the life draining away from her as the blood spread on the ground, Constance wanted to die with her. Panic had seized hold of her and her thoughts were frantically scrambling inside her head.

It was then that I made myself known to her. I told her that her beloved Florence wasn't dead; there was still breath in her body. After her initial horror subsided, she calmed herself. She became aware of my presence, there, in the yard, watching over her. She understood I would take care of everything.

Constance held her sister's hand in the ambulance as they wended their way through murky streets to the Poplar Infirmary, not half a mile away. Florence opened her eyes when they were wheeling her into the examination room, and Constance stroked her head and told her she was safe.

We shall rejoin her now as she waits anxiously for news of her sister. Mr. Bartleby is to return to Whitechapel to fetch the girls' mother. Gilbert Johns offers to remain at the infirmary. He's been kind to Constance, even trying to put his arm around her as they wheeled Florence into the hospital, but she shrugged him off. She knows she is weak at the moment and she doesn't want him to take advantage of the fact. Not now. It's been agreed he should also leave.

CONSTANCE

The corridor is long and drafty and filled with the chatter of nurses and the sound of coughing. It smells of carbolic, too. I'm watching Mr. B and Gilbert disappear through the door, and then, from out of a side passage, I spot two men. One's a copper and the other, I realize when he's only a few yards away, is Sergeant Hawkins. It's all I can do to keep myself from leaping up and running toward him. I'm that relieved to see him, but it's not a mutual feeling, I can tell.

"Miss Piper." He raises his hat most formally. "Your sister—"

I break him off. "She's being cared for. Pray God she'll recover."

"Indeed. My officers have notified me about events in Clarke's Yard, but I'm afraid I do hope you understand that I'll need to question Miss Florence when she is stronger." He glares at his constable, who beats a sharpish retreat, leaving us alone in the corridor. "Shall we?" he says, gesturing ahead of him, like he wants us to take a Sunday afternoon promenade. Only I can tell this isn't a social visit. He's looking very serious.

We've just taken a couple of paces down the corridor in silence when, from out of nowhere, he says: "The dead man."

I stop in my tracks. He stops, too. *"The dead man?"* I repeat. My look tells him I'm not sure what he's on about.

"Ah," he grunts. "You haven't been told?"

"Told what?"

There's a couple of nurses standing next to a trolley nearby. It's clear he doesn't want our conversation to be overheard. He moves on and I follow. "A man's body was found in the blacksmith's workshop, the same time as your sister."

My mind flashes back to the mayhem in the yard. I was so caught up in helping Flo that I'd no notion of what was going on around me.

"I . . . I didn't know. . . . Who?" Just as the question leaves my lips, I think of the blacksmith. I pray it's not him.

Detective Sergeant Hawkins inhales deeply. "The body is not yet identified, but at the moment, we believe it to be Adam Braithwaite."

I gasp and stop in my tracks. "Oh, God!" My fears for him, it turns out, were real, and now it's too late to save him.

Seeing my face, the sergeant looks sympathetic. "I'm sorry. The news must come as a shock."

I picture the smithy and hear his gritty voice. "I was going to warn him," I mutter.

"Warn him? About what?" Sergeant Hawkins is on his mettle. "Is there something you haven't told me, Miss Piper?"

"How? How was he killed?"

He thinks for a moment. I know he's going to say something that he supposes will shock me, and it does. "This is why we can't yet be sure that it is Mr. Braithwaite." He works his jaw. "I fear the dead man had been decapitated." I gasp again. "His head was found in the furnace."

I think he half expects me to swoon. But I don't. Just because I can put on a lady's manners when I want to, it doesn't mean I've gone all soft. There's more to me than frilled petticoats and powder puffs.

The sergeant narrows his eyes at me. "You think you might know who did this?"

"Perhaps," I reply. "That's why I was about to go to Clarke's Yard myself."

"To warn him, you said. About what?"

"Not *what. Who*, Sergeant. About Will Mylett."

One of his brows shoots up. "Catherine's brother?"

"Yes."

Sergeant Hawkins looks at me all wary. I can see his mind's working away as he carries on walking, his hands clasped behind his back. "Can you think why Miss Florence might have been in Clarke's Yard?"

For a moment, he's taken me aback. I get the feeling he thinks my sister might've been up to no good. Flo can be fiery at times—he's seen that for himself when she had a fit at him down at the station—but she's no murderer. The only reason I can imagine is to lay flowers where Cath fell. I know it sounds silly, but I remember she once said that's what she wanted to do: to see the place where her best friend died. I tell him so, but even as I say it, the excuse sounds lame. His eyes tell me he knows that I'm hiding the real reason why I think Flo went to Poplar.

"Might it have anything to do with that baby farmer of yours in the vicinity?" he asks.

For the second time in as many minutes, I'm stunned. "You seem to know a lot about Flo's comings and goings, if I may say so, Sergeant Hawkins." I don't care if I sound full of myself. Now I think it's me who deserves some answers.

He nods as if agreeing he should be a little more forthcoming. "Some residents called a constable earlier to complain about a young woman behaving oddly. She was banging on a door and creating a disturbance."

"Not Woodstock Terrace!" I blurt out. I'm suddenly picturing Flo hammering on Number 9's front door, cursing and turning the air blue with her foul mouth and her accusations. All the same, I've just broken my own cover and I suddenly feel as though I need to run to safety.

It's Sergeant Hawkins who stops this time. He looks deep into my eyes, pinning me with his gaze. "Perhaps you should tell me everything you know, Miss Piper?"

CHAPTER 37

EMILY

So that is exactly what Constance does. Together with Detective Sergeant Hawkins, she finds a quiet seat in an alcove, set away from the busy hospital wards and clattering trolleys, and she tells him everything. She discloses what Adam Braithwaite told her (Will Mylett killed his own sister over money) and that it was supposed he'd fled abroad. Now, it seems, he has not.

She also recounts the sorry tale of Louisa Fortune's missing baby—although she is careful to mention no names—and she informs him about the woman she knows to be a baby farmer, who she fears is also a murderer.

For several minutes, Detective Sergeant Hawkins listens attentively, although he has not taken out his notebook. He is hearing what Constance has to say without wishing to intimidate her, albeit he is starting to understand that she is one not easily intimidated. Now and again, he nods, or interjects with an "I see" or a "Can you clarify?" But just when Constance has told all there is to tell about Mother Delaney and her daughter and son-in-law, the detective is still left puzzled.

"But this still doesn't explain why your sister was with Adam Braithwaite," he puts to her.

I watch Constance bristle with indignation on Florence's behalf. She can't believe her sister may be under suspicion. "I'm sure Flo will give you a perfectly good explanation, just as soon as she is strong enough, Sergeant Hawkins," she tells him.

CONSTANCE

Someone calls my name. I look up to see a nurse standing close by. "You may see your sister now." Sergeant Hawkins and me are both on our feet like a shot. "Follow me."

So I leave the detective and hurry to the ward where they've put Flo. There's a curtain round her bed to make it more private. The surgeon, a tall, lean man with jam jar glasses, stands taking her pulse. He's looking serious.

"Your sister, yes?"

I nod. "She's going to be all right?"

"She's lost a lot of blood, but she should pull through." He pushes his glasses up his nose. "However, I fear she's lost the baby," he says in a low voice.

"Oh" is all I manage.

"Did you know?" He peers over his spectacle rims.

Slowly I shake my head, even though I did. I've known since Miss Louisa asked me to hold a séance and the pinprick of light settled on Flo's head. Granted, it was only for a second, and it could've been explained away as the light from the copper's lantern, but I knew. In that moment, I saw she was carrying a child inside her, and the odd things she'd done since now made sense to me: the sickness, the swing of her moods, and her pining after that slimy creep Danny were pieces in a puzzle that suddenly all fitted. It's why she was so keen to see the baby farmers brought to justice, too. She wasn't just angry for Cath's baby Evie, she was angry for her own unborn child, as well.

"You'll break it to her?" he asks me.

"Yes," I say.

"She may even thank you," he adds, glancing back at Flo.

"*Thank me?*" I repeat, all confused.

"There's no ring on her finger," says he with a smirk.

Once the surgeon's gone, I settle myself in the chair by her bed. I'm angry and on edge, but I want to be the first person Flo sees when she opens her peepers. It's almost midnight when she does. I watch as her lids flicker and she moans a little. Quickly I pour some water into a tin mug and hold it to her lips. She raises her head to sip it, then slumps back. Her eyes widen and she stares at the ceiling.

"Where . . . ?"

"You're in Poplar Infirmary, my love," I tell her, clutching her hand.

The thought seems to comfort her; and for a moment, she is calm, but her peace is short-lived. I can see she is remembering. It's like the past is flashing before her eyes and she cries out. "No!" she screams as her head jerks up and she grasps hold of my hand.

I lay my free hand on her shoulder and press down gently. "It's all right. No one is going to harm you, darling," I assure her, but there's still fear in her eyes.

Suddenly her breathing comes in short pants, like she's reliving something terrible. "He tried to kill me," she murmurs, clutching hold of my arm.

I don't understand. "Who did?"

"The man with the tattoo." She points to her hand.

It takes me only a second to realize what she's talking about. "The man with the tattoo. The one in the George?"

"He killed Cath."

"What?! How do y . . . ?"

"He told me," she groans. "He grabbed me in an alley, and when I tried to get away, he said, 'Your friend didn't make a fuss,' and then he put his hands round my neck and . . ." Her eyes begin to brim and I worry she'll do herself more harm.

"Don't talk now, my darling," I whisper, trying to soothe her. I stroke her head, but she's still flighty.

"That's why I went to Clarke's Yard," she sobs. "I knew it was nearby. I had to tell someone, and I knew Adam Braithwaite was a good man. I called and I called, and then I saw . . . !" Her voice splits into a faint scream at the recollection of what she stumbled upon.

So that was the reason she was in the yard—she was fleeing from the lech with the tattoo. She was seeking protection from Adam Braithwaite. A thought shoots into my mind. Perhaps this man, her attacker, had been to the forge before her. Perhaps he had killed not only Cath, but Adam Braithwaite, too. I digest the notion for a moment. It makes perfect sense. I need to tell Sergeant Hawkins, and quick, before this tattooed fiend gets his filthy hands round someone else's neck.

CHAPTER 38

Monday, January 14, 1889

EMILY

Sir William Sampson, the owner of Number 9, Woodstock Terrace, has wasted no time moving in new tenants to his Poplar property. The Webleys arrived early this morning, and while Mr. Webley has gone to work, his wife has been left to unpack their belongings and mind their children. They are a respectable family. Father is a warehouse supervisor at the nearby docks. Mother is an active member of the Temperance Movement, and their three offspring are all under the age of eleven.

They also have a dog, a fox terrier, and the children are delighted to discover their new house has a small patch of garden at the rear. It is a very narrow area, mainly laid to lawn, but there are shrubs at the far end: laurel and lilac. The previous occupants obviously had no interest in the garden's upkeep, as the grass was left to grow and the weeds were free to flourish.

Mrs. Webley is, however, a keen gardener, and once the men have unloaded their trunks and boxes—the house is already furnished—she is keen to inspect her new domain. She has dressed her children in their coats and, despite the cold, has ushered them outside into their new garden. The dog, which goes by the name of Patch, accompanies them.

For a few minutes, the terrier is content to play fetch with the children, while Mrs. Webley surveys the briars in the shrubbery. But then his attention is caught by something else. His ears prick up and he sniffs the air before bounding toward the laurels. He begins to bark; then he begins to dig, much to the delight of the children. His front paws scrabble away at the earth beneath the thick foliage close to where Mrs. Webley has been standing, and it's not long before clumps of soil are being flung into the air.

"Patch, what on earth have you found?" asks Mrs. Webley, shaking her head disapprovingly, but with a wide grin on her face. She carries on inspecting some shriveled roses.

By now, the children have joined her: Susan, aged ten, Jonathan, eight, and Becky, six. They think it most amusing to watch their dog thus engaged. They have never seen Patch dig so enthusiastically before.

"He's got something," cries Jonathan suddenly as a fragment of material suddenly emerges from beneath the soil.

The children cluster round the dog to peer closer as he keeps on digging frantically. Then little Becky lets out a delighted cry: "It's a doll, Mummy. Patch has found an old doll!"

Mrs. Webley smiles. "Really, dear?" she says unthinkingly. She carries on inspecting the shrubs. However, it's only when Patch's bark suddenly turns to a growl that she gives his discovery her full attention. She strides over to see what the terrier has uncovered. By this time, he has dragged whatever he has found from out of its hiding place and is wrestling with it in a frenzied fashion.

"Mummy, he's killing the doll!" screams Becky.

"Patch, no!" yells Susan.

"Move back, children," says Mrs. Webley as she finally draws

close enough to see what has so excited the terrier. It takes a moment to realize what it holds within its jaws; but when she does, her hands fly up to her face. "Oh, God!" she exclaims.

"What is it, Mummy?" asks Susan, who already knows what Patch has discovered is not a doll.

Grabbing the dog by its collar, Mrs. Webley pries open his jaws so that he's forced to drop whatever he is attacking. She picks him up, still growling and squirming, and thrusts him into Susan's arms. "Get into the house. All of you. Now!" she yells.

The children have never heard their mother raise her voice before, let alone shout, and they immediately do as she says. They do not wait to see her bend down to inspect the decaying contents of the white napkin that's just been mauled by the dog. Nor do they see her vomit in the shrubbery.

CONSTANCE

"The suspect is a sailor. Officers are at East India Docks as we speak, Miss Piper, with orders to arrest him on sight for the murder of Miss Mylett and Mr. Braithwaite." Sergeant Hawkins, like me, hasn't slept much. There are bags as big as traveling trunks under his eyes, but he's on the ball.

"Does this mean that Will Mylett is in the clear?" My mind's in a whirl and it's hard for me to think straight.

"We'd still like to question him. After all, Mr. Braithwaite did accuse him of Catherine's murder."

"So that means Will had reason to kill him," I say. I'm thinking out loud, but the sergeant gives me a nod.

"Yes," he tells me. "And, of course, if there are any developments . . ." He picks up the papers he has in front of him and taps them on the table, so they're all neat and lined up. We're sitting in the interview room away from the hubbub of the big office, but he's as good as telling me to go. Questions race through my brain. I'm not finished yet.

"But what about the baby farmers?" I ask as he stands.

He shakes his head. "Miss Florence was right. It seems they have also fled." He sees my shoulders slump. "I'm sorry. I know how important it was for you to see them brought to justice. But for now, we must concentrate our efforts on finding Adam Braithwaite's killer. I must get up to Clarke's Yard now."

I stand up. "Of course," I say, even though I think my heart will sink to my feet. I'm turning toward the door when there's an urgent knock.

"Yes?" calls Sergeant Hawkins.

Constable Tanner's eager face cuts in. "Excuse me, sir. But you're needed right away up in Poplar."

The sergeant nods. "I know. Clarke's Yard. I shall be on my way shortly."

But Tanner shakes his head. "No, sir. Not the blacksmith case, sir." He shoots a look at me, as if what he has to say should be heard in private, then says softly: "They've found a baby's body at Woodstock Terrace."

Sergeant Hawkins fixes me with wide eyes.

"Oh, God!" I let slip. I desperately need to see for myself. I want to go with him, and as if he can read my thoughts, he asks me: "Miss Piper, will you accompany me in the police carriage?"

The journey to Poplar takes no more than ten minutes, but we spend much of it in silence. PC Tanner comes with us; but it's clear from the queer look he gives me, he don't approve of me muscling in on the investigation. We're met at Woodstock Terrace by another constable, and Sergeant Hawkins tells him he wants to see the site of the grim discovery first. We're shown through the hallway and into the back garden, where two more uniformed officers are waiting, alongside a bloke in a long-sleeved vest. He's armed with a shovel and a pickax, ready to start digging.

I watch Sergeant Hawkins stride the length of the garden to

the shrubbery. It's clear where the body was found. There's a mound of fresh soil just under a large laurel bush and a shallow hollow at its side. Crouching down, he picks up a handful of earth and weighs it thoughtfully in his palm.

"Take them all out," he orders, nodding to the shrubs and bushes. I think I'm the only one who hears him say under his breath: "God knows how many more babes there may be."

EMILY

Meanwhile, back in Whitechapel, news has spread of the horrific murder of the blacksmith in Poplar. The killing is the gossip on every street corner and in every shop, including Greenland's, the poulterer's. In the yard at the rear, Gilbert Johns is keen to see what Mick Donovan thinks of the brutal killing. Making sure his master is out of earshot, Gilbert has reason to believe that the Irishman might have more than a passing interest in the murder.

"You knew 'im, didn't you?" he asks, loading crates of dressed birds onto the cart.

"Who?" Donovan is chopping the heads off chickens with a cleaver. They're falling into a pail below.

Gilbert heaves another full crate onto the trailer. "The blacksmith. Braithwaite," he begins, pausing for breath. "Weren't he the bloke you vouched for when he was nabbed for that brass nail's murder?"

The head of another foul falls into the pail; then Donovan lays the bird to one side. "What if I did? I just told the truth."

Gilbert wipes his forehead with his sleeve. "Got any ideas then?" he asks, picking up another crate.

"Any ideas?"

"About who done it?"

Again the cleaver falls. "No."

Gilbert can take no more. He strides over to the Irishman

and seizes his jaw in his hands, jerking his face up toward his own. There's fear in his eyes. Gilbert can see it as his gaze bores into him. He thinks he may be telling the truth, but he won't let him get away with anything. "You better go to the police," he growls. "Tell 'em what you know, afore I do."

Chapter 39

Tuesday, January 15, 1889

Emily

Just as Number 9, Woodstock Terrace, in Poplar was an unremarkable house in an unremarkable row, so, too, is Number 7, Lenton Road. It stands in a street in the village of Tillingford-on-Thames, peopled by hardworking souls: artisans mainly—decent, God-fearing men and women, who pride themselves on earning honest livings. All of them, that is, except the occupants of the said Number 7.

The Charltons only moved in last week. They are a seemingly respectable couple in their late twenties. The wife's mother is a heavily-built Irishwoman in her early sixties. The couple's two children also live in the house: Isabel, a pretty, blond-haired, blue-eyed girl, on the plump side, always immaculately turned out and often to be seen on her mother's hip, and a baby boy with a shock of red hair and a birthmark on his leg, known as Georgie.

Should anyone ask, the latter was adopted when his missionary parents, who were close friends of the couple, were both murdered by savages in Africa. Should anyone ask, such a yarn usually puts paid to any casual admirer's awkward questioning as to who has endowed the child with such flame-colored hair by replacing suspicion with sympathy. Georgie is proving a troublesome child, but his griping is nothing a good dose of laudanum can't remedy. Otherwise he is manageable, eating one meal a day and progressing reasonably well, if a little slow to grow.

Explaining away the steady stream of visitors, almost all young women with babies, is a little problematic, however. The advertisement in the local newspaper, the Reedhampton Mercury, *inserted the day they arrived in Tillingford from Poplar, is proving most fruitful. Their new location looks as though it could be a very rewarding hunting ground.*

As ever, however, there is a cloud on the horizon. They cannot afford to give rise to misgivings among their neighbors, especially after what happened in London. That's why Mother Delaney—or should I call her Mother Noonan? *That is the name she now goes by—has decided that collecting her prospective charges from the railway station remains the best policy, except in cases where her midwifery skills are called upon. This time, she will dispense with the services of a doctor, too. There'll be no need for any more death certificates. Three moves and three changes of name within the year are too much for any family.*

CONSTANCE

I'm on my way to Commercial Street Station. I've left Ma to look after Flo. She only came home from hospital yesterday. Her body's mending, but it'll take longer for her mind to heal. Mine too. I jump at every unexpected sound, shudder at every shadow. Until the man who strangled Cath and near killed her, then went on to cut Adam Braithwaite's head off, is behind bars, neither of us will sleep easy at night.

There's Mother Delaney and her family, too. They've disappeared into thin air. By now, they'll be miles away, but they'll set up in business again, trading on the heartache and the shame of desperate women. As for Miss Louisa and her husband, I expect they'll forever grieve for their lost son, even though there's no body to bury. It's hard to keep hope alive when there's nothing to cling to, but I don't suppose they'll ever give up looking.

That's why I dread hearing what Sergeant Hawkins has to say. He's sent word he wants to see me regarding the dead baby they found in Woodstock Terrace yesterday. I left the grisly sight before they'd finished digging, so I'm praying they've found some clue that might lead to wherever Mother Delaney has gone. I'm also praying it's not little Bertie Sampson that the dog dug up.

When I arrive at the station, Sergeant Hawkins shows me into the interview room. My guts roil as my eyes settle on a familiar-looking box on the table. I steel myself to glance in, but there's no body. I'm that thankful. Instead, I see a white napkin, a bloody handkerchief, and the yellow binding that's become so familiar to me.

The sergeant catches my curious gaze. "They're to be photographed," he explains, motioning me to take a seat. "There's already been a postmortem."

"A boy?" I ask, all fearful.

He shakes his head. "A girl. A newborn mulatto."

I feel my shoulders slump, even though I hate myself for showing my relief at the news. Any dead babe is a tragedy, but I'm grateful this latest-found child can't be the Sampsons' Bertie.

"As you see, she'd been strangled with the same sort of binding and a rag had been stuffed in her mouth." His eyes skate across to the box.

I am no longer surprised, but I can tell there is something

else Sergeant Hawkins wants to share with me. From out of his coat pocket, he brings out a cloth bag.

"Our search of the garden at Woodstock Terrace also revealed this, Miss Piper." He tips up the pouch and out onto the desk falls a knife. "Is this the one that Miss Mylett had about her person the night she died?"

For a moment, all I can do is stare at the blade that's still smeared with blood. I recall the wildness of Cath's eyes as she showed it to me in the George and how I feared she might harm someone. All I can do is nod.

"It had been buried in the bushes," the sergeant tells me. "It is proof of a link between Miss Mylett and Mother Delaney and her associates, but no more. You told me, at the hospital, that Miss Mylett attacked the haberdasher."

"So the man with the tattoo is still your main suspect for Cath's murder?" I ask.

The inspector nods. "As I told you, Miss Piper, there are officers stationed at the East India Docks with orders to arrest this man and Will Mylett, too."

"The docks, yes," I say, suddenly rising to my feet.

"Miss Piper?" The sergeant is trying to read the look on my face. He knows an idea has just taken root in my head. He's starting to read me like a book. "Miss Piper, I must warn you the docks are no place for . . ." He stops himself. He almost said "a lady," but he didn't. He still doesn't think I'm worthy of the name, like he did when we first met and he thought me Miss Beaufroy's companion. But his attitude toward me only strengthens my resolve and makes me more determined to win his respect.

"My sort can take care of ourselves," I tell him straight. I may not be a real lady, but I can surely handle myself. "Good day, Sergeant Hawkins," says I. I know exactly where I'm going next.

I'm angry as I head out of the station, walking sharpish,

when who should I bump into but Mrs. Greenland, the old poulterer's wife? But she doesn't seem to notice me. She's in that much of a blather as she makes for the duty sergeant's desk. I stop to watch.

"Someone come. Pl-please, someone come q-quick," she stammers.

Sergeant Halfhide deals with her calmly. "What seems to be the trouble, Mrs. Greenland?" he asks.

The poulterer's wife shakes her hatless head. "The most shocking thing. The most shocking thing," she says over.

"Shocking, eh?" The hirsute sergeant raises one of his bushy brows. "What would that be, madam?"

Mrs. Greenland leans forward, as if she doesn't want anyone else to know her business, and says in a loud whisper: "A murder, Sergeant. He's dead."

I can't hold back. I rush up to the old woman and look at her straight. "Who?" I say. "Who's dead?"

Mrs. Greenland fixes me with dazed eyes. I can see she's in shock. Her whole body's started to shake. "One of the boys," she replies. "One of the boys."

I know I'll not get any sense out of the poor woman, but I don't want to wait for the coppers to get their act together. Instead, I rush out the door and down the road to the high street, where I can see the red-and-white–striped awning of the shop. I break into a run, and in a couple of minutes, I'm down the alley at the side of the shop.

A huddle of men stands in the little yard, outside the hanging shed, clustered around Mr. Greenland, but Gilbert's not there. "No. Please, Miss Tindall, no," I find myself muttering again as I barge my way to the front, toward the shed. One of the blokes tries to stop me. He grabs hold of my arm.

"You can't go in there," he yells at me. But it's too late.

I duck down through the door. Gilbert's the first person I see; and for that, I'm so thankful. He's standing among all the dead chickens and geese on hooks, his eyes wide and fixed. There's flies everywhere and a stink, too. I hold my breath, but then I turn to follow his gaze to see Mick Donovan. He's there, all right, only like the fowl, he's dangling from the rafters; eyes bulging, tongue lolling, hanging from the end of a rope. I can't hold my breath no longer. It comes out as a scream.

Chapter 40

Emily

We shall leave Constance to recover from her terrible shock in the capable hands of Gilbert Johns while we venture to the village of Tillingford. It's a pretty settlement on the banks of the Thames, three miles downriver from Reedhampton, the county town of Brentshire. Mist rises up from the river and there's still a nip in the air. The ground is muddy underfoot. There's been a fair bit of rain overnight, and the path is already churned up by horses' hooves as they heave barges laden with beer and seeds to London. One such barge is slowly hoving into view, heading toward the bank.

A silver-haired bargeman is at the back. He's pulled the rudder toward him as he rounds the bend, bringing his vessel closer to the reeds. He's fixed on the bank close by, making sure he steers well clear, when suddenly he lurches forward. Wait. He's spotted something in the rushes. He's coming alongside and peering down into the reeds. Grabbing a punt hook, he pokes about in the dead stalks and branches that the winter storms have broken off.

A parcel, *he thinks as he jabs.* Linen or some such. *He sticks out his tongue from between a grizzled beard as he concentrates. Suddenly he manages to get a purchase and starts to drag the parcel slowly and carefully closer to the boat. "Gently does it," I hear him say. Then I see his arms tense and, in one swift movement, he hauls the parcel onto the deck of the barge. He's unwrapping the brown paper now, tearing at it with his hook. When that's out of the way, there's a layer of thick flannel fabric underneath.*

"What 'ave we 'ere?" he asks himself, pulling at a large white handkerchief with his calloused hands.

I want to close my eyes, but I cannot. I have to watch as the bargeman peels away the flap of white cotton to realize with horror that what he's looking at is a little human face, its eyes mercifully closed. The bargeman utters a most terrible sound. It's a cross between a wail and a retch.

"No! Oh no! Oh, God!" he cries, over and over.

There's a length of yellow floral binding tied tight around the baby's tiny neck and fastened behind its left ear.

Chapter 41

Wednesday, January 16, 1889

Emily

The borough constabulary at Reedhampton may not enjoy the prestige of the Metropolitan force, but they are proving themselves every bit as adept, if not more so, at tracking down criminals. An eagle-eyed constable, when examining the wrappings in which the latest infant was found, detected a local address written on the brown paper. Subsequent inquiries have led him and his sergeant to a house not three miles distant. It's no surprise that the address is Number 7, Lenton Road.

Although the new occupants have only been in situ for a few days, they're already getting a reputation among their neighbors for being a most welcoming family. Indeed, so eager is the matriarch of the household to encourage visitors to her home that when she hears her daughter answer the door to yet another knock, she is really quite gratified. It's only when the young woman appears in the company of two police officers from Reed-

hampton Borough Constabulary that she becomes a little less welcoming.

"Bridget Delaney, you're under arrest," says the sergeant.

As Philomena protests and feigns her innocence, her mother turns belligerent. She suspects the game is up.

"What the hell do ya think . . . ?" she curses as she's clapped *in handcuffs.*

"Save your breath for the station, old woman," advises the sergeant. "You've got a lot of explaining to do."

CONSTANCE

There's a knock at the door. It never brings good news these days. When I see Mummy's boy Tanner standing on the doorstep, my heart misses a beat. I'm expecting to hear they've found another dead baby, but no.

"'Morning, miss," he greets me, all friendly. "I'm sent to tell you that Detective Sergeant Hawkins wishes to see you at the station," says he.

I can't hide my worry. "Is something wrong?" I ask.

Tanner leans toward me, all confidential-like. "Between you and me, it's nothing to fear," says he.

So I wrap myself in my shawl, don my hat, and don't waste a minute getting to the station. The duty copper on the desk even smiles at me when I say I'm here at Sergeant Hawkins's bidding. He shows me to the large office, where I see the detective sitting at his desk.

"Ah, Miss Piper," he says, rising to greet me with a smile. I can't recall him ever looking so at ease with himself. "I have some news."

"*News?*" I repeat. I'm hoping it's good, although it's not something I'm accustomed to, but the sergeant's manner leads me on.

"You probably saw the police carriage waiting outside."

"No." I shake my head. I was that fixed on what I was about to learn that I never noticed it.

"Well, there is one," he tells me with a nod. "And it's to take Mr. and Mrs. Sampson to the hospital in Reedhampton." His words puzzle me, until he adds with a smile: "Five babies have been discovered and rescued from a certain minder's home."

At the news, I feel my face lift. "You've tracked down Mother Delaney?"

"Not me, but my colleagues at Reedhampton Borough Constabulary, yes."

I gasp with joy. "So Bertie is alive?"

"Ah." He's stumbling over his reply and my heart sinks. "That I cannot say, but there is, of course, a chance that he is one of the five. And you, yourself, will be one of the first to know."

"Me? How?"

I see his lips twitch. "Because I suggest you accompany the Sampsons."

I'm not half flattered by the idea, even if I do think it's right and proper, though Mr. Right and Mrs. Proper are strangers to most in Whitechapel.

"Yes." I reply, adding a heartfelt: "Thank you," even though I'm not sure what part, if any, he played in tracking down the baby farmers.

Sergeant Hawkins reaches for the door handle. "There's one more thing you should know, Miss Piper," he tells me, all earnest.

"What's that, Sergeant?"

His expression has switched back to seriousness. "When they conducted a thorough search of Delaney's house, they found a dead child. A boy of about three months." He works his jaw. "Don't let the Sampsons get their hopes up too much."

EMILY

While Constance awaits the imminent arrival of Miss Louisa and her new husband, there is activity in the Mylett household in Pelham Street. Fanny tiptoes quietly upstairs, holding aloft a candle. Once on the landing, she opens the door into Cath's old room. A fully dressed man is lying on the bed, his hands clasped behind his head on a pillow, and his feet, clad in boots, are on the counterpane. Fanny frowns at the sight.

"Get your ruddy great feet off there," she hisses, keeping her voice low.

The man smirks. "Relax, my gal," he tells her, swinging his legs off the bed. "Remember, Adam Braithwaite is dead and buried."

Ignoring him, Fanny picks up a tin mug from the floor by the bed and slams it on the nearby chest of drawers. It's clear she's not happy.

"The Irish lad's dead. Hanged himself, so they say." She shakes her head. "You wouldn't have had a hand in that, would ya?"

He shoots her a wounded look, then shrugs. "It's probably for the best. He'd have talked in the end."

She walks to the window and crosses her arms as she looks out onto the warren of squalid slum dwellings, silhouetted in the moonlight.

"And I told you Auntie says she heard footsteps." Fanny turns sharply and looks pointedly at his boots.

The man is dismissive. "No one'll take notice of her," he replies, with a shrug, pointing to his temple. "Besides, this time tomorrow, we'll be on that ship, won't we, my darlin'? Bound for America." He sits up, pulls her toward him and begins to kiss her neck, but she fends him off and manages to squirm free.

"It's a good bleeding job we are," she tells him, straightening her blouse. "It's getting too close for comfort round 'ere."

Constance

Lord knows poor Sergeant Hawkins has his work cut out for him. I'm waiting by the main door of the police station for Miss Louisa and her husband to arrive; all of a sudden, I hear this rumpus. Two coppers are wrestling with a bloke, who's cussing and hollering. His hands are cuffed behind his back and they're dragging him toward the cells. As they draw close by, I catch a glimpse of his face—and he of mine—and my body goes stiff with fear. I look down at his hand. He's the lech I saw in the George that night: the man who nearly killed Flo.

Sergeant Hawkins appears at his door to find out what all the noise is about and reads the look of terror on my face.

"It's him," I bleat. "The sailor with the tattoo."

The sergeant comes close. "I'll deal with him, Miss Piper. You are required elsewhere." He shoots a look behind me and I turn to see Miss Louisa and her husband walk toward the desk.

"Yes," I reply. I know there's nothing more I can do here and at least I can leave safe in the knowledge that the lech can't hurt no one else, for the time being at least.

EMILY

There is strong liquor on the sailor's breath. Normally, he'd be put in the cells to let its effects wear off, but Sergeant Hawkins knows that this sort of man could drink a whole bottle of rum and not feel any worse. He stands over him in the interview room.

"Where did you find him?" he asks one of the constables.

"In the George at Poplar, sir."

"Let me see his hand," he instructs. The prisoner, now more compliant, is uncuffed and the officer grabs hold of his hand and thrusts it out on the table in front of Hawkins. On it, inscribed in blue ink, is a large tattoo of a naked woman. Hawkins knows it's going to be a very long night.

CONSTANCE

As we head out of the city in the police carriage, I tell Miss Louisa and her husband all I know. It's early evening and the highway is quiet. We're soon on the Bath Road, a little way short of Slough. The couple sits side by side, with me opposite. Miss Louisa is most fretful. First she smiles at the thought of seeing her son; then she dissolves into tears for allowing herself to be hopeful.

And me? I'm mindful of Sergeant Hawkins's words: *"Don't let the Sampsons get their hopes up too much."* But that's easier said than done. Both Miss Louisa and her husband have been treated so cruelly by Mother Delaney that they don't know which way to turn.

"Perhaps a dose might calm your nerves, my dear?" suggests Mr. Sampson to his wife. She nods and opens her reticule to bring out a small brown bottle of laudanum. She uncorks it and swigs it back. Within five minutes, she is fast asleep.

So now it's just Mr. Sampson and me. My skin prickles. He makes me feel uneasy, and I him. I know he's remembering what happened the last time we were alone together, when Miss Tindall came inside me and I became her for a moment. I've been calling her all evening, but I've not sensed her. Perhaps she'll come to me now so that she can speak to Mr. Sampson on his own.

Despite the darkness, the carriage blind remains open. The lights of Slough have come into view and I'm watching them grow nearer so that my face is turned away from Mr. Sampson. Taking advantage of his wife's sleep, he reaches for his silver cigarette case. It seems he wouldn't ask the likes of me for permission to light up. From the corner of my eye, I see him open the case, choose a cigarette, and tap the tip twice on the cover before taking out his vestas. As he strikes a match, I turn toward him; and in that moment, the flame lights up my face. It's then that I feel her presence. Miss Tindall comes to me like a rush of wind.

"No," murmurs Robert Sampson as he looks at me. I know from his changed features that it isn't Constance Piper, the flower girl, who's staring at him from out of the darkness. Emily Tindall wants to speak to him and bids me take my leave. She has control of my mind and my body and my world grows dark. I remember nothing. I must've blacked out for a moment, because the next thing I know is that we've hit a pothole and my head jerks up again. I blink as I try to focus. The lights of Slough are behind us.

"You all right, Mr. Sampson?" I ask, aware that he is gazing at me, openmouthed.

"Miss Piper?" He needs to make sure it's me.

"Yes, Mr. Sampson," I reply. "I must've dozed off."

"But you just . . ." He shakes his sleek black head as he fingers the rim of his topper. He takes a deep breath and starts over, like I've just walked back into the room. "I want to thank you for all that you have done."

"I am glad to have been of service, sir," I reply with a nod. I don't know what Miss Tindall has just said to him, but he seems more at ease. Nevertheless, I pray this long and uncomfortable journey will end well.

We arrive at Reedhampton Hospital shortly before nine o'clock. The five babies have been put in a little room all to themselves. The doctor, a kindly old man with a monocle and hunched shoulders, wears a white coat that almost reaches to the floor. He shows us into the room. A policeman stands at the door.

A plump little girl, dressed in pink frills, sits on a nursemaid's knee, playing with a floppy rabbit. For a second, I'm hopeful that perhaps the babies have been cared for, after all; but then the doctor breaks the news that this child is, in fact, Mother Delaney's granddaughter.

"I warn you the other children are not as healthy," he says sternly.

I dart a look at Miss Louisa and see her swallow hard and

brace herself as we are directed toward five cots ranged against the wall. I feel my stomach knot as the moment of truth arrives. She peers over into the first cot. A tiny girl lies asleep; her little arms are like sticks. Next to her is another painfully thin babe, who is shaking violently.

"What ails the child?" asks Mr. Sampson, a deep frown creasing his brow.

"Laudanum," explains the doctor. "She is displaying typical withdrawal symptoms."

Miss Louisa gasps at the thought as she gazes on the baby in the next cot: a boy with blond curly hair and sores on his hollow cheeks.

"Marasmus," says the doctor.

The fifth and final cot contains another boy, bigger than the other one and with a shock of red hair. He's kicking his legs, and although he's bony, it's clear he's got a bit of life in him.

I look at Miss Louisa, but she only has eyes for the baby in the cot. Without a word, she bends low and scoops him up in her arms, tears streaming down her face.

"Bertie! Oh, God! My darling little Bertie!" she cries, nuzzling her cheek against his.

Mr. Sampson puts his arm on her shoulder and peers over to see his son for the first time through a mist of pent-up emotion.

"You're sure he is your son?" asks the doctor with a smile.

Miss Louisa, choking back tears, manages to point to the baby's thigh. "The birthmark," she says. "He is our Bertie."

I feel myself choke up, too. I think my heart will melt. I've never seen such love and joy on anyone's face. Mr. Sampson's having a little weep as well, and I can see the old doctor's struggling, too. It's an amazing moment, and one I feared I'd never see. I just wonder how many other young mothers won't ever have the chance to see their lost babies ever again.

We spend a few more minutes at the hospital, weeping and smiling, before we part: the Sampsons, and Bertie, for a nearby inn and me back to London in the waiting carriage. But just before I go, Mr. Sampson draws me aside. I fear what he might say, but he looks at me with those piercing blue eyes of his and whispers: "Tell Miss Tindall I'm so very sorry and thank her for me, too. I cannot express . . ." He wells up again.

I pat him on the arm. "I understand" is all I say.

EMILY

Detective Sergeant Hawkins is beginning to think he is on a losing wicket. It soon became evident to him that despite his initial assumptions, the sailor with the tattoo, although undoubtedly a violent man, is probably innocent of Catherine's murder, although he does admit to being one of her regular clients. Nor can the detective find any connection with Adam Braithwaite.

The sailor is not charged with murder, although he is detained until such a time that Florence can identify him—or not—as her attacker. Once again, in the hunt for Catherine's murderer, Detective Sergeant Hawkins finds himself at a loss.

CHAPTER 42

Thursday, January 17, 1889

CONSTANCE

The police carriage reaches the East End in the small hours. Try as I might, I haven't been able to sleep a wink. Don't get me wrong, I'm so happy for the Sampsons. That little Bertie is alive and safe, well, it makes my heart leap for joy. But now that old Irish witch is behind bars, I've still got my work cut out for me. Cath's killer remains at large and I can't rest until he's found.

I pull up the blind in the carriage to see a familiar landscape of brick warehouses and workshops and I realize we're traveling back through Poplar, near the docks. And there, on Commercial Road, at the junction with Jubilee Street, I see the George Tavern. There's lights still burning.

I knock on the roof, then open the window to shove my head out.

"Stop here, if you please!" I yell up at the driver.

As soon as the carriage comes to a halt, I tell him I'll find my own way home, but first I've got a call to make. With all that's happened, I'd forgot, until now, how I'd told the little lad with freckles that if he saw or heard anything about Will Mylett, he should leave word here, at the tavern. I never expected he would, of course, but when I speak with the landlord, it turns out he has. Freckles left a message, all right, yesterday evening.

"You'll find 'im at low tide, under London Bridge," the landlord tells me. That's about now, so that's where I head. I can't believe I'm doing this. I know I shouldn't, but I'm pushing the fear of an East End night to the back of my mind, I'm so set on solving Cath's murder.

The sight of Mick Donovan in the hanging shed has seared itself on my brain, and all. I can't unsee those bulging eyes, or the look of anguish on that face. Gilbert told me he knew Mick was in trouble; he'd delivered a sack from the docks for someone—he didn't know who. They're waiting on the postmortem report. The coppers are saying Irish Mick hanged himself, but I think different. Moreover, I reckon whoever killed him could've killed Adam Braithwaite, too. My money's still on Will Mylett.

That's what drives me on through the darkness and down to the Thames. That's what brings me here, to this filthy stew pot, against my better judgment. I only hope I don't regret it. The smell of the river is scouring my nostrils and the reek's stinging my eyes. I'm praying Miss Tindall is watching my back as I step gingerly down the slimy watermen's steps to the cluster of vagabonds and ruffians that congregate in this church of the damned after dark.

The miserables, as the better-off refer to them, have lit a fire from driftwood under the pile. It's not big, but it's where they all huddle, young and old alike. Some's come out of the clink; some's not right in the head, but all of them seem to have lost everything, even any hope of making some sort of life for themselves. The flames light up a few faces, but throw others into shadow. There's no chatter, neither. It's like cold and hunger have gagged their sorry mouths.

I'm not sure how I'll find the little kid. I'm peering into the straggle of doomed souls, when I suddenly feel a tug at my skirts. At first, I think one of the rascals is filching from me and I strike out, but when I look down, I see it's him. It's Freckles—and I'm so pleased, I want to hug him.

I bend down to his eye level. "You want to tell me something?"

He nods, but he's looking afeared. "Not here," he says.

"Let's walk."

We clamber back up the steps and shelter in the doorway of a warehouse nearby. I feel in my apron pocket and take out a farthing and show it to him. I think he'll snatch it, like he did before, but he don't. He's scared. I can see it in his eyes. He's not the cocky little sod I first met on the docks. He's shivering, too, and I'm not sure it's just with cold.

"You know where Will Mylett is?" I ask.

He shakes his head.

"If you want this, you'll have to do better than that," says I, holding up the coin.

He swallows hard. "I did know. He was 'iding, miss."

"Hiding?"

"In a place near here."

"He's not there now? What happened?"

The boy looks down at the ground and scuffs his old boots, which are way too big for him, through the dirt. "Someone came."

"Who?"

He shakes his matted head. "I told Mr. Will about his sister, that the court said she were murdered."

"The inquest?"

He nods. "So he says he'd leave after that and he'd need me no more. He gave me a shilling and that's the last I saw of 'im, I swear. God's honest. Only . . ."

"Yes?"

"Only as I was going down the stairs this other gaffer came up. He pushed me away and I fell. He frighted me, so I hid."

"What happened to Will?"

Freckles frowns. "I don't know, but I 'eard noises."

"What sort of noises?"

"Angry voices and then something fell. I didn't know what to do, I were that frit. I waited awhile, until the bloke came down the stairs again."

"Was he alone?"

He nods, but then I see him chew his cracked lip. "But he 'ad a sack over 'is shoulder."

I gasp. "Oh, God!" I try and think straight. "This man with the sack? What did he look like?"

Freckles shakes his head. "Hard to say, miss. Not big. Dark hair, oh and . . ."

"Yes."

"He had a patch over his eye."

EMILY

Constance is not the only one up and about when most God-fearing souls are abed. Detective Sergeant Hawkins is still at his desk as dawn is poised to break. He is poring over the medical examiner's report into Michael Donovan's apparent suicide. That, at least, is what his officers at the scene told him at the time. He is ashamed to say he was relieved. It meant one less crime for him to solve. Now, however, he has come to the summation of the report and does not like what he reads: A blow to the back of the head possibly rendered the victim unconscious before he was hanged to make it appear a case of self-murder.

He slaps his palms on his papers and pushes away from his desk, as if wishing to put distance between himself and the report. Another murder to investigate is the last thing he needs right now. Just as he does so, PC Tanner, who's just about to go off duty, walks into the office to tell him Miss Piper is asking to see him urgently.

"Constance," he says under his breath. His mind darts back

to their last encounter. He has learned from experience that he ignores Miss Piper's opinions—or rather her intuition—at his peril. Inspector McCullen's been on his back. Three more unsolved murders in six weeks—Mylett, Braithwaite, and now Donovan—don't sit well with the Assistant Commissioner, nor with any resident of Poplar and Whitechapel, for that matter. He needs all the help he can muster—divine or otherwise. He frowns, grabs his jacket from a nearby chair, scrambles into it, and leaps to attention as soon as his unexpected visitor marches in.

Constance

"Miss Constance, I thought you might stay in Reedhampton with the Sampsons."

Detective Sergeant Hawkins is certainly not expecting my early return. Tell the truth, I can't believe I'm here, neither. The thing is, what I've just discovered is so important, it can't wait.

"I was, but I'm back now," I snap. "Do you have the medical examiner's report on Adam Braithwaite's body, Sergeant Hawkins?" There's no time to stand on ceremony. I know my behavior must look unseemly, but what's arrived in my brain could prove crucial to the investigation.

"Yes. Yes, of course, but this is highly irregular." I can tell he's put out.

"Please, you have to trust me," I tell the sergeant.

He fixes me with an odd look. "You've had another vision?" I'm not sure if he is taking me seriously.

"More intuition," I counter.

He brings the file from a nearby drawer and hands it to me. "Here."

I flick through, until I find the part where it estimates Adam Braithwaite's time of death. I look up. "This says the blacksmith had been dead between ten hours and three days."

"Why is that noteworthy?" asks Sergeant Hawkins.

"He had a wife, didn't he?" I come back. "The one who gave

him an alibi on the night of Cath's murder. Why didn't she come looking for him?"

He frowns in thought. "I remember she was nursing her sick aunt before. Perhaps she was staying with her again?"

"And where was that?"

I can see I'm grating on his nerves. "I'm afraid I couldn't tell you offhand, Miss Piper. Inspector McCullen has some of the earlier paperwork."

I can't let it rest. I try another tack. "Have you spoken with Gilbert Johns? Has he told you about Mick Donovan taking the cart out at night?"

The sergeant nods. "Yes, I know about the cart and the sack."

This is too important to let go. I'm like a dog with a bone. "It's clear there was a body inside, but whose? It can't have been Adam Braithwaite's. The sack was collected the day before you arrested him."

His eyebrows shoot up in shock. "Surely, you're not saying we should be looking for another body, Miss Piper?"

"I am," I snap. "Unless . . ." My eyes stray back to the report into Braithwaite's death. "You told me his face was so badly mutilated, he could only be identified by his wife."

"Yes, that's right. The head was partly burned in the furnace. We also found a bloodied eye-patch nearby."

"But what if the body was someone else's?"

The sergeant's jaw drops. It's like he's just had a revelation, like the scales have just fallen from his eyes. "Of course!" he mutters. Suddenly he's hurrying to the door. "Tanner!" I hear him shout. "Tanner!" He disappears for a moment, then returns with Mummy's boy at his side.

"It was you who tracked down Mrs. Braithwaite to her sick aunt's house, was it not?" he asks.

"Aye, sir," replies the bewildered copper, looking at me all put out. I know he was just about to go off duty.

"Do you still have the address?" asks his boss.

He takes out his notebook and thumbs through. "Yes, sir. Pelham Street, sir."

Sergeant Hawkins balks and pins his look on me as he asks: "Not Number 11?"

"Yes, sir."

Tanner has barely had time to return his notebook to his pocket before Sergeant Hawkins is grabbing his own topcoat and hat. "I'll need a couple of men," he yells, hurtling through the door.

"Righto, sir," calls the constable.

"What about me?" I cry, heading after him.

He pauses in the hall. "This could be dangerous, Miss Piper. You'd best stay here," he tells me. And he's off. Course his words is like a red rag to a bull. I'd rather eat my hat than sit around and twiddle my thumbs waiting for him to be a hero. I'll follow on, and he can't stop me.

Emily

Dawn has just broken when, a few minutes later, Detective Sergeant Hawkins raps on the door of Number 11, Pelham Street. His knock is answered quickly. He does not, however, expect the door to be opened by a recently widowed woman.

"Mrs. Braithwaite!" he exclaims as soon as he sees Fanny standing there.

She does not expect to see him, either. In a moment of unthinking panic, she tries to slam the door in his face, but he thrusts his boot across the threshold and jams it open.

"Let me in!" yells Hawkins.

Fanny manages to sidestep and pushes against the door from the inside. Twisting toward the stairs, she screams: "Coppers. Get away!" But her strength is no match for the detective's and he shoulders the door, ramming it backward and shoving Fanny away in its wake. She staggers and stumbles to the floor, allow-

ing Hawkins to bound over her. He's poised to leap up the stairs, when she grabs his coat and tries vainly to drag him back, but he fends her off with a blow to her hand. In five strides, he's on the landing.

One door is halfway open, the other shut. He tries the handle on the closed one. It seems locked. He rattles it, then realizes it's been blocked from the inside. "I know you're in there, Braithwaite!" he yells. He takes a run at the door and shoulders it. There's a loud thud as a chair that's been wedged under the handle crashes to the ground; this time, he manages to force the door open to see the blacksmith escaping through the sash window.

"Police!" he cries, lunging toward the window as Braithwaite flies into the air. Hawkins sees him land flat on his stomach against the pitched roof of a privy a few feet below. A drainpipe saves his fall, and although he lands awkwardly, he soon picks himself up.

"Braithwaite!" shouts Hawkins in vain.

Ignoring the detective, the blacksmith jumps down onto the boundary wall of the house, teeters along it for a few steps, then lowers himself down into the narrow alley at the back. Hawkins starts to follow, but not before he's summoned help, blowing his whistle twice.

You'll remember how the sergeant has no love of heights and has to summon all of his courage to set off in pursuit. Somehow he manages to lower himself onto the pitch of the privy, but his legs betray his fear. He cannot run, only walk along the top of the wall. Thankfully, it is but a few paces until he is able to jump down onto the footpath that leads toward Brick Lane, but he is glad to return to terra firma. He's also just in time to see his quarry turn left up ahead.

Running full pelt, and ducking under the narrow archway to the alley, he finds himself on the main thoroughfare as Braithwaite shoots across the lane and careens into the path of a passing brewer's dray, sending barrels toppling from the cart. The shire horse is unsettled and rears up, but the blacksmith sidesteps it and carries on through the great wrought-iron gates of the Black Eagle Brewery. Dodging a stray barrel and ignoring the angry shouts of the drayman, Hawkins runs after his quarry.

The courtyard is already busy and noisy with morning deliveries. Four carts are being loaded and for a moment the blacksmith is lost among the barrels, casks, and horses. Gasping for breath, Hawkins scans the courtyard. Fast footsteps approach from behind him. He turns and is relieved to see PC Tanner.

"Over there!" shouts the constable, pointing to Braithwaite as he disappears up a flight of steps into the malt house entrance.

"Get men on the main doors," orders Hawkins. "I'll go after him." He begins to ascend the treads of the wooden staircase just as the wanted man dives through the open door at the top.

Constance

I've given Sergeant Hawkins a few moments to get ahead before I'm on his tail. Unbeknown to him, I followed him out of the station, heading for Margaret Mylett's house. The chimney stack of the Black Eagle Brewery looms up ahead and I'm almost at the junction with Pelham Street, where she lives, when I see three or four coppers inside the loading yard of the brewery. Something's going on.

I look through the great wrought-iron gates and watch the rozzers run helter-skelter. Somehow I know I'll find Sergeant Hawkins here. My head turns this way and that as I enter the yard. Barrels are rolled onto dray carts. Sacks are being winched up from a wagon to the third floor. Men are everywhere. A wall of noise bombards my ears and clatters inside my skull, but my eyes fix onto the big double doors to the brew house ahead of me.

"Oi, miss! You can't go in there!" I hear a voice yell behind me. I take no notice, only quicken my step. Inside there's a huge steam engine, which is powering some of the machinery.

Chains jangle, whistles blow, and the steel rakes churn up the mash. Great vats stand in a row like giant cauldrons; next to them, swathed in steam, are the shallow trays where the scalding wort cools down. It's hot and humid inside. As my eyes adjust to the light and the steam, I see a clutch of men looking up at a gantry above them. They're pointing at a lone man. I strain to look. It's Sergeant Hawkins.

His head switches up and down, and from side to side. He's on the prowl as he creeps gingerly along the narrow iron walkway that lies at least twenty feet above the ground. He's vulnerable. I remember he don't like heights, and one slip and he'll fall. What's more, there's no cover and nowhere to hide. Suddenly, from out of the corner of my eye, I see a flash of movement above him as a pulley swings out, a sack dangling from its huge hook.

"Look out!" I shout.

The sergeant's head cracks up and he jumps back just as a hundredweight bag of grain comes hurtling down from a great height. It misses him by inches and bursts on the walkway in front of him, spraying barley into the air. I catch a glimpse of a man framed by iron girders, high up in the roof space, but it's hard to make out his features. In a flash, he's gone again.

I switch to Sergeant Hawkins as he climbs the flight of stairs up to the next level that runs along the side of the mill engine. It's a massive machine that grinds the hops between rollers. They run in opposite directions to crush the husks and spit them out on a moving belt.

I can hardly hear myself think as I watch him edge his way along the side of the mill, and then I catch sight of the man, again. He's ducked down below a gantry rail and lowered himself onto the same level as Sergeant Hawkins. I think he's heading for the chute they roll the barrels down, on the outside wall. He's at least fifty yards ahead, level with the sparing tubs, where they spray hot water onto the mash. But he takes one look at the chute and decides he's too high up to risk a jump, so he keeps on running along the narrow walkway. I can see he's tiring. I can see, too, that if I take another staircase, I can head him off. He'll be trapped. Sergeant Hawkins is catching up with him; so, quick as a flash, I hurry to the far end and start to climb, two steps at a time.

"Miss! Come back!" I hear PC Tanner cry after me, but I'm too fly for him.

The man has nowhere to go. If he carries on, it'll be straight to me. If he turns back, he'll run into Sergeant Hawkins. Out of breath, I reach the landing, blocking his path. It's too late for him to turn. I think we've got him trapped, when he stops dead in front of me. We come face-to-face for the first time. I gasp when I realize the man's right eye is dead and unseeing in its socket.

I was right. It's not Cath's brother from the photograph. It's not Will Mylett. It's the man who everyone thought was already dead—the man whose face everyone believed was smashed so bad, only his wife could recognize him. It's Adam Braithwaite. He looks down at the four steaming vats that lie eight feet below. There's a gap of about three feet between each one. He has to surrender. Or jump. Instead, he lunges at me and grabs me by the neck.

"Come any closer and I'll kill her!" he shouts below.

"Just like you did Catherine Mylett!" shouts back Sergeant Hawkins.

I feel the blacksmith's stinking breath on my cheek; then his grip loosens and he steps back. I turn to see him hesitate before taking a gulp and launching himself off the gantry. My hands fly up to my eyes. I can't look. I wait for the splash, my heart pounding faster than the steam engine, but it don't come. He's not landed in the vat, but on the ground between. Only he's just lying there. He's not moving. Men are rushing forward now, closing in on him. Sergeant Hawkins runs back along the gantry and down the stairs.

"Move back!" calls PC Tanner, clearing the way for the detective.

By now, I've managed to squeeze past the huddle of brewers to the front. Braithwaite is facedown. I catch Sergeant Hawkins's eye just before he gives Constable Tanner the nod to turn him over onto his back.

"Adam Braithwaite," mutters Sergeant Hawkins. It's the first time he's seen his face up close. He bends low and checks for a pulse in his neck. After a moment, much to everyone's surprise, he declares him to be alive. "Call a doctor," he orders.

There's a bloody gash on the blacksmith's left temple, where he caught his head on the vat; while below the left knee, his leg lies at right angles to his thigh. It's clear it's a bad break.

"Will he live?" I ask.

Sergeant Hawkins looks up at me. "Let's hope long enough to talk."

CHAPTER 43

EMILY

The doctors are used to dealing with industrial injuries at Poplar Infirmary. Every day, a docker is brought to them, with a flattened leg or a broken arm or rib. Injuries at the brewery are not unheard of, but usually involve scalding or crushing.

Adam Braithwaite's condition is, nevertheless, serious. The glancing blow he suffered to his head was severe, but not life-threatening. His leg, however, was necessarily amputated in theater and now a fever has taken hold.

Sergeant Hawkins has asked to be notified when the injured man is capable of being interviewed. Many questions remain unanswered, and Braithwaite, he believes, holds the key to most of them. The detective only hopes that he is able to answer them before he takes a turn for the worse. If he lasts the night, it'll be a miracle.

CONSTANCE

I'm hardly over the threshold of our home when Flo rushes up to me and gives me a big hug. Ma's there, too, and plants a kiss on my cheek.

"It's good to have you back," says Flo. "What news?" she asks fretful-like, still holding me tight.

So much has happened in the last few hours that my head's a jumble. But at least I've brought some good news back with me.

"Bertie's alive," I tell her.

"Oh, Con!" Flo hugs me again.

Ma pats me on the back. "Oh, my days!" says she, her eyes filling with happy tears.

Gently I push my big sis away, but take both her hands. "They've arrested the baby farmers." I can hardly believe it's true myself.

"And the other babies?" asks Ma, dabbing her eyes with her pinny.

I nod cautiously. "They found five alive."

Flo frowns. "*Alive?* Does that mean . . . ?"

I think of what the doctor at the hospital told me. When they searched the house in Tillingford, they found dozens of letters from mothers asking for their children to be adopted. There were other documents: vaccination certificates and clothes, too. There are so many babies unaccounted for, there's an order to dredge the Thames for bodies. It makes difficult listening. Flo's lips tremble at the thought. She shakes her head.

"So Cath was right about little Evie and the others."

"It seems that way," I say, letting her hands fall. "There's something else you need to know, too," I begin. I have a long tale to tell her and Ma, but I don't yet know it's ending until I hear what Adam Braithwaite has to spill; that is, if he's willing or able to speak at all. "Let's sit down," I say.

Chapter 44

Emily

Adam Braithwaite lies in a small room away from the main surgical ward. PC Semple stands guard outside, even though there is no prospect of the prisoner escaping. Sergeant Hawkins is not alone when he enters the room. Constable Barrett, one of the officers who found Catherine Mylett's body, has accompanied him. It will be his job to record the injured man's statement—or rather, it is hoped, confession. A nurse is also in attendance to ensure the patient is not unnecessarily taxed or fatigued by this interview.

Hawkins leans over Braithwaite, whose head is bandaged. His good eye is closed. "Can you hear me?" The man's features screw up, as if in pain. After a moment, he grunts. "It's Sergeant Hawkins, here." Another grunt. The detective leans in, close to the man's left ear. "You've been lying, Mr. Braithwaite, have you not? You lied to Miss Piper when you told her that Will Mylett murdered his sister. It was you, wasn't it?"

A groan escapes the blacksmith's lips. Undeterred, the inspector continues.

"Mylett found out, and when he threatened to expose you, you murdered him. Isn't that right?"

On the pillow, Braithwaite's head stirs. "Water!" he croaks.

The nurse fills a cup and holds his head so that he can take a few sips. "You killed Catherine, didn't you?" the detective asks sharply. "You spun all those lies to Miss Piper about how you cared for her, and yet you killed her. Why?"

"I loved Cath."

Sergeant Hawkins arches his brow. "Is that why you fought over her? Is that why you assaulted Joseph Litvinoff?" he asks, recalling the blacksmith's previous conviction for affray.

Braithwaite swallows down a sob. "Yes." He is becoming very agitated and the nurse feels it is time to draw a halt to the proceedings for the sake of her patient.

"If you please, Sergeant . . ."

She need say no more. Reluctantly Sergeant Hawkins concedes that his questioning might only serve to hasten Braithwaite's decline.

"I shall return tomorrow," he tells the nurse. He only hopes his prisoner will survive the night.

For Constance, the night holds its own demons. While Florence and her mother have retired to their respective beds, fully versed in all that has passed over the last two days, she lies wide awake. She has not slept in more than thirty-six hours; yet she has never felt more alive. She is on the alert because she senses I am close.

You see, the time has come to reveal the truth to her. Adam Braithwaite's life will shortly come to an end; but before it does, he will divulge what really happened that night. Constance will need to help him in his recollections and coax him through his account. It will then be up to her to piece together the shattered fragments of the sorry tale so that justice can be done.

As I enter the room, she sits upright in bed. She knows I am here. A warmth spreads throughout her body; a fire burns in her eyes. It's time to tell her what I saw when I was sent to Poplar the night Catherine Mylett was murdered. She needed to collect the pieces of the puzzle for herself before I could help her put them in order.

"You are here," she mouths in the darkness.

She is listening, so I shall begin.

Constance

A moment ago, I felt warm, but now the room is so cold that I'm drawing my shawl around my shoulders. My feet, too, feel like ice. I look down at where the blanket should be and I see I'm no longer in bed, but out on the street.

I look around me. The place is oddly familiar, but it brings no comfort. I'm fearful as I stand opposite the entrance to an alley. It's dark and the only light comes from a lamppost opposite its mouth. All around are boarded-up houses, although on one side of the alley is a tobacconist's and on the other an ironmonger's. It's then that I realize I'm standing across the road from Clarke's Yard, in Poplar. I'm not alone, neither. Squinting into the shadows, I think I see someone else standing, shivering in the cold, hotching from one foot to the other. Hatless and hunched, I make out Cath Mylett and she's waiting for someone.

"Cath!" I cry. "Cath!" But she can't hear me. I try and run to her, but my feet are clamped to the spot. No, she can't hear me, but she can hear and see a wagon as it approaches. Wait up! There's writing on the side of the trailer. It's Greenland's cart trundling by. I look up at the driver. It's Mick Donovan. I gasp as I see him pulling up just past Cath. He cocks his head at her, then jumps down and lopes up to her. There's a sort of swagger in his manner. When I hear what he says, I understand why. He thumbs his hat to the back of his head.

"You couldn't say no to a fine young Irish fella, now could ya?"

"You was in the pub with Flo," I hear her say. She's wary of him.

He strokes the whiskers that cling to his top lip. "So I was.

You was looking at me, weren't you now? Givin' me the eye." He winks at her.

Cath's used to dealing with his sort. Think they've got something we women lust after. He'll want something for nothing. "Not tonight," I hear her say. "On yer way." She turns her head and tries to ignore him. But she can't get rid of him that easy. It seems he won't take "no" for an answer. He's moving in on her. His hands are on her waist.

"But you're a fine figure of a woman, to be sure," he tells her, and he bobs low to try and find her mouth, just as he did to me. I can feel the bristles from his pathetic moustache scrape against my skin and I want to scream to Cath, but my tongue is tied. She turns her head this way and that, trying to push him back, but he presses her hard against the wall. But just as she's buckling under his weight, a voice comes from nowhere.

"Get away!" comes the cry. "Get away from her!"

A man in a billycock hat suddenly appears and grabs Mick Donovan by the shoulder, turning him round to face him. "On yer way, if you know what's good for you," he snarls.

"No!" Cath cries suddenly. It's like she's had a change of heart. "Stay. Stay if you want," she tells Mick, reaching out for his arm.

I'm confused. Why should she change her mind just like that? A second later, all is clear as the man in the billycock pulls out a short-bladed knife.

"Get away, I say," he hisses, the knife pointing at Mick's neck. Glancing down, the Irishman sees the blade and a hand, wrapped in a bloody bandage, clamped on his shoulder. He's no choice. He backs off, then runs to the cart and is out of sight in a moment, leaving Cath to face the man in the billycock alone.

The blade is returned to his pocket with his bandaged hand. Up until then I'd thought this shadowy thug must be Will Mylett, Cath's brother. She was due to meet him that night to hand over the money she'd blackmailed from the baby farmer. But now I know different.

"Give me my money," he says, looming over her small frame. "Give it back, here." His right hand is outstretched, but Cath's still pressed against the wall and she's shaking her head.

"No," she says softly. He comes closer. "No!" she says, louder this time.

"You'll give me back my cash, you whore," he scowls, but she darts away from the wall and starts to run down the alley. He lurches toward her and snags her by her collar. "You will give it back to me," he growls as her hands fly up to her neck. She's making a strange, gurgling sound, but the man's grip only tightens. Suddenly he's lifting her tiny body up from the ground so that her legs are flailing in the air.

I can't believe it. She's kicking madly as he shakes her like a rag doll. "Give it to me!" he cries, over and over again—until, after what seems like ages, Cath stops kicking and her body goes limp.

"Cath!" I scream, but no sound comes out, even though my cheeks are wet. Through my tears, I see the monster throw her small body to the ground and bend over her. He's panting for breath as he looks down on her, crumpled against the wall. I'm not sure he knows what he's just done. He crouches low to check for a pulse, as if he can't quite believe what he's just done, either. It's like his anger was in charge of him and he didn't know his own strength.

I see him shaking his head as he looks on Cath's lifeless body; then a second later, he's rifling through her pockets to bring out a wad of notes. The pressure he put on Cath's poor neck must've made his wounded hand seep again and fresh blood drips down his fingers. Peeping from Cath's apron pocket is a hankie, so he filches it and wraps it round his hand to stem the flow.

That's why Miss Tindall has brought me here; to make sense of the knife and the bloody handkerchief dug up in the garden at Woodstock Terrace. Now I can see for myself what I should've worked out before: that Cath wasn't murdered by her brother, or by Adam Braithwaite, but by the baby farmer's son-in-law. The man who's just ended her life is Albert Cosgrove. After he gave Cath the lucre, he must've gone looking for her, combing the streets to get his money back. When he found her, and she refused to hand it over, he lost his temper and throttled her. Dr. Bond wasn't wrong when he said she was choked by her own collar, but what he didn't realize was that it was pulled tight by another's hand. I've got to get help. Cath might still be alive. It might not be too late to save her.

"Help! Help!" I scream.

"Con. Con. Calm yourself." Flo's voice breaks through my vision. Suddenly I'm not at Clarke's Yard, but in the bedroom, and Flo and Ma are standing over me. I glance at the window and see a cold dawn is breaking. I try and stand, but I'm stiff as starch. It's then I see I've been lying on bare floorboards.

I struggle to prop myself up. "What the . . . ?"

"Come on, my gal," says Flo. "You must've fallen out of bed. Found you there, I did." She scoops her arm under mine and she helps me to my feet before I slump back down onto the bed.

I shake the sleep from my head as Ma huddles me in my shawl.

"You must've had one of your bad dreams," she says, trying to comfort me. Only there's no solace in her words, rather she reminds me of what I've just seen and what I have to do. I leap up from the bed and grab my clothes from the nearby chair.

"What you fink you're doin', Con?" Flo shouts after me as I rush downstairs, pulling on my jacket as I go. "What's up, Con? Con?"

Ma's words blew away the cobwebs in my mind. I can see clearly now. Miss Tindall has shown me what happened to Cath. I know exactly where I must go and exactly what I must do. I only hope I'm not too late.

Chapter 45

Friday, January 18, 1889

Emily

Constance is not too late, even though Adam Braithwaite has certainly taken a turn for the worse overnight. Detective Sergeant Hawkins resumed his interrogation at his hospital bedside about half an hour ago, but has made little progress.

"I swear I didn't kill her."

The detective is a patient man, but he knows that his prisoner's time on earth is finite and that the truth needs out before Braithwaite makes his exit. "Why won't you admit it?"

The blacksmith winces in pain. "I'm telling the truth."

"He is," says Constance, blustering in, past PC Semple on the door. The officer follows close behind. "I'm sorry, sir," he bleats apologetically.

"Miss Piper. Come in, please. I'm glad you are here," Hawkins greets her, shooting the ineffectual constable a scalding look.

Constance seats herself by Hawkins at the bedside.

"I thought it would be easy to obtain a confession from a man who knows he is about to die," he tells her, heedless of his prisoner's sensibilities. "But Mr. Braithwaite insists he is innocent."

"I didn't kill Cath, I tell you. I swear," he reiterates from his bed.

Constance casts a compassionate eye over the man who lies before her in his death throes. "He's right," she says.

"What?" *The sergeant's head whips round to face her.*

"He's telling the truth. He didn't kill Cath Mylett," she confirms.

Hawkins frowns. "I don't understand."

"Then let me explain," offers Constance, her gaze on Adam Braithwaite. It is time for her to relay all that she knows; all that she has discovered for herself and all I have shown her. She takes a deep breath to steady herself and addresses the blacksmith.

"Little Evie was yours, wasn't she?" she says. I am still with her, but she has managed to deduce these conclusions herself. I have merely shone light into the darker corners of her mind, where her suspicions have been loitering. She goes on: "But you couldn't afford to keep her. So Cath was forced to turn to a baby farmer for help."

Braithwaite groans at the thought of Cath's suffering, but Constance refuses to stop. "After Evie died and Cath got sick and had to go to the asylum, you settled for the next best thing."

Sergeant Hawkins, who has followed Constance's thread up until now, looks puzzled. "What are you suggesting, Miss Piper?"

She spits out her reply. "I'm suggesting that while Cath was out of her mind with grief, Adam Braithwaite here married Cath's cousin."

Sergeant Hawkins knows what she's saying makes sense. He nods to Tanner. "Bring Mrs. Braithwaite in, if you please."

Fanny is escorted into the room, looking pale and expressionless as she is shown to a seat on the opposite side of the bed. Constance glares at her. She first suspected her duplicity on her last visit to Pelham Street. She thought she was hiding her cousin Will. She'd not realized that Fanny had been leading a double life, until she'd seen the medical examiner's report on the mutilated man she'd supposed was Adam Braithwaite.

Constance keeps Fanny in her sights. "You said the body was your husband's, when you knew it was Will Mylett's. His face was so badly smashed up that no one could argue. You even planted a bloodied eye patch nearby so there'd be no doubt." She shakes her head in disgust. "You played the grieving widow as well as you played the devoted niece!"

Fanny does not respond, but simply hangs her head as Braithwaite's fingers crawl across the blanket to reach for her hand. She looks at it, but refuses to take it.

"You bastard. You lied to me," she tells him through clenched teeth. She shakes her head, then starts to speak. "Cath introduced us, see." She huffs a bitter laugh. "He was her 'man,' she said. But when she found out she was pregnant, he didn't want nothing to do with her. That's when we started courting. Within three months, we was wed."

Hawkins glances over at Constable Barrett to make sure he's taking notes. Satisfied that he is, he asks: "Did you know that Catherine's baby died at the hands of a baby farmer?"

Fanny nods. "She told me. I visited her just after she went into the asylum. Mad, she was, but with good reason. She told me that this old woman was starving all the babies in her care and even killing some of 'em. She said she'd told Will about her and that when she felt better, he'd help her get her revenge."

"Get her revenge?" *echoes Hawkins.*

Fanny nods. "Cath wanted to settle her score, so she asked Will to help her. Only thing was, the old witch got wind of trouble and moved."

The sergeant nods. "So that's why Catherine waited so long to make her move. She'd lost track of the baby farmer's whereabouts."

Constance, who has been listening to Fanny in silence, suddenly remembers the newspaper cutting she found among Cath's belongings. "But when she saw an advertisement in the local newspaper, she knew the old woman was back in business in Poplar."

Fanny nods. "That's when she and Will hatched the plan to get money from them." She shakes her head. "You couldn't blame her, after what she'd been through."

"Blackmail," says Sergeant Hawkins, fixing Fanny with a glare. "And you knew about this plan?"

"No," Fanny snaps back. "Not then. Not till later, I swear."

"It's true," comes Braithwaite's thin voice from the bed. "The first I knew of it was that night—the night she . . ." He stops himself short, choking on his own words. "She'd arranged to meet Will outside Clarke's Yard at two o'clock. It was about eleven when she came to me in such a state as I'd not seen afore. Wild she were, and with blood on her hands and face. I cleaned her up and calmed her down. Gave her a couple of slugs of gin. She told me she'd lost it with this bloke where the minder lived. She'd gone at him with a knife, but he'd snatched it from her and cut his hand, quite bad. Then she showed me the money." Braithwaite flinches as he tries to move.

"How much?" asks Hawkins.

"A lot."

"How much?" he asks again.

"Thirty quid."

"Thirty pieces of silver, more like," snarls Fanny.

The sergeant shoots her a disapproving look. "Then what happened?"

"I'd never seen that much money before. Nor had she. And it were there, in her hands. It were late and we'd both had a bit to drink." He gulps down a sigh. "I told her we could leave London behind. Together, just the two of us."

"Oh, for the love of . . . ! " Fanny directs her searing gaze at her husband.

"Go on," urges Hawkins.

"She wouldn't have none of it. She turned on me. She said if I'd been a decent father, then little Evie would still be alive. That hurt." Another tear breaks loose from the blacksmith's eye. "That's when we started to row—"

"And that's when you strangled her," Hawkins butts in.

Braithwaite's face crumples. "No," he wails. "It weren't me. I never killed her. I swear. I just left her there, on the street."

Sergeant Hawkins is growing irascible. "I've told you before, Braithwaite, don't play games. You killed Will Mylett, and you killed his sister."

"No," snaps Constance. Hawkins's head whips round again. "He's telling the truth," she says more calmly. "He didn't kill Cath. This is what I wanted to tell you." She's fixing the sergeant with a determined look.

"It were that bastard brother of hers," mutters the blacksmith.

Constance cuts in. "What makes you so sure? Did you see him attack her?"

"No," comes Braithwaite's reply. "But it had to be him. She were meeting him, to give him the money. That's why she stayed in the yard and I left for home."

Now it's Hawkins's turn. "But did you see Will Mylett that night?"

Pain is etched on Adam Braithwaite's face. The sweat is breaking out on his forehead. "No, I didn't, but who . . . ?"

It's time for Constance to unburden herself. "There was someone else," she says suddenly. She holds the key to this case and now is her time. She straightens her back.

"That night, the night Cath was killed, Mick Donovan . . ."

"Donovan? The Irishman found hanged?" Hawkins breaks in.

"Yes," confirms Constance. "Mick Donovan was making deliveries and drove past Clarke's Yard. He saw you leave"—she's looking at Braithwaite—"but he saw Cath stay, so he thought

he'd try his luck with her. He stopped his cart and went to ask her if she was willing, but just as he did, a man came up to him and threatened him with a knife if he didn't make himself scarce."

"I told you, it must've been Will," groans Braithwaite.

"It wasn't. Mick Donovan didn't get a good look at his face, but he did see his hand. He saw it was bandaged."

Sergeant's Hawkins's eyes widen. "The haberdasher."

"Yes," says Constance. "Albert Cosgrove. He came to get his money back. He'd been out looking for her and was sure he'd find her on the streets. He knew she was a regular at Clarke's Yard. He didn't intend to kill her, but he lost his temper. He took her by the collar—a collar lined with binding to stiffen it."

"Dr. Brownfield's four-thread cord," mutters Sergeant Hawkins.

Constance nods. "Cosgrove didn't intend to silence Cath for good, and he may even have left her alive, but he wanted his money back. And he got it."

Hawkins follows through. "He traced Donovan to Greenland's by way of the cart and made sure he was silenced, too. He hit him over the head, then strung him up to make it appear that he'd killed himself."

"Exactly," confirms Constance. Earlier, when she was recounting the baby farmers' grisly deeds at home, Florence told her of her encounter with Albert Cosgrove at the poulterer's shop. Constance deduced that he must have been on a mission to mark out his prey.

Despite such a convincing theory, the detective does not, however, appear entirely won over. "But where is the proof, Miss Piper? This sounds very plausible, but we need hard evidence."

"You already have it, Sergeant," she counters.

"We do?"

Constance takes a deep breath. "In an evidence box in your office, you'll find a bloody handkerchief with a pink rose em-

broidered on it. As Cosgrave was attacking Cath, the stab wound she'd given him earlier began to bleed again, so he snatched her handkerchief from her. He wrapped it in the parcel with the dead babe that was left at the market the following day."

Braithwaite winces as he lifts his head. "So what about Will?"

"Will came later," Constance continues. "He found his sister lying dead, but when he saw the law coming, he panicked and fled the scene. He went into hiding, as you well know," she tells Braithwaite pointedly.

Sergeant Hawkins is frowning. "But how have you ascertained this, Miss Piper?" His voice is low.

Constance is happy to reveal her sources. "A boy at the docks. He was helping to hide Will. I think you must've followed me." She throws a scowl at Braithwaite again. "I led you to the nipper, who led you to Will. You killed him, then paid Mick Donovan to transport the body back to your forge, where you smashed his face, then tried to burn his head so everyone would think it was you who was attacked."

"So Will Mylett was dead while you were in custody?" cuts in Sergeant Hawkins. "That explains the medical report that stated he might've been dead for up to three days," he mutters with a nod.

"Yes," replies Constance. "But, meanwhile, Mick Donovan was getting nervous. He was already fearful for his own life after Cosgrove tracked him down to the shop, and then when the body was found at the forge, he was terrified he might be accused of murder." She switches her gaze to Fanny. "He tracked you down to Pelham Street. He'd no idea the man who hired him to transport a dead body was in hiding upstairs."

From the bed, there comes a sob. Adam Braithwaite is a broken man. He became a murderer because of a mistaken belief. He was convinced that Will Mylett had killed the woman he loved. Remorse is written on his face. He will die bitter, but contrite.

The nurse, who has been present throughout the proceedings, addresses Sergeant Hawkins. "I think he's had enough, sir," she says, watching tears flow from her patient's only eye.

The detective nods and looks at Constance. "We are finished here." He nods at Constable Barrett. "Charge him, will you?"

Together, he and Constance leave the room.

CHAPTER 46

Friday, March 1, 1889

EMILY

It was the last Constance and Detective Sergeant Hawkins saw of Adam Braithwaite. He lingered on in stinking agony for another three days, but at least his death from gangrene spared him a trial and the rope. His wife, Fanny, was given a ten-year prison sentence for perverting the course of justice and conspiracy to murder.

Mother Delaney, on the other hand, has not been so lucky. For the past few days, she has been furiously busy in Reedhampton Jail, writing letters to the authorities, proclaiming the innocence of both Philomena and Albert. They were briefly arrested, but freed before Detective Sergeant Hawkins could issue a warrant for their arrest. It seems they have now disappeared.

About her own fate, however, Bridget Delaney appears sanguine. When all hope of being declared insane was lost, she resigned herself to her execution. Now that the day is come, however, if she believes in the Almighty, she does not call on him at the hour of her death. As the hangman finally puts the rope around her neck and asks her if she has anything to say, she replies simply: "Nothing."

On the final stroke of nine, the lever is pulled. It's all over in a second. The short drop proved efficient and the woman, with surely the coldest heart in Christendom, has been dispatched straight into the fires of hell.

CONSTANCE

They're calling Mother Delaney "the Angel Maker" in the newspapers. She's sent more than twenty to heaven, so the latest reports say. And there'll probably be more. Of course, it wasn't just her. That evil son-in-law knew exactly what she was about. When I told Flo that it was him that killed Cath, she looked sad and said: "So he didn't only make angels, but saints, too."

There's one thing for sure—there certainly won't be any angels where Mother's gone, and at least there's a happy ending to the story of one of those little ones.

That's why I'm in my best bib and tucker to meet Mr. and Mrs. Sampson, on Platform Twelve at Euston Station, to be precise. They've decided to start a new life in America and I want to wave them off as they board the train to Liverpool. The 10:53 will take them to the docks, where they'll be first-class passengers on a ship of the Cunard Line and will sail to New York.

Little Bertie's looking smart in his blue sailor suit and jaunty little hat, which he keeps pulling off. Miss Louisa—sorry, I ought to be used to saying Mrs. Sampson by now—is quite radiant. That gaunt, haunted look that etched itself on her face is nowhere to be seen. She's holding Bertie in her arms, where he belongs. I doubt she'll ever let him go again.

As for Mr. Sampson, I think he's redeemed himself by his actions. It's clear that he loves his wife and son very much. I suppose everyone should be given a second chance and this is his. He'll probably never tell his new wife about the part he played in Miss Tindall's death. He'll have to live with his own guilt for the rest of his days, but perhaps it'll make him less willing to see the faults in others and understand that we are all, after all, only frail humans.

As the whistle blows and the steam billows out across the platform, the locomotive chugs off. I'm standing by the Sampsons' carriage and wave to them as it pulls away. A few moments later, when the clouds of steam are slowly clearing and the well-wishers are turning to leave, I spot what seems to be a familiar figure standing quite still, talking to a gentleman. For a second, I think it's Miss Tindall, but then I tell myself not to be so stupid. I've been wrong so many times before. She's not noticed me, and a second later, she's gone. The strange thing is, the gentleman she was talking to is now walking toward me. Quite fast, he's moving, tucking his fob watch into his waistcoat pocket as he approaches. He's wearing a bowler, which hides his eyes, and it's not until he's a few feet away from me that I realize who it is.

"Miss Piper!" he calls, whipping off his hat.

"Sergeant Hawkins! What . . . ?"

He draws near and seems agitated. "It's my day off and I thought it would be fitting if I bid the Sampsons farewell. But I had trouble finding the right platform."

"So you stopped to ask a lady."

"Ah, yes." He nods sheepishly. "You saw. Most curious."

"*Curious?*"

"Yes. She told me I'd missed the Liverpool train, but that the person I sought was still on the platform."

I try to stifle a smile. "Very curious," I say.

"So . . . I have missed the Sampsons?"

"I'm afraid you have."

"But I have found you." His eyes are bright and full of promise. "And I am glad of it because I wanted to thank you."

"Thank *me*?"

"I fear I doubted your"—he casts around for the appropriate word—"your *intuition* at times." I know what he means. It can't be easy for a man of his reasoned mind to believe that my gift means my visions can trump all the logic in the world. He pauses. "I saw a pleasant tearoom on my way in. I don't suppose . . ."

There's no doubt in my mind. "I'd like very much to join you," I say.

EMILY

While Constance, Sergeant Hawkins, and, of course, the Sampsons can all take some comfort from a sense of closure to this whole terrible affair, more than a hundred miles away, at a railway terminus in Norfolk, another crime is about to be uncovered. On that very same morning, a railway examiner on the Great Eastern Line is passing a carriage, which had been shunted into sidings the previous evening. He hears a noise and stops to listen. Unless he's very much mistaken, it sounds like a baby's cry. Dropping to his knees, he is inspecting underneath the carriage, when he realizes that the noise is coming from within a compartment.

Alarmed and perplexed in equal measure, the examiner informs the foreman, who carries a master key, and together they open the locked carriage door. The cry persists and they follow it until, to their utter disbelief, they find a brown paper parcel tucked under one of the compartment seats. Inside lies a tiny baby, soiled and cold, but miraculously very much alive.

Further investigations will reveal that the carriage, where the baby was abandoned, had been occupied by a smartly-dressed young woman and a man with wispy sideburns and a billycock hat. Because of the important role he has played in bringing to justice the baby farmer Bridget Delaney, Detective Sergeant Thaddeus Hawkins is informed. Thanks to his diligence and good record-keeping (and, in part, to Constance's assistance, although there is no official mention of this), it does not take long to trace those suspected of leaving the child to die. The male is also wanted in connection with the murders of Catherine Mylett and Michael Donovan. The suspects went by the names of Edith and Edmund Blunt. You, however, would know them better as Philomena and Albert Cosgrove.

AUTHOR'S NOTES

My first encounter with the real "angel maker" was ten years ago in a bookshop (now closed) not a mile from where, just over a century before, she used to live near Reading, and just a couple of miles away from my own children's school. It was the photograph of her on the front cover that first attracted me. It was as if I was staring evil in the face; here was an image of a Victorian woman in her late fifties, slightly jowly and wearing a bonnet, but it was her eyes that I found so mesmerizingly frightening.

It was only when I began to read the blurb on the back of the book that I discovered I had every right to be disturbed by the way she looked. Her name was Amelia Dyer. She was a baby farmer—a person, usually a woman, who accepted custody of a child in exchange for payment. The difference between the usual Victorian baby farmer and Dyer was, however, that she murdered literally scores of children in her care, many in cold blood. There had been other women before her who had been hanged for allowing their charges to die, usually through willful neglect, but this baby farmer was in a league of her own.

When she was young, her own daughter, Polly, asked her mother where all the babies that she cared for went when they left their house. Dyer's reply was that she was an "angel-maker." When police dredged up babies' corpses from the River Thames, she even admitted: "I used to like to watch them with the tape around their neck, but it was soon all over with them."

One of the most troubling aspects of this case—and there are many—is that Dyer's motivation was never discovered. True, she spent two short stays in asylums, but this was only when she was dangerously close to being arrested. The court rejected her plea of insanity and she was hanged at Newgate Prison on June 10, 1896. Although she made money from her evil exploits, she lived a very frugal lifestyle. While her daughter, Polly, and her husband, Arthur Palmer, were never charged as her accomplices, it's fairly certain they should have been. Palmer was, however, given three months' imprisonment with hard labor for abandoning a small girl the previous year.

The case of the governess in my novel is also based on fact, although the true identity of the young woman was never made public. She suffered unimaginable cruelty at Dyer's hands, which I chronicle in my novel, although I do admit to changing the final outcome. Sadly, in real life, the story did not have a happy ending.

As for Catherine Mylett, more commonly referred to as Rose, there is much speculation as to whether she was yet another victim of Jack the Ripper's. The general consensus among historians, however, is that she was not because of the modus operandi of her killer. There has been speculation, specifically by William D. Stewart in his 1939 book, *Jack the Ripper: A New Theory*, that it was Amelia Dyer who killed the Whitechapel prostitutes through botched abortions. In other words, she might have been Jack the Ripper. There is, however, no evidence to connect Dyer to the Ripper murders.

The streets of Victorian London are clothed in shadows and secrets in Tessa Harris's gripping new mystery featuring flower seller Constance Piper . . .

London, July 1889. Eight months have passed since the horrific murder of Mary Jane Kelly. The residents of Whitechapel have begun breathing easy again—daring to leave windows open and walk about at twilight. But when old Alice McKenzie is found dead, throat slashed from ear to ear, the whispers begin once more: Jack the Ripper is back.

Constance Piper, a flower seller with a psychic gift, was a friend to both women. With the supernatural help of her late mentor, Miss Emily Tindall, and her more grounded ally, police detective Thaddeus Hawkins, she uncovers links between the murders and a Fenian gang. The Fenians, committed to violence to further their goal of an independent Ireland, are also implicated in a vicious attack in which the Countess of Kildane's uncle was killed. Could the Whitechapel murders be a ruse to make the British police look helpless?

Soon, Constance is called upon for help. But there are spies everywhere in the city, and a bomb plot intended to incur devastating carnage. And as Constance is fast discovering, the greatest evil may not lurk in the grimy alleys of the East End, but in a conspiracy that runs from Whitechapel to the highest office in the land . . .

Please turn the page for an exciting sneak peek of Tessa Harris's next Constance Piper mystery A DANGEROUS DECEPTION coming soon wherever print and e-books are sold!

CHAPTER 1

London, Wednesday, July 17, 1889

CONSTANCE

It was the footsteps that woke me. From the cradle of my deep sleep, I supposed the noise to be rain splattering the window, or maybe even a trotting horse. Opening my gritty eyes, I looked up at the square of light on our moldy ceiling and thought perhaps I'd dreamed the sound. But then I heard the cry; the cry that we all know round here too well. That's when I knew it was real. "Murder! Murder!"

Scrambling out of bed, I rushed over to pull up the sash and there he was, in our street, a little nipper, shouting at the top of his voice. "Murder! Murder!" Cupping his hands round his mouth he called out once and then he cried again. He hollered words that turned my blood even colder, and everyone else's too. "Jack's back!" he bellowed and a chill ran down my spine quicker than a rat along a drain pipe.

For a moment I was numb. I couldn't believe it. Still can't. Just as we were all feeling safe in our beds, just when we dared leave our windows ajar at night on account of the warmer weather, just when we could walk out at twilight again, we hear there's been another killing. Of course the cry made us all sit up and take notice. If Jack is back, none of us is safe.

Flo was quick off the mark. Pushing me out the way, she shoved her head out the window.

"Where?" she yelled. "Where's the murder?"

The lad turned and, still running backwards, gulped and yelled up, "Castle Alley, by Goulston Street Wash'ouse."

Ma shuffled in with her shawl drawn round her shoulders and a frown on her brow. "What's amiss?" she wheezed, all blurry-eyed.

Flo and me swapped glances. We knew she wouldn't take it well.

"There's been another killing," I said, as soft as I could, but it still didn't stop her from gasping for air, like a fish out of water. I feared the shock would bring on another attack, and it did. I rushed over to her and sat her down beside me on the bed.

"I'll go and see what's what," Flo told her, pulling on her skirt. She tried to act all cocky, as if she could make things right, but of course she couldn't. We both knew that if Jack was back to work, then no amount of brave words would help soothe the terror that'd return. There's been nothing since November; not since Mary Jane Kelly was found on the day of the Lord Mayor's Parade. She was Jack's fifth, or some say sixth victim. 'Course after her came poor Rose Mylett. At first we all thought she was one of his too. With the help of my friend Acting Inspector Thaddeus Hawkins I proved Rose's murder weren't Jack's handiwork after all. So that's why, eight months on from the foulest murder of all, it's come as the most terrible shock to everyone to think the fiend stalks among us again.

EMILY

Yes, eight long months have passed since Jack last struck. Eight months in which the people of Whitechapel and beyond have tried to rebuild their lives. Yet the brutal killings still cast their shadow. I well remember the morning they found the body of what everyone prayed would be the Ripper's last victim; Mary Jane Kelly. In a squalid room in Miller's Court it was. I was there when the rent collector first put his eye to the broken pane, but couldn't quite comprehend the scene at first. He'd been banging on the flimsy door for the past few seconds, fearing it might splinter under his fist. He'd even called the tenant's name. "Mary Kelly. Mary Jane." He was used to her scams; the way she'd pretend she didn't know what day of the month it was, or how she'd sometimes just flutter those long lashes of hers and beg a favor. Her wiles were enough to make a grown man weak at the knees. Or how she'd call him "dear Tommy" in that sing-songy voice of hers that reminded him of a sky lark on a spring morning. But six weeks is a long time in any landlord's book and Mr. McCarthy wasn't having any more of her shilly-shallying, so this time Thomas Bowyer was under instructions to return with the rent, or not at all.

His knocking having met with no response, Bowyer went around the corner of the premises to where he knew the window pane was broken. Carefully he reached through the jagged glass and drew back the curtain so that he could see inside. It was a sight that would come to haunt him for the rest of his days. He withdrew his hand so quickly from the broken pane that his skin was caught and torn by the glass as he staggered back. Yet he did not make a sound, save for a violent retch in the gutter nearby. Despite his dizziness and nausea, he managed to alert his boss to what he had just seen; to the two pieces of cut flesh on the table and to the blood on the floor and to the fact that the body of Mary Jane Kelly, the prettiest and sweetest of the street girls he knew, lay mutilated beyond all recognition.

That was last November. On the ninth day of the month to be precise. Not that time means anything to me. It is but a ticking of a clock. I am no longer of this earth, you see. I am what they call a revenant. I died—or, more accurately, was murdered, because I tried to expose a secret society of powerful men that preyed on my young pupils. I was handed over to a cruel bully, whom I now know went by the name of the Butcher, and paid the ultimate price for my discovery when he cracked my skull against a wall. Now, however, I have returned to right the wrongs committed against me and so many others who cannot defend themselves against the powers which control their lives.

London's East End, where this shocking crime against Mary Jane Kelly was perpetrated, is where I usually roam. Unseen by nearly all, I am to be found underfoot in the cobbles of Whitechapel, on the panes of grimy glass, in the fabric of people's clothes, on wood and on brick, even floating on the air you breathe. There are traces of me all around—of what was, what is and what will come—but only the chosen few can sense them. Constance Piper is one of them and I am able to live on through her.

CONSTANCE

This time the killing's even closer to home; just a couple of streets away from us. The washhouse is where Ma, Flo and me go for a bath now and again. 'Course we have to go second class: a cold bath and a towel for your penny. Someday I'll treat myself to first class: that's two towels and warm water. Someday.

"Let's get the kettle on," I say, guiding Ma downstairs. I sit her in our one good, horse-hair armchair by the empty hearth just as Flo steps over the threshold to find out what's what.

"I won't be long," she calls back to Ma, trying to reassure her, only she's wheezing that much, I'm not sure she's heard. So we sit and we wait.

Already there's a dreadful brouhaha outside. People are coming down our way to get to Castle Alley. You wouldn't ever catch me down that dingy rat hole. Never gets any sun, even when there's some to be had. In shadow all day, it is. It's where some of the local costermongers park up their barrows for the night. You get all sorts coming and going and all manner of diseases lurking there, so they say. Some ragamuffins and unfortunates even kip down under the carts. If you can put up with the stink I suppose it's out of the rain. But I needs hold my breath just when I'm passing, the stench is that bad.

At least half an hour goes by before Flo's back. She takes off her shawl as she blusters through the front door. "It's Bedlam out there," she tells us, like she's the one who's having it hard. "There's crowds all round the mortuary, as well as where she was found."

It's been raining in the night and there's mud on her boots. She's all flushed as she sits down to ease them off. I'm watching her and I'm waiting for her to say something more. It's like she's trying to think of how to get something off her chest. But she just gives me the eye and bites her lip.

"Oh God!" I mutter, watching her stand up real slow, like she's trying to put off what she knows she must do. "It's someone we know, ain't it?" I keep my voice low, but Ma, still in the chair, knows something's amiss.

"Well, Flo?" she asks, all breathy.

Dread flies up like a black crow from somewhere deep inside me. My whole body tenses as I watch my big sister stand in front of Ma, take a deep breath and say, "Word is it's Alice Mackenzie."

CHAPTER 2

Thursday, July 18, 1889

EMILY

As Acting Inspector Thaddeus Hawkins walks up Commercial Street toward the police station, he carries the weight of the world on his shoulders. His normally quick step is slowed by thought, and his invariably pleasant, yet serious, demeanor has been severely compromised.

It's nine o'clock in the morning. He managed to grab just a few hours' sleep in the section house last night. This latest murder has put everyone back on their mettle. All his men had finally returned to their normal beats after the terror that the depraved killings of the previous year had wrought. Petty theft, drunkenness, and the usual abhorrent abuse to which women are continually subjected by their menfolk were all habitual crimes starting to occupy his constables' time once more. Most of the men were relieved to return to the basic business of policing;

the policy of "prevention rather than the cure" is what the new police commissioner, James Monro, is so keen to pursue. But Alice Mackenzie's murder has certainly set the cat among the proverbial pigeons again.

Nevertheless, despite this latest killing, life continues as normal on Commercial Street.

"Parnell Commission latest. Read all about it!" shouts a young newspaper vendor. Hawkins stops to buy a copy of the Telegraph. *He will peruse it later. These days the goings-on at the Parnell Commission appear to have replaced talk of Jack the Ripper in the fashionable clubs and drawing rooms of the West End. It seems the Establishment has put the Irish nationalist leader Charles Stewart Parnell "on trial" for allegedly supporting violence to further the cause of Irish Home Rule. The* Times *newspaper, Hawkins knew, had published some articles that showed him to condone outrages committed by the Fenian Brotherhood, and these were subsequently proved to be forgeries. Politics is a messy business, the detective knows, but he'll read about it later.*

Folding the newspaper under his arm, Hawkins continues down the road, passing deliveries of fruit and vegetables to the greengrocer and crates of fish to the nearby fishmonger.

"'Morning, Inspector," greets Mr. Bardolph as he guts a herring on a marble slab outside his shop. His sharp knife slits the fish's gullet with a ruthless efficiency that is all too familiar to the detective. The sight of the blade triggers an old and unwelcome feeling in him. Although he tries to conceal his unease, the shock comes again, the stab in his abdomen. He'd thought he'd be able to consign that terrible, sickly reaction, which he used to suffer during these awful cases, to the recesses of his memory. But in the past two days those old presentiments of dread and the rising nausea have returned. He knows he must inure himself to them. He touches his hat and manages a smile.

"Good morning, Mr. Bardolph."

Thaddeus Hawkins is a familiar face to most of the shopkeepers and costermongers round here. He's made it his business to get to know the local community, to share their concerns and fears. Up until two days ago he'd been convinced that the world had heard the last of this Jack the Ripper. He'd seen for himself the conviction held by Commissioner Monro that Montague Druitt was the fiend behind the killings and that his suicide last December had put paid to his nefarious deeds once and for all. Rumor had it, however, that any public announcement on the subject had been barred by the suspect's brother. William Druitt, it was said, had threatened that if his brother was exposed, he would reveal that there were homosexuals in high positions in the army, in Parliament, at the bar, and in the Church.

Now, however, with this latest unfortunate's murder, that whole hypothesis had been thrown into the air. It has come as a huge blow and, Hawkins is convinced, will resurrect the terror felt by so many East End residents last autumn. Of course, it is not yet proven that Alice Mackenzie was felled by the same killer. Indeed, within the force itself, there are conflicting opinions—some say Jack the Ripper is returned; others that this murder is unrelated. Whatever the veracity of either claim, the press is already sharpening its metaphorical knives and pointing them at H Division once more.

Events, however, are about to take an even more challenging twist. Sergeant Halfhide, with his unfeasibly large whiskers and bluff manner, is behind the duty desk as Hawkins walks into the police station.

"'Morning, Inspector," he greets the young detective, but his eyes, shaded by bushy brows, are brighter than usual. There is something conspiratorial in his look that makes Hawkins linger. And then it comes. A white envelope slides across the counter. "I'm to personally see you get this," says Halfhide, his tongue

suddenly bulging against the inside of his mouth in a show of self-confidence. "Came not an hour ago."

Hawkins picks up the envelope, looks at the back, and as soon as he registers the crest of the Metropolitan Police, his head jerks up again in shock. "From the commissioner!"

Sergeant Halfhide nods, raising his brows simultaneously. "From the very top, sir."

Wide-eyed, the young detective also nods and, letter in hand, marches into his office, shutting the door firmly behind him. Such is his curiosity he can't even wait to sit down. Standing over his desk, he takes a paper knife and slices into the top of the envelope with surgical precision. Extracting the contents, he unfolds the single sheet of paper. The handwritten letter reads thus:

> Dear Acting Inspector Hawkins,
>
> It is with great concern that I learned of the latest killing in Whitechapel. I would therefore be most grateful if you could meet with me in my office at your earliest convenience to discuss the case.
>
> I am sure you will understand the confidential nature of my request.
>
> Yours,
>
> James Monro (CB)
>
> Commissioner of Police of the Metropolis

Hawkins leans on his desk and considers this rather unorthodox summons from his superior. He wonders why he, an acting inspector, not even a full-fledged one to boot, should be singled out for such a confidential briefing. His former boss, Inspector Angus McCullen, has been on leave since earlier in the year, citing stress due to the exertions of the Ripper investigations. Yet, there are others far more senior than him: Fred Abberline and

Edmund Reid, to name but two, whose knowledge of the Whitechapel murders is just as detailed as his own. Nevertheless, who is he, he asks himself, to turn down such a request? An urgent one at that. Whatever the commissioner has up his sleeve, he clearly doesn't want to involve any senior officers.

Visit us online at
KensingtonBooks.com
to read more from your favorite authors, see books by series, view reading group guides, and more.

Join us on social media
for sneak peeks, chances to win books and prize packs, and to share your thoughts with other readers.

facebook.com/kensingtonpublishing
twitter.com/kensingtonbooks

Tell us what you think!

To share your thoughts, submit a review, or sign up for our eNewsletters, please visit:
KensingtonBooks.com/TellUs.